PRAISE FOR THE NOVELS OF C̶ ✄ **P9-CLD-265**

THE SUICIDE HOUSE

"Gripping . . . the book's real strength is the idiosyncratic Rory, who suffers from OCD and is on the autism spectrum, a deeply developed character readers can't help rooting for. Hopefully, she'll be back soon." —*Publishers Weekly*

"Charlie Donlea is a superb psychological suspense writer . . . the book has a fast-paced plot and main characters unlike any typically found in this genre." —*Seattle Book Review*

SOME CHOOSE DARKNESS

"In Donlea's skillful hands, this story of obsession, murder, and the search for truth is both a compassionate character study and a compelling thriller." —*Kirkus Reviews*

"Part 1970s serial-killer thriller and part contemporary Chicago crime novel, this deceptively quick read has something for everyone." —*Booklist*

"Suspense builds, clues mount and dangers lurk seemingly everywhere as the story nimbly toggles between then and now in Donlea's twisty-turny mystery." —*Bookpage*

DON'T BELIEVE IT

"You can't blame Charlie Donlea if the ending of his novel makes your jaw drop. The title alone is fair warning that his characters are no more to be trusted than our initial impressions of them." —*The New York Times Book Review*

THE GIRL WHO WAS TAKEN

"A fast-moving page-turner. . . . Donlea skillfully maximizes suspense by juggling narrators and time all the way to the shocking final twists." —*Publishers Weekly*

SUMMIT LAKE

"Donlea keeps readers guessing throughout. The whodunit plot is clever and compelling . . . for fans of nonstop mysteries with a twist." —*Library Journal*

Books by Charlie Donlea

SUMMIT LAKE

THE GIRL WHO WAS TAKEN

DON'T BELIEVE IT

SOME CHOOSE DARKNESS

THE SUICIDE HOUSE

TWENTY YEARS LATER

THOSE EMPTY EYES

Published by Kensington Publishing Corp.

THE
GIRL
WHO WAS
TAKEN

CHARLIE DONLEA

KENSINGTON
PUBLISHING CORP.

www.kensingtonbooks.com

KENSINGTON BOOKS are published by

Kensington Publishing Corp.
119 West 40th Street
New York, NY 10018

Copyright © 2017 by Charlie Donlea

This book is a work of fiction. Names, characters, businesses, organizations, places, events, and incidents either are the product of the author's imagination or are used fictitiously. Any resemblance to actual persons, living or dead, events, or locales is entirely coincidental.

To the extent that the image or images on the cover of this book depict a person or persons, such person or persons are merely models, and are not intended to portray any character or characters featured in the book.

All rights reserved. No part of this book may be reproduced in any form or by any means without the prior written consent of the Publisher, excepting brief quotes used in reviews.

All Kensington titles, imprints, and distributed lines are available at special quantity discounts for bulk purchases for sales promotion, premiums, fund-raising, educational, or institutional use.

Special book excerpts or customized printings can also be created to fit specific needs. For details, write or phone the office of the Kensington Sales Manager: Attn.: Sales Department. Kensington Publishing Corp., 119 West 40th Street, New York, NY 10018. Phone: 1-800-221-2647.

The K logo is a trademark of Kensington Publishing Corp.

First Kensington Hardcover Edition: May 2017

ISBN-13: 978-1-4967-0101-5 (ebook)
ISBN-10: 1-4967-0101-1 (ebook)

ISBN-13: 978-1-4967-3698-7
ISBN-10: 1-4967-3698-2
First Kensington Trade Paperback Edition: July 2021

10 9 8 7 6 5

Printed in the United States of America

For Mary
Sister, cheerleader, friend

ACKNOWLEDGMENTS

Special thanks to my Kensington family, who made me feel like a superstar as they waited anxiously for my next creation. To my editor, John Scognamiglio, who refused to let me screw up this story, despite my best efforts. Thanks for your guidance and insight, and for letting me know when enough was enough. To my publicist, Morgan Elwell, who does a stellar job getting the word out about my books, and even stashes a few copies in the right places. To the art department for designing a fabulous cover. And to Steven Zacharius, thanks for your encouragement.

Much appreciation to my agent, Marlene Stringer, who took a frantic call from me during the writing of this novel and talked me off the ledge. I've officially added "counselor" to your résumé.

"Write with the door closed. Rewrite with the door open," says Stephen King. When I open the door, the first people I invite in are my wife and sister. You guys are the best First Readers I could ask for. To Amy, for reading the same story over and over and pretending to love it more each time. No matter how good a book may be, you only read it twelve times if it's a classic or if your husband wrote it. Thanks for your ideas on how to make the early drafts better, and for letting me know when I finally had the ending correct. To Mary, for the timely brainstorming and late-night texts. I sometimes feel that you put more thought into these stories than I do. And one thing is for certain—you have a sinister mind, which came in very handy for this story.

To Abby and Nolan. I love that you think I'm "really good at writing books," even though you haven't read any of them. But the day is coming when you sit down to read one of my books, and it's a moment of happiness (and angst) that waits in my future. To my parents—Brian, Sandee, Fred, and Sue—your support and encouragement mean the world to me. And if you keep rearranging my novels on bookstore shelves, you're going to get me in trouble. So knock it off!

And finally, to the readers. Thank you for taking a chance on my book. I hope it provides you hours of entertainment (and makes you check the locks at night). Please consider writing a review of this book on any of the many outlets where other readers may find it.

Amazing grace how sweet the sound
That saved a wretch like me.
I once was lost but now I'm found
Was blind but now I see.

The Abduction

Emerson Bay, North Carolina
August 20, 2016
11:22 p.m.

Darkness had forever been part of her life.
She looked for it and flirted with it. Became quaint with it and charmed it in a way foreign to most. Morbidly of late, she convinced herself about the joys of its company. That she preferred the blackness of death to the light of existence. Until tonight. Until she stood in front of an abyss that was dead and blank in a way she had never encountered, a night sky without stars. When Nicole Cutty found herself in this chasm between life and death, she chose life. And she ran like hell.

With no flashlight, the night blinded her as she broke through the front entrance. He was just an arm's length behind, which caused adrenaline to flood her system and drive her for a few strides in the wrong direction until her eyes adjusted to the tarnished glow of the moon. Spotting her car, she reoriented herself and ran for it, fumbling with the handle until she ripped open the door. The keys hung from the ignition and Nicole cranked the engine, shifted into drive, and stepped on the accelerator. She gave the engine too much gas and nearly sideswiped the vehicle in front of her. Her headlights brought to life the ink-black night, and from the corner of her eye she saw a flash of color from his shirt as he appeared from around the hood of the parked car in front of her. She had no time to react. She felt the thud of impact and the awful rocking of the car's suspension as the wheels absorbed the unevenness of his body before regaining traction on the gravel road. Her response came without thought. She pushed the accelerator to the floor and twisted a tight U-turn, then raced down the narrow road, leaving everything behind her.

Nicole jerked the wheel as she skidded onto the main highway, swaying in the driver's seat as the fishtail settled and ignoring the speedometer as it climbed past eighty mph. She flexed her arm from where he'd grabbed her, a deep purple bruise already forming, while her eyes bounced from the windshield to the rearview mirror. Two miles went by before she eased off the gas pedal and the four-cylinder quieted down. Being free gave her no relief. Too much had happened to believe fleeing could make the problems of tonight disappear. She needed help.

As she turned onto the access road that led back to the beach, Nicole ticked off the people she couldn't ask. Her brain worked that way, in the negative. Before deciding who could assist her, she mentally crossed off the people who would do her harm. Her parents were at the top of the list. The police, a close second. Her friends were possibilities, but they were soft and hysterical and Nicole knew they would panic before she explained even a fraction of what had transpired tonight. Her mind churned, ignoring the only real possibility until she had ruled out all others.

Nicole paused at the stop sign, rolled through it while she grabbed her phone. She needed her sister. Livia was older and smarter. Rational in a way Nicole was not. If Nicole dismissed the last stretch of their lives and ignored the distance between them, she knew she could trust Livia with her life. And even if she wasn't sure about this, she had no other options.

She stuck the phone to her ear and listened to it ring while tears rolled down her cheeks. It was close to midnight. She was a block from the beach party.

"Pick up, pick up, pick up. Please, Livia!"

The Escape

Two Weeks Later

Emerson Bay Forest
September 3, 2016
11:54 p.m.

She pulled the burlap from her head and gasped for air. It took time for her eyes to adjust while amorphous shapes danced in her vision and the blackness faded. She listened for his presence but all she heard was the splattering rain outside. Dropping the burlap bag to the ground, she tiptoed to the bunker door. Surprised to see it opened a crack, she put her face to the crevice between the door and the frame and looked out into the dark forest as rain pelted the trees. She imagined a camera lens trained tightly on her eyeball as she peered through the sliver in the door, and then the camera's focus backing out in a slow reverse zoom that captured first the door, then the bunker, then the trees, and eventually a satellite view of the entire forest. She felt small and weak from this mental picture of herself, all alone in a bunker sunk deep in the woods.

She questioned whether this was a test. If she pushed through the door and stepped into the woods, there was the chance he would be waiting for her. But if the open door and the moment free from her shackle were an oversight, it was his first misstep and the only opportunity she'd had in the last two weeks. This was the first moment she found herself untethered from the wall of her cellar.

With her hands trembling and still bound in front of her, she pushed open the door. The hinges creaked into the night before the slapping rain overwhelmed their whine. She waited a moment, held back by fear. She squeezed her eyes shut and forced herself to think, tried to push away her grogginess brought on by the sedatives. The hours of darkness from the cellar came back to her and flashed in her mind like a lightning storm. So, too, did the promise she made to herself that if an opportunity for escape appeared, she'd take it. She decided days before that she'd rather die fighting for her freedom than walk like a lamb to the slaughter.

She took a hesitant step out of the bunker, into the thick and heavy rain that ran in cold streaks down her face. She took a moment to bathe in the downpour, to let the water clear the fogginess from her mind. Then, she ran.

The forest was dark and the rain a torrent. With tape binding her wrists, she tried to deflect the branches that whipped her face. She stumbled on a log and fell into the slippery leaves before forcing herself up again. She had counted the days and thought she'd been missing for twelve. Maybe thirteen. Stuck in a dark cellar where her captor stowed her and fed her, she may have missed a day when fatigue sent her into a long stretch of sleep. Tonight, he moved her to the forest. Dread had overwhelmed her as she bounced in the trunk, and a nauseous feeling told her the end was near. But now freedom was in front of her; somewhere beyond this forest and the rain and this night, she might find her way home.

She ran blindly, taking erratic turns that stole from her all sense of direction. Finally, she heard the roar of a semi truck as its wheels splashed over the wet pavement. Breathing heavily, she sprinted toward the noise and up an embankment that led to the two-lane highway. In the distance, the truck's red taillights sped on, fading with each second.

She stumbled into the middle of the road and on wobbly legs chased the lights as though she might catch them. The rain pelted her face and matted her hair and drenched her ratty clothing. Barefoot, she continued in a push-slap, push-slap gait brought on by the deep gash on her right foot—suffered during her frantic march through the forest—which trickled a crooked line of blood behind her that the storm worked to erase. Driven by panic that he would come from the forest, she willed herself on with the sensation that he was near, ready to fast-step behind her and pull the sack over her head and bring her back to the cellar with no windows.

Dehydrated and hallucinating, she thought her eyes were deceiving her when she saw it. A tiny white light far off in the distance. She staggered toward it until the light splintered in two and grew in size. She stayed in the middle of the road and waved her bound hands over her head.

The car slowed as it approached, flashed its high beams to illuminate her standing in the road in wet clothes and no shoes, with scratches covering her face and blood dripping down her neck to dye her T-shirt red.

The car stopped, wipers throwing water to each side. The driver's door opened. "Are you okay?" the man yelled over the roar of the storm.

"I need help," she said.

They were the first words she'd spoken in days, her voice raspy and dry. The rain, she finally noticed, tasted wonderful.

The man walked closer, recognized her. "Good God. The whole state's been looking for you." He took her under his arm and led her to the car, carefully seating her in the front passenger seat.

"Go!" she said. "He's coming, I know it."

The man raced around to the other side, shifting the car into drive before his door was closed. He dialed 911 as he sped along Highway 57.

"Where's your friend?" he asked.

The girl looked at him. "Who?"

"Nicole Cutty. The other girl who was taken."

The Book Tour

Twelve Months Later

New York
September 2017
8:32 a.m.

Megan McDonald sat spine-straight in the chair and watched Dante Campbell read through interview notes without a hitch while a stylist dabbed her nose with a powdered brush, and general chaos occurred around her as producers shouted orders and lighting changes and the time remaining in commercial break. The shoulder shrugs and the deep breaths had done nothing useful, and had actually caused a knot to form in her trapezius, which was starting to spasm. Megan startled, a quick flinch, when a different makeup artist touched her cheek with a brush.

"Sorry, sweetheart. You're too shiny. Close."

Megan closed her eyes while the woman ran a brush over her face. A voice off in the darkness, beyond the television cameras, began counting down. Her mouth went cotton-dry and a noticeable tremor took control of her hands. The makeup people melted away and suddenly it was just Megan sitting in the bright lights across from Dante Campbell.

"Five, four, three, two . . . you're live."

Megan stuffed her shaking hands under her thighs. Dante Campbell stared into the camera and spoke in the practiced pitch and varied cadence perfected by morning-show hosts, among which her show was the top rated.

"We all know the harrowing story of Megan McDonald. The all-American girl, daughter of Emerson Bay's sheriff, who was abducted in the summer of 2016. One year later, Megan is out now with her book, *Missing*, the true-story account of her abduction and courageous escape." Dante Campbell pulled her gaze from the camera and smiled at her guest. "Megan, welcome to the show."

Megan took a hard swallow of dry nothingness that nearly made her choke. "Thank you," she said.

"The country and, of course, Emerson Bay, has wanted to hear your story for more than a year. What inspired you to finally share it?"

Since booking this interview, Megan struggled with the answers she would give. She couldn't tell the great Dante Campbell the truth—that writing the book was the simplest way to tame her mother's sorrow and buy some breathing room. It was a way to get her mother, neurotic with worry and angst, off her back for a few months.

"It was just time," Megan said, deciding finally on the answers that would best get her out of the bright lights. "I needed to process everything before I was ready to tell people about it. I've had a chance to do that, and now I'm ready to tell my story."

"Time to process and to *heal*, I'm sure," Dante Campbell added.

Of course, Megan thought. Because, after all, it had been a whole *year*, and certainly such a time frame was sufficient to heal. Surely, a full year would make her complete again. Because, if Megan didn't come across as healed and happy and recovered, Dante Campbell—queen of morning television—would look wicked while drilling her for details. *Please,* Megan thought, *tell your audience again how mended and restored I am.*

"That too, yes," Megan said.

"I'm sure something like this takes a long time to get over, and in some ways documenting the events in your book was therapeutic."

Megan stopped herself from rolling her eyes. She had many adjectives to describe the process that created her book. *Therapeutic* was not one of them.

"It was." Megan smiled with her lips pressed together. It was her new smile, the best she could do and so different from the beaming pictures she saw the other day when she paged through her senior yearbook. Back then, her smile was wide, with straight, bright teeth filling the space between her curved lips. She tried at first, but it was too hard to fake that big smile so she came up with this new one. Lips together, edges turned up. Happy. People were buying it.

"What can people expect from reading your book?"

Megan wasn't completely sure, since she hadn't written much of it—that distinction went to her shrink, who snagged a byline on the cover.

"It, uh, you know, covers the night it happened."

"The night you were abducted," Dante clarified.

"Yes. And the two weeks I spent in captivity. A lot of it is stuff in my head that I thought about while being held. About where I was kept, and all my failed attempts to get away. And then about the night I, you know, ran out of the forest."

"The night you escaped."

Megan hesitated. "Yes. The book documents my escape." The thin smile again. "And a whole chapter about Mr. Steinman."

Dante Campbell also smiled. Her voice was soft. "The man who found you on Highway Fifty-Seven."

"Yes. He's my hero. My dad's hero, too."

"I bet. We had Mr. Steinman on the show, not long after your ordeal."

"I saw, and I was happy that he got the recognition he deserves. He saved my life that night."

"Indeed." Dante looked down at her notes before smiling again. "It's no secret the country has fallen in love with you. So many people want to know how you're doing and what's next for you. Will they get any of that from the book? About your plans for the future?"

Megan pulled her hand from under her thigh and rotated it in the air to help her think. "There's a lot about what's happened since that night, yes."

"With you and your family?"

"Yes."

"And with the ongoing investigation?"

"As much as we know about it, yes."

"How difficult is it for you to know your abductor is still out there?"

"It's hard, but I know the police are doing everything they can to find him." Megan made a mental note to thank her dad for that answer. He fed it to her the night before.

"Before this all happened, you were on your way to Duke University. We're all curious to know if that is still an option for you."

Megan rubbed her tongue around the inside of her sandpaper lips. "Um, I took a year off after this happened. I was trying for this fall but that didn't work out. I just . . . couldn't get things organized in time."

"It has to be hard, of course, to get back to normal. But I understand the university has extended an open invitation for whenever you're ready?"

Megan had long since stopped questioning people's fascination with her abduction, and the public's unquenchable thirst for the morbid details of her captivity. And now, their lust for her to proceed as though nothing happened. She stopped questioning all of these things when she finally understood the reasoning behind them. She knew attending Duke University and carrying on a normal life would allow all those who feasted on the morose details of her ordeal to feel good about themselves. Her normalness was their escape from sin. Otherwise, how could they or Dante Campbell yearn so badly to hear the disturbing details of Megan's abduction if she were still reeling from that event? If she were a broken girl whose life was a wreck and would never be the same, their vigor for her story would simply be unacceptable. They couldn't allow themselves to be so attracted to her narrative if it ended any way but beautifully. If she were *healed*, however, if she were moving on with her new, *therapeutic* book and taking a shiny seat in the freshman class at Duke University, and if she were a *success* . . . well, then they all could burrow like maggots into the meaty flesh of her disturbing story and fly away clean and pearly as though no metamorphosis had occurred.

Megan McDonald needed to be a success story. It was as simple as that.

"Yes," Megan finally said. "Duke has given me many options for next semester or even next year."

Dante Campbell smiled again, her eyes soft. "Well, I know you've been through a lot, and you are an inspiration to survivors of abduction everywhere. And we know this book will certainly be a beacon of hope for them. Would you come back and talk to us again sometime? Give us an update?"

"Of course." Thin smile.

"Megan McDonald. Good luck to you."

"Thank you."

After repeating where *Missing* could be purchased, Ms. Campbell sent things off to commercial break and the studio was again loud with voices from the dark area behind the cameras.

"You did really well," Dante Campbell said.

"You never asked about Nicole."

"It was just a timing thing, hon. We were running late. But we'll put a link about Nicole up on the website."

And with that, Dante Campbell was up and past her, offering a gentle pat on Megan's shoulder. Megan nodded, alone in the studio chair. This, too, she understood. Today's interview could only include the *pretty* details. The *inspiring* parts. The heroic escape and the bright future and the girls who were sure to be helped by the book. This morning's interview was a conclusion to the Megan McDonald drama and it had to end with success. It could include none of the ugly elements that still lingered about that summer. Especially about Nicole.

Nicole Cutty was gone. Nicole Cutty was not a success story.

PART I

"A life might end, but sometimes their case lives forever."

—Gerald Colt, MD

Chapter 1

September 2017
Twelve Months Since Megan's Escape

W*hy forensic pathology?*
  It was a question asked of Livia Cutty at each of her fellowship interviews. Generic answers might have included the desire to help families find closure, the love of science, and the craving to tackle the challenge of finding answers where others see questions.

These were fine answers and likely given by many of her colleagues who were now in fellowship spots just like her own. But Livia's response, she was certain, was unlike any of her peers'. There was a reason Livia Cutty was so sought-after. An explanation for why she was accepted by every program to which she had applied. She had the grades in medical school and the achievements in residency. She was published and came with sterling recommendations from her residency chairs. But these accolades alone did not set her apart; many of her colleagues possessed similar résumés. There was something else about Livia Cutty. She had a story.

"My sister went missing last year," Livia said at each interview. "I chose forensics because someday my parents and I will get a call that her body has been found. We will have many questions about what happened to her. About who took her, and what they did to her. I want those questions answered by someone who cares. By someone with compassion. By someone with the skill to read the story my sister's body will tell. Through my training, *I* want to be that person. When a body comes to me with questions surrounding it, I want to answer those questions for the family with the same care, compassion, and expertise I hope to receive someday from whoever calls me about my sister."

As the offers came in, Livia considered her options. The more she thought, the more obvious her choice became. Raleigh, North Carolina, was close to where she grew up in Emerson Bay. It was a prestigious and well-funded program, and it was run by Dr. Gerald Colt, widely considered in the world of forensics as a pioneer. Livia was happy to be part of his team.

The other draw, although she tortured herself when she considered it, was that with the promise of performing 250 to 300 autopsies during her year of fellowship training, Livia knew it wasn't outside the realm of possibility that a jogger somewhere might stumble over a shallow grave and find the remains of her sister. Every time a Jane Doe rolled into the morgue, Livia wondered if it was Nicole. Unzipping the black vinyl bag and taking a fast glance at the body was all it usually took to dispel her fear. In her two months at the OCME, many Jane Does had entered her morgue, but none left under the same anonymous name. They had all been identified, and none as her sister. Livia knew she might spend her entire career waiting for Nicole to arrive in her morgue, but that day would stay somewhere in the ether of the future. A moment suspended in time that Livia would chase but never catch.

Capturing that moment, though, was less important than the chase. For Livia, perusing a fictitious time in the future was just enough to lessen her regret. Soften the edges so she could live with herself. The hunt gave her a sense of purpose. Allowed Livia the feeling that she was doing something for her younger sister, since God knew she hadn't done enough for Nicole when her efforts could have been noticed. Vivid dreams of her cell phone occupied Livia's nights, bright and glowing and carrying Nicole's name as it buzzed and chimed.

Livia held her phone while it rang that night but had decided not to answer it. Midnight on a Saturday was never a good time to talk with Nicole, and Livia had decided that night to avoid the drama waiting on the other end of the call. Now, Livia would live without knowing if taking that call the night Nicole disappeared would have made any difference for her younger sister.

So, imagining a time in the future where Livia might find redemption, where she might help her sister by using whatever gifts her hands and mind possessed, was the fuel needed to get through life.

After morning rounds with Dr. Colt and the other fellows, Livia settled into the single autopsy assigned to her for the day. A straightforward junkie who died of an overdose. The body lay on Livia's table, intubation tubes spilling from his gaping mouth where paramedics tried to save him. Dr. Colt required forty-five minutes to complete a routine autopsy, which ODs were considered. Two months into her fellowship, Livia had brought her times down from more than two hours to an hour and a half. Progress was all Dr. Colt asked from his fellows, and Livia Cutty was making it.

Today, it took one hour twenty-two minutes to perform the external and internal examination of the overdose in front of her, determining the cause of death to be cardiac arrest due to acute opiate intoxication. Manner of death: accident.

Livia was wrapping up paperwork in the fellows' office when Dr. Colt knocked on the open door.

"How was your morning?"

"Heroin overdose, unremarkable," Livia said from behind her desk.

"Time?"

"One twenty-two."

Dr. Colt pouted his lower lip. "Two months in, that's good. Better than any of the other fellows."

"You said it wasn't a competition."

"It's not," Dr. Colt said. "But so far, you're winning. Can you handle a double today?"

Supervising physicians routinely performed multiple autopsies in a day, and all the fellows would be expected to increase their caseloads once they brought their times down and got the hang of the overwhelming paperwork that went along with each body. With her fellowship running twelve months—from July to July—working five days a week, with stretches of time away from the autopsy suite observing other subspecialties, two weeks dedicated to ride-alongs with the medicolegal investigators, plus days spent in court or participating in mock trials with law students, Livia knew that to reach the magic number of 250 autopsies the program promised, she would eventually have to log more than a single case each day.

"Of course," she said without hesitation.

"Good. We've got a floater coming in. Couple of fishermen found the body out by the flats this morning."

"I'll finish my paperwork and get on it as soon as it comes in."

"You'll present your findings at afternoon rounds," Dr. Colt said. He pulled a small notepad from his breast pocket and jotted a reminder as he walked out of her office.

Chapter 2

The body arrived at one p.m., which gave Livia two hours to perform the autopsy, clean up, and gather her notes before three o'clock rounds. Afternoon rounds were the bewitching event each day, when the fellows presented the day's cases to the staff at the OCME. The audience included Dr. Colt and the other attending MEs under whom the fellows were training, the subspecialists in pathology who assisted in nearly every case, visiting medical students, and pathology residents. On a given afternoon, thirty people stared at Livia as she presented.

If fellows were confused about the details of the cases they were presenting, it was painfully obvious and very unpleasant. There was no faking it. Hiding was impossible when you were in the cage, as was termed the presentation room where afternoon rounds took place. Surrounded by ugly metal chain links that belonged in someone's 1970s backyard, the cage was a feared place for all new fellows. Standing in front of the large crowd was meant to be stressful and challenging. It was also, throughout the course of the year, supposed to get easier.

"Don't worry," one graduating fellow told Livia when

they swapped spots in July. "The cage is a place you'll hate at first, but later love. It grows on you."

After two months on the job, the love affair had yet to blossom.

Livia finished her paperwork on the heroin overdose and headed back to the autopsy suite. She gowned up in a disposable blue surgical smock over her scrubs, triple-gloved her hands, and pulled a full shield over her face as the investigators rolled the gurney through the back door of the morgue and parked it next to Livia's autopsy table. In a sterile operating room, the surgical dressings were meant to protect the patient from the doctor. In the morgue, the opposite was true. Cotton, latex, and plastic were all that stood between Livia and whatever disease and decay waited inside the bodies she dissected.

With one at the head and the other at the feet, the two scene investigators lifted the body—zipped in the standard black vinyl—onto the autopsy table. Livia approached as the investigators gave the scene details to her—male floater discovered by fisherman at just past seven a.m. Advanced decomposition, and an obvious broken leg from wherever he'd jumped.

"How far is the closest bridge from where the body was found?" Livia asked.

"Six miles," Kent Chapple, one of the scene investigators, said.

"That's a long way to float."

"He's ripe enough to suggest a long swim," Kent said. "Colt's giving this to you, huh?"

Water leaked from the body bag and dripped through the holes of Livia's table, collecting in the basin below. A body pulled from salt water was never a pretty sight. Jumpers usually die on impact, and eventually sink. They were termed *floaters* only after the body began the decaying process where intestinal bacteria fester and eat away the insides, releasing noxious gases captured within the abdominal cavity that, literally, raise the dead. This process could take hours to days, and the longer the body sat underwater before floating to the surface, the worse condition it was in when it finally arrived at the morgue.

Livia smiled from behind her clear plastic face shield. "Lucky me."

She slid the zipper down and watched as Kent and his partner slipped the bag gently away. She saw immediately the body was badly decomposed, worse than any floater she'd seen before. Much of the epidermis was missing and, in some areas, the full thickness of the integumentary system gone entirely with only muscle and tendon and bone visible.

The investigators took their dripping body bag and placed it on the gurney.

"Good luck," Kent said.

Livia waved her hand but kept her gaze on the body.

"I see it every year, Doc," Kent said at the door. "Around September it starts. They break you in with drunks and overdoses. Then the ugly ones come. Decomps and kids. Doesn't let up until January or so. Colt does it to all the fellows to find out what you're made of. You'll get some juicy homicides eventually. I know that's what you're all after. A nice gunshot wound or strangulation. But you'll have to wait until winter. Deal with the messy ones first. Prove you can handle them."

"That's how it works around here?" Livia asked.

"Every year."

Livia lifted her chin. "Thanks, Kent. I'll let you know how this one goes."

"Don't bother."

The investigators wheeled the empty gurney out of the morgue, shaking their heads with suppressed smiles and sideways glances at the mess they'd left on the table that would surely make most people vomit, and would be a challenge for even a seasoned ME to get through. They knew Dr. Cutty would be at it for a while. Lots of work and trouble, and likely a few dry heaves, all to scribble on a death certificate that internal organ damage or aortic dissection was the cause of death; suicide the manner.

The back door to the morgue closed and with the investigators gone Livia was the only physician in the autopsy suite, just her and the jumper, still dripping on her table. Mornings saw most, if not all, of the autopsy tables crowded with pathologists garbed up and in various stages of examination. Others milled around as well, subspecialists weaving between the tables and around the autopsy suite to offer their expertise. The morgue was not a sterile environment and all that was required for entry was an OCME badge or a police shield. Detectives routinely peered over a pathologist's shoulder, waiting on a crucial nugget of information that would either set them off on an investigation or give them clearance from one. Technicians wheeled away bodies for X-ray or picked up specimens for neuro-path or derm-path or dental-path. Other technicians completed the autopsy process by sewing closed the gaping incisions made by the physicians. Scene investigators came and went, sometimes delivering new bodies to empty tables. Overseeing it all was Dr. Colt, who strolled the autopsy suite, hands clasped behind his back and cheaters hanging at the tip of his nose. Mornings were organized chaos.

But today was Livia's first double, the first time she was in the autopsy suite during afternoon hours. This was the time of day usually spent on paperwork, gathering notes and preparing for three o'clock rounds in the cage. With just her and the body in the quiet morgue, Livia sensed the eeriness of the place. Every sound was amplified, her tools clanking off the metal table and reverberating in the corners, the body dripping like a leaky faucet into the basin below. Usually, bone saws from adjacent tables or conversation from her colleagues overwhelmed these noises. But today her movements were magnified and obvious, and it made for a most unpleasant experience as she manipulated the body in front of her and listened to the sucking and sloshing of tissue. It took some time to adjust to the solitude, but when she got deeper into the external examination, the hollowness of the morgue faded and soon skepticism was all that remained.

Suicide jumpers typically presented with internal organ bleeding. The impact of the fall, depending on the height of the jump, brought death in a number of ways. Oftentimes, a broken rib impaled a lung or pierced the heart, and exsanguination—bleeding to death—was the cause of death. The impact could dislodge the aorta from the heart, or shear another vital vessel to cause the bleeding. In these cases, Livia would open the abdominal cavity to find pooling blood trapped in one of the compartments surrounding whichever organ had suffered the damage. Other times, the body was in decent shape with the internal organs having been protected by the skeletal shell. When Livia saw this presentation, she knew to look at the skull and the brain, which would likely show fractures and subarachnoid bleeding.

As she looked at the body in front of her, which had been presented as a floater found drifting in Emerson Bay, Livia knew it wasn't so. First, in order for this body to reach such a level of decomposition—there was barely a flap of skin present, and what was there was rancid and black—it had to have been in the water for months or longer. If that were the case, it would not have been floating, as Livia was certain this body had not been. The intestinal gases that float a body need to be contained in the abdominal cavity, and this body had no such cavity. All that was left of the gut was a wall of muscle and tendon that held the organs in place but certainly was not airtight to hold gases. Second, the broken leg the investigators had documented was not typical of a jumper who landed feetfirst. Those bodies showed impact injuries and upward compression of bones, sometimes with the tibia rising past the knee and into the thigh; and the femur displaced into the pelvis. The body in front of Livia held a horizontally fractured femur that suggested localized trauma, not full-impact trauma of a body landing sideways on water and definitely not a feetfirst landing.

Livia jotted notes on her clipboard and then started the internal exam, which showed a lack of any damage to the organs. The rib cage was in full working order. The heart was healthy, with the aorta and inferior vena cava well apposed. Liver, spleen and kidneys showed no damage. The lungs were empty of water. She was meticulous with her documentation and careful as she weighed each organ. An hour into the autopsy, perspiration covered her brow. She felt her scrubs sticking to her arms and back as she checked the wall clock—just past two p.m.

Moving to the head, she checked for facial fractures and inspected the mouth and teeth. If an ID were made on this body, it would come from dental-path, since this John Doe possessed no skin for fingerprints. And with no dermis present, there were no distinguishing tattoos that might aid in the identification.

It was during the examination of the head that Livia noticed them, the circular holes poking through the left side of the skull. She counted twelve holes randomly seated through the bone, and she racked her mind for a potential etiology. No obvious answer came to mind, besides an atypical bacterial infection that had reached the bone. But surely, had this been the case, there would be peripheral damage to the surrounding skull and some mass loss or erosion. This skull looked perfectly healthy but for the holes, which Livia quickly determined could not be from bullets or shrapnel, but might be blamed on pellets from a shotgun.

She went back to her pad and made more notes. Then, with the aid of the bone saw, she performed the craniotomy and removed the top of the skull the same way she'd do to a pumpkin at Halloween. The brain was soft and syrupy and had not been vibrant for some time. Much of working on a decomp was more difficult than a traditional autopsy. Removing the brain was the exception. If still intact, it usually came out of the skull without much effort, the dural lining no longer enclosing it. After severing the spinal cord, Livia placed the brain onto a rolling metal cart next to the autopsy table. The brain, normally laced with an intricate network of blood vessels, was usually a red mess that pooled blood beneath it when placed on the scale. This one was different. The vessels that ran through it had long since bled dry, and now the tissue was sloppy only from the water in which it had been submerged.

Examining the brain closely in the area underneath the skull piercings, Livia located corresponding holes in the tissue. Rooting deeper into the left parietal lobe, Livia was convinced after ten minutes of exploration that no shotgun pellets were present. She wiped her brow with the back of her forearm and looked up at the clock. She was due in the cage in ten minutes and didn't have a prayer of finishing the autopsy by then, let alone being prepared to stand against the assault of Dr. Colt and her supervisors.

In front of her was a body pulled from the bay that had no internal injuries besides a non-jumper's femoral fracture and piercings through the skull. Despite the panic Livia felt, she had the urge to call Kent Chapple, the scene investigator, and tell him he had things wrong. Not just about the body—this clearly wasn't a jumper. But also about Dr. Colt's timing. He'd dumped a homicide in front of her and it was technically still summer.

Chapter 3

It was close to four p.m. when Livia completed the autopsy. Rounds in the cage had been running for an hour. Currently, she was both tardy and ill prepared, and Livia had seen the consequences of wearing these qualities into the cage. An unexcused absence bore less wrath than a poor performance, so in lieu of rounds Livia dropped off her specimens for further analysis by the dental- and derm-path labs, then picked up the X-rays she had ordered and headed upstairs. She skated past the cage, where the lights were dimmed and Jen Tilly was presenting. Dr. Colt and the other attendings had their backs to the entrance and their attention trained on the screen, making possible Livia's stealth escape behind them. She took the stairs to the second floor, where the neuropathology lab was located, and found Maggie Larson behind her desk and busy with paperwork.

Dr. Larson ran all things in the Office of the Chief Medical Examiner that dealt with brains. She had a single neuropath fellow assigned to her for the year, who was likely down in the cage listening to Jen Tilly.

"Dr. Larson?" Livia said from the doorway.

"Livia," Dr. Larson said, eyes squinted. "No rounds this afternoon?"

"They're going on right now but I was assigned an afternoon case and I need some help before I get murdered down there."

Dr. Larson lifted her chin, noticing the transport container Livia carried by her side like a pail of water.

"What've you got?"

The woman had a sixth sense for brain tissue, and Livia and the other fellows knew a conversation could not be had with Dr. Larson if an unanalyzed brain was nearby. It was like trying to talk to a dog while holding a bone-shaped biscuit.

"I'm confused by something I found on exam and was hoping to get your opinion."

Dr. Larson stood from her desk and pointed to the examining table. A short woman whose hair had long ago sprouted gray roots and was now marble-streaked with the few dark strands that refused to give way, Margaret Larson held a PhD as well as a medical degree, which told Livia she'd spent years in paperwork and research labs. Livia placed the container down as Dr. Larson clicked on the overhead lamp.

"What do we have?"

They snapped on latex gloves as they gathered around the table, Dr. Larson stepping onto a stool to gain height over the specimen.

"The investigators brought in a supposed floater found by fishermen this morning. From external exam, I know the body wasn't floating." Livia took the brain out of the container and placed it on the table, dripping the pungent formalin solution along with it.

"While examining the skull, I found this." Livia handed Dr. Larson the autopsy photos of the skull piercings.

With no hesitation, Dr. Larson juxtaposed the photo next to the brain. She stuck her gloved pinkie finger into one of the holes in the brain tissue.

"I was thinking maybe pellet wounds from a shotgun blast, but could find no foreign bodies."

Without talking, Dr. Larson grabbed her slicing knife—which looked much like a long, serrated bread knife—and began cutting the brain into one-inch sagittal sections. She made it through, end to end, like a seasoned chef on a reality cooking show. Livia watched the slices fall to the side, soupy and wet and old.

Dr. Larson inspected each of the sections.

"No pellets. And the pattern isn't quite right for a shotgun blast. You'd see more randomness, and the angle of the pellets could come from only one direction." She pointed back to the autopsy photo. "See here? This set of holes is temporally located over the ear; this other set is located more posteriorly. Pellets from a shotgun can only go straight, they can't curve."

Dr. Larson looked at Livia to make sure she understood. Livia nodded.

"X-ray?" Dr. Larson asked.

Livia pulled black-and-white scans from a manila envelope, which Dr. Larson held up to the light. "No foreign bodies in the brain, so let's move on from the shotgun theory. What else?"

"Infection was my other guess," Livia said, knowing it was incorrect but wanting confirmation from Dr. Larson, as she was sure Dr. Colt would request.

"No peripheral or collateral melting or bone loss," Dr. Larson said, looking back at the X-rays and the autopsy photos of the skull. "What else?"

Livia shook her head. "Congenital?"

Dr. Larson shook her head. "Doesn't explain the concurrent piercings into the brain."

"I'm out of theories."

"That's not enough ammunition for the cage."

"Agreed," Livia said. "Any suggestions?"

"Not from this. I'll need to have a look at the skull. Get my hands on it. But one thing I can tell you: He didn't die recently. The brain is soft and the decomposition is from more than water penetration."

"The dermis was ninety percent eroded," Livia said. "How long do you think?"

"Muscle mass?"

"Full and complete, not much erosion. Ligament and cartilage present throughout."

Dr. Larson held up a sagittal section of the brain, placed it flat on her gloved palm. "I'd say a year. Maybe more."

Livia cocked her head. "Really? Would the body last that long underwater?"

"In the condition you're describing? Definitely not."

Dr. Larson waited for Livia to piece it together. Finally, Livia lifted her gaze to meet Dr. Larson's. "Someone sunk him after he was dead awhile."

"Possibly. Any clothing on the body?"

"Sweatshirt and jeans. I put them in the locker as evidence."

"Smart girl. I'll go examine the skull, see what I come up with. You might think about involving Dr. Colt."

Livia nodded. "I'll head down and let him know."

When Livia entered the autopsy suite with Dr. Colt twenty minutes later, Dr. Larson had the body out of the cooler and was examining the piercings in the skull.

"Maggie," Dr. Colt said. "I hear we have a complicated case."

"Intriguing, for sure," Maggie Larson said through her surgical mask as she stood over the body. She wore loupes that magnified the area of the skull she was interested in. Dr. Colt snapped on latex gloves, tied his mask, and went straight to the broken leg.

"This is not the fracture of a bridge jumper."

"No, sir," Livia said.

"Did you measure the height?"

"Femoral shaft fracture, twenty-seven inches from the heel," Livia said.

"Make sure to include that number in your autopsy report. Homicide will want to compare that to the height of various car bumpers, since I'm quite certain this fracture is from a vehicle-to-man impact."

Livia filed several things away in her mind. First, to include the height of the leg fracture in this report, and all subsequent ones. Second, horizontal femoral fractures can be caused when a car strikes a standing pedestrian, an impressive conclusion had she come up with it herself. And last, to research other vehicle-to-man traumas so that she never again made the same glaring omission in an autopsy report.

"Got it," Livia said.

Dr. Colt moved to the abdomen. "Broken ribs?"

"None. And the body was so decomposed, there's no way it was floating. Abdominal cavity wasn't able to hold gases."

"What did the investigators' report state?"

"Floater, but I believe that was based on the statement of the fisherman who found the body. I think he likely snagged the body off the bottom, hauled it to the surface, and called the police when he saw his catch. The investigators took the word of the cops and the fishermen that the body was floating. Plus, they noticed the broken leg and made the conclusion he was a jumper."

"So you think he drowned?"

Livia shook her head. "No water in the lungs."

"So peculiar," Maggie Larson said from the top of the table. Cradling the skull in one hand while peering through her magnifying lenses, she probed the holes with an instrument Livia had never before seen in the autopsy suite.

Dr. Colt moved to the front of the table and took a spot next to Dr. Larson. "What do we have?"

"Twelve random holes through the skull."

Dr. Larson extracted the probe she had been roto-rooting through the skull and set it to the side. Livia looked closer and swore the foreign tool was a skewer she'd find in her kitchen drawer. In her two months of fellowship she'd learned that MEs regularly brought personal tools to the morgue, whatever was most comfortable and got the job done.

"Too random to be gunshot pellets, and on different planes. Plus, no foreign bodies found."

"Drill holes?" Dr. Colt asked.

Maggie Larson pouted her lips. "Morbid, but possible."

Dr. Larson backed away from the skull and allowed Dr. Colt to take her spot. He, too, pulled surgical loupes from his overstuffed breast pocket and slid them onto his face. He was quiet for several seconds before he let out his characteristic "hmm." Finally, Dr. Colt removed his loupes and dropped them back into his jacket pocket. He snapped off his gloves and rubber-band shot them into a garbage can across the room.

"Penetrating wounds of unknown etiology through the skull and dura and into the brain. Looking at the rest of the body and with Livia's autopsy findings, he bled to death from these wounds. The inside lining of the skull is remarkable for left-side blood staining, indicating the victim never moved from a supine position after suffering these wounds. Put those conclusions in your report as well, Dr. Cutty. Make sure it's detailed. Keep the cause of death as exsanguination. Manner, undetermined."

"Undetermined?" Livia said. "I thought we were on the same page that this was a homicide." Livia felt her bragging rights slipping away. The fellows fought each morning for the most interesting cases. A homicide was by far the best any of them had seen in their first two months. "Someone hit this guy with their car, and then . . ." Livia looked at Dr. Larson. "Drilled him in the head, or something. Dropped him in the bay when they were done with him."

"We provide the facts, Dr. Cutty. The detectives sort them out. 'Or something' is not part of our survey or our vocabulary. Get his clothing to ballistics for analysis."

Livia nodded.

"You did good work, Livia," Dr. Colt said. "Sometimes, the findings point a strong finger at what exactly happened. Other times, they simply tell us what did not. This guy did not jump from any bridge, that's what we know for sure. The rest is out of our hands."

Chapter 4

In the following days, with help from the anthropology department, Livia discovered her non-jumper was approximately twenty-five years old. The body had not been vital for at least a year, and it had likely been in the water for only three days before the fishermen jigged it off the bottom. Police dredged the flats of Emerson Bay, a long sandbar popular to striped bass and sheepshead fisherman for the sudden depth change, and found near the site where Livia's John Doe had been discovered a green tarp that had been tied by rope to four cinder blocks. Fibers from the rope matched evidence samples Livia had collected from the man's clothing. Dr. Colt had also pointed to postmortem wounds—chafing to the muscles around the ankles and calves that Livia had originally missed. These, he explained, were the likely tie points for whoever tried to sink the body.

With help from the ballistics lab that analyzed the clothing, it was determined that the body had originally been buried. Soil analysis suggested the burial was in a place high in clay content and gravel. Adding weight to the burial theory, Livia described in her report two "shovel contusions"— a term coined by Dr. Colt, who suggested they trademark it—to the left upper arm. According to Dr. Colt's analysis, the digger had become too aggressive during the excavation and stepped the pointed end of the shovel into the body instead of the dirt.

With no fingerprints available due to the state of decomposition, Livia relied on dental-path to do whatever they could to make a formal identification. It was the middle of October, three weeks after the body came to the morgue, before she heard anything. Livia was in her office completing paperwork on her morning case and preparing for afternoon rounds when Dennis Steers from dental-path poked his head in.

"ID'd your John Doe from last month," he said.

Livia looked up from her work. "Yeah?"

"Homicide guys worked with Missing Persons and went back month to month. Your guy went missing last year. Reported by his landlord."

"Landlord? No family?"

"I guess he was a bit of a drifter. MP detectives said his mother lives in Georgia and hadn't talked to him in years. Didn't know he was missing until she got the call."

"That's sad."

Dennis dropped a thin file onto Livia's desk. "Here's what we have on him. Arrested just once, but had some detailed dental work completed a while back that allowed a positive ID."

"Thanks, Dennis. I'll be happy to get this off my desk."

When he was gone, Livia pulled the file folder over to her and opened it. She saw in the top left corner a small square photo of a young, good-looking man. She read farther down and saw he had been reported missing in November of 2016.

Livia pulled out the death certificate to finalize her notes so it could be printed up and sent off to this young man's mother in Georgia. Her first homicide was an interesting and challenging study, a case that required much guidance and one that taught her a great deal. Dr. Colt had apologized a half dozen times over the past month whenever he heard Livia was spending time on the case, either talking with the homicide detectives or preparing reports for Missing Persons or working with the ballistics lab on the soil analysis and cloth and fiber findings. It was her first *clinger*—a case that no matter how hard she tried, she couldn't get rid of.

A life might end, Dr. Colt told her, but sometimes their cases live forever.

Two days later, Livia completed the file and delivered her final report to the homicide detectives. The name of the man "floating" in the bay was broadcast to the public by every news anchor in Emerson Bay and North Carolina. The exact details about his death were kept vague as the investigation was in the preliminary phase, and he was still being reported as a "floater" whom fishermen had stumbled upon. The newspeople ate up any morsel of information they could find about this twenty-five-year-old man named Casey Delevan. They presented it dramatically on the evening news, but the sad truth was that no one had missed Mr. Delevan, and no one was looking for him. The story had no staying power. After a day, the identification of the body pulled from Emerson Bay was old news, overshadowed by Oktoberfest, changing leaves, and Halloween festivals.

It was ten p.m. when Livia started her bag work at the gym. In a tank top, shorts, and bare feet, she went at the Everlast bag with everything left inside her. It was soft but solid when her shin connected with it. As she brought her leg down, she danced on the balls of her feet before unloading a combination of three punches—two straight left jabs and a powerful right hook. Another kick followed. Sweat poured down her long, lean frame. Always athletic, Livia had formerly been a treadmill and Nautilus regular. Running and light strength training had been enough during medical school and residency to stay in shape and give her mind a break. But since she started her fellowship, something more than long runs was needed to offset the overwhelming volume of information her brain absorbed each day. She needed, too, an escape from the eerie morgue, where bodies lay on autopsy tables, the piercing cry of bone saws echoed off the walls, and the smell of formaldehyde hung in the air. Livia needed a release from the close quarters she shared with death, and evidenced by the sculpted body she witnessed in the mirror over the last few months, she'd found her refuge.

Bag work was how she spent the last fifteen minutes of her workouts. Livia had long ago given up on the "cooldown" feature of the treadmill. Cooling down now was saved for the shower.

"Good!" Randy said. He, too, was dripping with perspiration. His T-shirt clung to his hulking body and his arms tensed as though he'd like to get involved in the action. "Mix it up. You throw the same combination over and over, your opponent will anticipate it."

About to release another side kick with her dominant right leg, Livia instead offered an axe kick with her left, followed by a spinning backhand right.

"There you go," Randy said. "Variety gets you out of trouble. You stay stale with that side kick, and your opponent will see it coming." He checked his stopwatch. "Time!"

Livia bent over, breathing heavily, and put her gloved hands on her knees.

Randy patted her on the back as he walked away. "Good workout. I'd take you back home with me as my bodyguard. The streets of Baltimore would never be the same."

"I'm sure."

"See you next week, Doc."

Livia showered at the gym and was home and in bed by eleven thirty p.m. She grabbed the book off the nightstand, disgusted with herself for reading it. She'd spent twenty-seven bucks on the thing and knew some portion of her cash would find its way to Megan McDonald. The previous evening, Livia made it through half the book, which covered Megan's stellar life and all her accomplishments. It covered in detail the summer retreat she championed, and all the girls she had helped in her young life. Livia read page after page about the driven person Megan McDonald was, the entire narrative implying, without frankly stating, what a loss it would have been had she not escaped from that bunker.

Livia hated the writing and the vocabulary and the foreshadowing. She hated that the book turned such a tragedy into a suspenseful true-crime noir. She hated that Nicole, who disappeared from the same beach party on the same night, was barely mentioned. She couldn't stomach the implication that her sister was the *other* girl, the lower-profile, less-special girl who did not have the town's sheriff as a father or a résumé that compared to Megan McDonald's. Livia detested the suggestion that the world would be less a place had Megan McDonald not escaped, but would continue just the same without Nicole. Most of all, Livia was saddened that no one remembered her sister any longer. The country was transfixed, not by the girl who was gone, but by the one who made it home.

Over the past year, Livia watched every interview Megan McDonald had given. She was torn between believing Megan's grief over Nicole, and thinking she was full of herself. Reading this money-grab was not swaying her low opinion of the girl. Why, Livia wondered, would someone put on display her innermost thoughts and horrors for the reading public to devour if not for attention and celebrity?

And despite all this, Livia couldn't stop reading. The story was the closest thing she'd gotten to real details about the night Megan and Nicole were taken. Just as Livia turned the page to begin a new chapter, the phone rang. She answered on the second ring.

"Hello?"

"Livia?"

"Yes?"

"It's Jessica Tanner."

Livia remembered Nicole's friend. Ten years separated Livia and Nicole, and a strange relationship had developed between the two sisters. Livia was very close in a maternal way with Nicole; this motherly relationship lasted until Livia went off to college. Nicole was eight years old at the time, and their relationship blossomed whenever Livia came home for holidays and summers. Some of the greatest memories they shared were those times when Livia was home from college. Livia's mind drifted to those nights, when Nicole would sneak into Livia's bedroom. One late night, she lugged a thick *Harry Potter* novel with her and stood by Livia's bed.

"You've got to go to sleep. You've got soccer in the morning."

"Just for a little while," Nicole said. "Just one chapter."

Livia smiled. "Fine. Hurry up."

She moved the covers to the side, and Nicole climbed into her older sister's bed, tucked her head into the corner of Livia's shoulder as they both lay on their backs. Livia found where they'd left off, marked with a Taylor Swift ticket stub from the previous summer.

Livia opened the book and read. One chapter turned to three and soon she heard Nicole's breathing become deep and rhythmic. It wouldn't have taken much to carry her nine-year-old sister to the bedroom next door, but Livia never minded sharing her space with Nicole. She stuck the stub back into the book, a new location farther along, and couldn't help feel as though the same was happening to them. Each time, they got further along in their story together. Livia wondered what would come next when the book ended. Would another follow, or would the latest one simply end? Sisters don't share beds forever.

Years later, Livia was finishing medical school when Nicole started at Emerson Bay High. Livia's pathology residency occupied much of her life during Nicole's high school years. Their relationship drifted during this time, the formative years of Nicole's adolescence. The realities of life and work sent the sisters in different directions. Reading *Harry Potter* novels was a distant memory tarnished by time. Still, Livia knew most of Nicole's friends from that time, and knew Jessica Tanner had been one of her sister's closest. The last time the two had talked was at a vigil for Nicole more than a year before, and another time briefly when the town gathered to futilely search the wooded areas of Emerson Bay just after the disappearances.

"Hi, Jessica. Everything all right?"

"Yeah. Sorry I'm calling so late. I mean, is this late?"

"It's fine. What's going on?"

"I'm at school. At North Carolina State. My mom just told me about this guy they found back home. Floating in the bay."

"Uh-huh," Livia said, wondering how Jessica had gotten wind that Livia was involved with the case.

"Do you know about it?" Jessica asked.

"Do I . . . yeah," Livia said. "I heard about it."

"Some fishermen, like, found the guy floating or something. But people are saying maybe he didn't jump. Maybe he was killed."

"Okay."

"So I saw a picture of the guy. The dead guy."

"What kind of picture?"

"You know, on the news. My mom sent me the article

from the paper. She still doesn't get that all of that stuff is on-line."

Livia waited.

"So anyway, I just wanted to tell you because . . . I figured you'd wanna know."

"Know what, Jessica?"

"The dead guy? Casey? That they pulled out of the bay? He was the guy Nicole was dating that summer. Before she disappeared."

SUMMER 2016

"Let 'em drool."
—Nicole Cutty

Chapter 5

July 2016
Five Weeks Before the Abduction

They sat on the edge of the pool, feet bathed in the cool water and the high summer sun on their shoulders. Emerson Bay was in the distance, just down the flight of stairs carved into the hillside and which ran down from the pool to the water's edge. A pontoon and speedboat floated next to the dock, and two umbrella bays were vacant of the Jet Skis they stored. Rachel's brother and a friend were streaking the bay on the Yamahas, hopping waves made by the wake of powerboats, the screaming engines audible from the poolside patio where the girls sat. It was Friday afternoon and Emerson Bay was busy. Already, there were boats pulling waterskiers and tubers, sailboats angled from the wind, and music blaring from pontoons anchored out by Steamboat Eddie's.

The three of them—Jessica Tanner, Rachel Ryan, and Nicole Cutty—had been friends since freshman year. At first a reluctant friendship, formed when previous friends from middle school splintered off into various factions created by sports or neighborhoods or popularity or the hundreds of *other categories that separated high school girls. Jessica, Rachel, and Nicole—along with handfuls of other girls— were left to fend for themselves at the beginning of freshman year. A lesson learned in high school, just as in the wild: There was strength in numbers. These three found one another and stuck together. As the other cliques grew, from the cheer team to the scholars, the chemistry geeks to the beauty queens, Nicole and her friends formed their own inseparable union. Only recently, as summer wound down and college beckoned, had things begun to change.*

Rachel's house sat on the edge of Emerson Bay, along with 987 other homes whose owners were lucky enough and wealthy enough to hold such a piece of prime real estate. Although the homes came in various shapes and sizes, most were elaborate structures with sprawling lawns and rolling greenery that spilled down the hillside to the banks of Emerson Bay. Most had pools and beach access and some sort of motorized water toy, from speedboats and pontoons to Jet Skis and fishing boats.

Rachel's home was where the three had spent each summer since freshman year, lounging poolside or cruising the lake on Rachel's ArrowCat. It was where they had become friends. Rachel's house and the pool and the bay and the summers all held their secrets. The pool house was where Jessica had hooked up with Dave Schneider. The boat garage was where Rachel puked the first time she'd gotten drunk. And on the Ryans' docked pontoon was where Nicole claimed to have lost her virginity during a party last summer, although the story had changed so many times no one knew the truth any longer.

"What's up with you lately?" Jessica asked.

"What do you mean?" Nicole said.

"You've been MIA. You don't post anything. You barely return texts. So what's up with you? I know you're not hooking up with anyone."

Nicole smiled and splashed the water with her feet. Shrugged.

"Get. Out! Who?"

"Yeah," Rachel said, forehead wrinkled. "Who?"

"You guys don't know him."

"A Chapel Hill guy?"

"God no! He doesn't go to school."

"Doesn't go to college? How old is he?"

"I don't know. Like, twenty-five?"

Jessica stared at her. "What the hell, Nicole?"

"What? I'm seventeen. It's not illegal. Gotta be fifteen or younger."

"I don't care if it's legal. What's a twenty-five-year-old doing with us?"

"He's not doing anything with us. Just me."

"Whatever," Jessica said. "Does he have a job?"

Another shrug. "I don't really know. Construction, or something."

"So what, he holds the stop sign at construction sites?"

"I don't know what he does."

"Sounds serious," Rachel said.

"Screw you guys. I'm so sick of Emerson Bay boys. And high school boys, in general. Totally predictable. Totally boring."

"When do we get to meet him?"

Nicole made an ugly face. "Great idea. I'll suffocate him with neediness. Please meet my friends so they can love, love, love you!"

"Tell him to come to Matt's party next Saturday," Jessica said, almost a challenge.

"Right. Like he wants to go to a high school party."

"You're still going, aren't you?"

Nicole shrugged again. She could have yawned to get her point across. "Yeah, I guess. The bitches will be there, so I might not stay long."

"*Come on,*" *Jessica said.* "*They're not bitches, they're just . . .*"

"*Perfect. Little. Bitches,*" *Nicole said.* "*And so fake it makes me want to puke.*"

"*Megan McDonald? She is always super nice to you.*"

"Yeah, in a super-fake way. Like: I'm so much smarter than you and prettier than you and more popular than you, I think I'll act really nice to you so you don't feel so sorry for yourself. And if I could find a way to document my charity to you on my résumé, I'd do it because it might get me into a better school."

Jessica and Rachel laughed at the mimic.

"*That's not Megan at all,*" *Jessica said.*

"*If anything,*" *Rachel said,* "*she comes off as too nice. So I can see why you think she's fake. But it's real. It's the way she is. And she created the summer retreat, so you can't make the argument that she's dumb. Girl's smart-smart. Like thirty-six-on-her-ACT-smart.*"

"*Exactly. She created a retreat to help incoming freshman, yet during our freshman year she was the one who was bitchy and cliquey and made people feel like shit.*" *Nicole stood from the pool and moved to a lounge chair.* "*She bothers me.*"

"*She bothers you* lately *because she's hooking up with Matt. I thought you were* 'so over' *him,*" *Jessica said, making air quotes.*

"*I am. But Megan McDonald? Really? I mean, after me, he gets with her? He'll need a crowbar to get in her pants, so what's the point?*"

"*You're disgusting,*" *Jessica said.*

Nicole unhooked her bikini top and lay bare-chested on the lounge chair, closing her eyes and absorbing the sun. "*Tell me when your brother comes back with his perv friend. I don't need them drooling when they see me topless.*"

Jessica and Rachel looked at each other with quizzical stares and suppressed smiles as they watched their friend lay half naked by the pool. They had both discussed Nicole's transformation this summer. They defined it as rebellion before heading off to college. A severing of ties, perhaps, to make the process of leaving her family and friends easier.

"Megan's off to Duke next year," Jessica finally said. "And I'm sure she'll be in Ethiopia or somewhere next summer saving sick kids, so you won't have to worry about her for long."

With closed eyes, Nicole raised her hand in a thumbs-up gesture. "You know what? I am going to Matt's this weekend. Think I'll start a little summer fling with him. See what the little prude does when she sees her boyfriend all over me."

The rev of Jet Skis filled the summer air and Rachel looked down at the bay. "My brother and his friend are back."

Nicole kept her eyes closed as she lay on the patio chair, her breasts glistening with tanning oil and perspiration. She didn't move. "Let 'em drool."

Chapter 6

July 2016
Four Weeks Before the Abduction

The night before Matt Wellington's party, Jessica and Rachel got together to sit by Rachel's pool. Nicole told them she couldn't make it, marking the first time all summer the three hadn't spent Friday on the bay. Nicole used as an excuse her visiting aunt and the ensuing dinner her parents required her to attend. Had she thrown a fit, the way she typically did when forced into something as stupid as dinner with her aunt on a Friday night, she might have wiggled out of it. But the truth was, Rachel's house and the pool and the bay and spending the summer on the water flirting with high school guys she had no interest in just didn't do it for her anymore. Those times felt like they had passed her by. The summers on the bay were in the past, and the magical moments that seemed to come every day when they were younger came less often now, until the whole scene became pointless and boring.

Nicole got home from dinner around ten p.m. She promptly locked her bedroom door and logged on to her computer. She was supposed to talk with him tonight, and it caused her to ache with anticipation.

A few minutes into her solitude there was a knock on her door.

"What?"

"Are you going to say good night to Aunt Paxie?" Nicole's mother asked.

"Good night, Aunt Paxie!" she shouted from her desk.

"Good night, Nicole."

Nicole listened to her mother and aunt shuffle away from her closed bedroom door. She'd seen, earlier in the evening, her mother shake her head at the restaurant when Aunt Paxie asked about Nicole's black hair and black eyeliner and black lipstick. "Just ignore it," she heard her mother say under her breath.

That's all her mother and aunt ever did, ignore things. What else could explain Aunt Paxie's presence in North Carolina for the past three days without mentioning Julie? Ignore anything long enough, and it will go away. It was her mother's unspoken motto.

When Nicole heard no more whispers outside her door, she pecked at her keyboard and found the chat room where they normally talked. Sometimes they moved around, at his urging, to different spots online, as if someone were stalking them and spying on their conversations.

Hey. You around? *she typed.*

It took a few minutes, but then the response came.

Nikki C! Where you been?

Trying to find you. You've been hiding from me.

Ha! LOL. You're the mysterious one. So what's going on, sweet thing?

Not once had Nicole heard his voice, but still she loved when he called her that. No boy at Emerson Bay High would have the courage to talk to her that way. Most could barely hold eye contact, let alone engage in a full conversation. Flattering her with a nickname was something out of the realm of high school banter, which was why Nicole had no FOMO about anything happening tonight on Emerson Bay. This was the only place she wanted to be, and the only person she wanted to talk with. She typed.

Been busy with my friends, but they're getting SO boring lately. Do I sound like a bitch?

A hot one. I saw the picture you posted. You've got a great body, and your face is gorgeous.

Thanks. When can I see you?

I'm way too shy to post a pic.

How about we meet, then?

Much better idea. Your aunt still visiting?

Yeah. Leaves tomorrow. Had to do the whole dinner thing. So over her being here.

She's the one whose kid got snatched?

Their conversations always ended up here. This was a big topic for them and they talked—or typed—for hours about it. He was the only one in Nicole's life who was willing to engage her about the subject. Aunt Paxie had been here since Tuesday, and hadn't once mentioned her daughter. Fine, Nicole reasoned, it was eight years ago. Fine, it still depressed her. Paxie didn't want to turn the visit—her first since Julie went missing all those years ago—into a sobfest. All understandable. But Aunt Paxie hadn't even mentioned Julie. Not once. Ignore, ignore, ignore, and the problem will go away.

Nicole finally typed. Yeah.

What was her name?

Julie.

Your cousin?

Yeah.

You guys were close?

We used to visit each other when we were kids. Mostly it was just our moms getting together, but Julie and I always considered them *our* trips. I remember riding on the airplane next to my mom and just feeling so excited to see her. Then, with our mothers pre-occupied, catching up as long-lost sisters who only saw each other twice a year, Julie and I would stay up until midnight, chase fireflies, and sit around the bonfire while our moms got drunk on wine and relived their childhoods.

Nicole watched the screen after typing so much of her heart and her childhood onto the page. Finally, the reply came.

Sounds fun.

It was.

How old was she?

When she disappeared? Nine.

Tell me about it.

God it felt good to finally talk to someone about this.

Don't really know a lot 'cause my mom never gave me any de-tails. Guess she thought I was too young. I've looked for stories about her on the Internet, but there's not much. They never had any leads. Julie just disappeared one day walking home from school.

Common route.

Nicole looked at the screen for a moment before replying. What's that?

Perps use common routes to take kids because they're pre-dictable. Whoever took Julie knew she would be walking that exact route on that exact day. Guy probably watched her for a long time while he plotted the take.

That's freaky.

Totally. He probably waited and watched and calculated who Julie walked with and at which points during the walk home from school she was alone. Framed his window of opportunity per-fectly, then . . .

There was a small pause in the typing.

They ever find the guy?

No.

Julie?

Another short pause before Nicole typed again.

No one ever saw her again.

Sad.

Nicole stared at the screen and at the word sad *as it popped up in the dialog box. She typed.*

Still miss her.

Ever think about what Julie went through? Try to put yourself in that situation?

Nicole watched as the question popped onto her screen. This was why she was helplessly addicted to their conversations. She'd thought about this very thing for years. She wondered how Julie was taken and how she felt when she realized she wasn't going home. She wondered if Julie climbed into his car by herself, or if he forced her. She wondered where he took her and what he did to her. Morbidly, she thought about these things. During the days and sometimes when she slept at night. Mostly, she and Julie chased fireflies in her dreams, but within the darker imaginings were murky images of Julie crying in a dim closet, too scared to push open the door and run for help.

Finally, Nicole's fingers moved over the keyboard.

All the time.

Long pause.

Me too. I think about my brother, Joshua. Picture him in some dark place, scared and all alone. It makes me want to cry but I can't stop thinking about it. Does that make us weird? These thoughts?

I don't know. I don't think so. Better than pretending Julie never existed, the way my mother and aunt do.

Nicole sat still and waited for a reply. Finally, it came.

I've got a secret, if you promise to keep it.

I promise.

Nicole stared at the screen. There was a short pause before Casey's reply popped up.

I know a club.

Oh yeah? What kind of club?

The kind I think you'd really like.

Chapter 7

July 2016
Four Weeks Before the Abduction

Actually a chain of four lochs connected to one another by channels, Emerson Bay was the largest and most populated, and ran via the Chowan River to the Atlantic Ocean. Homes colonized the shores and were stacked deep inland away from the bay. Matt Wellington's house sat on the banks of Emerson Bay and, like Rachel Ryan's, was a sprawling hillside estate whose backyard spilled down to the water's edge. By ten p.m., Saturday night's party was in full swing.

The Wellingtons' pool was dug into the side of the hill, with boulders and granite creating a backdrop where the bulldozer had cut into the earth. Spotlights highlighted the granite, and underwater bulbs made visible the kicking legs of kids treading water in the deep end. Girls screamed as they sat on guys' shoulders for chicken fights. Matt Wellington's parents made an appearance every so often, walking out to the pool to check on things. The kids resorted to sneaking beers down by the bay. Stairs cut through the hill and led to the water. Out of sight from the house, a cooler filled with cold Budweiser was quickly losing its bulk as kids chugged beer, squashed the cans, and tossed them in the bay.

Megan McDonald sat with her friends at a patio table. Some girls walked around in bikini tops and cutoff shorts. The bolder ones lost the shorts and paraded around in full bikinis.

"She's a total slut," Megan said. "Look at her."

Megan was hanging with her cheer team friends, a huddle of ten girls. They watched Matt hoist Nicole Cutty onto his shoulders by dipping his head underwater and swimming between her legs before standing, his hands firmly planted on her thighs. Nicole screamed as she wrestled Jessica Tanner, who was sitting on Tyler Elliot's shoulders.

At some point during the chicken fight, Nicole reached over and pulled Jessica's bikini down to expose her breast. The boys hooted at the skin show before Jessica screamed and fell backward into the water, one arm crossed over her bare chest, the other extended straight at Nicole with her middle finger raised until the deep end swallowed her.

"Who does that?" Megan asked.

"They're so desperate for attention," Stacey Morgan said.

"And they're getting it. She's going to end up pregnant before she's twenty. Just watch."

"They call her Slutty Cutty for a reason. Half of Emerson Bay would have to take a paternity test to determine the father."

This got the cheer team laughing. Megan and Stacey split off and headed down toward the bay. They each grabbed a Budweiser and sipped the awful-tasting stuff for ten minutes while they watched boys skip crushed empties across the water. From behind her, Matt grabbed Megan around the waist and hugged her tight. Soaking wet from the pool, he dripped all over her.

"You haven't even said hi to me yet," he said in her ear.

"*That's because you've been too busy with the topless girls in your pool.*"

Matt picked her up, Megan's back pressed firmly to his chest. "*I'm throwing you in the bay for that comment,*" he said as he penguin-walked her along the dock.

"*Throw me in and you're dead,*" Megan said calmly.

Matt kept walking closer to the water. At the edge of the dock, he rocked her back and forth. "*One. Twoooo. Three!*" He lifted her up and pretended to throw her in the water. Megan screamed. When he let her go, she turned with a smile and slapped his shoulder.

"*I would've killed you,*" Megan said.

"*Yeah,*" Nicole said, coming down the stairs. She was also soaking wet, just out of the pool. With her breasts spilling from her bikini top, her bottoms straight across her flat stomach, and the string of dock lights reflecting off her skin, Megan admitted she was gorgeous. On the outside. Inside, Nicole Cutty was ugly. She was a bully. The type of person Megan's parents always taught her not to be, and not to be around. Nicole Cutty was the type of person Megan had created the retreat to fight against.

"*How would she explain to her police-chief daddy that she ended up in the water with all her clothes on?*"

"*I wasn't going to throw you in,*" Matt said, still smiling and ignorant of the rivalry.

"*Where's your bathing suit, anyway?*" Nicole asked. "*You know this is a pool party?*"

"*Thanks,*" Megan said. "*I figured that out.*"

"*So where's your suit?*"

"*On my body, I just don't feel the need to parade around in it.*"

"*Figures.*" Nicole laughed. "*It doesn't take a bikini top for everyone to see you're flat-chested.*" Nicole grabbed a beer *from the cooler.* "Get over it or ask Daddy for some implants."

"Shut up, Nicole," Stacey said.

Nicole popped the beer. "Or, since you guys are so scared of swimsuits, maybe you'll join us later when we go skinny-dipping in the bay." She laughed again. "Right! The cheer princesses skinny-dipping." Nicole walked up the stairs. "Matt, tell your buddies we're getting naked at midnight."

Stacey made an ugly face as Nicole walked up the stairs. "It must be tough when everything you have going for yourself is in your tits."

Ignoring the comment, Nicole looked over her shoulder as she ascended the stairs, hips swaying back and forth, and stared at Matt. "You better be in that water with us."

Megan looked at Matt once Nicole was gone. "She's such a slut. I can't believe you hang out with her."

"Nicole?" Matt said, laughing it off. "She's cool. Just has, like, a chip on her shoulder about something. Wants to fit in like everyone else. Blow her off."

Jessica Tanner came down the stairs, smiling as she watched Nicole saunter past. Jessica grabbed a beer. "Don't let her bother you," she said to Megan. "She's got a thing for you."

"For me?" Megan said.

"She thinks you're an elitist. . . ." Jessica opened her palms and shrugged her shoulders. "Or something. Too good to hang with anyone but, you know, your little group. Like Matt said. Just blow her off. She's harmless."

"Isn't she your friend?" Stacey asked.

"Yes. Best friend." Jessica smirked. "But I'm not a zealot. I can admit when my friend is being a bitch." Jessica popped her beer. "I think that's what Nicole hates about your clique. Defending each other no matter what. It irks her." Jessica took a sip of beer. "Me too, sometimes. But hey," Jessica said *as she headed back up the stairs. "Wanna shut her up? Call her bluff about skinny-dipping."*

It was eleven thirty p.m. when the first group swam out to the raft. It floated twenty-five yards off Matt's dock and, lighted by a halogen bulb stuck to the top of the flagpole that stood in its center, the raft was a beacon of light in the otherwise dark bay. Made from thick pinewood, it was a small patio deck floating on Emerson Bay, attached and secured to the bottom by a long chain. Two of the guys floated the cooler out and hoisted it up on the deck. It was only a few minutes before a melee broke out among the guys, pushing one another into the water, backflipping and belly flopping. The girls screamed as they huddled on one side of the raft and allowed the boys to play King of the Hill, which Matt—captain of the wrestling team—won without contest. Next was the girls' turn, as the guys playfully pushed them into the water. Some fought back, but resistance brought the attention of two or three guys who carried the girl by the armpits and ankles to heave her over the side.

Once things calmed down, they all sat around the edge of the raft dangling their feet into the water. Beers were popped and chugged and things quieted down. The same scene played out every time this group got together at a bay party; someone always talked about skinny-dipping. The boys outnumbered the girls on the raft—twelve to eight—all hoping for the girls to magically slip out of their suits and jump in. They would all do the same, they promised. Dares and challenges and compromises were usually laid down before the group finally got bored and swam back, the journey to the raft resulting in nothing more than a good swim and some laughs.

At Matt's urging, Megan and Stacey, along with three other cheerleaders, had floated out to the raft. Jessica, Nicole, and

Rachel also took the swim, and together they made up the group of eight girls. Now, with the twenty kids sitting around, legs dangling in the water and the raft ebbing with the subtle waves of the bay, they broke off into separate conversations. Megan sat next to Matt and they talked about Duke. He, too, was headed there in the fall and they were each happy to know a familiar face would be close. They had never formally dated, although last summer they got together a few times with mutual friends and had gone to see The Martian *together*, which was termed a date only after they kissed in Matt's car. But as popular as they each were, they somehow never managed to be comfortable with each other. So senior year passed with them as friends, both waiting for more to happen, but never getting there.

"So who's doing it?" Nicole asked the group after twenty minutes on the raft. "Didn't we all swim out here for a reason?"

"You go first," one of the guys challenged.

"Please," Nicole said with a dismissive smirk. "I'm not worried about me, I just don't want to be the only naked person in the lake. I want naked guys with me, but you're all too scared to drop trou." Nicole looked at Jessica and Rachel. "Shrinkage? It's so dark, we won't be able to see your little guys anyways."

Jason Miller stood up and walked over to her. "You go, then I'll go."

Another ugly face. "Right, I'll get naked so you can watch me jump in. Then you'll sit down with your buddies, too scared of the woody in your shorts to jump in yourself."

"You're all talk, Cutty. We'll do it at the same time."

The debate went back and forth about who would remove their swimsuit first and in what order. Then came the rules about where to place the discarded clothing, and that no one could touch the suits or there would be hell to pay.

During the back-and-forth, Megan turned to Stacey. "Let's just do it."

"Really?" Stacey said with a smile.

Matt joined in. "Let's just friggin' do it, shut them all up."

"Yeah," Tyler Elliot said, looking at Stacey.

"Fine," Stacey agreed, and in one unified movement of twisting arms and legs they each dumped their suits onto the deck of the raft before anyone knew they had done so.

"See you, suckers!" Matt yelled as they all jumped in the lake. When the group looked over, they saw a brief glimpse of bare butts, shadowed by the night, until the splash erased everything from view. The four of them laughed as they swam away from the raft, protected by the dark water.

This sent the others onto their feet, all straining for a better view of the four who had finally done it. A mass disrobing began, as guys dropped their shorts and jumped into the lake. Nicole was naked a few seconds later, but in no hurry to find protection in the water. She shielded her breasts with her arm as she jostled Jessica and Rachel to join her. The remaining guys who stayed on the raft whistled at the show. Jessica and Rachel quickly undressed and jumped in. Nicole slowly turned to the guys who stood staring at her, uncovered her chest, and stared back at them for a few seconds, her eyebrows raised. It shut them up quickly as the boys blinked and could think of nothing to say.

"Only ones left," Nicole said. She began to fall backward off the raft. "Must have the littlest guys in the group."

A splash followed and she was gone.

In the end, two guys who never dropped their shorts claimed the beer was running low and wanted to keep their buzz going. Megan and Matt, after taking a lap around the perimeter and treading water, grew tired and swam to the safety of the raft, holding on to the side and placing a foot on the bar that ran underwater and encircled the float. Megan was careful to stay underwater, keeping just her head visible.

"That was crazy," Matt said.

"It's senior year, we had to do it eventually."

"I love that we started it."

The water splashed between them as kids swam and kicked around the raft.

"I'm really glad we'll be at school together next year," Matt said.

"Yeah? Me too."

He leaned his face toward hers, careful not to get too close—not to get too much skin-on-skin contact—and kissed her. Megan, balancing with her right hand on the raft and right foot supporting herself on the bar, kissed back, rubbing her left hand through Matt's hair. Without warning, Megan felt a hand run up the back of her thigh and grab her butt with a hard squeeze. She pulled away quickly.

"Take it easy you two," Nicole said. "Grabbing ass in the lake? Get a room, already."

Megan pushed Nicole's hand away. Matt laughed because he wasn't sure what else to do. Nicole swam off as quickly as she had appeared.

"That wasn't me," Matt said as soon as Nicole was gone.

"No kidding."

Spent of energy from treading water, everyone slowly reconvened at the raft. Awkward and shy now that swimming away was not an option, the girls mostly congregated on one side, boys on the other. Matt reached up and grabbed Megan's suit.

"Here you go," he said in a disappointed tone. "Looks like the party's over."

Megan took her bikini and strapped it around her neck, watching out of the corner of her eye as Matt pulled himself out of the water to his waist to retrieve his shorts. She pulled on her bottoms, climbed back onto the raft, and handed out suits to her friends in the water. Everyone did the same except for Nicole Cutty, who climbed up the ladder and stood on the raft, squeezing water from her hair in no particular rush before bending over to pick up her bikini. From the depths of the lake, the guys helplessly stared.

Megan noticed Matt, like every other guy, unable to peel his attention away until Nicole stepped both feet into her bottoms and pulled them up.

PART II

"I'm back, my Love. I'm back."
—The Monster

Chapter 8

October 2017
Thirteen Months Since Megan's Escape

The dorm was a three-story red brick building with a security door and card-key entry. Livia waited outside until she saw Jessica Tanner walk through the lobby. Livia pushed open the door after Jessica unlocked it and they ducked into an empty study room. Close to midnight, about an hour after Livia had received Jessica's phone call, the dormitory lobby was dark and quiet.

"How's medical school?" Jessica asked.

"It was good. I graduated a few years ago."

"Oh, that's right. Aren't you a pediatrician?"

"Pathologist."

"That's what I meant," Jessica said. "I remember Nicole telling me about it. Don't you, like, examine bodies and stuff?"

"Something like that. Can I see the picture?"

Jessica produced a photo from her pocket. Livia took the picture and felt her heart ache when she saw Nicole, black hair weeping from her scalp and dark eyeliner painted thick and heavy onto her lids, transforming her eyes into ovals of coal with sapphire hidden inside. Standing next to her in the photo was a guy who draped his arm over Nicole's shoulder. It took only a few seconds for Livia to match this man's face to the photo of Casey Delevan from her case file, a bit longer to imagine that the decomposed body from a month earlier was the same man posing with Nicole.

Dr. Colt encouraged all the fellows to work on the flaw of seeing their cases only from the side of death. Counseling the deceased's family was an important part of their occupation, and visualizing vibrant souls instead of lifeless cadavers would help the fellows deliver news with compassion. Despite her efforts, all Livia saw when she looked at Casey Delevan was the putrefied body with the leg fracture and the strange piercings in the skull.

"I didn't think Nicole was dating anyone," Livia finally said.

"She was really secretive about it. I never even met the guy. Nicole showed me that picture to sort of, I don't know, prove she had a boyfriend. I was giving her shit about it because no one ever met him. I don't know why I kept the picture. Nic just never asked for it back. Then, when my mom told me about the guy floating in the bay and I saw him on the news . . . it's the same guy."

"Did you know him at *all*?" Livia asked.

"No. Nicole was very private about him. We used to tell each other everything." Jessica shrugged. "I don't know. That was a weird summer for us."

"When was this taken?"

"Last summer, I guess. I mean, after senior year. That's when she started dating him. Our friendship drifted that summer. I always thought it was because of this guy, but I sort of think she was going through some other stuff."

"Like what?"

"I don't know. Rachel and I had a hard time reading her. She was really rebellious and started doing things I've never seen her do before."

"What kinds of things?"

"Like, I don't know, she was really mean to some girls at school. Especially to . . . Megan."

"Megan McDonald?"

Jessica nodded.

"How so?"

"She hated all the attention Megan was getting for the summer retreat program and her scholarship to Duke. Nicole tried to get with Megan's boyfriend, and that caused a big problem."

Livia held up the photo. "I thought she was dating this guy. Casey?"

"She was. The thing with Matt was just to piss Megan off and, I don't know, prove that she could get anything she wanted. I know she hooked up with him that summer."

"With Megan's boyfriend?"

"Yeah. Lots of drama."

"What was this guy's name?"

"Matt Wellington."

"And when you say 'hooked up' what are we talking about?"

"What do *you* think?" She took a deep breath. "Listen, Nic was my best friend. But she was different after senior year. Really promiscuous. Skinny-dipping. I mean, we all did it but Nicole was blatant about it. Making sure everyone saw her naked." Jessica shrugged. "Something was off, you know? With all the black makeup and clothing, whatever that was about."

Livia remembered a trip home during the summer of 2016, and Nicole's startling jet-black hair and the heavy black eye-liner and black clothes. Livia had ignored it. Made a point of saying nothing about it, and was almost obnoxious with her feigned ignorance of her sister's physical change. Tonight wasn't the first time Livia wished she could go back and offer the help Nicole was so clearly begging for.

Livia held up Casey Delevan's picture again. "Nicole ever say this guy would hurt her or anything like that?"

Jessica shook her head. "No. She barely talked about him at all."

"You ever tell the police about him?"

"Yeah," Jessica said. "When they interviewed me, I told them she was dating someone. But I never knew his name and I forgot about the picture until I went through some of my stuff this past summer and found it. Why? You think he had something to do with Nic disappearing?"

"I don't know." Livia stared at the photo, held it up. "Can I keep this?"

"I guess." Jessica lifted her chin. "Do you know what happened to him?"

"Casey? Yeah. He jumped off Points Bridge and was found floating in the bay."

Chapter 9

Trouble sleeping the night before, with thoughts of Nicole and Casey Delevan running through her mind, Livia was at work early on Friday morning. She finished paperwork in the fellows' office until nine a.m., when she was due in the autopsy suite for morning rounds. In front of her locker she pulled the blue smock over her scrubs and stuffed her hair under a surgical cap. She entered the autopsy suite, dropped her surgical gloves and face shield onto the table, and walked over to the whiteboard where the day's cases were labeled and assigned.

She saw her name scribbled in blue dry-erase:

Dr. Cutty — Jean Marie Miller: 89 y/o female fall victim.

The other fellows similarly had cases assigned to them, as did four of the attendings. She read through the list to see if anyone had a more interesting assignment. All the cases that morning looked mundane, except for Tim Schultz. He had a gunshot wound, and Livia was unhappy about it. She knew, however, with little sleep and her mind so firmly preoccupied with Nicole, that today was not the right time to tackle a challenging case. Or even an interesting one. An elderly fall victim felt appropriate for her current mindset.

"You look like shit," Jen Tilly, one of the other fellows, said as she walked up to the whiteboard.

"Thank you," Livia said.

"Were you crying?" Jen asked.

"No. Just up all night."

"What's wrong?"

Livia lifted her chin when Dr. Colt strolled into the morgue. "Long story."

Tim Schultz jogged through the door just after Dr. Colt and hustled past him to the dry-erase board. Dr. Colt, with his hands behind his back, walked to the board and scrutinized it as if he hadn't written every word an hour earlier.

"Late for morning rounds, Dr. Schultz, and you don't get a case for that day."

"Yes, sir," Tim said.

"Cutting it close, no?"

"Had a bathroom emergency."

"Um-hmm," Dr. Colt said, still reading the board, head back and peering through his cheaters. "There are certain things I don't need to know about my fellows, Dr. Schultz. You've just touched on one of them."

Dr. Colt walked to the whiteboard, picked up the eraser, and wiped clean the assignment next to Tim Schultz's name. "That was a gunshot wound that might have been interesting, but I think I'll give it to Dr. Baylor. An overdose came in overnight, and with your stomach already sour, Dr. Schultz, I think that's a better assignment for you."

Dr. Colt began writing on the whiteboard. Livia and Jen smiled while Tim turned his palms upward.

"Dr. Colt, my stomach feels just fine."

"Not for long. The OD is a decomp found in the projects,

suspected to be a week old, or more. The investigators should be wheeling him in soon."

Tim looked over at Livia and Jen, who were doing their best not to laugh. He mouthed, without making a sound, *I wasn't late!*

An hour into her autopsy of the elderly fall victim, Livia was struggling to get through the morning. She had completed the external examination to discover ecchymosis on this eighty-nine-year-old woman's left side, from her rib cage to her shoulder to her skull. She noted and photographed a likely broken ulnar and radius on the left side. The internal examination was unremarkable, as she suspected it would be, and Livia started the process of weighing the organs. Today was the first time in her fellowship—the first time since her early days of path residency—when the smells and noises of the morgue bothered her.

Tim Schultz's decomp arrived just as Livia was detaching the lower intestine from the rectum. As soon as the investigators unzipped the bag, the odor hit her as it wafted through the autopsy suite.

"Christ Almighty, Tim," Livia said. "Turn on your overhead."

Tim switched on his ventilation fan as the investigators positioned the body on his table and quickly fled the morgue.

A few minutes later he sliced open the abdomen, releasing the noxious fumes of intestinal rot. The odor hit everyone in the morgue, and a collective sigh came from each of the doctors.

"Seriously, Tim," Livia said. "Turn up your fan."

"It's on high, Cutty. Since when did you become so odor intolerant?"

Livia tried to block the smell from her mind as she went back to work. The woman in front of her had been discovered yesterday afternoon by her son, who stopped by for his weekly visit and found her lying on the bathroom floor. What Livia needed from this portion of the exam was a time of death, which she calculated from the stomach contents. She noted lividity on the left side, which suggested the fall had likely rendered the victim unconscious since she hadn't appeared to move after the incident. Specifically, she hadn't rolled onto her back as many fall victims tend to do. Livia confirmed the fractured wristbones, and then moved to the skull, where she knew the full story would be told.

With the bone saw in her hands, she worked hard to ignore the mess that was unfolding on Tim Schultz's table. It reminded her of her own decomp from last month, and she tried desperately to stop thinking about Nicole smiling happily in that photo. Livia tried not to think about Casey Delevan's arm draped over her sister's shoulder—the same arm she and Dr. Colt discovered to have suffered "shovel" wounds when someone dug him up. She tried not to think of the abrasions on his wrists and ankles from cinder blocks that pulled him to the bottom of Emerson Bay.

With all these thoughts coursing through her mind, Livia's movements were sticky and fat. She moved the buzzing bone saw over her patient's head and performed the ugliest craniotomy of her short career, forgetting to design the cut asymmetrically so the skullcap would fit back into place without sliding off. Family members were never happy to see their loved one with a deformed skull at the funeral, a lesson every first-year pathology resident learned.

"Shit," Livia said to herself as she switched off the bone saw and watched the skullcap slide off the top of her patient's head.

Dr. Colt—standing at Tim Schultz's table with his hands behind his back, cheaters on the tip of his nose, closely observing the internal exam—looked up. "Dr. Cutty? Is there a problem?"

Livia pushed the skull back into place. She'd now have to run thick sutures through the scalp and, if possible, place a few staples into the skull when she was finished.

"No, sir," Livia said. Dr. Colt drew his attention back to Tim's decomp.

When she let go of the skullcap, it sloughed back onto the autopsy table and Livia peeled away the dura. She examined the brain and quickly documented the findings she knew would be present. A subarachnoid hemorrhage with midline shift of the brain—very typical of head trauma when elderly people fall and are not fast enough or strong enough to break their descent.

Worried about the extra time she needed to suture the skull, Livia performed the neuro exam quickly, removing and weighing the brain, and then taking appropriate photographs for afternoon rounds. With everything completed, she got busy putting the body back together. Making the head pre-sentable proved challenging and time-consuming. When she finished—one hour and fifty-two minutes later—she was em-barrassed by her work. A mediocre technician could have done a better job pulling the Y-incision together, and the skull was simply a mess of running sutures and staples the mortician would have to make presentable. Thankfully, Tim Schultz's decomped overdose distracted Dr. Colt the entire morning.

With her paperwork completed, Livia created a zipped file of her fall victim's case for afternoon rounds. As soon as she finished, she sat at her desk and cruised the Internet, search-ing for anything she could find about Casey Delevan. Pick-ings were slim as Mr. Delevan had little to no online presence aside from the fact that he was recently ID'd as the man fished from the bay at summer's end.

"Well," Tim said as he entered the fellows' office. "That's the last time I use the bathroom before morning rounds."

Livia abandoned her search as Tim and Jen walked in.

"It's been a while since Colt has doled out reprimands," Jen said. "I think he was waiting for his first chance to stick it to one of us. Wrong time, wrong place."

"No kidding," Tim said. "That was the worst case I've seen."

"Smelled like it," Livia said.

"You'd better have your facts straight for rounds," Jen said. "Your decomp is sure to get all the attention. And Colt is on a rampage."

They worked through lunch and then made rotations through dermatopathology and neuropathology before meeting back in the cage for afternoon rounds. Indeed, Tim's case got much of Dr. Colt's attention. Tim spent a full hour in the front of the cage, albeit a calm sixty minutes where he successfully navigated the onslaught of questions. Tim had made obvious progress since fellowship began in July, and was no doubt aided today by Dr. Colt having spent the entire morning at his table.

Jen Tilly presented next. A fifty-year-old woman had died of cirrhosis due to chronic alcohol abuse. The presentation was fast and streamlined nicely by Jen's meticulous preparation. Livia switched spots with her. It suddenly felt odd to be in the front of the cage. Although lately Livia had striven to be here, in front of Dr. Colt and her other teachers, today was an anomaly. All morning, throughout the autopsy and then during the afternoon when she prepared her presentation, her thoughts had been with Nicole. Like a computer application running in the background and drawing down her phone's battery, the left-side analytical portion of her mind had been working all day on Casey Delevan and his connection to her sister. But now, with thirty sets of eyes on her as she stood in the glow of the Smart Board projector, Livia was finally forced to focus her mind on the fall victim she had autopsied. She was surprised to find such a scant amount of information to work from, as if suddenly she was taking that final exam from her dreams for a class she had never attended.

She fumbled through the findings of her external exam, covering the left-side lividity, the bruising, and the broken wrist. She went through the mostly unremarkable findings of the internal exam, noting the presumed time of death based on stomach content and suspected time of last meal. She moved to the neurological findings, covering with some confusion the midline shift she presented as the cause of death.

"What did the QuickTox tell you?" Dr. Colt asked from the darkened gallery of the cage.

Shit.

A QuickTox was an abbreviated toxicology report that quickly identified chemicals in the bloodstream, and was a precursor to the full toxicology report that typically took days to return. Livia had sent samples to the lab, but hadn't run a QuickTox.

"I didn't think to run one. I felt pretty certain in this case that the cause of death was midline shift."

The moment of silence that followed her statement was the most uncomfortable time Livia had spent in the cage. She knew what was coming.

"Is that how we practice medicine, Dr. Cutty? By being 'pretty certain' about things?"

"No, sir."

"Why is there no QuickTox in your presentation?"

"An oversight," Livia said.

"A startling one, Dr. Cutty. Can you please tell us which medications your patient was taking?"

Livia stumbled with her words as she shifted through her notes. "I don't have that information with me."

"You don't have that information with you?" Dr. Colt repeated. He referred to his notes. "This patient was taking eight different medications. One of which was a new Rx for OxyContin, given for recent onset of neck pain and headache. So we have an eighty-nine-year-old woman with a new onset of headache symptoms, prescribed likely too high a dose of an opioid analgesic, who possibly fell as a result of a drug interaction. And you don't have that information in front of you?" Dr. Colt went back to his notes for reference. "She was also taking the acid reducer cimetidine, which is not meant to be taken with OxyContin. Cimetidine increases the blood levels of OxyContin, which can cause dizziness, low blood pressure, and fainting. All quite relevant to a fall victim."

Dr. Colt continued as his voice elevated. "Or, we have a stroke victim who's been having headaches for the past week and collapsed as a result of said stroke. However, the very examination performed to determine if any of these mechanisms played a role in her death didn't actually cover any of these possibilities. So I ask you, Dr. Cutty: This morning, did you see someone's mother on your table? Did you see someone's wife? Or did you simply see an old woman who fell in her bathroom and hit her head?"

He looked back at his notes. "Did you simply see one hour and fifty-four minutes out of your day lying on that table? Because with the reckless manner in which you handled this case, I'm betting on the latter."

The cage took on a heavy quiet when Dr. Colt finished his rant. He stood up and walked to the front of the room, taking a place next to Livia.

"Let Dr. Cutty's case be an example for all the fellows in this program. We want you to make progress during your training. And with progress comes respect. But when you rest on your laurels and put up shoddy work under the cover of that respect, you will be called out. Keep it up, and you might *lose* the respect you've worked so hard to earn over the past three months. Every single human body that comes through this place is someone's wife, brother, son, uncle, sister. Treat them that way. That's why we hired you, and that's what you promised us."

Dr. Colt walked out of the cage and left each of its occupants quiet and uncomfortable as they slowly shuffled papers and headed into the weekend.

An hour later, Livia was sweating as she punished the Everlast bag. Randy leaned a shoulder into the leather to steady it as Livia went after it.

"Because you're in such a nasty mood," Randy yelled over the pounding. "I won't mention your crappy form."

"Good." Livia grunted as she punched. She danced on her feet. "Tonight's not about form, just anger."

She released a combination of punches and kicks for the next twenty minutes until her fists were sore and her shins raw.

"Okay, Doc. That's all my shoulder's got in it."

Livia put her hands on top of her head, breathing heavily. "Thanks, Randy. I'm done anyway."

"Get it all out?"

Livia grabbed her water bottle. "Probably never get it *all* out."

"Wanna tell me about it."

She sipped from the bottle. "What would that do to my membership fees?"

Randy threw her a towel and waited.

"You have regrets in life, Randy?"

"Too many to list."

"Name your biggest."

"Let's see . . . I've got an eighth-grade education 'cause I thought selling drugs on a Baltimore corner was a career path. I've got this"—he pulled down the collar of his shirt to reveal a shiny gray scar across his dark black skin—"because somebody shot me. And I gotta wake up each day knowing I'm alive 'cause I killed the guy who wanted me dead."

Livia stared at him a moment, then slowly nodded her head. "Okay, you trump me."

Randy laughed. "Impossible. Not with regret."

"No?"

Randy shook his head. "Nope. Regret, it's got no size. Mine can't be bigger than yours. My daddy always said: 'You either got it, or you don't.'" He pointed at the bag. "And you're not gonna get rid of it by punching a bag."

"Probably true."

"So what is it? What's your regret?"

Livia looked at the bag, then back to Randy. "Not answering my phone."

That night Livia Cutty woke in her childhood bedroom under the same ceiling fan that kept her cool during the hot summers of her youth. After her trip to the gym, she decided to get out of Raleigh. With Casey Delevan's picture in her purse, she headed to her parents' house in Emerson Bay. Her original plan was to ask them about Nicole in the months before she disappeared. To ask if her parents knew anything about the guy Nicole was dating. Livia had planned to show them Casey Delevan's picture and tell them his body had been pulled from the bay and slapped on her autopsy table. That he was likely dead for more than a year, and if the timing added up he had been killed about the same time Nicole went missing. Livia's original plan had been to confess her suspicions that the man in the picture was somehow connected to Nicole's disappearance. She needed her parents' help to figure out what Nicole was up to in the months before her death because, alone, Livia knew little about Nicole from that summer. The sad truth was that her sister had fallen into the shadowed corners of Livia's life in the years before she was taken. Nicole's rebellious attitude had driven Livia away. She blamed her absence from Nicole's life on her residency and the looming decision to pursue a fellowship or move straight into the workforce. She claimed to have no time for her sister, even when Nicole had asked that summer to stay with Livia for a week.

"*I just need to get out of Emerson Bay for a while,*" Nicole said.

"*And come here? Nic, there's nothing to do here,*" Livia said.

"*I don't care. I'm okay doing nothing. As long as I'm not here.*"

"*I spend twelve hours a day at the hospital.*"

"*I don't care. We can hang out when you get home at night.*"

"*Nicole, I get home at eleven o'clock. Sometimes later. Then I get up early and start it all over again. It's what you do in residency. I'm not going to be able to entertain you, or take you out.*"

"*I don't care, Liv. I just want to get away from everyone here.*"

"*I know high school is hard, but you're done with that now. You'll be off to school in the fall and you'll make new friends. Trust me. Coming here will depress you.*"

Silence.

"*Nic?*"

"*What?*"

"*It's your last summer before college. Enjoy it, okay? Just give up on all the drama. It's pointless.*"

"*So I can't come see you?*"

"*In three weeks I'll be home for a long weekend. We'll talk then.*"

Nicole went missing from the beach party a week later.

Livia had tucked that conversation into the dark recesses of her mind and covered it with a heavy dustcloth. It was a protective measure: compartmentalizing the times she had failed her sister.

When Livia arrived home Friday night, her parents were thrilled to see her. They were anxious to hear about her first months of fellowship. Livia handled a battery of questions and apologized for how busy she had been, and for being out of touch lately. What she couldn't tell them was that her forensics fellowship offered very manageable hours and was, in fact, one of the best lifestyle choices in medicine. The truth was that she had never been so busy that she couldn't return home. But the excuse of a hectic schedule was an easy lie, and her parents never questioned her long absence. Either they were oblivious to the fact that Livia had trouble walking through the door of her childhood home because it reminded her so much of her younger sister, or they knew damn well the trouble she was having and gave her a pass. In this first year since losing Nicole, they all suffered from the same feelings of inadequacy and failure—stuck between needing to do something every minute of the day to prove they hadn't given up, and allowing themselves to let go so they could move on.

Whichever it was, ignorance or a free pass, Friday night's impromptu visit was spent discussing her new life as a forensics fellow and never touched on her absence over the past year. None of Livia's concerns or suspicions about Casey Delevan came to fruition Friday night. Having aged greatly in the last year, her parents shouldered the heavy burden of their missing daughter, and it would be unfair for Livia to present any of these developments before meaning could be assigned to them.

Before bed, Livia had ducked her head into her parents' room. They sat up in bed reading the way she always remembered them doing as a child. She wished them both good night and, backing out of the doorway, noticed Megan Mc-Donald's book on her mother's nightstand.

She sat now in the dark hours of night when sleep would not come, and watched that red ceiling fan spin and soothe her sweaty skin. Her parents had never believed in air-conditioning, and Livia carried memories of her and Nicole sleeping on damp sheets with windows yawning and box fans humming through the night. Warm Septembers saw her off to school with red cheeks and sweaty strands of stray hair plastered to her forehead. October now and unseasonably warm, Livia's bedroom was the same as it had always been.

As the grandfather clock in the downstairs foyer chimed to indicate two hours past midnight, Livia sat up in bed. The room had not changed since she left for college more than ten years ago. Pictures of her youth still stood on her dresser, and stuffed animals hung in a net in the corner. Her old beanbag chair where she used to do her homework sat deflated next to the bed. The room looked like that of a dead child her parents didn't want to forget. Nicole's room next door was the real thing, and Livia sensed why she hated coming home.

At her old desk, Livia pulled out her MacBook and sat in the subtle glow of the screen. She typed *Megan McDonald* into the search engine and found thousands of hits. She pulled up articles from 2016 when Megan and Nicole went missing. The stories exhaustively covered Megan's background. Her shining future was known to the world. The reporters loved that such an all-American girl had been kidnapped. It made for great reading, how such a smart young girl had outfoxed her abductor, escaped from the unsettling bunker the entire country got to know so well through pictures and tours on the morning talk shows, whose journalists had all converged onto the small town of Emerson Bay. Livia found a video of Dante Campbell clambering out of the bunker in a skirt and high heels and looking like a complete fool.

The country fell in love with Megan McDonald. She was the girl who made it home. Megan became a star. She was the brightest of Emerson Bay High, and after the abduction she was the doll of the country. That Nicole Cutty was also a part of the story was only news initially. That Nicole's abandoned car was found down the road from the beach party where both the girls had gone missing was only newsworthy until Megan McDonald resurfaced. Megan's stunning return home and heroic escape overshadowed everything else. Eclipsed the fact that Nicole was still gone.

As Livia sat in her childhood bedroom, she realized how much had changed in the last year, and how much had stayed the same. Her room. Her parents' love of humid, stuffy homes. And Livia's unwavering guilt that during her sister's time of need, she had turned her back on Nicole.

Livia typed the name *Casey Delevan* into the search engine and hoped for more luck than she had earlier in the day. Mr. Delevan was a twenty-five-year-old construction worker reported missing by his landlord in November of 2016. Estranged from his mother, and with an MIA father, he had no family looking for him and no one who ever knew he was gone. The article stated that Casey Delevan's mother lived in a town outside of Atlanta called Burlington. Livia checked the map. I-95 to I-20, about eight hours.

The drive looked easy. A straight shot and a good place to start.

Chapter 10

With her parents still sleeping, Livia snuck out of the house at six a.m. By noon, she entered Georgia. Bald cypress trees stretched into the afternoon sky, and river birch shadowed the road. The last two hours of the drive were easy, and Livia allowed the GPS to guide her through the town of Burlington.

Casey Delevan's mother lived in a dilapidated house with peeling paint and dirty windows. There was no garage, but a rusted-out Toyota Corolla was parked in the gravel driveway. It was the middle of the afternoon on a Saturday. Three hours earlier Mrs. Delevan had answered the phone when Livia called and asked if she were interested in purchasing a magazine subscription. Now Livia parked in the street and walked to the house. The doorbell made no audible sound and after the second try Livia knocked instead. A moment later, a middle-aged woman answered the door.

"Barbara Delevan?"

"Yes?"

"Hi, ma'am. My name is Dr. Livia Cutty. I'm here to talk to you about your son."

The woman regarded Livia through the screen door, then pushed it open and held it for Livia to enter. "C'mon in."

Livia walked through the door, which led directly to the living room. On a sunny autumn day, Mrs. Delevan's home was dark and drab. A forced blackness brought by drawn shades that allowed only an outline of boxed light to enter. No lamps helped Livia's vision, and the result was a dingy brown glow her eyes needed time adjusting to.

"Can I get you something? Water or soda?"

"No, thank you."

"Beer, or something?"

"I'm fine."

"C'mon in and have a seat."

Livia walked into the living room and took a seat in the recliner. The couch, Livia could tell, was Mrs. Delevan's domain. It was split into three sections, and the middle cushion was well worn, trampled down and stained with various colors—food and coffee. Mrs. Delevan fell into the spot and brought her feet up onto the coffee table. There, too, was evidence of a sedentary life. The finish on the table was absent from where the woman's feet constantly rested as she watched television—a giant monstrosity that stood in the corner and predated flat panels, it was the very definition of a "large screen" television. It was blaring an episode of *Housewives* from somewhere, and in the same movement that Mrs. Delevan sat down, she muted the television.

The cushion to her right was stacked with papers—Livia guessed they were bills or financials of some sort, organized roughly in piles and by a slider where envelopes rested upright. Covering the cushion to her left was food and beverages. Cartons of takeout and plastic bottles of Coke, the current one wedged between the cushions. A bottle of vodka stood in the corner of the couch and a white Styrofoam coffee cup, the rim bitten and marred, rested on the table.

Mrs. Delevan slopped some vodka into the coffee cup and topped it with Coke, then looked at Livia.

"If you're here to talk about Casey, I'm gonna need one of these. Sure you don't want nothin'?"

"Yes, thank you." Livia looked around the small home. "You live here alone, Mrs. Delevan?"

"Call me Barb. Yeah, it's just me. Alan down at the store thinks he lives here sometimes, till I set him straight." She smiled to reveal a set of rickety teeth and necrotic gums.

Livia noticed a pack of Marlboros on the end table and had smelled the stale odor of nicotine as soon as she walked in the door. The last years of Livia's life had been spent analyzing the lifeless human body, its tissue and cells, and witnessing the destructive nature of the world—the things the human race does to one another and to themselves, the substances that are ingested, the air that is breathed, and the manner in which our organs malfunction as a result of it all. The consequence of this education and the postmortems she'd conducted was that Dr. Livia Cutty saw death before it arrived.

She watched Barb take a gulp of vodka and Coke and imagined the fatty liver that sat inside the woman's body. Livia knew exactly what that organ would feel like in her hands, bloated and greasy with hardening vessels snaking along its surface, abused for so long by the toxins that washed through it. When Barb reached for the Marlboros and put one between her lips, pinching her lips together as she ignited the tobacco, Livia watched in her mind's eye as the smoke traveled through the trachea and into the lungs. She imagined the epithelial cells and goblet cells lining the airway, streaked now with yellow soot and slowly dying. She saw the small bronchioles of Mrs. Delevan's lungs already stenosed from years of abuse, and the tiny clusters of alveoli tight from necrosis and unable to expand and transfer oxygen into the bloodstream. Put this woman on a treadmill and

Livia could see her heart working in overdrive to push oxygen into those dying lungs.

"You have one of those?" Barb asked. "A guy who thinks he can come and go as he pleases?"

"Can't say I do, ma'am."

Barb waved her hand to dismiss the thought. "You with the police?"

"No, not exactly. I'm with the Office of the Chief Medical Examiner in North Carolina. I was the one who performed the autopsy on your son."

"Oh yeah? Cops said I could call you if I had any questions." Mrs. Delevan turned and paged through the papers to her right, gave up after a minute. "They gave me a card, it's in here somewhere."

"Here," Livia said, handing her a new one. "I'm always available."

"You come all the way down from Raleigh?" Barb said, reading the card.

"Yes, ma'am."

"Long way."

"It was a pretty drive. Trees are starting to change," Livia said. "And I don't like talking to family over the phone about something so delicate."

"Well, I appreciate it. Police tell me my Casey didn't drown, that maybe somebody killed him."

"Yes, ma'am. That's what my examination revealed."

"Somebody stabbed him, they said?"

Livia nodded. "That's what it looks like, yes."

Homicide detectives, Livia was learning, were notorious for leaving out "unimportant" details when talking to victim's families. Livia could imagine the two Raleigh detectives setting foot in this home and knowing two things immediately. First, Barb Delevan had nothing to do with her son's death. And second, she wasn't going to be useful to their investigation. To streamline their visit, the detectives had left quiet the details about the suspected manner in which Casey Delevan had died. "Stabbed" carried the connotation of a sharp object to the gut. As awful as that image may be, unidentified holes to her son's skull were worse.

Barb Delevan shook her head, took a sip of vodka and a long drag from her cigarette. "You sure he didn't drown like the newspeople say? He wasn't really stable. Mentally, I mean. I could see him jumping from that bridge before I could see him . . . well, before I could imagine someone hurting him."

"I'm sure, ma'am. Your son did not drown."

"But on the news, they say he might have."

"I understand, but the newspeople have it wrong."

"How can you tell?"

"Lots of ways. But the strongest evidence we have is that your son had no water in his lungs. This tells us without question that did not drown. And he had no injuries consistent with a long fall from a bridge."

"So it's true? Someone stabbed him?"

Livia nodded and Casey's mother wiped her eyes before taking another hit from her cigarette.

"He suffer?"

Livia had no way of knowing this. But based on Maggie Larson's report that whatever was used to penetrate Casey Delevan's head had breached the brain tissue as deep as an inch and a half in four different locations of the temporal lobe—responsible for hearing and cognitive ability—there was a very good possibility that Casey Delevan suffered a long, slow death while bleeding out and completely conscious. The only good news was that he might have been deaf and unable to comprehend what was happening. Then again, he might have lost consciousness, making his death truly painless. This long afterward it was simply impossible to know for certain. Still, Livia's answer was immediate.

"He died instantly."

Barb nodded. Knowing that her son had not suffered relieved some of her burden.

"I'd like to ask a few questions about Casey, if that's all right," Livia said.

Barb shrugged. "Sure."

"Police said you two were estranged."

"We didn't talk, if that's what you mean."

"May I ask why?"

Another sip of vodka. "Long story."

"I drove a long way."

"Why's it important?"

Livia thought for a moment. "About a year ago, summer before last, a couple of girls went missing from up where I live in Emerson Bay."

Barb pointed two fingers at Livia, cigarette between them and smoke twisting behind. She nodded her head. "I 'member that. That one girl is still all over the news. One that got away."

"Correct. The other girl? She was my sister."

"Other girl who was taken?"

"Yes."

"That was your sister?"

Livia nodded.

"Well, shit on that. Sorry to hear, Doc."

"Thank you." Livia shifted in the recliner. "The reason I mention it is because Casey and my sister, Nicole, were dating when she disappeared. My examination of the—" Livia stopped herself. She almost said *body,* something Dr. Colt had lectured them about. Relatives didn't want to hear about bodies. The deceased were still very much alive in their memories. "—of your son indicates that he likely died around the same time that my sister went missing. End of the summer of 2016. Maybe fall. So for my own selfish reasons, Barb, I wanted to find out a little about Casey. About the person my sister was dating."

"You're not sayin' Casey had something to do with those missing girls, are you?"

Having built a good rapport to this point, Livia didn't dare reveal her suspicions. And the truth was that she had no idea what to think about Nicole and Casey. "Of course not. I'm just looking for anything I can find about that summer. Anything I can learn about my sister before she went missing."

"You know," Barb said, pouring more vodka into the white Styrofoam cup, "we're a lot alike, you and me."

"Oh yeah? How's that?"

"My older boy, Joshua, he went missing. He was nine. Out with Casey and their daddy at the fair. Their father was such a piece of shit, excuse me. Worthless as a husband and no good as a father. Knowing this about him, I still let him take my boys to the fair that day. He came home with Casey. Never saw Joshua again."

Livia paused at the revelation. "I'm very sorry to hear that."

"Me too. So I know how you feel. About your sister. Casey would've known, too."

"When did that happen? Your other son?"

"July twelfth, 2000. He'd be twenty-seven now, but I only know him as that nine-year-old boy stuck in my mind." Mrs. Delevan looked off into the corner of the room.

"Joshua was never found?"

Barb shook her head. "My Joshua is gone. Police questioned my husband for a long time, but they finally gave up on that angle. There was a predator at that fair, and he waited until Joshua drifted far enough away from his daddy.

That's all it was. The police checked in with me for a year to tell me about their leads and about the case. But they stopped calling eventually. After a while, I gave up hope. Me and their daddy were never the same. I still blame him. He didn't have nothin' to do with Joshua's disappearance, but he was the one supposed to be watchin' my boy that day. He knows it, too. So he took off about a year after we lost Joshua. Casey and me never seen him again. Casey hung around until he was eighteen, then he took off like his daddy. Ain't talked with him for three, four years. Then I get a call from the police. Now both my boys are gone."

Livia listened to the sad life of Barb Delevan. The self-destruction and drawn shades and dark house and reclusive lifestyle made a great deal more sense. And so, too, did Nicole's attraction to Barb's son. Their cousin Julie's disappearance—a turning point in Nicole's childhood—was something Casey Delevan would have related to. Livia imagined Nicole finding comfort in that connection, something she hadn't found from her family. Livia had been off at college when Julie disappeared and didn't see the ramifications until the following summer when Nicole was withdrawn and confused. A nineteen-year-old kid herself, Livia wasn't equipped with the tools to comfort her younger sister about something so tragic. Her parents tried to shield the horror of it by moving on and hiding the details from her.

"I'm really sorry for your loss," Livia said. "I won't take up any more of your time. If you need anything, or have any questions, please call me."

"Thanks for coming all the way down, Doc. And for setting my mind to rest that my boy didn't suffer."

"Of course."

"And it does get easier," Barb said, sitting up and pouring more vodka. "Day by day, I miss him less and less."

Livia stood. She knew Barb Delevan was talking about her

missing son whom she hadn't seen for nearly twenty years, not Casey. That Barb and Casey had lost touch, Livia was sure, had to do with the nine-year-old boy trapped in Mrs. Delevan's mind.

"Thank you," Livia said as she headed for the door and the fresh air outside.

Chapter 11

Megan McDonald pulled up to the house in West Bay. It was dark and dreadful, but she'd never had the heart to tell Mr. Steinman how hard it was to come here. He was lonely, and Megan understood that if *she* didn't visit him, no one would. His wife was a number of years older than he, the love affair originating from two separate marriages and now, on the downhill side of life, culminating with Mr. and Mrs. Steinman in separate rooms much of the time.

It was a sad life that Mr. Steinman had described to Megan over the past year, and she had decided not to let him live out his days alone. She owed him something, and company is what she had to offer. That she needed to drive along Highway 57 and past the spot where Mr. Steinman had found her staggering the night she escaped from the bunker was an added element to the silent sacrifice Megan made to visit the man who had saved her life. But Megan couldn't claim full martyr status for her visits to Mr. Steinman. With all her friends away at college, she actually looked forward to their cribbage games.

She climbed from her car and knocked on the door.

"Come in, my lovely young lady," Mr. Steinman called from his couch. He sounded in a jovial mood this evening.

Megan pushed through the front door to the smell of old people, a combination of talcum powder and antiseptic. Some might be turned off by the home. It was less than organized, and with some neglect could be featured on a hoarding reality show. But Megan was always flattered when she visited Mr. Steinman. He was not elderly, just sixty, and his self-awareness had not abandoned him. She knew the stacks of clutter in the corner were his way of tidying up for her presence. The smell of rubbing alcohol and antiseptic, she knew, could not be avoided.

Mr. Steinman sat in his worn green recliner, a deck of cards neatly arranged on the coffee table next to the cribbage board. This was, Megan knew, the highlight of his week.

"Hi," Megan said.

"Long one or short one?"

"Short. Sorry, I've got to get home and then to therapy."

Mr. Steinman leaned forward and shuffled the cards. "Sit," he said. "Soda?"

"Sure."

The cards fluttered together as he shuffled them. "Help yourself."

Megan grabbed a soda from the kitchen and then she sat at the corner of the couch. Mr. Steinman dealt six cards.

"I'll let you have the crib to start," he said.

Megan smiled and analyzed her cards. "Go easy on me."

"Never. Where've you been lately?"

"Book stuff. Interviews and all that."

Mr. Steinman regarded her over the top of his cards. When their eyes met, he looked back to his hand and discarded two cards into the crib. "You're not fooling me, you know that?"

"We've just started playing, I haven't tried to fool you yet."

"I mean with the interviews."

Megan paused briefly, but then discarded her own cards to the crib.

"It's the way you smile," Mr. Steinman said. He looked up, held eye contact this time.

"How's that?" Megan asked.

"When you're here and you get a good run or a string of fifteens, you smile. You *really* smile. Not that fake thing you do with your lips together when you're on TV."

"Oh, I have different smiles?" Megan let out a halfhearted laugh that *she* didn't even believe.

"Yeah, like that. It's as fake now as it is when you're gabbing with Dante Campbell. I don't like it."

She played her first card, a ten of diamonds.

"Don't lead with a ten or a face card. I tell you the same thing every time." He laid a five on top of it and moved his peg two places on the cribbage board. He threw down a four of hearts. "And don't think you can purposely play badly to distract me. Why do you smile like that in interviews?"

He was old and reclusive, but Megan could never argue that Mr. Steinman was anything but observant.

"I don't know. 'Cause I don't like doing them."

"Then stop."

"I can't. Everyone wants me to do them."

"You go through life doing all the things everyone *else* wants you to do, and you'll wake up one day realizing your life's passed you by and you've got a list of stuff you've never gotten to."

Megan threw a nine onto the table.

"Yeah, well, I'm doing what I need to do at the moment to earn myself some freedom. I've got other things I'm working on, too."

Mr. Steinman threw a card. "Like what?"

"Like trying to figure out what happened the night you found me."

Mr. Steinman paused, lowered his cards. "How are you doing that?"

Megan shrugged.

Mr. Steinman stared at her. "Speak."

"With my doctor. We're getting closer to figuring some things out about where I was held."

Mr. Steinman dropped his cards onto the table. "I was talking about getting on with your life as far as doing things that *you* want to do. Like going to college. Or taking that trip to Europe you keep talking about."

Megan shrugged. "Maybe."

There was a loud crash from another room, and Mr. Steinman was up in a flash. Megan had never seen him move so quickly.

"Wait here," he said. He scampered through the kitchen. The keys he wore clasped janitor-style to his belt loop jingled as he moved.

Megan heard a door open and his footsteps pound on the stairs. Sitting in the living room by herself, Megan tossed her cards onto the table and took a deep breath. If she wasn't fooling Mr. Steinman during her book tour, she certainly had everyone else guessing. *Missing* was climbing the best-seller list and Megan was waiting to hear where it landed. Whether Mr. Steinman approved or not, she'd have to use her fake smile for the foreseeable future.

Mr. Steinman returned a few minutes later, slightly winded and with a glistening layer of perspiration on his forehead.

"Everything okay?" Megan asked.

"Not entirely. I'm afraid I'll have to take a rain check on tonight's game."

"Oh, of course." Megan stood up.

"Or . . . I don't mean to kick you out . . ." he said. "Would you like to finish your soda?"

"No. I'll take it with me."

"I'm sorry. I'm terribly embarrassed."

"Don't be. I'll come back and we'll play again."

"When?"

"Um, next week?"

Mr. Steinman nodded. "I'll look forward to it."

"Are you sure you don't need any help? I promise I don't mind."

With an ushering hand on her shoulder, Mr. Steinman led her to the door. "I'll be fine. Come again next week. Please."

Megan sat in her bedroom and scrolled though her phone. A year and a half ago, she couldn't pick up her phone without several text messages waiting for her. Now all she managed were a few e-mails from friends who still kept in touch. But e-mails were a distant way to communicate, meant for parents and old acquaintances and readers of her book who stalked her and hoped for a reply to the desperate praise they typed in the too-long messages.

"Honey?" her mother said in a whispered voice as she poked her head into Megan's bedroom.

The word *honey* had never crossed her mother's lips until after the abduction. And the whispered calls into her bedroom were the definition of regression, as though Megan were an infant waking from an afternoon nap.

Oh, there she is! Megan could almost hear her mother squeak in the annoying baby voice of a new parent. *Look who's awake.*

"What's up, Mom?" Megan said, looking up from her empty phone.

"Claudia's on the line. She has some exciting news."

Claudia was the literary agent her mother had sought out when she came up with the idea for Megan to collect her thoughts about her abduction and stick them between a hardcover binding, which displayed on its cover the eerie forest from where she had escaped, and Megan's thin-smiling face on the back flap like a James Patterson novel.

Megan's mother walked into the room and handed her the phone. She smiled. "You'll want to hear this."

Megan took the phone and placed it to her ear. "Hi, Claudia. What's going on?"

"Dante Campbell is pure gold! We knew there would be a big regional audience, but since the interview your book has taken off. I just got word that you will be eleven on the *New York Times* Best Seller list for next week."

Megan looked up to see her mother's smile, wide and steep across her face.

"That's . . . awesome," Megan said in a monotone.

"I've set up another interview for you. There are lots of requests coming in. I need to know your schedule so we can book them."

"I work eight to four."

"Of course, but would your dad give you a little time off if I set up a phone interview?"

"I guess I could ask."

"It's no problem," Mrs. McDonald said, loud enough for Claudia to hear.

"Okay, Miss *New York Times* best-selling author!" Claudia said. "I'll get a few of these set up, and we'll touch base next week."

There was silence for a few seconds.

"This is a big deal, Megan."

"I know," Megan said, trying for conviction. "I'm psyched."

"We'll talk next week."

Megan handed the phone back to her mother.

"So?" her mother said with wide eyes.

Megan let out a sigh of disbelief. "I don't know. It's crazy."

"*So* crazy. I'm very proud of you, Megan. You're helping so many girls who have gone through a similar experience."

Megan shrugged. She doubted that if every abducted person in the country purchased a copy of her book the number would be large enough to launch it onto any bestseller list. The readers who were buying *Missing* were not in need of any insight the book might offer on recovering from abduction. The majority of readers lusted after an eerie story of survival and escape, and they were happily eating it up.

"You can tell your father. He's coming home today."

Megan's mother quietly closed the door, twisting the handle so the spring mechanism didn't pop when the door caught. The same way a nursery door would quietly be closed.

Alone again, Megan reactively scrolled through her empty phone until she finally threw it onto the comforter next to her and lay down on her bed. She had badly miscalculated, figuring that after more than a year no one would still care about her story. Now the book she didn't write but which carried her name and image was a best seller. She had originally agreed to the book on her mother's urging. It would pay for college, her mother told her. And would help other victims of abduction. Megan's father was indifferent about the idea, struggling in his own way with the circumstances of their new lives. But once the idea of helping other victims came about, everyone else jumped on board. From Claudia the agent to Diane the editor to Dale the publicist, and eventually to the sales force at the publishing house. No one could admit that Megan's story offered an opportunity for profit. The same way Dante Campbell could not perform her interview without first establishing that Megan was healing, none of them could stick a dollar in their pocket from the sale of the book without first referencing all the "girls" it was helping and all the semesters it was financing.

The book was born only because Megan needed something to give her parents that reminded them of their daughter. She needed something to work on that showed them the
old Megan still existed. The Megan they loved and clung to.
The smart Megan, ambitious and talented. The all-American
girl filled with determination and bursting with potential.
She had nothing else to offer her parents after the abduction,
so Megan agreed to write the book with Dr. Jerome Mattingly, a noted psychiatrist who'd written a hundred other
books, and on whose couch Megan lay twice a month. Whatever. It kept her busy, and kept her parents mostly out of her
hair. Her mother so desperately longed for the girl Megan
used to be that the desire practically oozed from her eyes
whenever she saw Megan editing Dr. Mattingly's work.

There was no combination of words to explain the phe-
nomenon Megan had undergone. She had yet to find a way
to tell her parents that the daughter they remembered from
before that summer was gone. Cynthia and Terry McDonald
would need to come to this conclusion on their own. Until
then, Megan played along. She allowed her mother to hope
somewhere in the chapters of a morose autobiography that
the child who once existed would be found, and that the old
Megan would spill back to her from the pages. Megan owed
her mother the courtesy of the illusion that the great Dr. Mattingly would tease the old Megan from the prickly vines of
the new world she had returned to after her escape. Brush off
the burrs and the dirt and the pain and the memories to deliver Cynthia McDonald's daughter back to the world as
though the last fourteen months had never happened. As if
those two weeks in that cellar were nothing but a distant,
transparent memory easily looked past.

The problem was that Megan didn't want the help. The
only girl she wanted to save was long gone. Megan was sure

no book, best-seller list, or fantasy about other girls being inspired by her story would be enough to erase the image she held of herself running to safety while Nicole Cutty sat alone in that dreary cellar waiting for the man to come at night. Waiting for the keys to rattle and the floorboards to squeak. So many noises announced his presence. The soft hum of the car's engine. The thump of the door slamming. The keys jangling and the door scraping across the floor when he opened it. His steps—the gentle drumming of soft-soled shoes against the dusty, wooden stairs as he descended to the cellar.

All these sounds came at night. It was his favorite time.

"Tell me about it," Dr. Mattingly said. "Tell me about *that* sound."

Megan sat in a plush chair in Dr. Mattingly's office. This was her twenty-eighth session, two each month since her escape, and she was finally starting to buy into the idea of hypnosis. Before she met Dr. Mattingly, the only time she'd seen someone "hypnotized" was during a school variety show where the hypnotist pulled student volunteers from the crowd and made them hop around stage like frogs. Hypnosis, Megan was learning, was a real thing. It was a state of consciousness that allowed thoughts to surface which might otherwise stay buried.

It was immediately after one of Dr. Mattingly's hypnosis sessions that Megan had remembered so clearly the sound of airplanes that flew overhead during her captivity. And there was something else along with those airplanes, some other noise that had settled into the deep alcoves of her mind. A noise she was trying to retrieve. So delicate and draining was the process—like stretching under the bed for an object just out of reach, she drummed her fingers to gain that extra fraction of an inch. And now, on Dr. Mattingly's fat chair, Megan knew not to strain too hard. After twenty-eight sessions, she knew the process. To find success, she had to give herself to Dr. Mattingly's voice. Go only where he suggested. When she resisted, when she pulled her thoughts to where *she* believed they should go, the effect of hypnosis was lost and her mind drifted and she woke to find Dr. Mattingly snapping his fingers and repeating the word *no no no no*. Over the past year Megan had learned that getting into the correct mindset took time and patience, and once in that state, resistance could ruin the effect in seconds. She had only one shot during each visit and she found herself letting go of her rebellious attitude for two hours each month when she saw Dr. Mattingly. She was making progress, even if it was for a different purpose than Dr. Mattingly understood. His goal was to explore every inch of her mind to remove any repressed thoughts about her captivity. Shine light on all of it and it will eventually stop hiding.

Megan had a different goal entirely.

"It's the airplanes overhead," Dr. Mattingly continued. "Tell me again about the sounds."

Megan didn't want to talk about the airplanes again. This breakthrough had come last time. There was something else she wanted to reach for, something new, and she felt the proverbial fingertips of her mind stretch and strain for that other thing. The other sound she wanted so badly to identify. Something in her posture or her eyelids or her breathing betrayed her thoughts.

"Stay with me," Dr. Mattingly said in his calming voice. "Stay with what we can identify for certain. Just for now. We'll go to that other sound soon. Concentrate on the airplanes for now. Tell me about that sound."

"They were high, but not speck-in-the-sky high. Medium

high. They gave a low rumble like a far-off highway," Megan said, still with her eyes closed.

"And tell me the direction again."

Megan almost allowed the thought that she'd already been through this to pass through her mind. She resisted the temptation.

"It came from the back wall," Megan said. "Far away at first, then louder as it moved overhead. Then . . ." Long pause. "It faded."

"How did it fade?"

"From the windows. I could only hear the plane through the boarded-up windows in the back of the cellar. Once the plane was overhead, it faded away."

"Go to the other side of the room," Dr. Mattingly said. "Tell me what you see there. Tell me about that room. The cellar."

Megan had spent so much time in the cellar during these sessions—all her time, actually—that it was no longer disturbing to be there. At first, she blocked those images from the spotlight. Ran from them. But through her visits with Dr. Mattingly, she eventually understood that running from something implanted in your memory was like trying to pass a mirror without seeing your reflection.

It was not easy at first, but once she understood the possibilities of hypnosis, Megan gave herself fully to the process. So now, despite wanting to explore that other thought, the other sound that had just poked her subconscious, she instead put her trust in Dr. Mattingly to take her there in due time.

"Concrete floor," she said. "Gray floor. Cold at night, which felt good on my feet because it was so hot during the day."

"And the walls?"

"Same. Bare concrete with grooves or ridges every so

often. A bed in the back corner by the windows. No sheets, just a box spring, frame, and bare mattress."

"Now walk to the other side. Away from the windows. Follow the sound of the airplane. What is there?"

"It's a square cellar. My bed is there. Three windows boarded over. I can only walk for a short distance. I'm shackled to the wall by a strap on my ankle. I can go only as far as the chain will allow. There are stairs here, on the other side of the cellar."

"Can you see the stairs? Can you reach them?"

"No. They are around the corner and my chain is not long enough. The shackle allows me only to reach the small table near the stairs. He leaves my meals here."

"Good. Megan, I want to go back toward the windows now. Back to where your bed is. I want you to sit on the bed. The shackle is loose and you can move freely now. Tell me what you see and hear when you sit on that bed."

"It's dark. Always dark with no lights. The windows are boarded. Just a sliver of daylight spills through the tiny gap between the plywood and the edge of one of the windows. The bed squeaks when I sit on it."

"Tell me."

"The springs compress under my weight and creak when I adjust my position."

"Now stay very still. Don't move. Don't shift. Tell me about the squeaking now."

"It's gone."

"The springs are quiet?"

"Yes."

"Tell me about the stairs."

"They are quiet, no sounds."

"Tell me about the airplanes."

"They are gone, faded away."

"But there is *something*."

Long pause.

"Breathe in, slowly."

Megan did so.

"Through your nose and into your core, not your lungs, Megan. Center yourself."

Megan inhaled, centered the breath in that area below her chest, the center of her body. Then she blew slowly from her mouth.

"Again. This time, sitting on the bed in the dark cellar, listen to your breath. Listen as it enters your core."

Megan inhaled again.

"And listen to it leave your body."

Long exhale.

"Once more. Bring that air into your core and hold it there. Listen."

It was dead quiet in Megan's mind as she sat in the dark cellar of her captivity. This was how it mostly was during her weeks in the cellar, eerily quiet unless she broke through the silence. But then there was something. It was what she wanted. The sound she had been searching for since the session began. The sound she could never have found by herself, so buried, as it were, in the redundant folds of the memory center of her brain. But suddenly, as she held the latest breath in her core, the sound was there in her ears. She listened to it and explored it and let it run through her thoughts like the memory of the ocean tide from a tropical vacation.

"Tell me about it," she thought she heard Dr. Mattingly whisper.

"Soft. Far away. Really far. Just barely can I hear it. Like a long moan, but higher in pitch. A motorcycle without the rumble. No, this was smoother and fainter. A lawn mower, maybe. But on and off. Consistent. It starts and stops," Megan mumbled. "It's a long sound. Then it's gone. Then it's back again and it's long again. There it is." Megan was nodding. "There it is."

"Okay, Megan," Dr. Mattingly said. "I'm going to count from three, two, one. And you're here, Megan."

Her eyes blinked open and she sat up straight.

"What did you find, Megan? What did you hear?"

She looked at Dr. Mattingly. "A train. I heard the whistle on a train."

Chapter 12

He had the night to himself. He was out at the fishing cabins in Tinder Valley and would hole up in one of them overnight and fish in the morning before going home. It was easy cover and a solid story that would hold up to scrutiny. Logical and timely, his trip to Tinder Valley could be corroborated should she decide to check his story. It was what he needed—a night to himself. Enough time to have his visit, stay a while afterward to be respectful. Maybe share some dinner. He could take his time tonight, not like some other visits when things were rushed and abrupt and forced. Those visits were never fun. They typically ended in fights and arguments and resentment, and he never felt good about himself when he left. But time was on his side tonight. Time allowed them both to work through the things that got overlooked during rushed visits. Time prevented fights and scuffles. Tonight he had all the time he needed.

He pulled his car to the curb and turned off the headlights. It was dark here with no streetlights. Quiet, too. No highways. It would be a nice place to live, but that was not possible. For him, he could only visit this place. But what he found here he could find nowhere else. So empty was his life at home. There was no love there. There was no intimacy. He went through the motions when necessary. When she pressed him. But his thoughts were always here. He tolerated her touch because it was what he had to do to get by. He stomached her advances because he knew it was the only way to protect his secret.

But here, with his Love, he could play out his wildest fantasies. Here, he could service and please and pamper. Of course, it didn't always work the way he imagined it. Some didn't appreciate his efforts. Some even rejected his generosity. He was willing to allow rebellion initially, even put up with the early arguments and tantrums that came with new relationships. But ultimately, he expected this behavior to subside. Once his intentions were made clear, he wanted acceptance. He wanted gratitude. He wanted submission. More than anything, though, he wanted reciprocation. Sadly, for a few, this never transpired. And when his efforts were exhausted and he saw no hope on the horizon, he knew the end of the affair was near.

There was guilt when things culminated this way. Sadness when a relationship ended. He felt genuine remorse when he could not make things work. Regret, because he understood the finality of failure. After an unsuccessful relationship he allowed himself to bathe in those emotions. He gave himself that much—the opportunity to grieve. But then, like spring tulips, someone else caught his eye and those feelings of want and desire budded inside him, eventually blossoming into something new and hopeful. A fresh relationship was out there and waiting. He just needed to find the right person.

He stood from his car and adjusted himself. He walked inside with a frozen Stouffer's dinner, locking the door behind him. He listened for a moment, to make sure nothing was out of order. Then he walked to the cellar door, slid the lock, and clicked on his flashlight. He opened the door, which scraped against the wooden floor, and stared at the bare wooden stairs as a feeling of ecstasy burned in his loins. He started down the steps to his prize, who he knew would be waiting, shackled to her bed like a good and wanting servant. He had left a bucket and sponge for her to bathe, hoping tonight might be special.

"I'm back, my Love," he said as he took his first step down the rickety cellar stairs, his insides exploding with eagerness and lust. "I'm back."

SUMMER 2016

"Come out, come out, wherever you are."
—Casey Delevan

Chapter 13

Nicole Cutty pulled her car into the deserted parking lot behind a Walmart and turned off the engine. Across the street was a bar whose lot was still spotted with cars. She removed a joint from her purse and put the flame of her lighter to the end of it, listening as the tip crackled. Jessica and Rachel didn't like to smoke, so Nicole felt obligated to sneak her pot sessions in late at night. She had tried once to get them to smoke out by Rachel's pool one Friday afternoon, but Rachel threw a fit that her mom would smell it. Nicole loved her friends, but part of her couldn't wait to get away next year.

As people came and went from the tavern across the street, their headlights glared through Nicole's windshield. She wanted to feel alone and isolated, so she took her joint, climbed from her car, and walked to the park half a block away. It was just past eleven p.m. and her parents had no idea she had snuck out of the house. The yellow halogen lights had died an hour earlier and the park slithered with shadows from the streetlights twenty yards away. Nicole walked deep enough into the park so that she was comfortably within the penumbra of a row of maples that separated the playground from the road. The swing provided a nice cadence as she rocked back and forth and enjoyed the effects of the marijuana. The night before, she was skinny-dipping at Matt's party, and as she inhaled deeply now she relished that moment in her mind when all the guys stared at her and the other girls were invisible.

It took twenty minutes to finish her joint. She closed her eyes and swung for twenty more. Full swings like she was ten years old—knees cocked back and then flung forward to increase momentum, fists gripping the chains. She stared up at the night sky dotted with stars that blurred together. Finally, Nicole stopped kicking and let the swing slowly ease until she returned to a smooth rhythm where her feet dangled lazily, her toes barely touching the ground.

She heard a whistle that startled her. It came again.

"Roxie!"

It was a man's voice.

Nicole checked the ground to make sure she'd stubbed out the end of her joint.

"Roxie!"

From the shadows, a man emerged holding a leash.

"Come here, Roxie."

The man noticed Nicole on the swing and came over.

"Excuse me. Did you see a dog run through here? A little Jack Russell terrier?"

Nicole shook her head. "No, sorry."

"You been in the park long?"

"Half hour, maybe."

The man stood and turned in a circle as he surveyed the dark playground. "I knew I shouldn't have taken her off the leash."

Nicole stood from the swing, dizzy. The swaying had magnified the effects of the cannabis. She righted herself after a second. Felt good. "Roxie is her name?"

"Yeah," the man said. He pulled out his phone. "Here's a picture. Have you seen her before?"

Nicole moved closer to look at the man's phone, which glowed like a flashlight in the dark night. Her eyes narrowed and her lips separated when she looked at the photo. She stuttered her words until they finally formed.

"That's my cousin. Julie."

"It is?" the man said. "That's a shame. She's missing, too. And she's never coming home."

Before Nicole could react, a burlap bag came down over her head. Her muscles flexed and tensed, but the element of surprise was too great to overcome. Hands groped her and pulled her until she was shoved into the backseat of a car. She felt the momentum pull her into the seat as the car lurched from the parking lot and sped away.

The ride was twenty minutes, during which her hands were duct-taped behind her back and the burlap sack secured over her head. She cried and pleaded but got no response from the man who'd taken her. She knew there were others in the car.

"Why do you have that picture of my cousin?"

She heard the roll of duct tape unpeel. Then two hands reached inside the burlap and sealed the tape across her mouth. She bucked in the backseat, only to be subdued roughly by the man next to her.

Nicole finally gave in. Stopped moaning and fighting and kicking. She lay still under the weight of the stranger until the car ride ended and they lifted her from the backseat and dragged her through the woods. Nicole could feel the moss and sticks and leaves as they pulled her along, her feet barely *working. She thought she felt train tracks under her shoes. Down a steep slope, eventually the rattle of a metal lock filled her ears, and then a door squeaked open. She was dragged through an entryway and forced to her knees, with the man behind her. She closed her eyes despite the burlap sack over her head. His mouth was by her ear and his breath penetrated the sack.*

"How do you like it? Same as your cousin? What was her name? Julie?"

His hand slid along her waist and over her abdomen, then up to her chest, where he grabbed her breast and moaned into her ear.

Nicole tried to scream through the tape as she bucked wildly away from his grasp. The man released his grip and pushed her forward. She fell face-first to the cold ground, hands behind her back and unable to break her fall. The burlap was yanked from her head.

"We'll wait until you calm down. Ain't no fun when you fight the whole time."

The door closed before she could see his face. She stayed on her stomach and listened. No voices. No footsteps. Just silence. After a minute, she rolled onto her back and pulled her taped hands behind her legs and over her feet until her arms were in front of her. Then she ripped the tape from her mouth—a slow pull that distorted her lips and ruined her skin. She licked her lips and felt the sticky remains of adhesive.

Several deep breaths helped rid the shakes brought on by the man whispering in her ear. She tried to think, to pull reason from the darkness around her. The effects of the joint were not helping. On her feet now, she walked slowly to the door, feeling her way through the dark until her bound hands grasped the door handle. She shouldered it hard but found no trace of give. She threw her hip into it, then a wild front kick that knocked her backward and landed her on the ground. Then she cried. All she could imagine was Julie, young and scared and shoved in some dark place like this. Her stomach swam with nausea. Finally, Nicole sat up, pushed herself into the corner, and allowed the damp earth to seep through her jeans and suck the warmth from her body.

Chapter 14

July 2016
Four Weeks Before the Abduction

"Nicole."
The voice was far off and jovial, turning her name into a three-syllable word. Ni-coooo-ole.

"Come out, come out, wherever you are!"

Her eyes opened. She'd fallen asleep. Not sure if she was dreaming, she stood up and listened. The seat of her jeans was soaking wet and her upper thighs numb with cold. She'd been asleep long enough that the marijuana no longer had a hold on her.

"Oh, little Ni-cooo-ole. Where are you?" The voice was singsongy.

Nicole waited. The voice grew closer. Then a loud bang on the wooden door.

"You in there, Nicole? It's time to come out!"

The door flung open. Ten people stood outside the shed with flashlights, lighting the night and highlighting their faces like a pack of medieval tribesmen. The first two people to enter the shed were girls Nicole had never seen before, who raced in and bear-hugged her.

"*We love you, we love you, we love you,*" *one of them said.*

"*You fucking guys!*" *Nicole said.*

"*Freaky stuff, right?*" *the other girl said.* "*Did you piss your pants?*" *she asked, feeling Nicole's wet jeans.* "*Yes!*" *The girl turned to the group.* "*She pissed herself!*"

The crowd cheered. The girls led her from the shed and, once outside, the crowd cheered louder. A man walked from the ranks of the pack. His flashlight pinned under his chin so the light cast his face in an eerie glow. "*My little Nicole. You made it.*"

"*Casey?*" *Nicole asked.*

"*Who else would save you?*"

"*You're an asshole!*"

This brought the group to hysterics. There were loud whistles and catcalls.

"*What was with the picture of my cousin?*"

"*All part of the experience,*" *Casey said.*

"*And who was the guy? He grabbed my tits.*"

This brought more laughter and hoots.

Casey smiled in the glow of the flashlight. "*It wouldn't be very convincing had we just asked you to jump in the car with us.*" *He shrugged.* "*Missing cousins, groping, a little ear moaning. It's all part of the package you ordered.*"

He moved closer and grabbed her in a giant hug, whispering in her ear. "*You did great, sweet thing. Welcome to the Capture Club! I knew you'd love it.*"

Chapter 15

July 2016
Three Weeks Before the Abduction

Nicole lay on a beach towel on the bow of Rachel's Arrow-Cat. They had anchored an hour earlier and now allowed their bikinied bodies to absorb the warm afternoon sun while other boats slowly settled around them. Not far away was Steamboat Eddie's, a bar that sat on a very small island in the middle of the bay and served fried food and beer. Most summer days saw boats anchored and floating around the island, music blaring from the live band that played on the patio of Steamboat Eddie's.

"So where were you the other night?" Jessica asked.

Nicole lay on her back with her arms at her sides, sunglasses covering her closed eyes.

"Busy."

"With Mystery Man?"

"Maybe."

"So what do you guys do? Does he, like, take you to dinner?"

"He's not that cliché," Nicole said.

Jessica and Rachel waited.

"*We hang out.*" *Nicole didn't consider telling her friends about her adventure the other night. Not only would they not understand the club, but they'd likely judge her as unstable or demented.*

"*God,*" *Jessica said.* "*What's the big secret?*"

"*There's no secret. You guys just wouldn't get him. He's not like the guys we hang out with. Like all the losers last weekend who were too scared to drop their shorts at Matt's party. I mean, what's the big friggin' deal? It's a penis, get over it.*"

Rachel and Jessica laughed.

"*I'll never forget Chris Harmon's face,*" *Jessica said.* "*He was literally gawking at you on the platform. Like, he didn't even care that you noticed. I think he was in a trance.*"

"*I'm probably the first naked girl he's seen that wasn't on his computer screen. Little perv. And, of course, he was the only one who didn't do it.*"

"*Him and Brandon. Thank God,*" *Rachel said.* "*Could you imagine his scrawny little body all naked and wet?*"

"*Oh,*" *Jessica said.* "*Stop!*"

"*You're going to make me puke,*" *Nicole said as she pushed herself up onto her elbows and surveyed the growing pack of boats around them. It was Friday afternoon and the bay was packed.* "*What I'm more shocked about,*" *Nicole said,* "*is that those prudes actually got naked.*"

"*Who? Megan?*"

"*Yeah. Blew me away.*"

"*She was cool that night,*" *Rachel said.* "*She hung out with all of us.*"

"*She only came out to the platform because of Matt. She couldn't stand the thought of him out there all alone with me. God forbid!*"

"*Just tell her you've got a mystery boyfriend,*" *Jessica said.* "*Then she won't be so worried.*"

Just as Jessica said this, a water balloon fell from the sky and splattered on the deck next to them.

"*What the hell?*"

They looked around and saw Matt with his friends on the boat across from them.

"*Bombs away!*" *Matt yelled.*

Nicole raised her middle finger to them.

"*Better put that away,*" *Matt yelled from across the water. He stood shirtless on the bow of his boat, his toned stomach tapering to his swimsuit, the band of which rested low on his hips. His chest hair ran to his navel and then down to the band of his trunks. Nicole admitted, as tired as she was of high school boys, Matt Wellington still piqued her interest. She'd secretly watched all the boys last weekend, determining Matt to be the only man among them.*

"*Or what?*" *Nicole shouted.*

"*Or I'll come over there and put it away for you.*"

Nicole simply smiled behind her big aviator sunglasses and kept her middle finger raised, then lifted her hand higher. Without hesitation, Matt dove into the bay and freestyled over to Rachel's boat, lifting himself effortlessly out of the water and onto the back platform. His body poured water as he climbed onto the boat. Jessica and Rachel laughed as he approached.

"*You're screwed, Nic,*" *Jessica said.*

"*Don't fucking touch me,*" *Nicole said, but her smile betrayed the aggressive voice she fronted. And she meant for it to. She wanted his hands on her.*

Matt picked her up, towel and all, while Nicole screamed. With her in his arms, he jumped into the water. This brought some hollers from the surrounding boats as everyone watched the show. They splashed into the bay, Nicole grab-bing for her sunglasses before they sank, Matt collecting the towel as he surfaced.

"You're an ass," Nicole said in the water.

"You gave me the finger. Next time, heed my warning."

Nicole rolled onto her back and floated, her sunglasses back on her face. "I'm too tired to swim. Float me over to your boat."

Matt came up behind her, grabbed her lifeguard-style, and swam her to the back of his boat.

"You guys have beer?"

"Yeah," Matt said. "We snuck a few from my dad's stash in the garage."

Nicole rolled over in the water and wrapped her arms around his neck, her chest against his back. "Good. Carry me up, I need one."

Matt pulled his athletic frame up the boat's ladder with Nicole hanging on him. Once up, Nicole released her grip and Matt wrung out her towel, laying it over the railing to dry. He high-fived his two buddies when he walked into the cockpit.

"Meatheads," Nicole said. "Get me a beer."

Matt walked down three steps into the cabin and opened a cooler that was built into the countertop. He popped the top on a Bud Light and handed it to Nicole as he walked back up the stairs.

"Keep it low just in case the cops come around."

Nicole sat on the seat in front of the steering wheel. She chugged half her beer in a series of five swallows meant to impress Matt and his two wrestling buddies. She belched loudly.

"So what are you losers doing tonight?"

"Hanging here this afternoon," Matt said. "We might go to Sullivan's, he's having people over. Or maybe into town.

The street festival's going on. Supposed to be live music. How about you guys?"

Nicole shrugged. "Don't know yet. We're just hanging at Rachel's. We talked about the street fest." She chugged the rest of her beer. "You have enough for Jess and Rachel?"

"Yeah," Matt said.

Nicole looked over at Rachel's boat, which was twenty yards away. "Why don't you two sneak up on them? They'll freak," Nicole said to Matt's friends.

Matt's buddies laughed and then looked over at Jessica and Rachel, who were sunbathing, eyes closed and lying on their backs. Like two obedient dogs, Matt's friends nodded at Nicole's suggestion and quietly slipped into the water to start their stealth approach.

Nicole watched them for a minute as they made their way over; then she looked at Matt. "I need another beer."

"You drink like a sailor."

Matt headed below deck. Nicole stood from the captain's seat and followed him. There was little below deck, just a small space occupied by a half fridge, a small counter and sink, and cabinets for storage. But for Nicole, it was perfect.

"Boo," she said just as Matt was reaching for a beer.

He turned quickly and they were face-to-face in the small area. Nicole's body had partially dried in the sun while she drank her first beer, but her hair was still wet and slicked back and dripping down her shoulders. Quickly, she wrapped her arms around his neck and locked her fingers.

Instinctively, he put his hands on her waist. "What's up, Cutty?"

"You didn't even look at me the other night," she said in a pouty voice.

"When?"

"At your party when we all went out to the platform."

Matt laughed. "Trust me, everyone was looking at every-one. It was too dark to see anything."

Nicole smiled and raised her eyebrows. "So you did look?"

Matt nodded. "Guilty."

"Did I look fat?"

"That's a stupid question."

"Then how come you ended up hooking up with what's-her-face?"

"Megan? She's cool. We're both off to Duke after the summer."

"So she's your girlfriend?"

"I don't have a girlfriend."

"Good," Nicole said as she leaned forward and kissed his lips.

Matt kissed back for a few seconds. "This is not a good idea," he said.

"Why?" Nicole stared into his eyes. "I mean, if you don't have a girlfriend." She kissed him again and ran her hands down his back and then around to the front of his suit, pinching her fingers between his skin and the band of his trunks.

He grabbed her hands and laughed. "What's gotten in-to you?"

"You wanna go to college without getting any this summer?"

"Who says I'm not getting any? You don't know my his-tory."

"True. But I know your future if you keep hooking up with Megan McDonald. It's called celibacy." She leaned in and kissed him again, biting his lower lip. "But . . ." More kissing as she pulled her hand free from his grasp and ran her fingers over the front of his shorts. "If you need some action before you leave for school, just remember, not all Emerson Bay girls are prude princesses."

They heard screaming and laughing as Matt's friends ambushed Jessica and Rachel and tossed them into the bay.

"Uh-oh," Nicole said, flicking him in the crotch, which caused Matt to flinch. "You missed your opportunity." She pulsed her eyebrows and licked her lips, tilted her head and gave a sad face. "Too bad. Would've been fun."

She reached past him into the cooler, grabbed three beers, and walked up the steps and into the sunlight.

Chapter 16

July 2016
Three Weeks Before the Abduction

Coleman's Brewery was abandoned in the 1930s, ravaged by Prohibition and unable to overcome the Great Depression. The brewery tried to stay afloat by offering its customers a place to smoke cigars and play pool and snooker. Of course, the unspoken promise of bootlegger whiskey was the real draw. The occasional pint of Coleman's lager, which was secretly brewed and greatly sought after, made an appearance from time to time. It was just enough to keep the doors open during the Noble Experiment. But when the Depression hit, Cole Coleman was unable to stay current on bribes. By the mid-thirties, Coleman's closed its doors for good.

Eighty years later, the abandoned shell of the brewery still stood in the old industrial section on the west side of Emerson Bay. The Roanoke River ran north-south through Emerson Bay and separated the city into east and west halves. The east side flourished as a bayside community with yacht clubs and waterfront homes and beach access and a hip downtown area. The west side fell into disrepair. It was a place where freight trains passed in the dead of night, where streetlamps long ago spent their filaments and were never considered for replacement. West Bay was where weeds pushed through sidewalk cracks and potholes grew deeper in the streets. The police had given up patrolling the Cove, where Coleman's was located along with other forsaken buildings from long ago, because nothing much happened there besides winos taking shelter in the crumbling buildings and an occasional stray dog walking the streets. Dark and isolated, it was the perfect place for the Capture Club's meetings. And scary as hell, Nicole was discovering.

This journey to West Bay was Nicole's first meeting. Her only association with the club prior to her abduction had been through e-mails with Casey and the chat rooms where they sometimes went back and forth all night typing about the latest abduction in the news. Nicole obsessed with Casey over the details of these disappearances, her fetish for missing-persons cases birthed in childhood when Julie disappeared shortly after her ninth birthday.

There had been commotion and crying and hysteria that summer, and Nicole remembered going with her family to Colorado for the final time. Julie was not there, and no one would come right out and say where she was or what had happened to her. Instead, the adults used big words and promised one another Julie would be back. But besides in her dreams, Nicole never saw her cousin again. Thoughts about what happened to Julie became a festering curiosity Nicole secretly harbored. Livia had never showed much interest in their cousin. Julie was an only child and there was never a reason for Livia to tag along on the weeklong trips out west, so when Julie disappeared it was sad and disturbing but affected Livia in a different manner than it had Nicole. A freshman in college then, Livia was older and smarter and understood things more completely than Nicole. What Livia *never comprehended, however, was the loss Nicole felt after Julie was gone. Julie had no siblings of her own, and with ten years separating Nicole and Livia, the cousins considered each other sisters. There was a mutual understanding that they were learning things together, not simply being taught by an older sister or parent. And when Julie was gone, so too was Nicole's accomplice. She was left by herself to figure it out.*

The Cuttys never talked about Julie, and only lately had Nicole's mother reconnected with Aunt Paxie. The sisters' relationship was difficult for Paxie because seeing Nicole was a reminder of every milestone missed with Julie. With no one willing to answer Nicole's questions, she took to the Internet for information about Julie. Years had passed, though, and what little she was able to find about her cousin's disappearance was neither interesting nor pertinent. What Nicole did manage to locate was an online community just like herself— people obsessed with abduction and not afraid to talk about it. They spilled their secret thrill when someone went missing, offering theories about who took them and what was happening to them.

One night she met Casey in a chat room, and after two months of private messaging, Nicole was initiated into the Capture Club while she smoked a joint in the park. It was the craziest thing she'd done in her short life, trusting a stranger to abduct her and blindfold her and stick tape across her face. It was traumatic and thrilling. She still got chills now when she thought of that night. Like a gold nugget hidden away in a tiny satchel, those thoughts were all hers. New and unripe, they played over and over in Nicole's mind. The sense of danger that told her she had taken things too far. That she had allowed her fascination to overcome her judgment. In the dark of night, alone in her bed, she held on to the moment when she sat still and frightened in that shed behind Coleman's Brewery and felt real terror. She finally was able to relate to all the girls she had read about. She finally knew how Julie felt. For a brief moment, Nicole had reconnected with her old friend.

She parked, as instructed, at the train station and followed the freight tracks for half a mile out of town until she saw the old Coleman Brewery building down in the Cove. She took a path that led through the brush and down the gentle slope, hearing a train approaching from the north, running wood down from Canada. She wondered if this was the path they had dragged her through while the burlap sack was over her head. She made it to the intersection in front of the abandoned brewery just as the train chugged behind her, blocking the light that came from the streetlamps situated on the far side of the tracks.

A hundred years after the beige bricks of Coleman's Brewery were laid, they still stood. Mostly. She noticed one area toward the back of the building that was crumbling. Likely, it was where deliveries used to happen and one too many trucks had backed into the delivery bay and banged the foundation to rattle the bricks and jar the rebar, loosening joists to the point that a generation later the walls sagged and pried away the bricks.

Never having met anyone from this group before the other night when they all stood with flashlights under their chins and stared into the shed, Nicole wasn't sure what to expect from her first Capture Club meeting. She walked to the front entrance, past the debris on the ground—fast food Styrofoam and beer bottles. From inside she heard voices. Through a small atrium first, then past the open door, Nicole found a decrepit-looking room she assumed had once been a tavern. The waist-high bar still stood in the spot patrons used to sit and receive drinks across mahogany. No stools now, but Nicole noticed the group had brought two long folding tables and a dozen mismatched chairs. Two Igloo coolers held cold beers.

She spotted Casey standing near the head of the table. He smiled when their eyes met.

"Our lost girl has returned home!" he shouted.

Everyone looked toward the front of the brewery and cheered when they saw Nicole. She smacked her gum like this was the reception she had expected, then raised her hand. Casey came over and hugged her.

"Welcome to your first meeting. You're in for quite a treat."

The way he touched her, grabbed her like she belonged to him, sent a current through her body. He was so different from the boys at school, who broke eye contact if held too long, and who would never commit to anything for fear of rejection. Couldn't even take what was offered, like Matt the other day on the boat, too scared to act even when she was prepared to give herself to him. Casey, she was certain, took things even before they were offered.

For an hour Nicole stood by Casey's side as he took her around to each of the small factions and introduced her. She met guys with long hair and tattoos, girls with shaved heads and pierced everything—from noses to lips to eyebrows. They all drank canned beer and talked about random kidnappings from around the country. A college freshman was missing from Georgia and her boyfriend was suspected. A high school junior's body had just been found in the Florida Everglades. Another newlywed had gone missing from a cruise boat, and on and on. After she and Casey made it around to each group, he took Nicole's hand and pulled her into the barroom, sat her at the table as everyone gathered around and slid chairs to take their spots. Casey sat at the head of the table. Behind him was a chalkboard illuminated by a droplight, its large metal cone looking like a dog's surgical collar. A long extension cord ran to a gas generator outside. The hot summer night was thick with humidity, no breeze inside the old brewhouse.

"Okay," Casey said from the head of the table. "Listen up, people."

Slowly, everyone quieted and took seats.

"First, she's already done the tour tonight but let's formally welcome Nicole."

Everyone applauded and cheered.

"As we all know, Nicole took the overnight challenge, and despite pissing herself..."

A couple howls and a few screams of laughter.

"... She passed with flying colors. So Nicole caught a glimpse of what it's like to be abducted. It's something we're all fascinated with, good or bad, creepy or not. Is it a fetish? I don't know. Is it morbid? Probably. Would people outside the club understand? Fuck, no! Are they all liars who are just as intrigued as each of us? You bet your ass!"

Casey stood from his spot at the head of the table and picked up a piece of chalk. He tapped the chalkboard several times. "New business. For the last week we've spotlighted Reagan William Beneke. Serial killer from west Texas. Copped to sixty-four kills, implicated in thirty-eight. All women, snatched from Louisiana and Texas. Mostly young women, teens to late twenties. Stalked them at night, usually meeting them at bars and then seducing them. He took them to his house where he..." Casey looked around the room. "Use your imagination. When he was done, he strangled them and buried them in a Louisiana bayou, admitting to authorities that some of the bodies were taken by gators. This accounts for the discrepancy between how many he copped to, versus how many were found."

The club listened with focus.

"From his confession, corroborated by witnesses during his trial, we know he never took a victim by force. They all willingly followed him home. This reminds me of someone else who deployed a similar tactic. Anyone?"

There was silence in the barroom until Nicole finally spoke. "Dahmer."

"Yes," Casey said, pointing at Nicole. "Jeffrey Dahmer. Though he was completely psychotic and morbid in the manner by which he killed his victims, the way he took those victims is fascinating. Dahmer and Beneke lured their victims. Allowed them the choice to go with them, never taking any by force. So let's open tonight's discussion with this: What's a greater thrill? Brute force, or the soft hook?"

They talked for an hour about Dahmer's first victim, a hitchhiker who willingly climbed into the car and, later, entered Dahmer's house, where he was eventually killed. They moved to his other victims, mostly men picked up at gay bars and brought home to Dahmer's grandmother's basement. All his victims willingly followed Mr. Dahmer to his home— their eventual place of death. This type of take, Dahmer's version and Reagan William Beneke's version, was a different variety of abduction than the club was accustomed to. Up to this point, their mock abductions and initiations were done by force. Hood over the head, grab-and-drag style. Fast, efficient, and frightening.

"So Dahmer used his charm and his brains to get his victims to come home with him. Once they were in the basement, he drugged them and abused them and, ultimately, killed them. This club is interested in the hunt. I want us all to remember how slick Mr. Dahmer was in his approach. How charismatic he and Beneke were." Casey smiled as he stood by the chalkboard. "This will prove vital in the days to come."

A hushed anxiousness came over the Capture Club. Casey was planning the next abduction of a new member, and they all stirred with excitement.

Casey stared at Nicole. "The other night was a thrill for us to shove you in that shed out back. As a new member, your next stage is to turn the tables and become the abductor. Where you enjoy the thrill of stealing someone from the street, taking them to your own hideaway, and having them all to yourself. It's almost better than being the victim. Up for it?"

The crowd collectively trained its gaze on Nicole.

"Of course," she said.

"Good. We've got four prospects. All have confirmed their interest in the club."

"Guy or girl?" Nicole asked.

"Three guys, one girl. Preference?"

There was a bit of hesitation as Nicole's mind wandered to the dark closet in her dreams, Julie's eyes wide and peering from within. "Girl," she finally said.

Coleman's cleared out as the club's members slowly dispersed, dropping empty beer cans to the ground and leaving Casey packing up his computer and stowing away the generator. Nicole stayed behind, sipping a Miller Genuine Draft.

"I get to be part of it, right?" Nicole said.

"The take? Of course." Casey rolled an extension cord around his arm.

"What will we do with her?"

"Bring her back here, leave her in the ruins for a while." Casey gestured toward the back of Coleman's where the bricks were crumbling. "We could use the shed out back, where we put you. But I think we'll mix it up a bit. I'll throw an old mattress in the back room, make it look like we're going to have lots of fun with her."

"You gonna moan in her ear?" Nicole said, sipping her beer with a seductive look in her eyes.

Casey stopped packing. "That wasn't me."

Nicole stood and walked over to him. "Gonna grab her chest?"

"Wasn't me, either."

"No?" Nicole moved closer. "Kinda wish it were."

She was up against him now, their faces inches apart.

Casey glanced at the door. The last of the members had gone. He dropped the extension cord and grabbed her by the waist, pulled her into him.

"Don't tease if you can't deliver."

Nicole dropped her beer. It hit the ground and spouted fizz. She put her hands on the back of his neck. "I'm not a teaser." She pulled his face to hers and kissed him.

Casey's hands were all over her, and after a minute he pushed her backward onto the table. Her earlobe was in his mouth when he whispered, "How old are you?"

Nicole grabbed his face and looked into his eyes. "You duct-taped my mouth and threw me in a shed overnight. This can't be any more illegal."

He pushed her farther onto the table. Besides their voices and their moans, the only noise came from the generator outside that gave life to the single, isolated bulb that cast the brewery in shadows.

Chapter 17

August 2016
Two Weeks Before the Abduction

Diana Wells was good and buzzed. A nineteen-year-old freshman at Elizabeth City State University, getting into bars was never a problem. Her fake ID said she was twenty-two, the picture was close enough, and it hadn't failed her yet. The ID came from a friend's sister, and Diana flashed it to bouncers with confidence. She didn't like that it listed her fake self as 160 pounds. She was 145 since cutting carbs this summer, and could again fit into the skinny jeans from Christmas.

Out with two friends tonight, the flirting had started an hour before. First, the guy ordered them a round of lemon drop shots and waved when they all looked over. Then, he'd said hi on the way to the bathroom, ignoring all of them but Diana. With her two best friends, both size two and the ones who usually captured guys' attention, Diana loved the spotlight tonight.

He was older. Maybe a grad student, and Diana was happy to expand outside the circle they always hung with. It *was a drag to see her two friends flirt with a group of guys and casually pick the ones they thought were cutest. Diana was left with the scraps. The quiet guys who also hung in the shadows and waited for the end of the night to see what was left. Diana was it.*

Tonight, though, things were different. She was finally living the college social lifestyle, crushing on a guy who was into her from the beginning, not by default.

He was with another couple, a guy and a girl who were sitting next to him at the bar. They both were obviously in on what was happening.

"Are you going to talk to him?" one of her friends asked.

"I don't know," Diana said. "He looks older."

"Probably a grad student."

In the middle of their discussion, he waved his arm, inviting her over. Diana's eyes widened, and he waved harder. He gave her a look. Come here. I gotta beg you?

Her friends laughed and pushed her out of their circle. "Go! Lover Boy calls," her friends teased.

Diana, drink in hand, walked shyly toward him.

"I've only been buying you drinks all night," he said when she was close enough.

"Thanks for the shots," Diana said.

"I'm Casey," the guy said.

"Diana."

The bartender lined up four shot glasses and poured them full with a sticky red concoction.

Casey pulled them over. "Fuzzy navels. Here." He handed a shot to Diana.

The couple next to him grabbed the remaining shot glasses and held them up.

"These are my friends," Casey said. "Nate and Nicole. This is Diana."

"Cheers," Nicole said, and they all tilted their heads and slammed the shots.

"I'm so friggin' buzzed," Diana said. She took the shot in one swallow and laughed. "God, that's good."

"I could drink these all night," Casey said. "Or those lemon drop shots."

"Yeah," Diana said. "Those are good, too."

"Sit down with us."

Diana took a seat. They had to yell over the music. "You go to school here?" Casey asked.

"Yeah. You?"

Casey nodded. "I'm a grad student."

"Really?" Diana asked. "In what?"

"Math."

"Oh God! I hate math."

"Me too," he said.

Casey ordered more drinks and they talked for thirty minutes. He was so unlike the other guys she'd met at school who talked mostly to their friends and never directly to her. Casey asked all about her. When Diana had to use the bathroom he went with her, then waited until she was finished so they could walk back together. After another twenty minutes, Diana's friends came over.

"We're taking off," they said.

"Okay," Diana said.

Casey cocked his head to the side. "Total drag. But if you've gotta go, maybe we could hook up next week or something." Casey looked at his friends, then back to Diana. "Unless you wanna hang for a while here. I'll make sure you get home okay."

Diana smiled at Casey, then looked at her friends. "I'm gonna stay for a while."

It felt so good to be here at the end of the night, to be the one staying behind to talk with a guy while her friends headed back to the dorm.

"Cool," her friend said. "See you when you get back." Their faces carried smirks as they walked away.

"If you gotta go, that's cool," Casey said.

"No," Diana said, brushing a hand at her friends. "They're just going to get burritos."

Casey held up his beer and Diana clinked her vodka. "Cheers," he said.

Diana took a sip. God, he's gorgeous.

One o'clock came in a hurry. The bartenders hollered last call and a rush of students lined the bar to order one final drink before they spilled into the streets and headed to after-hours. There was talk of a Theta Chi late night. Diana laughed as the crowd squashed her and Casey into the bar to place their orders.

"We're gonna get trampled," Casey said. He took her hand and pulled her away from the bar, off her stool and toward the door. Diana felt his fingers intertwine with her own, the way she always saw couples on campus hold hands. She allowed him to pull her out the front door. The summer air was thick and sticky. Buzzed and dizzy from the shots, she felt herself walk the sidewalk with heavy, wobbly steps toward the end of the building and into the walkway that separated the bar from the dry cleaners next door.

Casey pulled her into the narrow space. "Sorry," he said. "I had to get outta there."

"Yeah," Diana said. "I needed some air."

"You thinking about going to the frat party?"

Diana shrugged. "I don't know. You want to?"

Casey came close to her, until her back was against the bricks. "Not really."

His face was close enough to smell the beer on his breath. Cigarettes, too. As if he could read her mind he said, "You smell like fuzzy navels."

This made her laugh. "That's 'cause you bought me, like, four of them."

Casey moved closer. "Smells good."

Diana stared at him until she closed her eyes and felt his lips on hers. She opened her mouth and their tongues explored in a sloppy, drunk kiss. She grabbed his head, ran fingers through his hair the way she always thought she would when she found a guy she really liked. They kissed on and off for fifteen minutes until the bar started to empty.

Diana rubbed her nose back and forth on his. Stared like a puppy dog into his eyes. "Wanna go to that party?"

"Not really," Casey said, giving her a quick kiss. "We could go back to my place. My roommates already headed home."

"Those were your roommates?"

"Yeah. Three of us live in a house on Park Street. They'll probably have people over, so we could hang for a while. Unless you wanna do something else."

Diana kissed him. "No. Let's go back to your place."

He grabbed her hand again and they found his car. Casey opened the passenger-side door and Diana climbed in and fastened her seat belt. Through her buzz she knew she shouldn't be in a car after so much to drink.

"You sure you're okay to drive?" she asked when Casey climbed in.

"Yeah, I'm fine. It's not far."

They pulled from the curb and headed to Casey's apartment. They stopped at a light and he again took her hand, held it while it rested on the console between them. The light turned green and he took off, then slowed and squinted his eyes.

"My roommates," Casey said, lifting his chin toward the windshield.

Diana saw them strolling on the sidewalk. "Oh, yeah."

He pulled to the curb and Diana rolled down her window. Casey leaned over, placed his hand on Diana's knee. "Hey, drunkos. Wanna ride?"

"Thought you were headed to the frat party?" the girl named Nicole said.

"We decided to go back to the apartment instead. Get in."

Casey's friends climbed into the backseat and Casey took off.

"Diana," Nicole said from the backseat. "Did this guy really convince you to come home with him? He's a total pervert who likes really strange things."

"My best friends," Casey said. "Throwing me under the bus."

"Ah," Diana said. "He seems trustworthy."

"If you believe that, then you're a very stupid person," Nicole said in a sullen voice. Serious. The drunkenness gone like it never existed.

Diana looked at Casey with a furrowed brow. Casey stared back with dead eyes and a solemn face. It was the last thing Diana saw before the bag came over her head.

She cried uncontrollably until the duct tape covered her mouth and muted her whimpering. During the brief scuffle in the front seat, they managed to secure her hands with zip ties, pulling them behind her back and clicking them tight. The car ride was fast and nauseating as Diana rocked back and forth under the momentum of sharp turns and sudden acceleration. Without her seat belt, and with her hands behind her back, she had no control over her body and she heard them laugh when she banged her head on the passenger-side window during a hard left turn.

Finally, the car screeched to a stop, skidding on gravel.

"Get her out," she heard Casey say in his new voice. The sweetness was gone. "Bring her around back."

Doors opened, hands grabbed her under the arms and pulled her from the car.

"Come on, stupid," Diana heard the girl say. What was her name, she couldn't remember now. "This is gonna be fun."

Still buzzed, if not outright drunk, Diana felt them drag her. She tried to keep up, tried to get her feet underneath her, but they were pulling too fast. She recognized the terrain as rock or pea gravel. They roughly sat her in a chair and quickly wrapped her with something, securing her to the chair. The material spun around her calves and arms and chest. Then the bag came off her head and she took a second to gather her setting. Maybe a warehouse, or an old building. She wasn't sure. The bricks were crumbling and there was a hole in the roof.

Casey stood in front of her. He stared with those dead eyes, his head tilting to the side. "You said you wanted to come home with me. Welcome home."

Diana tried to talk through the duct tape, tears spilling from her eyes.

Casey shook his head. "I don't want to hear you talk. It might ruin it for me. I want to keep the sweet voice in my head from back when you were digging me. It helps me through the difficult time you and I are about to have."

Diana looked around. The other two were out of view but she could feel their presence behind her. She noticed a ratty mattress on the ground.

Casey's face took on a devilish look. "But one thing I can't tolerate is snot and tears. So I'll give you ten minutes to get yourself together. When I come back, I want my sweet girl back, you understand?"

He turned and walked through a door at the far end of the room. When he was gone, Diana looked down at her body and realized the material they had secured her with was plastic wrap—clear cooking plastic wound tightly around her torso and legs. It looked eerie and disgusting and suffocating.

PART III

"Have you any idea how much it pains me when
you behave like this?"
—The Monster

Chapter 18

October 2017
Thirteen Months Since Megan's Escape

Early Monday morning, after a long weekend visiting her parents Friday night and driving to Georgia to see Casey Delevan's mother, Livia drank coffee and paged through her forensics textbook while the office was still dark and quiet. Her terrible performance Friday afternoon, both in the autopsy suite and the cage, still weighed heavily on her mind. She was determined to prevent it from happening again.

She read and reread postmortem findings in head injury victims. Reviewed anatomy she had long ago memorized, and studied the different effects of bleeding on the brain and midline shifts. She outlined the requirements of a thorough neurological postmortem, the types of tissue samples taken and the techniques used to sequester these specimens. She reviewed skull fractures and the different patterns of bone disruption that allowed a medical examiner to make educated guesses about the weapons used to cause the damage. Then she picked up a giant book titled *Clinical Therapeutics* and painstakingly reviewed pharmacology, specifically covering drug-to-drug interactions in the geriatric population. She re-discovered scores of medications with long, rambling names she vaguely remembered from medical school and committed them to memory. Finally, she studied cerebrovascular accidents—strokes—and the examination techniques that best uncover them when they are not as obvious as a large vessel bursting the middle of the brain.

When she finished, Livia still had thirty minutes before the office would fill with staff. She topped off her coffee and pulled Megan McDonald's book from her bag. Sitting at her desk in the fellows' office, she skimmed through the final chapters. She imagined her mother and father lying in bed, fingers tracing along the same book looking for clues that might tell them what had happened to their daughter. There too, in Livia's mind, was Barb Delevan's house with drawn curtains and the smoky haze and a half-spent vodka bottle. Her parents' picture-still house Friday night bore a striking resemblance to Barb Delevan's home—a place and its residents stuck in the past, unable to partake in the present.

The thing that prevented her parents and Barb Delevan from moving forward was the same relentless undercurrent of energy that prevented Livia from clear-minded thinking. It was the need for answers. The absence of closure was a tether anchored soundly to the past that caused an anachronism as time slowly chugged by—days and weeks and years—incarcerating a sliver of the soul while life continued on.

Livia turned the last page of Megan's book when she heard her name being called.

"Paging Dr. Cutty," Kent Chapple said from the hallway. "We are officially ready to roll."

Livia looked up from the pages.

"Time to roll, Doc," Kent said. "Call came in overnight, we've gotta hit the road."

Throughout the year of training, each fellow was required

to participate in two weeks of ride-alongs with the morgue investigators, formally termed Medicolegal Investigators, where they would observe scene-investigation techniques as well as the process of body sequestration. It was a week away from the morgue, strategically placed throughout fellowship to avoid burnout. During the course of autopsying 250 bodies in twelve months, every fellow needed a break. Livia was up first, and after Friday's dismal performance in the cage, the timing couldn't have been better.

Livia shuffled papers on her desk, gathered them and dumped them—along with Megan's book—into the bottom drawer as Jen Tilly and Tim Schultz came into the office. She stood up and, wearing jeans and a blouse in lieu of scrubs, grabbed her black windbreaker that held OCME in yellow lettering on the breast and MEDICAL EXAMINER across the back.

"See you guys," Livia said.

"Good luck," Jen said.

"Don't kill anyone," Tim said.

"Funny, Tim. Hope your stomach's okay this week."

Livia waved and was gone.

"Heard Colt opened fire on you in the cage last week," Kent said as they walked the hallway.

"Good news travels fast."

Kent laughed. "People are calling it a massacre."

"You've got to be famous for something, I guess," Livia said.

"Good timing for ride-alongs. Looks like I'm your savior."

"That's for sure. Get me out of here before Dr. Colt sees me."

They walked through the back door of the morgue and out into the sunny fall morning. Kent opened the sliding door to the morgue van and Livia climbed into the backseat. She wasn't sure what she expected, but the intimate quarters she found inside the van were not it. Although the past three months saw her face-to-face with corpses, she expected some separation from them here, a partition of some sort, but there was none. Directly behind the two captain's seats, the rear of the van held an empty gurney waiting to be filled with a body that would ride next to her for as long as it took to get back to the office.

"Good morning, Dr. Cutty," Sanj Rashi said from the driver's seat as Livia climbed into the van. Another investigator, Sanj was of Indian decent with dark skin, black hair, thick eyebrows, and a perfectly Brooklyn accent. He was born and raised in New York, and came to the North Carolina OCME after college at Rutgers—New Brunswick.

"Morning, Sanj," Livia said as Kent slid the door closed and climbed into the passenger seat.

"You're late," Sanj said to Kent.

"Yes, I am. And here's your coffee as my punishment." Kent placed a Starbucks coffee into the cup holder of the console.

"Sugar, no cream?"

Kent gave his partner an ugly look. "It's not the first time I'm late."

"Let me guess. A fight with the wife sent you to Tinder Valley for the night?"

"Traffic sucks when you're coming from the sticks."

"When the shit hits the fan at home, you can always stay at my place."

"Thanks, partner. But when I need to get away, I want my solitude."

Kent punched information into the GPS and shuffled papers on a metal clipboard. "First stop this week, Anthony Davis. Fifty-five-year-old male found dead by his landlord after NCFO."

Sanj started the van and the investigators buckled their seat belts.

Livia pulled the belt across her chest. "NCFO?" she asked.

Sanj put the van into gear and turned to Livia. "Neighbors Complained of Foul Odor. You didn't think we'd break you in with anything fresh, did you?"

The van lurched forward as Sanj and Kent laughed. It was going to be an interesting week, but at least she'd be away from Dr. Colt and the cage.

The apartment complex was on the border of Montgomery County. They parked in the lot and surveyed the three-story brown brick building that held twelve units. A small crowd had gathered near the front entrance and all eyes were trained on the morgue van as they pulled up. Kent and Sanj climbed out and opened the back doors to retrieve the gurney, on top of which rested a canvas bag containing everything they might need once inside. Livia followed them as they pushed the gurney past the police cars, whose lights were flashing, and climbed the stairs to enter the building.

An officer from the sheriff's department met them just inside the doors.

"This is the owner of the building," the officer said. "He'll escort you."

The man introduced himself. Sanj shook hands.

"Sanj Rashi." He pointed at Kent and Livia. "Kent Chapple, investigator with the Office of the Chief Medical Examiner. And Dr. Livia Cutty, Medical Examiner." He pointed down the hallway. "Where're we at?"

"Second floor," the owner said, and everyone packed into the elevator with the ominously empty stretcher.

When the elevator doors opened a moment later, Sanj inhaled deeply as if walking into a fresh spring morning. "And, there it is," he said.

The owner pulled out his handkerchief and put it over his

nose. "Yeah. Neighbors called two days ago to report the smell. I was finally able to get over here this morning. Opened the door and nearly lost it. Entire complex stinks now."

The owner led them down the hallway to unit 204, pushed open the door, and shook his head. "You need me for anything? Otherwise, I'm outta here."

"Go," Sanj said. "If we need anything, we'll come down."

"That smell ever go away?"

"So goes the body, so goes the smell. When we're gone, boil some coffee and a pot of vinegar. That'll eat it up pretty good."

The landlord hustled down the hall and into the elevator. Sanj looked at Livia, whose eyes were watering. "Welcome to ride-along week."

The apartment was a one-bedroom with a living room and a kitchen. Sitting on the couch was a very overweight and very dead Anthony Davis, dressed in shorts and a T-shirt, no socks, no shoes. Livia walked around the couch to get a better view while Sanj and Kent gathered what they needed from their canvas bag and took preliminary scene photos.

When Sanj stopped clicking his camera, Livia snapped on a pair of gloves and approached Anthony Davis. His skin was a pallid gray, his lips nearly white, and his eyelids slivered open to expose a hint of blue iris, the corneas long since dried and desiccated. Getting closer to the body, Livia greatly appreciated the overhead ventilation system at the morgue. It pulled more foul air than she understood until she found herself in a closed apartment with a rotting body. She put her hand to her mouth momentarily as if she might vomit.

"Here," Kent said, handing her a jar of Vicks VapoRub. "I can't stand to watch you anymore. Schultz? We'll let him suffer all week. For you, Dr. Cutty, we'll help you out. Smear some under your nose."

Livia took the jar and stuck her gloved finger into the petroleum, placed a small amount on her upper lip and inside her nostrils. The lemony-menthol odor immediately overwhelmed her, which was a much better alternative to the wet rot of Anthony Davis.

Sanj and Kent, donned now in gloves and protective eyewear, approached the body and began their investigation. Livia stood back and observed, which was how this week was meant to go.

"Moderate stage of putrefaction," Kent said. "I'd say five to seven days. Rigor is spent and the body is in a state of secondary laxity." He felt Anthony Davis's swollen legs. "Blood is fixed. Definitely a week."

Sanj took notes and more pictures, snapping shots of the body and the apartment from every angle as Kent moved around the body. "Definitely a heart attack risk."

"Or stroke," Kent said. "He died on the couch and never moved. Lividity in the butt and legs."

After they gathered everything of relevance and found nothing else to photograph, they managed Anthony Davis carefully into a black vinyl body bag and placed him onto the gurney. As they were securing the body, Livia took note of the couch and coffee table. A half-eaten pizza remained on the grease-stained box it was delivered in, and a Styrofoam container next to it sat suspiciously undisturbed. Livia carefully lifted the lid with her pen to find the dried, brittle bones of eaten chicken wings. A soda can was on its side on the floor, having stained the carpeting from where the syrupy liquid spilled.

She looked back to the gurney. "Can I check him?"

Sanj looked up from his clipboard. "The body? Be my guest."

Livia unzipped the bag to expose Anthony Davis's face,

then used her penlight to illuminate his mouth. Sticking her gloved fingers between his lips, she pressed down on his lower teeth and caused Anthony Davis's mouth to gape open. She put the penlight closer to his mouth to get a better look, the VapoRub losing some of its effectiveness this close to the rot.

"Got anything, Doc?" Sanj asked.

"Yeah," Livia said, staring down Mr. Davis's throat. "He choked on a chicken wing. I see the bones in the back of his throat."

Kent and Sanj had a look.

"That's why you're the doc, Doc."

"Anyone would have found it on autopsy," Livia said.

"Yeah," Sanj said. "But this makes us look smart."

"I bet he dropped his soda when he started to choke."

Sanj made sure to photograph the spilled soda can, then zipped up the bag and they pushed the gurney out of the apartment. Outside, the residents watched with morbid expressions as Sanj and Kent loaded their neighbor into the van. While the investigators talked with the police and finished their report, Livia found the building's owner.

"You're the landlord, is that correct?" she asked.

"Yeah. I'm the one who found him."

"Neighbors called to report a smell, is that right?"

"That's right, Doc."

"That ever happen before? Neighbors call with a complaint and you had to check on a tenant?"

"Tenants complain all the time. But I usually make a phone call and settle things that way. I called Tony for two days, and he obviously never answered. So I came over to see what was going on."

"How did you get into the apartment?"

"I've got a master to all the units. It's in the rental agreement that I can enter any apartment so long as I identify myself and give a reasonable lead time."

Livia nodded as she thought.

"Cops asked me about this stuff earlier this morning."

"Of course," Livia said. "You did the right thing. I'm curious for a different reason." Livia pointed to the parking lot, where Sanj and Kent were finished with the police and climbing into the van. "That's my ride. Sorry about Tony."

"Yeah," the landlord said. "You sure that smell goes away?"

"Give it a day or two," Livia said as she walked down the stairs.

They gathered two bodies on the first day of ride-alongs, and arrived back at the morgue just as another crew of investigators went out on an evening call. It was four p.m. Calls that came in this late in the day were dished off to the night-crew investigators. Livia thanked Sanj and Kent for their hospitality before she left, promising to see them in the morning. In her car, she plugged an address into her GPS. Anthony Davis's case and her discussion with the landlord had got her thinking. During the forty-minute ride back to the morgue, with the body lying behind her, she used her phone to get the information she needed. Casey Delevan had been reported missing not by friends or family, but by his landlord, much like Anthony Davis.

Livia jumped onto the highway and headed west toward Emerson Bay. When she took the off-ramp in West Bay ninety minutes later, the GPS spit out directions until Livia was in front of Casey Delevan's former residence, a long single-story building shaped in a blocked U that held eighteen units. She found the number to the management and dialed.

"Old Town Apartments," the voice said.

"This is Dr. Cutty from the medical examiner's office. We talked earlier."

"You here already?"

"I'm parked out front."

"I'll be right out."

A minute later, Livia saw the front door to the office open and a balding man walk out onto the patio. She stood from her car and approached him with a smile and an extended hand.

"Livia Cutty."

He took her hand. "Art Munson."

"You own the apartments?"

"The whole building. I'm only seventy percent full. You're not looking for a place to stay, are you, Dr. Cutty?"

"I'm afraid not."

"Didn't figure a doctor would want one of my little units. So which tenant are you interested in?"

"An old one named Casey Delevan."

"Guy they just pulled out of the bay?"

Livia nodded. "That's him. You're listed as the person who reported him missing, is that correct?"

"I called the cops, if that's what you're asking. Didn't know I was listed as anything."

"Why'd you call the cops?"

"He used to pay his rent three months at a time. I require it of some of my clients, especially the ones with bad or no credit. This prevents them from leaving me high and dry. He paid three months, missed his next installment. I sent two notices with no replies. So I went to check on things when he wouldn't answer his phone. Lot of these guys, they don't pick up the phone when I call. They forget I know where they live. Came by a couple of times, he never answered the door. Finally had to use my key to enter the unit. Knew right away he was gone."

"Why was that?"

"Place was dusty as hell. Rotten food in the fridge. Nobody had stepped foot in there for some time. I get it from time to time with this clientele. Something comes up and they split in a hurry. So, when I knew he was gone, I called the cops."

"When was that?"

"Just after Halloween. I went through all this with the cops. He prepaid for the summer, July through September. Never got anything from him for October. I chased him with phone calls for a couple of weeks before I discovered the apartment had been abandoned."

"And you called the police because you thought something had happened to him?"

"No. I called because I'm required to file a report with the police before I can clear the unit. I was already out a month's rent, so I wanted to move fast to find a new tenant. He didn't have any family listed on his documents, so I stored all his stuff—required by law—for three months. Then I started hocking it. Almost forgot about him until I heard he jumped from that bridge. Wish he'd written me a check before he jumped." Art Munson let out a small laugh that he quickly stifled.

"And you say the apartment looked unlived in for some time?"

"That's for sure."

Livia created a time line in her head. Casey could have disappeared anytime from July to November, confirming the OCME's suggestion that his body was twelve to sixteen months old when it came to the morgue.

"What did you do with his belongings?" Livia asked.

"Sold some of them to a few tenants. Tossed a bunch. Think a few things are still here in storage."

"Yeah? Think I could have a look?"

"Suppose so. What's the interest?"

"I did the autopsy on him. We're tying up some loose ends."

"Sounds like something the cops should be doing."

"My sentiments exactly. But here I am at the end of a workday, doing this stuff myself."

"C'mon in," Art said. "Storage is in the basement."

Livia followed Art Munson into the apartment building and through a door in the back, down a dark stairwell and into a large, cluttered basement. Fluorescent lights blinked to life and cast the space in a migrainous glow. It was a hoarder's paradise. Livia counted eight wooden desks at first glance before noticing another three under stacks of couch cushions and dusty plastic plants. A few old televisions were stacked in the corner along with two ancient refrigerators from when they were termed *ice boxes*, and dozens of framed pictures and hanging mirrors.

"Looks like a mess," Art said. "But it's more organized than you'd guess. Got everything separated by year. Delevan was last year, so that stuff's over here. He was my only AWOL tenant last year."

Art Munson pointed at a desk that held a stack of hardcover books, a microwave, and a computer.

"Most of his furniture sold. He had some halfway decent stuff, so it was easy to move. This is all that's left."

Livia walked to the desk and surveyed the stack of books. She saw a biography on Jeffrey Dahmer and an encyclopedia of serial killers. She paged through them to find they were heavily outlined and dog-eared. Livia pulled open the top drawer to a mess of pens and paper clips and unremarkable office supplies jostled and scattered during the desk's journey to Art Munson's storage space. She pulled open the other drawers and rooted around unimpressed. When she pulled on the bottom drawer, it was locked. She went back to the books and paged more carefully through them.

"You gonna be a while, Doc?"

"Maybe a few minutes."

"I'll be outside. Let me know if you need anything."

When Mr. Munson was gone, Livia pulled open the top drawer again and sifted through the junk. She looked for a key to the locked drawer but didn't find one. She looked around the basement at the other stacks of junk. The fluorescent lighting was starting to warm and the storage area was brighter now than it had been originally. On the third desk she found a toolbox. Inside was a flat-head screwdriver. Back at Casey's desk, she inserted it into the space between the locked drawer and desk frame, and pried with everything she had. Just as a grunt escaped her lips, the drawer splintered at the lock and sprung open.

Livia waited a moment to make sure Mr. Munson didn't come down to check the ruckus, then she paged through the upright files hanging in the drawer. Bank records and bills. The Old Town Apartments rental agreement. Then a thicker folder. She pulled this out and placed it on the desk. Newspaper articles spilled from the folder as she laid it down. Meticulously cut from the paper, they had sharp, ninety-degree edges and long horizontal rectangles that contained the headlines. Scanning them, Livia read articles chronicling the abduction of a Virginia girl named Nancy Dee. A sick and eerie feeling came over her as Livia paged through the articles, which first covered the initial reports of the missing girl and the search for answers. The police reports and speculation on how Nancy might have been abducted, where she had been the day she went missing—a time line of her life that pieced together her steps that day, the last time she was seen alive. The articles covered the police investigation, the town's search, and the vigils held by family and friends. The articles brought Livia back to Nicole's abduction. The Dee family had gone through the same process. The difference, however, came as Livia continued to page through the stories. Six months after Nancy Dee had disappeared, her body was discovered in a shallow grave in the Virginia woods more than one hundred miles from her hometown.

Livia stuffed the articles into the folder and rooted back through the drawer. She found a map of Virginia in one of the folders, pulled it out, and dropped it on the desk. Her fingers walked through the other hanging folders in the drawer, each labeled with a name. She saw *Paula D'Amato* and *Diana Wells* scrawled on the labels. She pulled the folders from the drawer.

"Doc?" Art Munson yelled from the top of the stairs. "You almost done?"

Livia stacked the three folders and the Virginia map into a pile and stuck them in her purse. She closed the drawer and brushed the splintered wood particles under the desk.

"Yeah," she said, rearranging her purse so it looked loose and casual before heading up the stairs.

Livia followed Art Munson outside. It was past six p.m. and dusk had settled over Emerson Bay, the fall sky lit by a fading lavender glow.

"Police ever look at any of Casey Delevan's belongings?" Livia asked.

Art shook his head. "Nope. Just took my statement, asked a few questions. Said they'd get back to me. After three months, I told them I was renting the apartment and moving his stuff. Never heard from them again."

"I'm still working with the detectives on this. Just making sure we don't miss anything." Livia handed him a business card. "If you remember anything else that feels important about Mr. Delevan, give me a call."

"Will do. I thought he jumped off Points Bridge. Something else going on with him?"

Livia shrugged. "That's it. We're just crossing t's and dotting i's. Part of the bureaucratic process."

Art held up Livia's card as she climbed into her car. "You find out he left any money behind, he still owes me a month."

Livia started the car. "If I find anything, I'll make sure you get a check. Thanks for your help."

Chapter 19

Megan McDonald worked at the county courthouse. It was a filing job secured by her father to keep her busy after the abduction. Sitting for long hours in her bedroom, Dr. Mattingly had warned, was unhealthy. But Megan countered, in the quiet of her mind, that filing marriage certificates and lawsuits in a stuffy office for eight hours a day was equally unhealthy. Again, though, like her book—and most things Megan did over the last year—the courthouse job was a way to calm her parents. Placate them and comfort them and make them believe everything would be all right. Her role as a daughter was ironic in this sense. She should be on the receiving end of comfort and consolation. But in this new, strange, post-abduction world, Megan found herself soothing her parents and making things workable so they could continue their lives.

She went to her sessions with Dr. Mattingly, she wrote her book, she did the interviews. She spent her days at her nine-to-five at the courthouse. At home, she listened to the only thing her mother was capable of offering—the whispered voice that gave updates on her book sales and relayed messages from readers who were touched by Megan's words. In reality, Megan knew, the main reason her mother periodically opened her door was to make sure Megan was there and safe and had not been taken again. It was becoming an obsessive compulsion Megan wanted to speak to Dr. Mattingly about.

It was too embarrassing for her mother to allow Emerson Bay, and the people who worked under her father, to see that Megan had fallen from stardom, so the filing position at the courthouse was termed an *internship*. To prepare her for what, exactly, was never clearly defined. But it was the only sufficient way to explain why a nineteen-year-old girl who was supposed to be studying at Duke University, a girl who was the valedictorian of Emerson Bay High and who had created one of the most successful mentoring programs the state had ever seen, was now weaving through middle-aged women in the back office of the county courthouse stuffing hard-copied documents into filing drawers.

The cafeteria was packed from eleven thirty to two o'clock each workday with county employees, lawyers, reporters, clerks, and herds of citizens who needed to stuff their faces with fried food before their court appearance for speeding or littering or DUI. The cafeteria was a noisy place with long picnic bench tables and orange cafeteria trays. An "intern" for the past eight months and Megan had not once stepped foot in the place. Instead, she spent her lunch hours in her car. She had developed a routine, which so far hadn't paid dividends. She wasn't sure yet, exactly, what she was looking for, but the alternative was to do nothing, which was no longer acceptable. Not when she believed she was so close.

It took twenty minutes to drive to West Bay, which, after factoring in the return trip, gave her twenty minutes to watch the sky. Pulling into a new park, one she hadn't visited before, Megan climbed from her car and leaned against the front bumper. After a few minutes a plane passed overhead on a southwest bearing toward Raleigh-Durham. She watched the image of the plane, the size of it in the sky and the direction it was moving. She listened to its sound. In her mind's eye, Megan superimposed this image with the ones she remembered from her two weeks in captivity. In the dark cellar where he kept her, she had been able to peek through a splinter in the plywood that covered the window to see the planes as they passed overhead. The small sliver of sky that was visible was usually vacant when Megan scanned it. But occasionally she saw a plane. At night, that slit in the plywood offered stars from which Megan made out constellations. During the day, she waited for those planes to make her feel not so alone. Those planes held people, and when she spotted them she felt like she was still part of their world.

As she watched now, leaning against her car in the park, she thought she was close. She had little to help her triangulate, but the sound of those planes burned in her mind told her the flight pattern she was now watching was the same one she'd seen and heard during her two weeks in that cellar.

She waited twenty minutes, then five minutes more, knowing the extra time spent would make her late for work. But still, she took the extra minutes hoping to hear it. Finally, she climbed into her car. She'd try another spot tomorrow. She was close. Here, the planes were at the correct altitude and bearing. Their engines at the right pitch. All that was missing was the train whistle.

Chapter 20

After her second day of ride-alongs, Livia made a quick stop home on Tuesday evening. Kent Chapple had so far dubbed Livia's time on ride-alongs as "rot week" since her third transport was also of a decaying body that had met with death days before. Today, she and the scene investigators had gone to the home of Gertrude Wilkes, a ninety-year-old woman who police found dead under the covers of her bed. Her body sat for nearly two weeks, they guessed, before the mailman reported the address to authorities when he couldn't stuff the mailbox any longer. With no family to check on her, the house was bubbling with the smell of death when police opened the door early that morning. By the time Livia arrived with Sanj and Kent, the odor had faded slightly, aided by the cops who had coffee fiercely boiling on the stove and every door and window open wide. Despite their efforts, when Livia entered the elderly woman's house, she had immediately reached for the VapoRub. Kent simply inhaled deeply as he walked past her.

The autopsy would later prove Mrs. Wilkes had died peacefully in her sleep of congestive heart failure, and though no family members were still living to hear this, it comforted

Livia that death had come so gently. It was also satisfying that no one besides the morgue crew and police would know this poor woman's body sat rotting for two weeks simply because no one was left in this world who loved her.

As Livia entered the foyer of her home on Tuesday evening, she unclipped the bobby pin that held her hair in a tight bun and let it fall to her shoulders. She reached for a strand and smelled it.

"Damn," she said.

Death had a way of permeating things—clothes and shoes were most common. But hair was the worst. Despite the tight bun Maggie Larson had taught her, some part of poor Mrs. Wilkes had come home with Livia. She checked her watch. There was time for a quick shower. As she turned on the water, she hoped Kent Chapple was wrong about the rest of the week. Death rot was getting old in a hurry.

Under the shower, Livia mentally reviewed what she had learned from her search the night before after returning home with Casey Delevan's files. She read every article he had collected on Nancy Dee, who disappeared from a small Virginia town without a trace and turned up dead six months later. Unlike Gertrude Wilkes, Nancy Dee had not died peacefully in her sleep. And sadly, she had plenty of family around to hear the morbid details. Her body was buried in a shallow grave in the woods and discovered by a roaming dog and its owner.

Livia also read about Paula D'Amato, a Georgia Tech freshman who went missing eight months before Nancy Dee, and whose whereabouts were still a mystery. Diana Wells, the third girl profiled in Casey Delevan's drawer, was harder to figure. Some quick Google stalking Monday night told Livia that Diana Wells was a student at Elizabeth City State University. Livia had managed to track down a phone number and, earlier in the day while she was on the way to Gertrude Wilkes's house, had reached Diana Wells.

Out of the shower and with the smell of death gone from her hair, Livia made the long drive back to Emerson Bay and entered the Starbucks in East Bay. For a place that sold coffee and pastries, it was packed at eight p.m. with kids on laptops plugged into tabletop outlets, students in various modes of study, and couples talking over cappuccinos.

Taking a seat at the bar, Livia gave three women expectant looks when they entered, offering eye contact and a small smile. They each ignored her. A fourth woman walked in with similar searching eyes, scanning the café until her gaze fell on Livia, who held up her hand in a gentle wave. The woman came over as Livia stood up.

"Diana?"

"Yeah. Are you Dr. Cutty?"

"Yes, thanks for meeting me."

Diana Wells held a confused look on her face, a deep crease forming between her eyebrows. "I guess I was expecting someone older."

"I just finished my residency. Can I get you a coffee?"

"Yeah, I'll have a vanilla latte."

Seated across from each other a few minutes later, Livia pulled out a yellow legal pad. She observed Diana Wells. An overweight girl, one side of her head was shaved nearly bald, with a sudden part that gave way to a wave of purple hair combed to the side. A nose ring and a lip ring and too much makeup begged for discovery and attention.

"I don't want to waste your time, Diana, so I'll get right to the point. How did you know Casey Delevan?"

"I didn't really know him. I mean, I didn't even know his last name until I saw him on the news as the guy who jumped from Points Bridge. I just met him once." There was a short pause. "You really pulled him out of the bay?"

"Not exactly. I did the autopsy on him. How did you meet him?" Livia asked, trying to find a way to elicit information from this girl without mentioning that Diana was profiled in Casey Delevan's drawer along with two other girls—one dead, the other missing—and not daring to discuss her suspicion that Diana Wells was next on his list.

"At a bar," Diana said.

Livia waited.

"Look, I talked to the police about this already."

"About Casey Delevan?"

"Yes."

"When?"

"That summer," Diana said. "The summer I tried to join the club."

Livia cocked her head to the side. "What club?"

Diana looked at Livia with another puzzled expression. "The Capture Club. I thought that's what you were calling about."

Livia contemplated the best approach to handle Diana Wells and decided honesty was easiest.

"There were some confusing findings in the postmortem exam. I'm trying to get some more information about Casey Delevan from people who knew him."

"Confusing, like, he didn't jump from the bridge?"

Livia opened her palms and shook her head. "We're not sure. Tell me about this club."

"He called it the Capture Club."

"Casey?"

"Yeah. It was a bunch of people who talked about missing persons cases."

"Talked about them, how?"

"I don't know, just, discussed them. All the details, what the cops knew, and their own theories."

"Cases from around here?"

"From everywhere. Around the country. Around the world, really. I found out about it after I started talking with Casey in online chat rooms."

"So you met him online?"

"Yeah. No, not really. I mean, I didn't know his name when I was talking to him online. In the chat rooms he just told me about the club and that he was into missing persons cases just like I was, and that if I was interested in joining the club I could become a member."

"And were you interested?"

"Yeah," Diana said, shrugging as if others' judgment meant nothing to her. "I was into that stuff."

"What stuff?"

"Kidnappings."

"In what way?"

"Curious about them. I wanted to know what happened to the people who were taken. I wanted to follow their stories and see what became of them." Diana shrugged again. "Same as anyone else who reads *Events* magazine when a missing girl is plastered on its cover."

"Okay," Livia said. "Did you join this club?"

"I wanted to but . . ."

Livia waited.

"To become a member you have to go through an abduction. A fake one."

"You have to agree to be kidnapped?"

"All I said," Diana continued in a defensive tone, "was that I was interested in the club. I never agreed to the abduction, just said that it sounded cool. Then they surprised me and made me believe it was real. I was drunk the night I met Casey. I had no idea he was the guy from the chat rooms. He made me think he was interested in me. He flirted with me. And at the end of the night, I went with him, got into his car thinking we were going to a late-night party. That's when it happened."

"When what happened?"

"They put a bag over my head, tied me up, and brought me to some abandoned building."

"Christ," Livia said.

"But I was so hysterical—I think I went into shock or something—they ended up driving me back to the bar and leaving me in the parking lot."

"He didn't hurt you?"

"No. Not physically."

"Did you ever see Casey again?"

"Never. Until he was on the news a few weeks ago."

"And you went to the police about this? Afterward?"

"My parents made me."

"What happened?"

"Nothing. They said they never found anything about the club, and that I was a willing participant."

Livia looked down at the notes she had scribbled. "You said Casey was with a friend. Did you know him?"

"Two friends. A guy and a girl. I didn't know them. The girl was the one who put the bag over my head after I got in his car."

"How many were there?"

"In the car? Just Casey and his friends. But after they brought me to that abandoned building, there were lots. Like, twenty or more. The whole club, I guess. But before I saw everyone in the club, it was just Casey and the girl. They tied me to a chair and whispered all these horrible things in my ear. The girl was telling me the things they were going to do to me. All these nasty, disgusting things.

"You ever see this girl?"

"No. She was at the bar with Casey, but I never paid attention to her. And when we were in the car, she was in the backseat and it was too dark to see her. Then she put the bag over my head."

Livia put her pen to the page. "You know this girl's name. The one who put the bag over your head?"

"Yeah," Diana said. "He called her Nicole."

Chapter 21

Two early-morning transports with the investigators had Livia back to the OCME by two p.m. on Wednesday afternoon. She sat behind her desk in the fellows' office and perused the Internet. She was looking for anything she could find about Casey Delevan or the strange group of twisted individuals Diana Wells had called the Capture Club, whose membership Livia was scared to admit included Nicole. Although Livia found no specific organization by this name, she did manage to locate a strong online presence of people interested in the details of current and past missing people.

After an hour of research, she turned her attention back to Casey Delevan. In a defunct website from 2015 that had not been updated for some time, Livia found an advertisement for Two Guys Handyman Service. Listed were Casey Delevan and Nathaniel Theros. There was a phone number and address. Livia wrote both down just as Kent Chapple poked his head into her office.

"We're done for the day, Doc. Any calls after three o'clock go to the second shift. I'll see you in the morning."

"Thanks, Kent," Livia said.

She ripped the sticky note containing Nathaniel Theros's

information from the pad and left the office. Mr. Theros lived on the west side of Emerson Bay, not quite a two-hour drive from Raleigh. Her brakes squeaked when she stopped in front of his house—a single-story ranch with overgrown shrubs, unkempt grass, and weeds pushing through the sidewalk cracks. Nathaniel Theros's house sat in a crumbling neighborhood of other dilapidated homes that made up the ruins of West Emerson Bay, where industry had died over the last few decades as factories shut down and moved overseas. The years had seen a great transformation take place in Emerson Bay, when shipping and port industries spread to the north and south, as if a drop of detergent had fallen onto Emerson Bay and pushed away the greasy factories and grimy shipping yards, leaving behind the squeaky-clean waterfront community of East Emerson Bay, called East Bay by locals, which was hip and young and booming. The waterfront homes attracted the wealthy, and tourism was rampant. Restaurants, shops, and galleries prospered as local residents and tourists walked the cobblestone streets and ate on verandas while staring at the bay and watching restored steamboats chug up and down the waterway.

But when tourism took root and sprouted to become the major economy in Emerson Bay, the west side suffered. Without the factories or the shipping yards, and without the benefit of a beautiful waterfront, West Bay became the dying side of town with crumbling shells of old refineries, and train yards that made for noisy living. What used to be a place where hard-working folk retreated after a day on the docks or in the factories, a place where a small yard for your kids and safe streets in the neighborhood were enough for a pleasant existence, West Bay now was somewhere only visited when necessary. And for Livia, today there was no way around it.

One last check of the address, then she walked up the steps

and rang the bell. Dogs barked incessantly and clawed the door from the other side. There was some yelling and corralling before the door finally opened.

"What's up?" the man said.

"Nathaniel Theros?"

"Only if I'm in trouble. Nate, otherwise."

Livia smiled. "No trouble. My name's Livia Cutty. I wanted to ask you a weird question."

The man was bent over, holding a large Rottweiler by its collar. Faded tattoos crept from under his T-shirt, down his arms and up his neck. He pulsed his eyebrows. "I like weird."

"You used to know a guy named Casey Delevan?"

Instant smile. "Oh, yeah. While back."

"Mind if I ask you some questions about him?"

"He in trouble?"

"You could say that."

"You a cop?"

"No, I'm a doctor."

Nate made a strange face. "Gimme a sec. I'll put Daisy away."

Livia waited on the porch while Nate disappeared into the house, dragging Daisy reluctantly with him as the Rottweiler growled and barked. She heard the rattle of a cage, then Nate was back. He pushed through the screen door and walked onto the front stoop, sat against the railing opposite her, and lit a cigarette that glowed in the October dusk. "So why's a doctor asking about Casey Delevan?"

"Curiosity, mostly. I work over at the OCME."

"What's that?"

"The Medical Examiner's office in Raleigh. I'm a fellow finishing my training."

"Oh, yeah? Like CSI stuff?"

"Sort of."

"Shit," Nate said with a smile. "What sort of trouble is Casey in?"

"There was a body pulled out of Emerson Bay a few weeks ago. You hear about that?"

Nate nodded his head. "Heard about it."

"ID came back as your pal, Casey."

Nate smiled as though Livia were putting him on, then put his cigarette to his mouth. "You telling me Casey's dead?"

Livia nodded. "Sorry. It's been on the news."

"I don't got a TV, just Internet. And I ain't been around the last few weeks. What happened to him?"

"Not sure yet," Livia lied. "He was found floating in the bay, so some people are guessing he killed himself. Jumped from Points Bridge. You two used to work together?"

"Yeah, like, I don't even know how long ago. Couple years, maybe. We had a carpentry company. You know, handyman stuff for rich guys in East Bay who don't know how to do any of that." Nate smiled as he reminisced. "We had some jobs lined up, too. Doing pretty good. Then one day, he stopped showing up. After a week, I knew he was gone."

"Gone, dead?"

"Shit, no. Just gone. Casey was a drifter. He'd been all over the place and I got the impression Emerson Bay was just a stop for him. When he didn't show for work, I figured he moved on to his next place. But I mean"—Nate shrugged—"I could see him jumping off a bridge. He was the craziest sumbitch I ever knew. Pretty dark, too, sometimes. Depressed, maybe, I don't know."

"When was that? That Casey stopped showing up for work?"

Nate gave a confused look, like Livia was challenging him with a calculus question. "Don't know. It was a while ago."

"Let's backtrack. When did you guys start Two Guys? Your handyman company. In the summer?"

"No. It was springtime." Nate thought for a moment and then shrugged. "Figured we'd try to get all the richies wanting to paint their big homes and remodel before summer came along."

"So spring of 2016, then? That was . . . let's say, twenty months ago?"

Nate wrinkled his forehead. "Yeah, I guess. Couple years, like I said."

"Okay. So you started in spring. And you said you had some work?"

"Oh, yeah. We were busy."

"Can you remember how long you and Casey worked together?"

Nate sucked on his cancer stick and rocked his head back and forth as if he were listening to music. "Few months. 'Member it being really hot that summer, and we were doing a lot of exteriors. We were painting a big house on the bay. It was so hot we had to hide from the sun, sort of follow the shadows throughout the day so we could paint in the shade." Nate shook his head now as it came back to him. "That's right. 'Member that now 'cause we were just halfway done when Casey took off. Left me to finish the sumbitch by myself. Big beach house. Yeah, now I got it. Guy paid me when I was done, and I even saved some cash to give Casey when he showed his face. After a few weeks, I figured the money was mine. He ain't comin' back."

"That was summertime," Livia said. "Do you remember which month?"

Nate thought for a minute. "I don't got the company no more. When Casey took off, I couldn't do it by myself. But I saved the paperwork for my taxes. Still got it in a folder somewhere. Want me to check when we did that house?"

"Would you mind?"

"Gimme a minute."

Livia stood on the front porch while Nate headed inside. He returned five minutes later.

"August," he said as he came through the screen door. He was holding a small calendar book he read from. "Job took three weeks. Started August thirteenth, finished by myself September fifth. Last time I saw Casey was that first week we worked on the house. He showed up that whole week, then never came back after the weekend. If I'm remembering right. So I guess that would be"—Nate consulted the old pocket calendar where he used to track his jobs—"Friday, August nineteenth. Last time I saw him." He looked up at Livia. "Best I can 'member."

Livia stared at the book in his hands. Her face stayed stoic but her mind was frantic. Nicole had disappeared on Saturday, August twentieth, from a beach party that most of Emerson Bay High seniors had attended. Livia remembered Art Munson, the landlord who reported Casey missing in November. With three months of rent prepaid, it's possible Casey disappeared in August along with Nicole. And it was possible that the time of death, determined by the anthropology department at the OCME to be twelve to eighteen months, was that same weekend.

Her thoughts veered in unorganized directions and for a moment Dr. Cutty, who was trained to take random discoveries and make sense of them, stood with no tools to collect the information she was gathering, no ability to put the pieces together into anything cohesive. The random bits of knowledge popped into her mind—about the weekend Nicole went missing and that it might have coincided with Casey's disappearance. About the two of them dating. About the perverse group called the Capture Club. About Casey Delevan's body turning up on her autopsy table. Her mind flashed back to Dr. Larson and the skewers she had used to probe the mysterious piercings in Casey's skull. The "shovel" contusions on his upper arms. His shirt caked in clay from the ground in which he was originally buried. The ropes and the cinder blocks and the fisherman who had pulled him from the bottom of the bay.

Livia's thoughts congealed into a single question. She asked it before she knew it was on her tongue. "Were you part of the Capture Club?"

"Shit," Nate said with a smile. He blew diluted smoke from the corner of his mouth. "How do you know about the club?"

"We're finding all sorts of things out about your pal Casey. I talked to a girl named Diana Wells. Know her?"

"Yeah, I know her," Nate said without hesitation.

"She doesn't have flattering things to say about your little club."

"That's 'cause she couldn't deal with it. Little psycho went ballistic during her initiation. Couldn't handle the take, so we had to cut her loose. First time we *ever* did that—stopped in the middle of an initiation. But we had no choice. She was throwing a fit. Thought she might have a seizure." Nate laughed as he reminisced. "Holy shit, it was a mess. We nailed her ass good."

"Sounds like it," Livia said. "Tell me about the Capture Club."

"Just a bunch of stoner kids out for a thrill. We were into that sort of thing back then. A fetish, I guess some people would say. Couldn't get enough of kidnappings and missing people. Used to talk about all the interesting ones. We *dissected* that shit. Like that girl who went missing in the Bahamas. 'Member her? Still, like six years later, everyone's trying to figure out what happened to her. Everyone's got a theory. There was an HBO special on her. Casey got a copy and we watched it at one of the meetings. The club, we made our own guesses and talked about all that stuff."

Livia nodded, trying to hide the ugly look her face wanted to make.

"I still read about that stuff all the time," Nate said. "It's just insane, you know, that somebody like, *steals* somebody else. Not their car, not their money. Actually steals the *person*! Yeah, the club was dark but so's the whole country. When someone important goes missing, or the case is interesting enough, everybody has the same fetish. Whole world, really. No one admits it, but it's true. In the club, nobody judged. We all understood." Another drag of his smoke and an amused look. "Everyone hides under the cover of news watching and sadness for the victim and their family. Fine. Be sad. That's normal. But don't pretend you're not curious."

"Tell me about the initiations."

"That was the thrill of the club. To get in, you had to agree to be taken. That a rush, on either side of it." He laughed. "We had some epic takes, too."

"Let me try to understand. You all agreed to kidnap one another?"

"Nah, it wasn't like that. You don't just agree to it, that wouldn't work. It wasn't anything you expected. Casey was the contact guy who went online and found people who were interested in becoming members. As soon as Casey was convinced that a new potential member would be up for the thrill and would be cool with it"—Nate raised his eyebrows—"the take was on. No one ever saw it coming. If you expected to get taken, what's the point? If it's gonna work, you gotta be scared. I mean terrified."

"Like Diana Wells."

Nate just smiled and blew smoke into the night air. "Not everyone was cut out for the club."

"And Casey was, what? In charge of the club?"

"He was the man."

"Who else did you guys talk about at the meetings? What other cases?"

"Shit. Lots. Some old stuff, like sixties old. But mostly current stuff."

"Like what?"

"Anything local, or even close, was always a big topic."

"You guys ever talk about Megan McDonald and Nicole Cutty?"

Nate looked at Livia, the corners of his eye creased slightly out of suspicion. "You sure you're not a cop?"

"I'm sure. You know who those girls are? Megan and Nicole?"

" 'Course I do."

"Yeah? Nicole Cutty was my sister."

"No shit?"

Livia cocked her head. "No shit. Casey and the club ever talk about Nicole or Megan?"

"You mean about them going missing? No."

"No? Why not? Can't get more high profile than Megan McDonald. Plus, they were local girls. Probably had you guys salivating with such a big case being so close."

"Totally. I was fascinated. Still am. Follow the McDonald girl online and watch her stuff. Even read her book. But there's no more club. Casey organized everything. So when he took off, the club broke up. We tried to get together a few times. Used to meet down at the old Coleman's brewhouse, but with Casey gone it wasn't the same." Nate smiled and shook his head. "So Nicole was your sister?"

Livia nodded. "She was."

Nate gave another crooked smile. "She was one of the club's most epic takes. She wanted it dark and dirty. Most people couldn't handle what we did to Nicole. She loved it."

Livia swallowed hard, pushing down whatever was trying to come up her throat. "So Nicole *was* part of your club?"

Nate frowned like everyone should know this. "Not just *part* of it. She had Casey all wrapped up. So whatever she wanted, she got."

Livia blinked and tried to make sense of what she was hearing. "I don't understand."

He finished the cigarette, tossed it in the grass with the dandelions and stray beer cans. "Just being straight with you, Casey and Nicole were screwing and running the club. Like, *together*. Whatever Casey was into, your sister was into. The whole thing with Diana Wells went bad because Nicole took it too far and Casey went along with it."

The words pushed Livia back half a step until she, too, rested on the railing opposite Nate. She tried to put on a casual expression. "You ever tell the police any of this?"

"I don't ever tell the police anything."

"They ever talk to you?"

"The police? Shit no."

"You sure?"

"I'd know if the cops talked to me, trust me."

"But Nicole goes missing, it's all over the news. Megan McDonald, too. At the same time, Casey stops showing up for work. You ever stop to think if there's a connection?"

Nate shrugged. "I just figured with Nicole being gone, Casey took off to avoid any heat from the cops. Boyfriend's always under the gun, know what I mean?"

Nate took out another cigarette, offered the pack to Livia.

"No, thanks," she said. "So this club, it's no more?"

"Poof," Nate said, lighting his Bic. He put the flame to the tip of his Marlboro. "Gone, just like that." He released his finger and the flame died.

"But you still follow the stories, right? Missing girls?"

"It's in my blood, or whatever they call it. You know?"

"DNA."

"Right. It's in my DNA. Ain't my fault, it's just part of me."

"You've got some sick DNA, Mr. Theros."

"So I've been told."

"You mind if I come back and ask some more questions if anything else comes up about Casey?"

"Sure, whatever."

Livia walked off the patio.

"So Casey's really dead?"

"Afraid so," Livia said over her shoulder.

"Sorry about Nicole. She was a cool chick."

Livia lifted her chin and walked across the trash-filled front lawn, a very different picture of her younger sister forming in her mind. Gone was the image of Nicole lugging *Harry Potter* books into her bed, shadowed now by the aura of a girl clad in black, desperate for attention and willing to go to great lengths to find it.

Chapter 22

Her ride-along week officially ended Friday afternoon at five p.m., but Livia managed, with a favor from Kent, to finish by noon. After the sequestration and transport of a forty-year-old suicide victim who had started his car in his closed garage and waited for the carbon monoxide to kill him, the morgue van pulled up behind the OCME where Sanj Rashi drew the gurney from the back and wheeled the body through the rear door of the morgue. In all, Livia recovered twelve bodies during ride-along week while learning the intricacies and tricks of scene investigation from Kent and Sanj. Although the past week had been fascinating, Livia found herself aching Friday morning to get back to the morgue. Back to her autopsy table and her tools and the controlled environment of the autopsy suite. What she learned during her first week of ride-alongs would prove invaluable as she continued her training, and she would return Monday morning more knowledgeable than when she left. She would also be refreshed and ready for her next case.

After Sanj wheeled the body inside, Livia stood outside with Kent. He pulled out a cigarette.

"You sure you don't mind if I take off early today?" Livia asked.

"You outrank me, Doc."

"Thanks. And I'd appreciate it if Dr. Colt didn't hear about my heading out today."

Kent smiled. "What happens in the morgue van, stays in the morgue van."

"I owe you one."

"Careful what you promise. I cash in on my favors. Trust me."

Livia pointed at his cigarette. "You know what this job's done to me in just three months?"

"What's that?"

"It's made me see people from the inside out. Or in reverse, I guess is a better way to say it. I see you dying of lung cancer as you suck on that cigarette. I see your lifeless body on my autopsy table, and I see all the necrotic tumors in your stenosed lungs. I see your trachea scarred and ash-strewn. I see your lips and tongue black with waiting death that crept down your throat and found your lungs. I see white pockmarks of cancerous tumors throughout your abdomen, and I feel your fattened lymph nodes swollen with—"

"All right, for Christ's sake," Kent said, dropping the cigarette and stomping it out.

"Sorry," Livia said. "I'm just telling you the perils of my job. Since when do you smoke, anyway? I've known you three months, first time I saw you stick a cigarette in your mouth was two days ago."

"Old habit," Kent said. "Just picked it up again."

Livia walked over to the van and leaned against it, taking a spot next to Kent. Ride-along week, much of which was spent in the van, provided many opportunities to talk. Fabricated beliefs about medical examiners were rampant, especially the idea that all MEs were tight with detectives, which Livia was finding to be a myth. The MEs worked most closely with the medicolegal investigators, and these were the people they got to know best. After five days, she realized much could be learned from sitting in the back of the morgue van. Kent was unhappily married to his high school sweetheart. His kids were the only reason he and his wife stayed together, and they had openly discussed the best time for divorce. Maybe when the kids were in high school, but that presented an awkward transition for the kids at an already challenging time. College was the next best time, but this was far off and the thought of "existing" together for that long was difficult. He didn't believe in counseling and straight-out refused to confess his annoyances and disappointments to a shrink. After all, Kent said in the middle of the week as he grumbled in the front seat and blew cigarette smoke through the barely open window, he had a never-ending supply of bodies that would listen to the stories of his shitty life.

"Things any better at home?" Livia asked.

"You can only stack a pile of shit so many ways, Doc."

Livia smiled. "Try a stress ball instead of cigarettes. They'll keep your hands occupied while you're in the van."

"I'll give it a shot."

"You talked all week about your wife, I wanted to make sure you knew I was listening."

Kent smiled, lifted his chin. "Noted. Just remember when you settle down, Doc. Wait for the right person, because once you have kids you're stuck with them." There was a short pause before Kent spoke again. "So, you seeing anyone?"

Livia shook her head. "This job is all-consuming. Sadly, I'm more interested in impressing Dr. Colt than a boyfriend. And my current outlet for pent-up energy is kicking a hanging Everlast bag held by a large black man named Randy."

Kent pursed his lips. "I'm not going to touch that answer."

"Good. It was meant to get me off the hook."

"You're off. So what do you have cooking today? Why are you cutting out early?" Kent asked.

"I'm making a run up to Richmond to meet with the chief medical examiner up there."

"Oh yeah? What about?"

"Probably nothing. It has to do with that jumper you dumped on me a few weeks ago."

"The one we pulled out of the bay?"

"That's him."

"That case still pending?"

"Yeah. I'm not involved with it any longer. Homicide guys have it. I'm just curious."

Kent ran his tongue along the inside of his bottom lip. "About what?"

"It's a long story, Kent. If we had a couple hours together in the van, I'd fill you in."

"We don't have that, so you can fill me in some other time," he said.

"You're on vacation next week?" Livia asked.

"Yeah. Heading up to Tinder Valley to fish for a few days."

"I'll see you when you get back?"

"For sure. You did good this week, Doc."

After her Emerson Bay runs to track down Diana Wells and Nate Theros, Livia had spent the past two nights concentrated on Nancy Dee, the girl profiled in articles she found in Casey Delevan's drawer. After two nights of researching the girl's disappearance, the search to find her, the leads that came and went, the people who were questioned, and, six months after she had vanished, the grisly discovery of her body in a Virginia forest preserve, there wasn't much Livia didn't know about Nancy Dee.

After Nancy's abduction from Sussex County, Virginia, in March of 2015, there was at first a group of the usual suspects that included her father and boyfriends. But the case quickly evaporated as everyone of interest provided solid alibis. An intensive search lasted for the first few weeks, and as Livia read Nancy's story the words took her back to the previous year when the folks of Emerson Bay looked for Nicole and Megan. Their search, too, was frantic. Filled initially with hope that there would be a simple explanation to their disappearances, the hunt slowly fell under a cloud of dread as the days stacked up. When Megan McDonald miraculously resurfaced, wandering down Highway 57 two weeks after she disappeared, a joy filled the town and elation flooded the country, sweeping from east to west like a rolling tsunami. Details soon followed about Megan's crafty escape from the dreaded bunker in the woods and her resilient character during her captivity. It was all everyone wanted, and the fact that Nicole was still missing fell into the shadows of Megan's celebrity.

There was nothing in particular that pushed Nancy Dee's story into the background other than time. The public's attention span was short, and there were plenty of other stories that came along to distract them. Until Nancy's body turned up in a shallow grave near the Virginia border in Carroll County, most had forgotten about this poor girl. Then, for a short, final burst, Nancy regained the headlines before she was gone for good, remembered only by family and friends and fetish groups that got off on such horrors.

Livia gathered everything she had on Nancy Dee and dropped it all on the front seat of her car. Virginia, like North Carolina, had a statewide medical examiner system in place, which meant any suspicious deaths would be handled by the OCME, as opposed to the smaller, coroner-run local facilities scattered throughout the counties. Livia had placed a call the day before to Dr. Angela Hunt, the chief medical examiner of

Virginia, to inquire about Nancy Dee. Dr. Hunt had agreed to meet with Livia if she could manage to get to Richmond by four p.m.

The ride from Raleigh to Richmond was two and a half hours, and a straight shot up I-85. Livia found the Madison Building and parked under two tall flagpoles where the American flag and Virginia state flag flapped in the afternoon breeze. It took a few minutes of introductions and displaying her medical examiner's badge until Livia was finally ushered to Dr. Hunt's office.

"Dr. Cutty?"

"Yes. Hi, Livia Cutty."

"Angie Hunt."

They shook hands and Dr. Hunt motioned for Livia to sit in one of the chairs in front of the desk. Taking her place behind the desk, Dr. Hunt asked, "What brings a Dr. Colt fellow up north?"

Livia smiled. "Not Dr. Colt. I'm on ride-alongs this week, and finished early so the timing just worked out. I wanted to ask you about that case from last year."

"Right," Dr. Hunt said, pulling a file from her bottom drawer. "Nancy Dee."

"Correct."

"I went back through it after you called. I'm happy to let you have a look. It was a sad case, but when I reviewed it I didn't see anything that jumped out at me."

"Just the same," Livia said. "I'd like to see it. For my own personal reasons."

Dr. Hunt smiled. "Whatever you need. You're welcome to use my office. Let me know if you need anything or if I can answer any questions."

"Thank you."

When Dr. Hunt was gone, Livia pulled the file toward her. She opened the front cover of the manila folder to find photos of the scene where Nancy's body was located. Livia had just witnessed hundreds of these photos being snapped by Kent and Sanj during the last week when they documented the bodies they were called to investigate and transport. Livia pulled the photos from the folder and laid them out in front of her. Depicted in them was Nancy Dee's lifeless body, as it lay partially covered by leaves and dirt. Her eyes closed, skin pale with death and pocked with dirt, hair matted and caked down like a sculpture. Livia could not help but superimpose Nicole's face onto the photos. The image caused her insides to ache and her stomach to sour.

A morning jogger, whose dog had taken off in front of him and raced through the woods apparently with a bead on the body's odor, had discovered Nancy Dee. She had been missing for six months, and the identification came quickly when the body was transported to Dr. Hunt's morgue.

Livia turned to the autopsy photos and perused the findings, cruising through the report like a speed-reader. She'd read hundreds of autopsy reports over the last four years, and had written plenty of her own in the first three months of fellowship. She expected to find this poor girl, abducted from the streets of Virginia and abused by a monster, to have died from some barbaric act of violence. Indeed, the autopsy revealed sexual abuse. But the photos Livia saw of the body were unremarkable. The external exam noted chafing and bruising to the ankles and wrists, likely from restraints, but otherwise there were no signs of physical abuse.

Livia paged through the autopsy report until she reached its conclusion. The cause of death made Livia's mind stumble. She turned back to the toxicology report and read it again. Her finger streaked down the page and came to rest on the sedative discovered in Nancy Dee's bloodstream. Because it was found in such high concentration, it was determined that Nancy's body did not have the chance to fully metabolize it, meaning she died shortly after it was ingested. Such a large amount was consumed that this drug had seized her respiratory system and caused fatal respiratory arrest. Whoever held Nancy for six months, by accident or with intent, had OD'd her on a drug called ketamine. Livia looked at the name of the drug for several seconds, drawing on her recently polished knowledge of pharmacology from her binge studying after her debacle with the elderly fall victim in the cage. Ketamine was used mostly by veterinarians for sedation before surgery, but had a limited role in traditional medicine. Called Special K by kids, it was also occasionally abused for its hallucinogenic effects. When combined with diazepam, as it was with Nancy Dee, the sedative effects were intensified.

Livia looked up at the ceiling of Dr. Hunt's office. Something else about the drug gnawed at her. She put her finger on the page and ran her nail under each letter. *K-E-T-A-M-I-N-E.*

When it came to her, it came quickly and with little doubt. She hastily reassembled the chart and pushed it across the desk. She tried briefly to find Dr. Hunt, but gave up after a few minutes of wandering the halls. Outside, she climbed into her car and let her phone's GPS take her to the nearest bookstore. She walked into the Barnes & Noble and, surrounded by the latest titles from popular authors, walked to the nonfiction best sellers display and plucked Megan McDonald's book from the shelf. Livia skimmed to the middle, where she thought she remembered reading it. It took a few minutes to find it, Megan's first-person recollection of her time in the hospital after her escape from the bunker. Her memory of that night had been foggy, Megan wrote, and much of what was recorded about her trek along Highway 57 and her reception at the hospital was documented with the help of Mr. Steinman, the man who had found Megan barefoot and bleeding and who had carried her away in his car and brought her to safety.

Livia skimmed the pages, frantic to find a single word, until she found the passage she was looking for. Megan's memory was altered that night, and she spent the first twelve hours of her hospital stay in a near-comatose state. Part of her trance was blamed on shock and dehydration. But mainly, the doctors determined, it was due to the large amount of sedative found in her system. A drug mostly used by veterinarians. A medication called ketamine.

Chapter 23

Megan sat with eyes closed and her legs positioned Indian style on the plush leather chair in Dr. Mattingly's office. Tonight's session was an add-on to her typical twice-a-month meetings. One Megan had specifically requested. Since her breakthrough session when she recalled the far-off train whistle as a recurrent noise from her time in the cellar, Megan was anxious to get back to hypnotherapy. She knew other things were buried in her memory, likely suppressed by the amnesic effects of ketamine, the drug that sedated her during those two weeks in captivity.

She believed there was enough there, in her own mind, to make sense out of what she'd been through. And since remembering the train whistle, she'd been up at night with something else that bothered her. Something about the cellar and her captivity that was knocked loose during one of the sessions but was not yet close enough to the surface of her memory to be useful. And since she'd started with Dr. Mattingly, Megan had learned to differentiate the important things from the meaningless. She learned which impressions to pursue and which to let go. Her restless nights were telling her this latest pining—that object her fingertips brushed against but could not grip—needed exploring.

"Describe the room again, Megan. Start with what you know for sure," Dr. Mattingly said.

The sessions took a familiar path each time, and Megan had learned to navigate this redundant road without protest or resistance.

"My bed is in the corner. Mattress, box spring, and frame. Across from me, against the wall behind which the stairs are located, is a table."

"This is the table where your food was placed?"

"No," Megan said with her eyes closed. "That table is closer to the stairs. This other table is against the wall."

"Go to it, Megan. Walk to that table. See it in your mind. See it three-dimensionally in your mind's eye."

"I try," Megan said. "I want to get there but my chain is not long enough."

"Don't force it. Just look, Megan. Look at the table and describe what you see."

"It's too dark to see."

"It's too dark only on the surface, Megan. Your eyes have adjusted themselves to the darkness. You see better than you believe you can. Look at the table. Take your time and tell me what you see."

Megan breathed hard through her nose. It took a minute before she answered. "There's a bottle. The table is empty except for a bottle."

Dr. Mattingly was quiet.

"It's a canister. . . . It's paint," Megan finally said. "A bottle of spray paint."

"Good, Megan. Now, leave that bottle alone. Move your eyes from that table you cannot reach. Go to the other table, Megan. The one where your food is left. What is there, Megan?"

Megan's crossed legs twitched while she sat in Dr. Mattingly's overstuffed chair as she walked in her mind as far as her shackles would allow. "There is nothing there. It's dark and I have to feel if food has been left for me. There is nothing now."

"Good, Megan. Very good. Now go back to the bed. Lie down there and listen to my voice . . . are you there yet?"

Megan nodded.

"Are you lying down now, Megan?"

Another nod.

"That table is empty, Megan. But sometimes it is full. Sometimes you wake to find your food having been set on that table. What is it that wakes you, Megan? What is the sound that pulls you from sleep?"

Megan shook her head.

"What is it, Megan? What do you hear that wakes you?"

"No . . . I don't know. The stairs, I guess. The stairs squeak when he walks on them."

"No guessing, Megan. There's no need to guess. Everything you need is right here, in this place. Just listen to it all and tell me what you hear."

"The stairs. I don't know! The stairs are squeaking. He's coming!"

"Ignore the squeaking stairs, Megan. Do you hear something else?"

"No. Just the stairs. He's coming!"

"Okay, Megan. I want you to wake up now. We're going to wake in three, two, one. And wake."

Megan's eyes blinked open and she stared at Dr. Mattingly. She was breathing short, quick breaths.

"Shit," she said after a few seconds.

"We've discussed this, Megan. Not every session will end with a breakthrough."

"It was right there. That thing I'm looking for."

"Megan, it's important at this stage of your treatment for me to protect you. To stop your mind from going too far in these sessions. Eventually, with each session, we'll go a little further and that will be considered progress. But journeying too far too soon will bring regression. Instead of moving forward, your mind will retreat and our progress will be lost."

"If I get close again, though, will you just leave me there for a minute longer? I hate it when you take control from me. You said I needed to feel in control for this stuff to work."

"I'm always considering what's best for you, Megan. When your body language and voice all coincide with it being the right time to take that next step, we'll do it. I'll leave you there. But when you're hyperventilating and your pulse is racing, your mind is not ready for that step. This takes time, Megan. And since you've given yourself to the process, you've made great strides. It's common to want to do too much. But as your physician, I need to keep you healthy throughout the process."

Megan took a deep breath. "You're the shrink."

Chapter 24

His last visit, so anticipated and carefully planned, had gone poorly. She had been in a particularly defiant mood that evening, and he knew it as soon as he entered the cellar. He'd walked down the stairs to find her standing with one side of the dismantled bed frame in her hand like a baseball bat. It hurt him to see her like that, so ready to fight him and strike him. All he had done was offer to love this one and take care of her. He wanted to give her a fair chance.

It was a burden for him that evening, with his hopes high on a pleasant night of companionship, to have to repair her meddling. First he overpowered her, which he did without difficulty, but the process put a damper on the evening. Then he tied her to the opposite side of the room so he could repair the bed in peace and without fear that she would attack him. Finally, worst of all, he punished her. This, he hated most. Such high hopes for the evening, it was a pity to have ended it that way. But if their relationship were to survive, they each had to follow the rules. He was not outside of those rules. Certainly not. He laid them out for her when they first started together, and promised he would never break the rules unless she forced him to do so. Unfortunately, with this one in particular, they were broken often. Much more than the others.

After that last evening ended so badly, he feared things were at a breaking point for them now. They were at that proverbial fork in the road he had reached with all of them. Despite each of their journeys being unique and lasting various lengths of time, they all seemed to reach this fork. In one direction, happiness and bliss. In the other, sorrow and grief.

That night when he found her armed and ready to strike, he calmly repaired the bed and delivered a swift and appropriate punishment. Afterward, he offered one more chance to make things work. He trusted and truly believed she was willing to try. She told him as much that night, nearly begged him for another chance. So he arranged tonight, another special evening when he had all the time in the world and no one was waiting for him at home and no one would question where'd he been. They wouldn't need to rush things.

When he descended the cellar stairs tonight, however, he knew immediately she had lied to him. He found her hard at work, having used the sharp end of the box-spring frame again to pry free one of the plywood boards that covered the window. It lay still on the floor, an open picture of her deceit. She had also pried apart the window frame—the heavy glass too thick to penetrate—to produce a gaping crevice through which she had managed to wedge half her torso until she trapped her head and neck and one of her arms outside the cellar window, her chest and lower body inside.

She looked pathetic, trapped, and helpless. Foolish, even, hanging halfway out the window with no means to go farther or to retreat back into the cellar. Did she even realize, in this wretched state, that he was her savior? The only one who could help her? He felt something for this one. Perhaps sorrow. Perhaps something different. But for the first time, he also felt fear. It would have been disastrous had she succeeded. Given more time she might have ruined everything for him. Panic washed over him at the thought of what her freedom would bring. The trail she would leave, like dropped popcorn kernels, would lead back to this place. The discoveries that would be made. It would spell the end, something for which he was not prepared.

As he entered the cellar, his mind worked quickly to correct his errors. She would no longer be granted access to the windows. He would rearrange her living quarters and restrict her movements. Sad, but necessary. Punishment tonight would be brutal. A statement that this behavior could not continue. The message would be delivered without remorse. He walked over to her and knocked softly on the window. Exhausted from her aborted escape, she lifted her head from the damp ground outside and stared at him through the thick glass block. She was stuck at the chest, with one arm wedged against her side and the other outstretched and supporting her head as she lay on the wet mud and pea gravel outside the window. He rubbed her bare leg, which hung inside the cellar.

He shook his head as he stared into her eyes. "Have you any idea how much it hurts me when you behave like this?"

With her teeth gritted, she violently kicked the side of his face. He recoiled in a sudden jerk, losing his footing and falling to the ground with his hand covering his cheek and a shocked look of insult on his face. He sat on the cold concrete floor and watched as she flailed, half in and half out of the cellar window—a feeble turtle on its back.

He stood and walked to the corner. On the table was a bottle of spray paint, which he shook violently, the small ball bearing rattling inside the bottle as it mixed the paint. He, too, gritted his teeth as he shook the bottle, staring at her as she looked back through the glass.

He walked to the far wall and pointed the canister at the concrete. In black spray paint he created a large *X* on the wall next to a previous one, whose thick black lines had dripped down the gray concrete to dry in frozen tears of paint. They both knew the rules. Three *X*'s meant the end of their relationship. The first had come last time, when he found her holding the dismantled bed frame and ready to fight for her freedom. Tonight, the second X. The rules were clear. After the third, a chance for redemption would not be granted, and a parting of ways would follow. The system was sophomoric and demeaning. But successful, too. History told him the second X brought them under control. There was always a joyous time after that second mark went onto the wall. It was a time of submission. A time of giving. A time when, in the past, he had fallen in love.

But love did not come easily. It needed to be earned. Betrayal needed to be snuffed out completely. He put the paint can back onto the table, inhaling the sweet chemicals as they saturated the air. Then he removed his shirt so as not to dirty it. Folded it neatly and placed it on the table. With his back to her, he took a deep breath and slowly exhaled. Then, removing his belt, he turned and walked to her, wrapped the leather around her ankles, cinching it tight, and then sadistically pulled her back through the window.

SUMMER 2016

"I'll be home for every holiday."
—Megan McDonald

Chapter 25

August 2016
Two Weeks Before the Abduction

He was seven years old when the man at the fair took his brother. With sticky fingers, Casey Delevan pushed cotton candy into his mouth and watched as the man with greasy hair placed his arm around Joshua and led him into the parking lot. There was no explanation to his silence that day. No way to explain why he didn't run for help. He should have found his father. Instead, he allowed the sugar to dissolve in his mouth until the man led Joshua across the gravel and out of sight.

Nearly twenty years had passed since that day at the fair, and still it lived inside him. He could sometimes go days without thinking of it, but that was rare. There were too many triggers in daily life that brought him back to the fair—sugar and sun and gravel—for him to forget what happened. That day had long ago stopped being simply an event in his life. That day defined him. It was what brought him now to the bunker in the woods. He tried to avoid this place, to resist its lure. But to go without filling the void brought misery *on a scale immeasurable. Taking the girls, he knew, was the best worst option.*

A very dark time came in the months after he took the first girl. From up north in Virginia, he'd never forget that first girl. Weeks of planning and hours of tedious strategy preceded his trip. And then, so shocking was the ease of it. The simplicity of locating her, and the smooth, carelessness of the take—no more difficult than walking a nine-year-old across a gravel parking lot. He knew instantly he could do it a hundred times over without growing bored of it. For a full week he sucked on the marrow, inhaled deeply the initial high from taking his first girl. But then remorse found him, descending like a black thundercloud. He stayed in his dark apartment and skipped work and didn't eat. He lost weight and gave up motivation to do anything but stare at the television. When days turned to weeks, he lost the urge to live. She ran through his mind, that first girl, and he was helpless to corral her.

Salvation finally came from a slow-building urge, a craving he came to rely on. It was the only thing that brought sanity. Inside him, like a small glowing ember in a smothered fire pit, was a growing hunger that needed feeding. Demanded it. That impulse lured him from his depression. The need to hunt and stalk and find the next girl. The thrill of the take and the execution of the delivery provided unexplainable contentment. Leaving the girls—bound and scared and helpless—for the one who requested them filled him with euphoria. The ritual was all that saved him.

He was not psychotic, he reminded himself. He never harmed the girls he took. Through the news he kept close track of them. Thus far, only one had surfaced. His first. The girl he so easily took from the streets of the small Virginia town, whose image ran wild through his mind during his first spell of misery. She had been found buried in a Carroll County forest a few months after he delivered her. The other two girls were still missing. He knew they were still out there, maybe in the same place he had left them, and this idea sparked an eerie feeling in his gut that even Casey Delevan was too timid to explore. He didn't want to examine whether this notion excited him or saddened him, so he left untouched that quiver inside him that begged for answers to where those girls were and what was being done to them.

To quell his need to explore their stories, he made the club aware of the latest details and joined in the discussions when the members speculated on who took the girls and what might be happening to them.

He parked his pickup now in the lot off Highway 57 and loitered around the rest stop. He used the bathroom and purchased a Coke from the vending machine. He paged through a few advertising brochures that rested by the front entrance, then took a seat at the picnic table out back. He waited thirty minutes until there was a lull in traffic and only one other car sat idle in the lot. Then he slid off the bench and walked into the woods. There was a trail he followed, and halfway along the beaten-down dirt path, he veered off into the dense forest.

The heavy foliage lasted for three hundred yards, all downhill, until he emerged from the thorns and the burrs to find the small ravine he followed for a mile and a half. It was August and muggy, with mosquitos plump and ripe after a summer of stalking. He swatted them from his neck and arms as he walked. Finally, he saw the bunker door. Dense brush and a pair of twin blue spruce trees camouflaged the entrance. Evergreen pines provided shade, and the thick wooden door the color of the land—brown and green and dirty—bled into the forest in a way that could be missed by a hundred people a hundred times. A casual glance would never pick it up. But obvious today was the red bandana tied to the door handle. A request, he knew, was waiting. Excite-

ment flooded his chest, as though his heart suddenly filled with a bolus of caffeine and nicotine and pumped it all at once into his system.

Casey calmed his body and sat on a fallen log. He watched the bunker and the woods, listened for anything out of the ordinary. Convinced after an hour that he was alone, he approached the door and pulled it open. Heavy and thick, the door served several purposes. If someone got to screaming while they were in this place, the door and the three other walls made from earth would mute their cries. The fat door also allowed hinges to be secured with three-inch carpentry screws that could not be whittled loose. And the massive bar that slid over the entrance to the bunker was certainly enough to stop anyone from escaping.

With the bunker door open, Casey saw the backpack and an urge overcame him, too powerful to quell. He entered the damp-smelling bunker and unzipped the pack. He ripped through the cash. Then, on the bottom, he found it. A single piece of white computer paper. He unfolded the request and read:

BROWN HAIR, SHOULDER LENGTH
THIN AND ATHLETIC, LATE TEENS
TALL

Casey read it again and again. He looked around, stunned by tunnel vision. He was, at last, here again. The desire boiling and tickling that part of him he knew no one else possessed—an eerie pond of dark and jagged emotions that made up his being. A black swamp in his soul he despised, formed years ago at the state fair when he ate sticky cotton candy and silently watched the greasy-haired man put his hand on Joshua's shoulder and lead his brother into the gravel parking lot.

The memories from that day—the sugary treat, the humid summer air, the stale smell of petting-zoo urine and pony manure—all mixed together over the years of his adolescence. Different concentrations of guilt bled into those memories. Remorse for his inaction that day. Shame for watching the stranger lead his brother away while Casey stayed mute and chewed on cotton candy. Those images and thoughts and memories all gelled together to form his humanity. He hated himself for allowing that dark swamp in his mind to define him. Hated when it boiled over and spilled from it banks. Hated it for controlling him. Hated it always. Except for the times he loved it.

He looked back at the page in his hand, read the request again. The hunt was on.

Chapter 26

Megan McDonald finished her senior year at Emerson Bay High with an impressive résumé. She captained her cheer team since sophomore year and took them to the state championship three times. A leader on the debate team, she played varsity basketball, and was ranked first in her class in grade point average. She spent part of the previous summer in South Africa assisting at a makeshift hospital run by Doctors Without Borders, a bullet point for her medical school application in the coming years. Her greatest achievement, however, was her effort in spearheading a mentoring program during the summer after sophomore year that, in total, included 80 percent of the incoming freshman class, and was created to help arriving first-year girls make the transition from middle school to high school.

Her determination to make the program perfect earned a write-up in the local paper. Teachers and administrators praised the mentoring program and the environment it created for freshman girls. Parents sent letters describing how *well adjusted their daughters were during such a big change-over year. The superintendent spread the word about the program's success, and neighboring high schools reached out to Megan for advice on creating their own summer platforms. Soon, an overachieving young man from a high school in New York called to ask for Megan's help in creating a similar program for boys. All the attention led to an article in* Events *magazine featuring Megan McDonald and how she was taking the anxiety out of high school for not only the incoming class at Emerson Bay, but—as her program became widely adopted—for thousands of kids around the country.*

She walked now from the high school where she had graduated valedictorian three months earlier. With her was Stacey Morgan, an upcoming junior who would take over the mentoring program this summer when Megan headed off to college.

"We've got another week to finish things up," Megan said as they walked across the parking lot. "I know you're stressed, but you're going to be fine. You'll likely do a better job than me, people like you more."

"Ha! Not true," Stacey said. "The younger girls idolize you."

"They'll feel the same way about you. You've just got to put it out there, you know? You're the leader of this event. Everyone during the weekend has to see it and feel it. If you do that, everyone will look up to you. Even the seniors. You're going to do great."

"Thanks."

They stopped at Megan's Jeep. "I'll miss you next year, you know that?"

"Yeah," Stacey said. "Me too. But you'll be making new friends and joining a sorority and you'll be on your own."

"Maybe," Megan said. "I'll only be in Raleigh. I'll be back on weekends and we'll hang out."

"Promise?"

"*Promise. You going to the beach party on Saturday?*" Megan asked.

"*Yeah. I think everyone's going. Isn't that when Nicole Cutty puked in the fire last year?*"

Megan laughed. "*Nicole's an idiot. She chugs five beers to impress . . . who? I don't know. Then tries to douse the fire with her vomit.*"

"*She was such a slut the other night, I don't understand her.*"

"*Nicole? I don't know. I'm trying to stay out of her way. She wants drama and I just wish no one would give it to her.*"

Stacey smiled. "*Will Matt be at the beach party? I heard you guys hooked up last weekend.*"

"*No!*" Megan said. "*We kissed in the bay, that's the end of it.*"

"*I thought you guys were together last year?*"

"*Sort of.*"

Stacey waited.

"*It's complicated. He was kind-of-sort-of dating this girl from Chapel Hill, but not really. And at one point, he was hanging out with Nicole. I don't know. I could never get the full story. So things are brewing but not, you know . . .*"

"*Fermenting?*"

"*Gross. I've got to run. I'm meeting my dad for lunch. I'll see you Saturday night.*"

Megan climbed into her Jeep and drove across town. As her father had grown increasingly depressed about Megan's upcoming college career, she was making the effort this summer to spend more time with him. It was hard to see him this way. The pride she saw in his eyes was unmistakable, and Megan knew he was excited for her. But she also felt her father's fear. Sadness came over him in the last few months since Megan had decided on Duke. The campus was just three hours away, but hours were not what upset her father. It was the idea that college was the first step in losing his *daughter. Megan had never been deceptive in her desire to get out of Emerson Bay and live in a big city. Fascinated by Boston and New York since she was a little girl, Megan had been vocal about those cities being her first choices for medical school after college. Her interests might change, but for the moment she was enamored of the idea of neonatology, and St. Luke's in New York had one of the best programs in the country.*

She pulled into the lot of Gateways, an Emerson Bay staple that served good salads and gourmet burgers. Parked out front was her father's cruiser, SHERIFF *stenciled across the side. Megan knew he was already inside chatting up the waitresses and bartenders and earning a free lunch from the owner. Her father had a certain charisma that made people comfortable. Some officers wielded their authority as a source of intimidation. Her father was never that way, which was likely why he was so successful as sheriff. Everyone in town knew him, most liked him, and the majority voted for him.*

She entered the diner and she saw the newspaper spread across the bar, a cup of coffee steaming next to it and the red-topped stool empty. As soon as she sat down, the waitress approached. "Hi, hon. Your pop's in the bathroom. What can I get you?"

"Diet Coke, thanks."

Megan scanned the paper. The sports page was open. She turned to the front page and skimmed the headlines. As Megan read, she heard the familiar jingle-jangle of her father's keys and holster as he walked up behind her. When conjuring a persona of their fathers, most girls pictured their dads' faces, hair color, or smiles. But Megan's dad had always been the swashbuckling sheriff of Montgomery County. She pictured him in his uniform more than she ever did "street" clothes—keys jingling and leather holster squeaking.

There was a part of her that was sad to leave for college.

Not nervous. She'd flown alone to Africa and found her way to a desert village where she worked alongside strangers in a country where she didn't speak the language. All the nervousness of her life had been spent on the Doctors Without Borders trip last summer. But there was a small ache of sadness when she thought of being away from her parents, and specifically her father, whom she'd worked her entire life to please.

"Hi, Daddy," Megan said when he kissed the back of her head.

"How'd the retreat planning go?"

"Good. Stacey's got it covered. A few other details to work out, but we've still got a couple of weeks." She swiveled on the barstool as her father sat next to her.

"I'm sure you'll get it all done."

She took a deep breath. "I'm kind of happy to hand it off, is that bad?"

"The retreat? It's a lot of work. There's no dishonor in being relieved to turn it over to someone else."

"I love the program. I just don't want that to be all I'm about."

"You're only eighteen, sweetheart. Plenty of time to build a legacy."

"That's not what I meant."

Her father looked down at his newspaper, now with ugly front-page headlines staring up at him. "What happened to my sports page?"

"Lots of things happen in the world besides sports, Daddy."

Her father grumbled as he rustled the paper.

"Hey," Megan said. "I got a big packet from Duke yesterday. Included was the basketball schedule. Just before Thanksgiving, we're playing North Carolina and it's a big rivalry game. You and Mom should come that weekend and we'll go to the game. It'll be fun."

"*Thanksgiving? That's a long ways off.*"

"*I'm not saying that's the first time you guys come to visit, I'm just telling you to save the weekend so we can go to the game.*"

"*What's the date?*"

"*It's the weekend before Thanksgiving. Then I'll just come home with you and Mom on Sunday for break.*"

Terry McDonald scrolled through his phone and set a reminder. How easy it was to think November would come without problems.

"*You ever hear from MACU?*"

Megan smiled and rubbed her father's forearm. "*Not yet, Daddy.*"

It was a long-standing joke, between just the two of them, for her father to ask about her status with the Mid-Atlantic Christian University, the closest college to Emerson Bay. He sometimes asked about Elizabeth City State, as well. Both schools were within thirty minutes. Megan had applied to neither.

"*Well, maybe they're just making you sweat.*"

"*You know I'll be home for every holiday, and even some long weekends.*"

"*MACU is twenty minutes. You could commute. Keep your room at home.*"

She raised her eyebrows. "*Sounds super fun for college. Keep checking the mail for me, okay?*"

They ordered lunch, two salads per Megan's request. Her father, now in his early fifties, had gathered an impressive bulge around his waist Megan was constantly on him to lose.

"*So what's going on this weekend?*" her dad asked.

"*End-of-summer beach party.*"

"*Adults going to be present?*"

"*It's right next to my friend's house, so her parents will be around.*"

"*Name?*"

"*Jenny Walton.*"

"*No drinking.*"

"*Got it.*"

"*And if you end up making a bad decision—*"

"*I'll call for a ride home.*"

"*And when you're at Duke, the same rules apply. I know kids drink, I'm not an idiot. I bust enough punks around town to know what's going on. But no drugs, and no drunk driving. And that means—*"

"*No drunk riding, either. Don't drink and drive, don't drink and ride. I got it, Daddy. I never have.*"

Terry McDonald leaned over and kissed his daughter's cheek. "As long as you keep that deal with me, anything else can be worked out."

"*Don't forget the deal I have with you," Megan said. "I get straight As first semester at Duke, you lose fifteen pounds by the end of freshman year.*"

Her father picked at the salad in front of him, pushing arugula to the side. "Yeah. Deal." He took a deep breath. "Got a feeling I'm going to be eating a lot of this crap."

They ate a quiet lunch together, two weeks before college, discussing the future—basketball games and Thanksgiving break and weight loss and medical school and big cities. The future was something taken for granted. It was always there, waiting to be lived.

Chapter 27

August 2016
One Week Before the Abduction

Nicole helped Casey pack the generator into the back of his pickup truck, along with the chalkboard and folding tables. They took one last pass through Coleman's to make sure the old brewhouse was empty of the club's presence. They were sure to sanitize the ruins out back where they had kept Diana Wells, removing the tape and plastic wrap they had used to restrain her, and tossing the chair that held her onto the tracks for the next passing freight to demolish.

When they were satisfied, they jumped into Casey's pickup and headed up Highway 64, leaving Coleman's as nothing more than a decaying brewhouse in West Bay.

"She looked like a goddamn zombie when we cut her loose," Nicole said in the passenger seat. "If she goes to the cops, they may not take her seriously."

"Either way," Casey said, "better to close things down for a while just in case."

"What are the cops going to do to us? She agreed to it," Nicole said. "Like all of us. You asked her if she wanted it, *just like you asked me. She's just mad because of how we did it. She was expecting us to grab her from a dark alley, and instead you seduced her."*

"Doesn't matter. All I know is that we're done with club stuff for a while."

"This is bullshit," Nicole said. "It's not our fault she's so soft."

Diana Wells's breakdown while bound and gagged at the brewery was proof that she expected none of it. Casey had misjudged her response to the ordeal when they finally cut her loose and welcomed her into the club. Nearly catatonic when they pulled the plastic wrap from her arms and wrists, Diana Wells could not walk. And when the gag came from her mouth, words never followed. Prepared to cheer and celebrate, the club instead dispersed quickly that night, some running with scared looks and coolers in tow when Diana collapsed to the ground and no one could rouse her. Casey finally drove her back to the bar and left her in the parking lot.

The Diana Wells situation now posed a problem. There were rumors that she would go to the police, and that her parents knew about the club. With his deadline approaching for delivering the next girl, Casey couldn't afford attention from the police. But he had to move forward. There were precautions he could take to cover his tracks should the cops hunt him down and ask about Diana Wells. Clearing out Coleman's was the first step. Today's errand was the next.

He pulled off the highway and turned right at the end of the off-ramp. A strip mall unfolded along the side of the road. Casey pulled into the lot and parked a good distance from the entrance of a Goodwill store.

"Here's the list," he said to Nicole, slipping her a piece of paper.

"Why'd we come all the way out here for this stuff?"

"Just go get it, okay? And throw some random stuff in with it."

"Like what?"

"Whatever. Just buy some junk."

With the slip of paper in hand, Nicole walked the length of the parking lot and entered the Goodwill store. She purchased a long-sleeved button-down shirt, a pair of cargo pants, and an ugly pair of sneakers—all the items from Casey's list that he would wear for the next take. He'd burn each item afterward, but should any evidence be left behind—from fibers to footprints—he would make sure it didn't lead to him.

For the random items, Nicole grabbed a jigsaw puzzle, an ugly plastic plant, and a set of barbecue tools that came packaged in a worn, wooden box.

PART IV

"I know you think everyone has forgotten about
Nicole. But I never have."
—Megan McDonald

Chapter 28

Monday morning, her first day back in the morgue after ride-alongs, Livia draped the surgical smock over her scrubs and slipped her feet into thin blue booties. She tied her hair into a tight bun and pulled on a surgical cap. Her face shield completed her personal protective equipment, and she approached the body that lay on her autopsy table. Carmen Hernandez was a forty-five-year old female who died during a house fire. As the deceased didn't have a single burn on her body, Livia already had a working diagnosis of asphyxiation secondary to smoke inhalation—after inhaling smoke-filled air, the victim's lungs filled with soot until she eventually suffocated. Her first case back after ride-along week, Livia had something to prove to Dr. Colt after her fall-victim disaster of ten days before. She blocked from her mind all she had learned in the last week about Nicole and Casey, the Capture Club, Nancy Dee, and the ketamine connection to Megan McDonald. She compartmentalized it all and went to work on the body in front of her.

After ninety minutes, Livia completed her autopsy of Carmen Hernandez and handed the body off to the autopsy technician who would begin the process of suturing the body back together, repairing the craniotomy, and making the body presentable for the mortician. Livia finished the morning assisting with other cases and observing in the derm-path lab. She spent time in the afternoon preparing for rounds, and when they all gathered in the cage at three o'clock, Livia was the first to present.

"Findings, facts, and feedback," Dr. Colt said, staring down through his cheaters as he read the chart in front of him.

"Forty-five-year-old female victim of a house fire last night. Pronounced dead on the scene by firefighters, found holed up in her bedroom. Transported by MLIs to the morgue last night. Autopsy performed this morning at 9:04 a.m."

"Length of exam?" Dr. Colt asked.

"Ninety minutes," Livia said.

Dr. Colt pouted his bottom lip and gave an approving nod.

"External exam was unremarkable for burn wounds. Congestion in the soft tissue of the cheeks and periorbital region was noted." Livia snapped the Smart Board to life and a photo of Carmen Hernandez's body appeared. A facial shot showed the swollen cheeks and eyelids. "There were slicing wounds found on the right hand and forearm." Another photo appeared, this one showing the jagged incisions on Carmen Hernandez's hand and arm. "Three, five, and six inches in length. All one half inch deep."

Another photo appeared of Carmen Hernandez's mouth and nostrils.

"Internal exam showed classic signs of smoke inhalation. Dirty airway, with soot lining the mucous membranes of the mouth, tongue, throat, and nose. Trachea was edematous and soot-streaked. Small bronchioles of the lungs were stenosed, with both lungs containing a large amount of ash.

QuickTox showed carboxyhemoglobin levels greater than seventy percent."

"The house fire occurred at night," Dr. Colt said. "Did you consider a blood alcohol level to see if the victim was under the influence during the fire, which may have hampered her escape and could have implications for insurance coverage?"

"Tox results were negative for drugs or alcohol. The victim was a healthy forty-five-year-old and was taking no prescription medications."

"The wound on the hand, Dr. Cutty? How is this explained?"

More photos appeared. These had been taken by Sanj and displayed scene details. In one was a broken window, and in another, Carmen Hernandez lying lifeless on the floor beneath the windowpane.

"From the scene investigator's photos, it appears the victim punched her fist through the glass window in an attempt to escape the bedroom. Based on the blood pattern, amount of loss, and clotting, she died soon after this act. Glass sequestered from the scene matches the size and shape of the slicing wounds to the hand and arm. Fire marshal informed me this afternoon that the house had been recently painted. The windows on the entire upper floor were, sadly, sealed shut by the paint. This explains why she tried to punch her way out instead of opening the window."

The room was silent as Dr. Colt read through the rest of the report. "Questions?" he finally asked the gallery. There were none.

"Welcome back, Dr. Cutty."

She had made the phone call over the weekend, on Saturday afternoon, and left a voice mail. Earlier today, as Livia pored through forensic textbooks and journals researching smoke inhalation cases, her phone rang. She was surprised by the nervousness she felt, unsure how to channel her emotions. But the conversation was quick, fifty-three seconds when Livia went back and checked. Livia had prepared a long statement about why they needed to meet and what she hoped to gain from the discussion. But it was unnecessary. The answer came immediately.

"I'll meet with you tonight," the quiet voice had told her.

So Livia found herself, just free from afternoon rounds at five p.m., driving east again toward Emerson Bay. It was close to seven p.m. when she pulled into the parking lot of the Montgomery County Federal Building. She walked to the plaza in front of the building with twilight still burning the horizon. As promised, Livia found her waiting on a bench outside the courthouse.

"Megan?" Livia asked to be sure, although she'd seen Megan McDonald's photo—dozens of them while she read *Missing*—and knew Megan's face well from the time immediately after the girl's escape. But this real-life Megan was different from the girl in the photos and on TV. That girl was happy and vibrant, with eyes filled by something missing from this real-life version of Megan McDonald. It took Livia a moment to define it, but when she came face-to-face with her, Livia was able to see it. The photos that covered the pages of the book were all taken—and likely carefully chosen—from before Megan was abducted. In them, Megan's eyes had a conquering effect to them. There was something in the pupil and iris that announced she was ready for the world and for the future. But more than that, those bright eyes on the page were enjoying the present life they were watching. These new eyes, however, the ones that were now the windows through which this girl witnessed the world, were vacant of passion and empty of the ambition that had so badly irked Livia as she read Megan's words. These true-life eyes were sad and lonely, and certainly had no propensity for optimism. They were stuck on today, and today was not as bright as it once had been.

"Hi," Megan said.

"I'm Livia. Nicole's sister."

Megan nodded. "I've met you before. A long time ago, when Nicole and I were in grade school." She allowed a small smile. "You seemed really old back then, I remember."

Livia had memories of her early high school days when Nicole, in third grade then, ran with her friends through the sprinkler in the backyard. Livia's mind wandered back to those sunny summer days, when Nicole danced with her friends through the twirling water, their skinny, childish bodies sporting swimsuits, their feet peppered with blades of grass, and their braided hair dripping before the sun could dry it. Livia imagined one of those girls as Megan McDonald, dancing with Nicole through the sprinkler. Livia had a powerful urge to go back to that warm summer day and broadcast to the world what was coming for those two innocent girls. She wanted to go back and warn them, protect them, and scoop them up and stop what was to come a decade down the road.

"I don't remember you and Nicole being friends," Livia said.

"Until middle school. Then we kind of lost touch." Megan avoided Livia's eyes. "In high school we didn't hang out much." Megan forced a laugh. "I actually think Nicole thought I was annoying, or something."

"Really? You guys didn't get along?"

"No. It wasn't like that. We just hung out with different crowds."

"Jessica Tanner told me Nicole was bitchy to you. Tried to steal your boyfriend?"

Another forced laugh from Megan. "Matt? No. We were never dating. That was just a confusing summer."

"Mind if we sit?" Livia asked.

They both sat on the bench and watched the activity outside the county courthouse, a scant two hours after the official close of business. Still, in the fading light, late-working lawyers walked the boulevard in blouses with their blazers hung on their shoulder bags, or with ties loosened at the neck and sleeves rolled to their elbows.

"I read your book," Livia said.

"Oh yeah?" Megan shrugged. "It's not really mine, but thanks."

"What do you mean?"

"I didn't write it, not much of it anyway. Most of it was my shrink."

"It's written in first person."

"Yeah. My publisher insisted on that. Made it more personal, they told me. But my doctor did most of the writing. He asked, like, a thousand questions and then pieced it together. I mean, I read through everything he wrote and made it accurate." Another shrug. "I was told that's how a lot of books are written. On the cover, Dr. Mattingly's name should be bigger than mine, but he's not the star, you know?" Megan took a deep breath and looked up into the evening sky. "I'm sorry about the book. I'm embarrassed that you read it."

"Why?"

Another shrug. "The book wasn't my idea. I never wanted to write it or be part of it. I never wanted the thing to exist. But so much was going on after that summer. My parents wanted their daughter back, and I haven't had the courage to tell them she's long gone. Haven't found a way to break it to them that that girl doesn't exist anymore."

Megan paused a moment.

"You know, I was missing for two weeks and was completely alone, never felt so alone. Then, when I escaped and came home, I never had a minute to myself. Someone was always with me in those first few months, too afraid to leave my side. My parents smothered me. My shrink was all over me to write the book. Then publishers approached me. Some agents. I used the book as a way to get them all off my back. I used the book to escape, as a way to buy some anonymity from those closest to me. It worked, too. As long as I was working on that stupid book, they all left me alone. My parents used the book as a distraction as much as I did. As long as my mother believed I was writing, it relieved her need to check on me every minute of the day and ask if I had decided on college and about what I was doing with my life and my future. As long as I was writing that book, my parents believed I was in some magical place of healing. And now look at me. The book that was supposed to bring me anonymity has brought celebrity. The book that was supposed to bring healing has only reopened all my wounds."

Megan looked at Livia.

"I wanted to include more about Nicole, but they all told me not to. Dr. Mattingly strictly warned against it, and my agent and editor greatly revised what I had written."

Livia heard through Megan's words the voice of a girl trapped and haunted by the past. It was a voice very different from the one her mind heard as she read Megan's book.

"Have your parents read the book?" Megan asked.

"I'm not sure," Livia lied.

"Don't let them, okay? It's not right for them. It's a goddamn celebration of my life and triumphs that completely ignores that someone else was lost that night."

"Thank you," Livia said. "I'll keep them away from it. Can I ask? Why was everyone around you so adamant about excluding Nicole?"

Megan shook her head. "Nicole is not a feel-good story. The editor was very specific that he wanted a triumphant story. He wanted the gritty, disturbing details because that's what sells. Because, really, that's why people buy the book. But the story needed to end with my victory, not with Nicole's tragedy. They have some formula they actually showed me about memoirs with dark themes that ended triumphantly for the victim versus the same books that ended in defeat."

"Based on sales, I'd say they know what they're talking about."

"Lucky me," Megan said.

There was a short pause. "I came here tonight worried that I'd hate you," Livia said. "Because I only know you from the book and your interviews. But I have a very different opinion of you right now."

Megan shrugged again. "You said you wanted to talk about the case. The funny thing is, besides Dr. Mattingly, no one has talked to me about what happened. Not for a long time. I mean, the police initially, and that was mostly my dad. Later, detectives. But after that initial surge? Nothing. I've tried to get updates, but there's not much to talk about. At least, that's what I've been told. I suspect it's partially true. They don't have much. But I also know it's this group of do-gooders around me, led by my parents, who want to protect me and help me move on. What no one understands is that I'm not capable of simply burying those two weeks as if they never happened."

"I'm sorry for what happened to you, Megan. And I *do* want to ask you some questions about that night, if you're comfortable talking with me."

"Yes," Megan said. "I mean, I'm comfortable telling you anything I know. You said on the phone you came across something?"

"I did. The night you were found wandering Highway Fifty-Seven. The night you escaped. At the hospital, a large amount of a chemical called ketamine was found in your bloodstream."

"Yeah. Dr. Mattingly tells me I was likely sedated to some degree for most of my time in captivity, based on my memory lapses and what he's discovered during therapy sessions. Through those sessions, with the help of hypnosis, I've been piecing things together about those two weeks. Which is another reason the book is such a joke. I know so much more now than I did when that book was written. But, you know, gotta strike when the iron is hot. So what about the ketamine is peculiar?"

"Do you know much about ketamine?"

"No."

"It's a unique sedative. It's fast-acting and, besides sedation and anesthesia—its two main uses—it can cause a number of side effects, including confusion, disorientation, memory loss, and impaired motor skills. When dosed correctly, ketamine causes conscious sedation, where the patient is awake but detached from their body and their surroundings. But if dosed incorrectly, if ingested in too great a quantity and combined with other drugs, ketamine causes respiratory failure and death."

Megan took her gaze from the evening sky and looked at Livia. "Dr. Mattingly told me some of this. That's why he thinks my suppression of certain aspects of my captivity has been so hard to overcome."

"Ketamine is also unique because we don't see it a lot in mainstream medicine. It's used mostly by veterinarians, not too often by medical doctors. So when we see it, it stands out. At least to me it does."

"Stands out how?"

"There was a girl who went missing a couple of years ago, more than a year before you and Nicole were taken. Her name was Nancy Dee. She was from a small town in Virginia and she disappeared one day after volleyball practice. This was back in March of 2015. Her body was found six months later and told a story of captivity—chronic bruising to her ankles and wrists commonly found when someone is restrained for long periods. Sexual abuse, as well. A jogger found her body in a shallow grave along a wooded running path. I had a look at the autopsy and toxicology report. Nancy died of respiratory distress from an overdose of ketamine."

Livia let the implication settle in.

"Ketamine?"

Livia nodded.

"You think my case is connected to this other girl?"

"I think it's a possibility," Livia said.

"Like, the same person who took me, took this other girl?"

"Yes. The same person who took you *and* Nicole."

An uneasy look came over Megan's face and Livia recognized it immediately.

"Look, Megan, I know I'm springing this on you, and I know I don't have much to back up my theory. But my sister is gone, and I need some answers to what happened to her. Some closure. At least some attention. I feel like this town has forgotten her. This town, the county, the whole goddamn state and country have forgotten Nicole Cutty ever existed. Maybe all these months later, I'm starting to forget, too.

"I want to look into this ketamine connection. See if there are any other similarities between your case and Nancy Dee's. I'm going to need help. My contacts include the detectives I work with at the medical examiner's office, but I know they won't give my theory much time. Especially since Nancy was from Virginia, which is out of their jurisdiction and beyond their interest. So, if you're on board here, I was hoping you might ask your dad for help on this."

Megan looked briefly at Livia and then diverted her eyes, nodding her head. "I can ask him. And I will, if we have to."

She paused. "It's just that my dad's had a harder time with this than anyone. I know he blames himself for what happened to me. Right afterward, before my mother became the zombie she is today—so focused on the book and the money and paying for the college I don't attend—I heard her mention to Dr. Mattingly how helpless my dad felt during my captivity. *Impotent* was the word she used. My dad is in charge of the county's police force and I know he still carries guilt for what happened to me. He's torn up that I was taken, as any father would be. But what killed him was not *finding* me. He used to tell me, right after I made it home, that he didn't sleep for the entire two weeks I was gone because his mind was working every second on ways to find me. I know he wants my forgiveness, but I've never blamed him for what happened to me so I don't know how to give it to him."

Megan shook her head and wiped her eyes before they had a chance to shed tears.

"He's not the same since this happened. None of us are. So, I'll ask him for help. I will," Megan said. "I promise. But if we want to look into my case, I'd rather start elsewhere first."

Livia nodded. "Okay. Where is that?"

"I work at the courthouse." Megan pointed at the building behind them. "If you want to look for a connection between my case—and Nicole's—and the girl in Virginia, I can get us access to my case file. I know right where to look for it. I've looked through it myself out of curiosity. I didn't find anything, but you'll be looking with fresh eyes. We'll take that route first and see what we find. If we come across anything relevant that connects the case to Nancy Dee, then I'll ask my dad for help."

"Okay," Livia said. "How exactly does one look at a case file and evidence?"

"I was able to find my case initially because I'm a snoop

and everyone's very awkward around me. I'm the sheriff's daughter and ever since the abduction people are afraid to talk to me. Before, this would have offended me. Now, I prefer it. I wander around the dark corners of that building and people avert their eyes. But I won't get that same treatment if I walk down to evidence with you next to me. To smuggle you in, we'll have to do it when the supervisor is gone and I'll have to ask for a favor. But I know an evidence tech who owes me one. I'll try for this Friday. Does that work?"

Livia nodded. "I'll make it work. What time?"

"Meet me here at noon? If I can't pull strings by then, we'll reschedule."

Livia stood from the bench. "Thanks, Megan. I appreciate the help."

"I'm glad someone's asking for it."

Livia turned to leave.

"Sorry I never got in touch with you or your parents after all this," Megan said.

"You've been through a lot. You've got to take care of yourself before you can be expected to reach out to others." Livia turned again to leave.

"Livia?"

Livia looked back.

"I know you think everyone has forgotten about Nicole. But I never have."

Chapter 29

Megan spread her cards onto the table. "Fifteen for two, four separate ways. That's eight. Plus two runs for three each. That's fourteen. The Knobs gives me fifteen total."

Mr. Steinman dropped his cards onto the table. "Fifteen, and the game."

Megan smiled. "Gotcha!" She moved her peg to the end of the cribbage board. "That's my first victory against you."

"Even a blind squirrel finds a nut every now and again."

"Don't! I played great! Everything you taught me, I did during that game. No leading with face cards, no pairs into the crib, all that stuff."

"I'd lose every game if it made you smile like that."

Megan blushed and shielded her teeth with her hand.

"How's the book doing?"

Megan shrugged, pulled her hand down. The smile was gone. "Climbing."

"You're a regular celebrity."

"Yeah, to people who love sick stories."

Mr. Steinman collected the cards. "I know you well enough now. There's a reason for that book. Something you won't admit."

"I'll admit it. The book gets my parents off my back."

"And allows you to do what?"

"Breathe." Megan pulled the pegs from the cribbage board and stored them. "And maybe find some answers for myself."

"I thought you were doing that in therapy."

"I am. I just need, I don't know, different answers than the ones everyone around me wants to give."

Mr. Steinman took the cribbage board and placed it with the cards on the end table. "I can't tell you what to do. A young, independent girl like yourself is not going to listen to an old man like me. Just remember, sometimes finding those answers comes with a new set of questions."

Megan nodded as though she understood perfectly.

There was a noise that came from another room. It sounded as though it came from the walls, perhaps the groan of a faucet being started. But there was something else that caused Megan to stiffen. If asked, she'd describe it as a moan but the whine of the faucet was enough to hide the exact origin.

Mr. Steinman, too, sat up straight when he heard it. "That's it for me, my lovely lady. Will I see you next week?"

Megan stood, feeling as though she'd overstayed her welcome. "Of course. Have a good night," she said.

Mr. Steinman hurried her to the door, his key chain chiming as it hung from his belt loop. "Good game," he said quickly. "I've never felt better after losing at cribbage."

"Need help?" Megan asked. "With, you know, whatever it is. Or company?"

"Not tonight."

"Are you sure? I don't mind helping. I'm not scared."

"One of these days," he said, grabbing the keys from his hip, "I'll take you up on your offer." He pulled the screen door closed as Megan walked onto the patio. "Good night."

Megan smiled with her lips together, nodded, and headed for her car.

Livia danced around the ring, thick headgear covering her jawline. Randy, six inches taller and twice as broad, stalked her carefully as they sparred. He'd been on the receiving end of a Livia Cutty side kick, an unpleasant place to be, and she'd kept him at bay with stiff left jabs. Everything considered, her technique was flawless and Randy was impressed.

He tried again to close the distance and get his hands on her, but the jabs were too straight. Then he saw it, the transfer of weight to her left leg. A side kick was on its way. The telegraph was her first mistake in nine minutes of sparring. When the kick came, he caught it in his left armpit, absorbing the impact and trapping her shin. In a flash, he knocked her left leg from underneath her and they both crashed to the ground. It was where Randy wanted the sparring session to be all along.

"Time!" the referee yelled just as they both crashed to the floor.

"Dammit!" Livia said.

Randy rolled off her. "Two-ninety vs. one-thirty. Physics are not on your side, Doc."

Livia sat up on the mat and leaned against the ropes, unsnapped her headgear. Her chest expanding with giant breaths.

"On a larger opponent, stick with those jabs. I couldn't get close until you announced that side kick. When they land, they're lethal. But I told you, they get stale after a while."

"Stupid," Livia said.

"Nothing wrong with being aggressive. Just don't go to the well so often."

Randy pushed himself up, offered his hand to Livia, and pulled her to her feet. They exited the ring as the next pair jumped in and started their session. Livia took a seat and pulled her gloves off. Randy handed her a water bottle.

"You seem like you're doing better than when you had your tantrum."

Livia smiled. "Can't get rid of regret by punching a bag. Isn't that what you said?"

"Something like that." Randy sat next to her. "All this frustration have to do with your sister?"

Livia shrugged. Randy listened more carefully than she thought.

"I sat around for a year doing nothing," Livia said. "At least now I feel like I'm doing *something*."

"Feels good to take some action, right?"

Livia nodded and took a sip of water. "I just don't know how hard to push."

"Because you're afraid of what you're gonna find?"

"Because I'm afraid I won't be able to do anything when I find it."

"Well," Randy said, wiping his face. "You go at it like that and you ain't gonna find shit. I'll tell you that much."

"Go at it like what?"

"With no heart. You want something, you gotta commit to it and go after it. Don't slow down, don't stop to think. Just keep moving forward."

Livia stood up. "And stop throwing my side kicks so often."

"That too."

Livia screwed the top onto her water bottle. "I've got to run, Randy. Thanks for the spar."

"Sorry I tossed you like a rag doll."

"Sorry I flattened your nose with those jabs."

Randy lifted his chin. "Hope you find what you're looking for, Doc. With your sister."

"Thanks."

"You know, when I was trying to get straight my daddy used to tell me a story about how life works in the Serengeti. Do you know?"

"The African Serengeti?"

"That's the one. You know how life works there?"

Livia shook her head.

"Each morning when the sun comes up, cresting the horizon and stretching shadows across the sand, every gazelle and every lion opens their eyes. They all understand something. Every gazelle wakes knowing that to survive the day they gotta run faster than the slowest gazelle in the herd. And every lion wakes knowing that to survive the day they gotta run faster than the fastest lion in the pack. That's life, young lady."

Livia stared at him. "So the fastest lion gets the slowest gazelle? That's the point?"

"No." Randy stood and headed for the showers. "The point is that no matter who you are, you gotta wake up runnin'."

Chapter 30

In addition to two weeks of vacation, forensic fellows at the North Carolina Office of the Chief Medical Examiner were allowed four personal days. Livia used one on Friday. She made the two-hour drive from Raleigh to Emerson Bay and found Megan waiting for her on the same bench outside the courthouse where they met on Monday. Late October, the temperature was in the sixties. The sun was high, the sky blue, and the plaza in front of the county building busy with lunchtime foot traffic. Livia walked onto the cobblestone court and took a seat next to Megan.

"You get everything set up?" Livia asked as she sat down.

Megan nodded. "We're good." She checked her watch. "We've got twenty minutes before the evidence supervisor takes lunch. Then we'll have about half an hour by ourselves."

Livia nodded and let a moment pass. "Megan, I want to ask you something about the night you were abducted."

"Go ahead."

Livia diverted her eyes momentarily, working up her courage.

"Look," Megan said. "I'm not going to fall to pieces if

someone other than my shrink asks me about that night. All anyone has wanted for the past year is to see me back to normal. See me healed. You're the first person who's asked if I know anything about the night I was taken. You're the first one who's bothered to include me in any part of figuring out what happened that night. Ask whatever you want, Livia. And believe me when I tell you that I think of Nicole all the time."

"I'm realizing that. And before we met, I never considered that it might be hard for you that you made it home and Nicole did not."

Tears welled again on Megan's eyelids, like they had Monday evening. "I'm not happy I escaped." She shook her head and exhaled loudly. "That's not true. I *am* happy. But part of me will always grieve for Nicole. The detectives haven't talked to me in months about anything new. When you called the other day . . . I don't know, a part of me woke up again. All this garbage about my book helping survivors of abduction is bullshit. But *this*. What you told me the other day. If we can find a connection between my abductor and the other girl who was taken . . . *that* will mean something."

Livia nodded. "In your book, you describe the night you were taken. How accurate is the description?"

"Not very. I remember more now than when it was written."

"But you never saw the man who took you?"

"Not his face, no."

Livia reached into her purse and pulled out the photo of Casey Delevan, his arm wrapped around Nicole's shoulder.

"You know this guy?"

Megan studied the picture. "No. Who is he?"

"He was dating Nicole that summer. His body showed up on my autopsy table a few weeks ago."

Megan squinted her eyes and waited for an explanation.

"He was found in the bay. He was originally thought to be a jumper. At the morgue, we determined that he'd been killed. A little fieldwork suggests the last time anyone saw him was the weekend you and Nicole were taken."

Megan stayed quiet as she tried to figure out the implication.

"So," Livia said. "Besides a connection to Nancy Dee, I'm looking for anything that will help me figure out what might have happened to him." Livia shrugged. "See if it has any connection to you or Nicole disappearing."

"I've never seen him before. And I didn't know Nicole was dating anyone. She was . . . I mean, there were some rumors that summer that she and, uh, Matt Wellington were hooking up."

"The guy you were dating?"

"We were just friends."

"Have you ever heard of a group called the Capture Club?"

"No, what is it?"

"A group of nuts who get off on abductions. Read about them, study them, discuss them, and even perform them. Mock abductions, anyway."

"That's sickening."

"I agree. This guy," Livia said, holding up the picture of Casey, "created the club. Nicole was part of it. I don't know what any of it means. Maybe nothing. But I haven't been able to calm my thoughts since he landed in my morgue."

Megan checked her watch. "Let's see if this helps answer some questions." She pointed to the courthouse. "We're late."

They both showed their IDs and passed through the metal detector without a hitch. They walked down the long hallways as justice was practiced beyond the heavy oak double doors of the courtrooms next to them. Lawyers counseled their clients on benches outside the courts, and a hundred defendants of DUI, littering, speeding, and alimony failure wandered the halls and searched for their destinations. Megan opened the door to a stairway and Livia followed her down to the lower level, where there were no windows and no foot traffic. They conquered another long hallway and came to locked double doors, above which read EVIDENCE AND PROPERTY.

Megan used her ID card to unlock the doors. Inside was a vestibule with another locked door and a glass partition next to it, the window slid open. A thirty-something man in an ugly brown uniform sat on a high stool behind the glass, paging through an auto magazine.

"Hi, Greg," Megan said.

"You're late."

"Sorry."

Greg looked behind him to make sure he was alone. "My supervisor takes an hour for lunch." He checked his watch. "Forty-five minutes, now. I'll give you half an hour to be safe."

Greg pressed a button from his perch behind the partition and the door buzzed.

"Thanks, Greg. I owe you one," Megan said.

Livia followed as Megan pulled open the buzzing door and entered the Evidence and Property storage area, where just about every piece of evidence collected from a Montgomery County case was located. In the back corner were rows of metal shelves stacked with cardboard boxes. Megan walked with efficiency to the M's and pulled a box off the shelf. She'd been here before, Livia determined. Within the aisles were waist-high tables. Megan deposited her case box onto one of them and lifted the lid.

"So, what exactly are we looking for?" Megan asked.

"I'm not sure."

They spent ten minutes looking through the contents of the "McDonald, Megan" evidence box, which contained several photos of Megan from the night she climbed into Mr. Steinman's car on Highway 57. From the hospital bed, Megan had been photographed from every angle. The camera isolated and highlighted her injuries—contusions on her ankles from two weeks in shackles. Friction burns on her wrists from the duct tape. Scratches on her face from her frantic run through the forest, and a gaping wound on her heel that required sixteen sutures to close. There were medical records and notes from the emergency-room doctors who initially cared for her. Livia read with interest until she found the toxicology screening, seeing that ketamine was indeed in her system the night Megan had escaped her captor.

Livia, standing within the quiet row of shelves, paged through pictures of the bunker from which Megan had escaped. There were photos of footprint impressions and random items found in the vicinity of the bunker. They included candy bar wrappers and beer bottles, an old rancid belt and a single Converse All Star shoe. The owner of either of the items unknown. Random fingerprints were sequestered from the door handle and from the objects found on the forest floor, but none matched each other or led to anyone in particular.

Stored in plastic evidence bags was the duct tape that bound Megan's wrists the night she journeyed through the forest. Other bags contained her blood-soaked shirt and shorts. The items retrieved from the forest were also sealed in plastic—the wrappers and bottles and a few other random items Livia pawed at on the bottom of the box.

She pulled out the file that contained the detectives' analysis and findings in the weeks after Megan had escaped. Livia had seen many such reports in her three months at the OCME.

Mostly, the file contained dictated interviews conducted by the two investigators assigned to the case. Livia skimmed through Megan's interview, where she recalled for the detectives her movements on the day she was abducted and everything she remembered about the night she was taken. Livia read briefly about Megan's time in captivity and about the night she escaped from the bunker. Most was redundant. She'd read all of this in Megan's book. There were other interviews of Emerson Bay High School kids, including Matt Wellington, but they were boring and mundane and led the detectives nowhere important.

Megan read Livia's expression. "I've been through it before and there's nothing in there that's useful."

Livia restacked everything back into the box and closed the lid. "You ever look at Nicole's case?"

Megan nodded, embarrassed to admit she had.

"Let me have a look," Livia said.

They walked two rows down to the C's and Megan pointed. Livia read the label on the box: CUTTY, NICOLE.

She pulled the box and placed it on one of the tables. She slowly opened the lid and pulled out a file that contained interviews and notes similar to those in Megan's box. More than a year before, Livia had given her statement to the two detectives who had come to her house and talked with Livia and her parents. She and her parents had received updates from these two detectives for the first few weeks of the investigation, but after a while the calls slowed and the updates became more random. Eventually, they stopped altogether. No one ever came out to the house to tell Livia and her parents that the case was stalled. But today, Nicole's case, sitting quietly on the shelf in the basement of the Federal Building, felt as cold as a body kept overnight in the morgue's cooler.

At the back of the folder were pictures that Livia flipped through. They were of Nicole's car, which was found abandoned on a frontage road near the beach where the end-of-summer party took place and from where Megan had established her abduction took place. Jessica Tanner and Rachel Ryan had confirmed having been in the car that night with Nicole when they all drove to the party together. The photos of the car made Livia's heart ache. It sat parked on the side of the road, pitched slightly to the right as the passenger-side tires rested on the gravel shoulder. The car looked ominous and lonely, and Livia fought hard to block the images her mind tried to produce about what her sister had gone through on this isolated frontage road. How soon after she placed her call to Livia, a call Livia overtly ignored, had Nicole's car become a crime scene?

The photos were of the outside of the car from every angle. Then, with the doors and trunk open, every inch was documented, inside and out. The tread of Nicole's tires was captured in the photos and imprints were taken. Prints were lifted from both inside the vehicle and from the door handle, but matched no one in particular besides Nicole. Fibers were taken from the floorboards, seats, and trunk. From the area around the car, items had been seized and included a can of Diet Coke and a Red Bull, cigarette butts, and the cap to a canister of lipstick. Shoe prints were found in the parking lot and captured with the use of a gelatin lifter. A random item was discovered from under the vehicle—a torn piece of green cloth had been recovered from the undercarriage of the car, just below the right front bumper.

Looking in the box, Livia located the sealed bag containing the green cloth lifted from the bottom side of Nicole's car. She removed it from the box and held it with her fingers. She studied it for several seconds as her mind worked.

"How much trouble would there be if we took this?" she asked Megan.

"Lots. What is it?"

"Something they pulled from Nicole's car. What if we get it back before anyone knows it's gone?"

"You're the medical examiner. But it breaks the evidence chain of custody," she said, spoken like the sheriff's daughter she was.

Megan looked down the fluorescent-lit row of shelves to the closed door where Greg was keeping watch for her. They'd been at it for close to the allotted thirty minutes and she expected him to pop his head in any minute to tell them to wrap it up. She pointed to Livia's purse. "Take it. Just get it back to me soon."

Livia slipped the clear plastic bag into her purse.

"Anything else?" Megan said. "Greg's gonna be pressing us soon."

Livia took a minute to look through the evidence log, reading through the other items confiscated from her sister's car. Nicole's sweatshirt and purse were in the front passenger seat. The rest of the car was empty besides the trunk. Livia stopped when she read the items found there.

Megan stirred next to her, walking closer when she sensed that Livia was interested in something else. "Find something?" she asked.

Dropping the evidence log onto the table, Livia reached back into the box to retrieve the photos again. She flipped quickly through them until she found it. Documented on the log, and captured in the photos, was a rectangular wooden box of barbecue tools. She looked at Megan.

"Where do they keep this stuff? The bigger pieces of evidence? Like this." Livia showed Megan the picture of the wooden barbecue set.

"In the property section." She pointed to the other side of the room.

"Take me there."

Greg stuck his head in. "Wrap it up. One more minute. It's my ass on the line."

They stuffed Nicole's box back onto the shelf and walked quickly to the other side of the evidence room, where large items were stored in plastic bags and meticulously logged.

It took them a long minute to find the C section and another few seconds before Livia found, wrapped and sealed in a clear plastic bag, the barbecue set taken from Nicole's trunk. She unzipped the bag and pulled out the worn wooden box.

She opened it and stared at the contents. Cased inside, seated within the contoured velvet mold, were a spatula, tongs, and an empty outline where a long, two-pronged barbecue fork once rested.

"Son of a bitch," Livia whispered to herself.

Chapter 31

Monday morning, Livia retrieved her case from the cooler with the help of two autopsy technicians who positioned the body on her table—a middle-aged woman who had died during a routine esophageal procedure when the doctor had accidentally lacerated the distal end of the esophagus and severed it from the stomach. As the doctor was unable to stop the bleeding, the woman died from blood loss. Livia and the fellows had been forewarned by Dr. Colt that when such accidental deaths—termed *therapeutic complications*—present themselves, the utmost diligence should be practiced since there was a very good chance the autopsy findings would be utilized in court when the family sued the physician.

This morning, Livia was thorough and patient as she performed her internal exam, not worrying about her autopsy time, only making sure she did everything that was required of her, and did it well.

Twenty minutes into the exam, she was carefully dissecting the strap muscles of the neck to obtain a view of the esophagus when Ted Kane from the ballistics lab walked into the autopsy suite. It was a typical Monday morning, with every autopsy table filled by the weekend's carnage. Tim Schultz and Jen Tilly were busy with cases, as were the other medical examiners who made up the staff at the OCME. The only thing missing was Dr. Colt, who'd taken a long weekend to spend time with his daughter, who was home from college. Livia took advantage of her boss's absence, arriving early and visiting Ted Kane in ballistics to ask for his help.

"Hey, Doc," Ted said as he approached the opposite side of Livia's table.

Livia looked up through her face shield. She stopped working briefly and raised her eyebrows. "Anything?"

"I've got a match."

"On which one?"

"Both. How long will you be?"

"A while," Livia said. "I'll come to the lab when I'm done. No doubt?" she asked.

"Not a shred. Come see me when you're finished."

Livia watched Ted leave the suite, and then went back to work. Her mind wandered with possibilities, but she refused to pay them any attention, refocusing her thoughts instead on the case in front of her. She took just over an hour to complete the exam before she handed her table over to the tech who would close and return the body to the cooler for transport to the funeral home. She spent another hour completing notes on the case, confirming that the patient had indeed bled to death due to a large esophageal laceration with blood deposition into the lungs and peritoneum. Cause of death: *exsanguination.* Manner of death: *therapeutic complication.* In layman's terms: The doctor killed her.

Livia typed the last of her notes, signed the death certificate, and hurried to the ballistics lab.

The ballistics lab was located on the second floor of the OCME. It was where techs analyzed everything from shoe imprints to glass shards, determining who walked through a crime scene in which type and size of shoe, to which direction a bullet penetrated a window. Ted Kane ran the ballistics department and Livia had delivered to him earlier in the morning the scrap of green cloth she had taken from Nicole's evidence box on Friday.

Livia walked into the lab and found Ted Kane in front of his computer.

"Ah, good," he said when Livia entered. He swiveled his chair and wheeled to a cluttered desk to his right. He handed Livia a piece of paper containing the fiber analysis completed on Casey Delevan's clothing from weeks before. Ted poked his eye into the microscope.

"Here's what we know. Spectral analysis tells us it's the same material. Same twine of cotton. Same fiber thickness. Same grade. The only difference is that the analysis on the clothing that came from your body was caked in clay." He looked up from his microscope. "This sample you gave me here is clean. Not a speck of clay on it."

"Otherwise?" Livia asked.

"They came from the same shirt. Exact match."

Livia had no time to contemplate the implications of this discovery. She thought briefly about the fact that a torn scrap of Casey Delevan's shirt was found under Nicole's car. But only fleetingly. Ted Kane was literally on a roll. He pushed himself away from the cluttered desk and his wheeled chair skated back to the glowing computer monitor.

"But this is better. Check it out," he said as he settled in front of the computer, which depicted the three-dimensional scan of Casey Delevan's skull that Dr. Larson—the neuropathologist—had obtained during her examination.

The image, taken by a scanning electron microscope, was one of the most impressive things Livia had witnessed during her training. Since the machine imaged the skull from both the outside and inside, it was able to extrapolate points to offer a "virtual tour" of the skull and the inner casings of the bone. Specifically, Ted Kane was interested in the twelve tunnels in Casey Delevan's skull.

When Livia found the evidence collected from Nicole's car, and the barbecue tool set in particular, it clicked immediately. When she saw the empty spot where a fork had once rested, her mind connected the tines of that missing fork to the mysterious holes in Casey Delevan's skull.

She spent the weekend perusing barbecue tools at various home improvement stores and learned the set found in Nicole's car had been discontinued. But Weber produced it, and with help from a nice young man at Burke Brothers Hardware, Livia obtained a model number for the out-of-date product. She brought it to Ted Kane earlier in the morning for tool analysis.

"So I went back to the original autopsy photos of the skull and the piercings," Ted said. "Then took some measurements based on extrapolated data. At first, we all thought these were twelve random holes through the skull. Now, as I examine them with your theory in mind, I see they're actually a group of six twin piercings. Look here." Ted moved his mouse and circled each pair of holes on the screen. Then he superimposed a computer-generated measuring protractor over the skull. "Each pair of piercings is exactly the same distance apart—one and a half inches. One point five four, to be exact. No variability. The pattern of distribution of each pair is random, but the pairs themselves are identical."

He pointed to the screen. "So check it out. I'm going to take you for a ride through one of the piercings." He moved the mouse and the image on the screen responded by shifting so that Livia's view was straight through one of the holes in the skull. Then the 3-D view shifted and Livia watched as though a small camera were moving through the channel in the bone. It reminded her of the hundreds of endoscopies she witnessed in medical school, as the probe's camera moved down the trachea.

"So a few things we can ascertain," Ted said. "Every channel is the exact same width, so we suspect they were all produced by the same instrument. But once we look beyond the width and analyze the actual walls of these channels, here's what we find." He pointed to the screen. "See this?"

Livia squinted her eyes at the monitor. "What am I looking at?"

"A small groove in the wall of the canal. It tells me the instrument used had a defect on it. It wasn't smooth. So probably during the lifespan of the fork, it was dropped or otherwise abused—wear and tear. It's significant because every pair of holes has a single channel—the left-side channel—with the exact same aberration. So beyond a doubt, all the piercings came from the same tool. This is important to the Homicide guys in case we recover that fork. We could match it beyond a reasonable doubt. But here's the money shot. This is what you'll be interested in."

Ted clicked through some other screens until the animated view of Casey Delevan's skull was again visible. "There were twelve piercings. Six sets of two, right? Each pair was exactly 1.54 inches apart. So we have the width of the tine, and the distance they are apart from each other. I did some research through our tool analysis database. We have a comprehensive list, and we have measurements on the fork you're interested in—based on the serial number you provided."

Ted clicked the mouse and again the 3-D image spun and then entered the burrow of one of the piercings.

"Every single channel pierced the full thickness of the skull. So, every one went from the outside of the skull, all the way through to the dura mater." He looked at Livia. "Except one."

He pointed to the screen where the image brought them into a channel and then to a dead end.

"There is one piercing that did not fully penetrate the skull. It simply lanced the bone and was then removed. This single channel gives us a great deal of information. Specifically, it shows the exact contour of the fork's prong. The contour, width, shape, angle of the tine's point, and the exact length of the tip of the tine. The angle of the point is key, because it is unique to the brand, design, and line of the product. It matches the fork you're interested in identically. So," Ted said, tapping the keyboard to produce a new image on his screen, "the missing fork from that barbecue set is what killed your floater."

Livia fumbled with her keys minutes later in the parking lot, started her car, and began the long drive east toward Emerson Bay. It consisted of two hours of solitude where her mind ran wild with speculation. It was past eight p.m. when she pulled into her parents' driveway. Livia walked to the garage and pushed through the side door, flicking the light switch as she entered. The car was parked in shadows. Livia's mind flashed back to Friday afternoon when she looked at pictures of this car from Nicole's case, doors and trunk open wide for the photographer to capture every detail from every angle. Now, it sat quietly in her parents' garage, seldom used since Nicole went missing.

From the workbench, Livia retrieved a tape measure. Crouching down, she ran the tape from the ground up to the bumper. Twenty-seven inches. The same height as Casey Delevan's femur fracture.

Livia let the tape measure snap back into place. She closed her eyes.

"What the hell, Nicole?"

Chapter 32

He sat in his car for a long while, uncertain about what the night would bring. The last time he was here, just a few days before, had been their worst moments together. It was when he had found her stuck in the window, some distance away from escape. Some distance away from ending it all. How exactly to measure that distance, he was unsure. A foot away? Twelve inches from the freedom she thought she wanted. An hour, maybe? If he had gotten a call or had been otherwise delayed, an hour was likely all she would have needed to work herself free. Or was that distance to escape measured by gumption? Some part of him wanted to believe she had failed because she hadn't wanted to succeed. Success meant she would leave him, and he knew there was a connection between them she held on to. She did not always show it, but it was there. She displayed it occasionally, this one, when she allowed him to lie next to her and hold her afterward. He had felt that connection. It was real. But still, she had come close to leaving him. Close to freedom. It rattled him. It could not happen again. He had endured last year's debacle. The bunker, the forest, and the heartache. But if this one escaped, if this one made it back to the world, his life would shatter down around him. Because of that, because she had been so immeasurably close to ruining it all for him, he had no choice but to be brutal last time when he served her punishment. He hated himself for it afterward.

So tonight, as he sat in his car, he was uncertain how the night would go. It was possible things could go back to the way they had once been. It was possible to get back to that point in their relationship. Part of his hesitation tonight came from not only his worry over how she would receive him after her last reprimand, but what that reaction would mean. Defiance and rebellion, per the rules, would result in her final strike. His reluctance now came from knowing that tonight could mark the end of their time together. This worried him because, despite everything, he loved this one. He loved them all, but with this one their relationship was so long in the making he was depressed that he hadn't been able to convince her of his love. He felt inadequate, that perhaps she was too good for him, a nasty revelation that left a bitter taste in his throat.

He took a deep breath and climbed from his car, surveying the area around him. It was dark and quiet and he wondered how long things would remain that way. He pushed through the front door, and his shoes clapped on the floor as he walked to the basement stairs. As soon as he opened the cellar door he smelled it. A sweet, pungent odor he knew all too well. Immediately, he knew he'd been too hard on her the other night, that he'd let his emotions overtake him. He'd spent the last few days worrying about her and debating if he should check on her. Now it was too late.

The stairwell was dark, and he clicked on his flashlight as he went. The odor grew stronger as he descended. Finally, when he reached the bottom of the stairs, he played his flashlight across the bed. She was there, the beautiful creature he could not convince of his love, pale and bloated and stiff. He sat on the bottom stair and cried. Why, he wondered, did they all end like this? What more did they want than to be loved and cared for?

He gave himself a full minute to wallow—moaning uncontrollably and rocking back and forth—before collecting himself. Then he went out to his car and retrieved what he needed from the trunk. He kept it under the floorboard with the spare tire. A half hour later, he carried up the cellar stairs the black vinyl bag that contained her body. Out into the night, he looked around again, but there was no one to disturb him. He loaded her into the trunk and slammed it shut in a violent motion that caused him to stumble backward. This single act of anger would be all he allowed himself for his failure. The moment called for efficiency and clear thinking. He sat in his car, leaving the door wide open as he ran his hands through his hair and closed his eyes. They welled again with tears but he would not allow himself to cry this time. Dead quiet, all he heard was his slightly labored breathing from hauling her body up the stairs. Between breaths, the still night was interrupted by a far-off noise. He listened for a moment. Somewhere in the distance, a train whistled through the night.

SUMMER 2016

"Are you guys coming back here
next year?"

—Rachel Ryan

Chapter 33

August 2016
Five Days Before the Abduction

"They have a website?"

"No," Terry McDonald said. "None that I can find. She said the guy found her in the comments section on a website that discusses missing persons. Invited her to a private chat room. Things progressed from there."

"Good Christ. I want to put my kid in a bubble when I hear this stuff."

"You and me both," Terry said. "Megan's off to Duke in a couple of weeks, so there's no bubble holding her for long."

He sat behind his desk at the Montgomery County Sheriff's Office and spoke with his deputy. Diana Wells, dragged in by her parents, had told her story the day before.

"Back in the day," Terry said, "parents used to worry about testosterone-filled teenage boys wanting to get laid, or about kids swigging peppermint schnapps. But now? There's so much crazy out there it's hard to keep track. The Internet has introduced a whole new predator. Like this group of idiots running around snatching people off the streets to initi-

*ate them into a club." He held up a sheet of paper. "Our op-
tions here, Mort?" Terry asked.*

*"Not many. Did you say she actually chose certain prefer-
ences for the abduction?"*

*"That's how she described it. Said she could choose to be
taken off the street or put in a trunk. She could have it rough
or gentle. She got to choose how long she was gone, too. The
minimum was three hours. The most was overnight."*

*"Lunatics," Mort Gleeson said. "So we have an underage
girl with a fake ID at a bar who was under the influence of
alcohol, who willingly climbed into the accused's car before
any of the mock abduction began. She was not physically
harmed. In the end, they dropped her off at the bar. And before any of it began, she agreed to the whole thing. Might be
able to charge the girl with stupidity, but going after this
club? There's not much there."*

*Terry McDonald leaned back in his chair, eyes fixed on the
pad of paper in front of him. There was a long pause.*

*"I've seen that look in your eyes before, boss. Don't get
yourself in trouble. This is an election year."*

*"Just gonna have a look at the links and addresses of those
chat rooms."*

*Mort Gleeson stood and rapped his knuckles on the desk.
"Keep me posted. I know your daughter is at that age, but
use sound judgment before you go knocking down any
doors."*

*Terry McDonald looked up from his notepad, nodded at
his deputy. When Mort was gone, the sheriff drummed his
fingers on his chin. He looked down at his notes. The Capture Club. He underlined it twice.*

*"Okay, ladies," Rachel said, walking down the steps of
the beach house and onto the pool patio. She carried smoothies on a round tray like a waitress. "My mom and I just made
these. Filled with strawberries and bananas and a shot of that*

THE GIRL WHO WAS TAKEN   263

protein powder. Supposed to help you lose five pounds in a week."

Rachel placed the tray on the patio table and handed out the extraordinary drinks that sported long straws and pineapple wedges stuck on the sides.

"None of us need to lose five pounds," Jessica said, lying on a lawn chair and soaking up the sun.

"The freshman fifteen is coming," Rachel said. "I'm fighting it off before it finds me."

"If you keep thinking you're going to end up fat and ugly, you will," Nicole said. "Self-fulfilling prophecy."

Rachel took a seat and they all sipped their smoothies, staring off at the bay and the boats and the wakeboarders ripping white streaks across the water. Occasional cotton-ball clouds spotted the blue sky. The scent of barbecued burgers sat on the shoulders of the afternoon breeze and mixed with traces of freshly cut grass, chlorine, and coconut sunscreen. A lawn mower buzzed from next door and, far off, an ice cream truck chimed as it chugged through the neighborhood. It was summer in Emerson Bay.

"Are you guys coming back here next year?" Rachel asked.

"Back where? Emerson Bay?" Jessica said.

"To my house. Are we gonna hang out next summer?"

"Why wouldn't we?"

"I don't know. New friends. Maybe one of us stays at college for the summer. Takes classes or something."

"Not me," Jessica said. "I'll be home. And if you're not, I'll sit right here with your mom all summer and text you pictures of us. But I don't think I'm the one you're worried about." Jessica looked at Nicole.

"What's that mean?" Nicole asked.

"You've been MIA all summer, preoccupied with the guy you won't let us meet."

"You guys wouldn't get him, and I don't feel like trying to explain him."

They had pushed all summer until Rachel and Jessica decided to finally give up. The closest they'd come to information on Nicole's boyfriend was a picture she showed them—a selfie of Nicole and Casey. They got some background one day when Nicole explained that Casey's brother had been abducted when they were kids. Jessica and Rachel knew immediately to back off the issue. Nicole had a strange childhood that included a cousin who had also gone missing. The mysterious summer fling made more sense to them.

"Before we get too concerned about next summer," Jessica said, "let's concentrate on this weekend. We're all still going to the beach party, right?"

"We have to go," Rachel said. "It's the unofficial end of summer in Emerson Bay. It's a tradition."

They waited until Nicole looked at them.

"What?" Nicole said.

"Are you going?"

"I guess."

"What are you going to do when Casey doesn't follow you to school?"

Nicole gave a fake smile. "I'll deal."

A boat cut through the water and drew its engine down as it entered the no-wake zone in front of Rachel's house. They all shielded their eyes from the sun as they looked toward the water.

"It's Matt," Jessica said. "That's another issue we need to discuss. Does Casey know you're hooking up with him?"

"Ha! Matt's too whipped by the princess to do much besides butterfly kisses. But I'll break him. He's a guy." Nicole sat up from the patio chair and adjusted her bikini top. Took off her sunglasses and held them in front of her to admire her reflection in the lens.

"Tyler and Mike are with him."

"Ah," Nicole said in a pouty voice. "It was so cute the other day when they ambushed you on the boat and threw you in the bay. It had been such a boring summer for you guys. But now . . . summer bummer to summer hummer?"

"Gross," Rachel said. She stood up and waved as Tyler and Mike jumped onto the dock and walked up the stairs toward Rachel's pool.

"Ladies," Tyler said.

"What's up?" Rachel asked.

They wore swim trunks without shirts, their chests carrying a bronzed glow that suggested they'd been on the bay for most of the day.

"Wanted to make sure you guys were going to the beach party on Saturday."

"Like we need an invitation from you guys?" Nicole said.

"We're going," Jessica said. "She's crabby."

"Matt too shy to talk to us?" Nicole asked.

"I don't know," Tyler said. "He's being weird."

Nicole stood and placed her smoothie on the table. "I'll go see what his problem is."

She sauntered down the stairs in her bikini and best seductive walk, knowing they were all watching her. She pranced along the dock and jumped onto the boat.

"You can't come up to say hi to me?" she asked Matt, who was rearranging water skis and wetsuits in a floorboard compartment.

"Hi," he said without looking at her. "Just stopped for a second because my boys have a thing for your friends."

Nicole sat in the captain's chair and playfully kicked Matt in the thigh as he knelt on the ground and wrestled with a wedged water ski.

"Give my offer any thought?"

Matt managed to free the ski and align it with the others, then shut the hatch and stood up. "What offer?"

Nicole cocked her head. "My offer from the other day,

when you and I were all alone. . . ." She pointed below deck. "Right. Down. There."

Matt grabbed a towel and dried his hands. He looked wholly disinterested. "You know something, Nicole? I can't understand why you need so much attention. But offering someone sex is a stupid way to get it."

Nicole swallowed hard when she heard his words, flashed her best persuasive grin to hide her embarrassment. "I figured you're not getting any from your girlfriend, so I'd help you out."

"Trying to convince me to cheat on my girlfriend is not the best way to get noticed. Do something original, Nicole. Then people will pay attention to you."

She stood up. "I thought you said you didn't have a girlfriend."

"Things change."

"Really? Megan McDonald?"

"Why do you care?"

"She's so not your type."

"You don't know my type."

"I used to, because I was your type."

"We dated last year, Nicole. Let's get over it."

"I was your type the other day." Nicole came up to him and put her hands around his waist. "I promise you, she's not going to give you what I can."

Matt grabbed her wrists and squeezed with his powerful forearms. "I'm scared to find out what you'd give me, and so are most of my friends."

Nicole tried hard to hide the pain he was causing in her wrists. "Let go of me."

"That's what everyone thinks about you, you know that? That you've become an STD-spreading slut. Slutty Cutty they call you."

"You're an asshole."

"And you're a whore." Matt pushed her away. "Get off my boat."

Nicole smiled. It looked forced and fake, worse than the last one. "You know what's going to be really funny? When I have a little talk with the princess about what happened between us right down there." She pointed below deck again. "I'm sure your Duke romance will flourish when she hears that you couldn't get your hands off me, or your tongue out of my mouth."

Now Matt smiled casually. His was better than Nicole's, more convincing as he walked slowly toward her. In one quick move like he'd used hundreds of times on the wrestling mat, he grabbed the back of her neck and pulled her face to within an inch of his.

"Talk to Megan, and you're going to see a side of me you've never known." He pushed her away again. "Now get off my boat."

The fake smile came back to her face, and she used the backs of her hands to wipe her tears. "You're such a loser."

She hurried up the dock, passing Tyler and Mike, who took awkward glances at her on the way by.

PART V

"People know me as the girl from my book,
or as the girl from before the abduction.
I'm neither anymore."
—Megan McDonald

Chapter 34

October 2017
Thirteen Months Since Megan's Escape

It was Friday before Livia could get back to Emerson Bay. As Megan sat in the passenger seat while they headed to West Bay, the horizon seared with the last efforts of the setting sun.

"Who is this guy?" Megan asked.

"A piece of work," Livia said. "The problem is, he might be useful."

Earlier in the week Livia had caught Megan up on her findings from the evidence room—the green fiber match to Casey Delevan's clothing, and the missing fork that Ted Kane had expertly identified as the tool used to end his life. Both findings created a link between Casey and Nicole on the night she was taken. By association, the findings had snared Megan as well.

Livia pulled through the light when it turned green, turned onto a side street a few minutes later, and stopped the car in front of the dilapidated house she had visited two weeks before.

"Useful how?" Megan asked.

"Here's the thing," Livia said. "When we go to your dad, I want ammunition. We've got the ketamine and the fibers and the missing fork. But for your dad to get on board, I need more. I need to convince him that Casey Delevan was taking girls."

"You mean Nancy Dee?"

"Maybe others, too."

"Other girls? Who?"

Livia pointed to the house. "I'm hoping to find out tonight."

They climbed out of the car and knocked on the rickety screen door. Daisy went wild, barking and clawing. Nate Theros held her at bay while he cracked open the door.

"Nate. It's Livia Cutty."

Nate smiled as he stared past Livia.

Livia followed his glance. "This is Megan McDonald."

His eyes unblinking, Nate carried the starstruck grin of a fan meeting his favorite movie star.

"Maybe you should put Daisy away," Livia said, interrupting Nate's moment as he gawked and grinned at Megan. "So we can talk?"

"Yeah," Nate said, nodding. "I'll be right back."

While Nate dragged Daisy to her crate, Livia spoke over the barking. "This guy was a member of the club I told you about. The one that studied missing persons cases. He's enamored of your presence. You're as famous as they get."

Megan raised her eyebrows. "I'm flattered."

"Just bear with me. I promised him you'd be here to sign a copy of your book and answer some questions for him. It's the only way he'd agree to talk."

Nate was back a minute later. "You guys wanna come in?" he asked, oblivious to the many things that would prevent two women from entering his house. Like that they were in West Bay at dusk, with a muddy purple sky just ahead of Halloween. Or that his T-shirt did nothing to contain the tattoos that traced his arms and neck. Or that the giant hoop earrings that weighted down his earlobes shouted bad intentions and mischief.

"No, thanks," Livia said. "Let's talk on the porch."

"Yeah, sure." Nate walked onto the front patio and put a cigarette between his lips. "Hey," he said to Megan.

"Hi."

"I read your book."

"Oh yeah?" Megan still hadn't found the right way to respond to this. "Thanks."

"Nate, Megan and I want to ask you a few questions about the club."

"Go ahead."

"You mentioned that the Capture Club talked about a variety of cases, old and new."

"Right."

"Who chose the cases?"

"Anybody. If you were curious about a case, you'd throw out a name."

"Like Jeffrey Dahmer?"

"Dahmer, Gacy, Bittaker and Norris, Beneke. You name it. But we didn't spend tons of time on them. They were old news."

"You guys talked about current stuff mostly?"

"A lot of the time, yeah."

"Anybody could bring up a topic or a name?"

"Yeah. Mostly we followed the news."

Livia nodded. "Especially if someone nearby went missing?"

"Right."

"Nancy Dee, for example."

"Yeah, we talked about her."

"You remember how the group got onto the Nancy Dee story?"

"I don't know. Probably Casey. He was the most up-to-date on the new stuff. Always had a bead on it right when the story broke."

"So, you'd say he knew about some of the cases before anyone else did?"

"Guess so, yeah."

"You remember any other cases, newer ones, that you guys talked about."

Nate wagged his head back and forth, eyes up to the sky. "Sure. Remember a bunch." He lit his cigarette. "Got a binder full of the ones we talked about."

"A binder full of missing girls?"

"Not just girls. Some dudes, too. Whoever the club thought was interesting."

"Where's this binder?"

"Inside."

"Can we have a look at it?"

Nate shrugged. "I don't know. That's my private stuff from back when the club was in full swing."

Megan cleared her throat. "I'd really like to see it." She smiled at Nate. "If that would be okay."

Nate inhaled from his cigarette and the smoke got lodged somewhere in his trachea, causing him to cough like a teenager taking his first drag. He avoided eye contact. "Be right back." He pulled open the screen door and disappeared inside.

"Interesting guy," Megan said.

"I think he's harmless. Thanks for throwing your star power around."

"What good is being famous if you don't use it?"

Nate was back a few minutes later with a black three-ring binder. It reminded Livia of the folder she'd taken from Casey Delevan's desk drawer. Nate handed it to her.

"Here're most of the cases we talked about. I've kept up on a lot of them. Plus a couple new ones." He looked at

Megan. "Got a bunch of your stuff." He shrugged, as if of-fering someone his life's work. "If you wanna check it out."

"Nancy Dee in here?" Livia said.

"Oh yeah. Got a few pages on her."

Livia found Nancy's pages and skimmed through them. Then she leafed through the binder, looking for information on Paula D'Amato, the other girl from Casey Delevan's file. Halfway through the pages she found newspaper clippings about her.

"You remember this girl?"

Nate looked at the page, saw Paula D'Amato's face. "'Course I do."

"How'd the club get onto this one?"

"Casey was into that one. He was on it right away, and we talked about her a bunch. He was sort of fixated on her."

"You remember much about this girl?" Livia asked.

"Georgia Tech freshman. Cops found her jacket in the woods off a trail that students take on the way back to cam-pus. Arrested her boyfriend, but let him go after a while. I guess they're questioning him again now. Plus some other fraternity guys. I've been watching that one closely since the other day, you know?"

"Since the other day?" Livia asked, holding the open binder. "What happened the other day?"

Nate let a slow smile form on his face as though Livia were playing a joke on him. He blew diluted smoke from the cor-ner of his mouth. "They found her body. Like, three or four days ago."

"Paula D'Amato?"

Nate nodded.

"Where?"

"You didn't hear about this?" His voice carried the excite-ment of a sports fan reliving an extraordinary play from the previous night. "Thought that's why you guys were here."

"No," Livia said. "We didn't hear."

He pointed his cigarette at the binder. "Details are still coming in. Her body was found in the woods, down in Georgia. It was zipped in a body bag and lying next to a hole in the ground. Like someone dug the grave but never buried the body. Really weird!" Nate smiled and then sucked again on his cigarette.

"This was a few days ago?"

"Yeah."

Livia handed the binder back to him. "We've got to run."

Nate pointed to Megan. "I thought you said I'd get to ask her some questions."

"Sorry. Some other time."

Livia took Megan by the wrist and hurried back to the car.

"What about signing my book?"

"Another time," Livia said before pulling away. She took a hard right and stepped on the gas. "Sorry to put you through that. You okay?"

"I dealt with worse during my initial book tour. Who's Paula D'Amato?"

"Another girl I think Casey took. I'm going to have to make a trip down to Georgia, see if I can meet with the medical examiner who did the autopsy. If the same findings are present that link you and Nancy Dee, you think we'll be able to get your father on board?"

Megan nodded. "Probably. But I don't understand. If you think this guy, the guy who was dating Nicole, was involved with these girls and had something to do with their disappearances, and mine . . . he's dead, right? So what are we looking for?"

"If Paula D'Amato's body was just found, I want to know when she died. If it was recently, Casey wasn't alone. Someone else is still out there."

Chapter 35

The thousand-watt twin adjustable LED lights brightened the forest as he dug. The earth was wet and the dig was easy, the shovel slicing effortlessly into the mud under the weight of his foot. The woods were quiet at night, its residents mostly tucked away under the cover of leaves or logs. Of course, the nocturnal hunters would be out—the owls and bats and coyote. But the lights by which he worked would hold them off, despite the lure of bitter odor her body gave off as it lay on the forest floor secured in black vinyl and waiting to be covered by the earth he was moving.

When he heard it, he stopped. With his foot on the shovel, he listened. Heard it again. He looked over at the black bag and then stumbled backward when he saw it move. Crinkling in the middle, the bag creased in a ninety-degree angle, as though she had sat up. He dropped the shovel and staggered away from her body until he fell into the shallow grave he had dug. He scrambled to get to his feet but his limbs were frozen with fear. She had unzipped the bag and her torso appeared above him. With unblinking eyes, she picked up the shovel and dumped dirt onto his shoulders. He clawed and begged, managing for a moment to get to his knees, but she was relentless with her efforts. The weight of the earth was finally too great, and he collapsed onto his stomach as she shoveled more dirt over him. The burden of the soil became so great that his lungs could no longer expand under the pressure. He looked up at her just before a final pitch of ground covered his face and his vision went black.

He sat straight up in bed now, grasping at the covers the way he'd been clawing at the sides of the grave in his nightmare. Inhaling deeply, he savored the air that was missing from his dream. Night sweats had soaked his clothes and sheets.

"What's the matter?" came the groggy voice next to him.

It was amazing how even her concern disgusted him. She did not love him, not any longer, and her feigned worry turned his stomach. Part of him blamed her for what he had become. Blamed her for the emptiness inside of him. The vacancy he tried so desperately to occupy with the girls he held captive and offered to love and care for.

"Nothing," he said, out of breath.

"Bad dream?"

Without answering he climbed from bed and walked down to the kitchen for a cup of water. His T-shirt stuck to his chest and he peeled it away as he swallowed the water. The last year had gone wrong. So terribly wrong. Things had gotten far away from him, and he didn't want to admit that it all might be falling apart. The debacle last year—with the bunker and escape, the hunt and the pressure and the media—should have been enough to stop him. To wake him up and bring to him the realization that things could not continue without great wreckage finding him. Yet he was helpless. He could no more convince himself to stop than he could convince the girls he loved to love him back. On this front, though, he was sure things were changing. He simply needed more time.

He knew, however, that he could not sustain this level of incompetence and expect to survive. His sloppiness since the bunker escape last year could not be ignored. He had spent his life on details, and warned his underlings against shoddy work. Taught those around him the need for precision and accuracy. The necessity of paying attention to every facet. Now he had fallen prey to the same careless errors he preached to avoid. The body turning up in the bay was a direct result of panic and inattention to detail. The knots securing the body to the cinder blocks were not closely considered; the consequences of this error were still unknown. The press had lost interest after the initial story broke, and the passing weeks had given him hope that he might be able to dodge the bullet. But more errors had followed. The careless application of the plywood that secured the cellar window had nearly allowed another escape. And his desire to make her comfortable by providing a frame for the box spring was an error so egregious he was sickened every time he thought of it. The quarrel that followed was unfortunate, and losing his temper was a sign of incompetence.

The sloppiness of his actions was dangerous, and he was scared. His trepidation had caused him to run from the woods the other night, too afraid to dump her body into the grave he dug. And now, so soon after their time together ended, she had been found. They called her Paula, and it sickened him. Just like before, when the jogger and his dog had disturbed the resting place he'd created for his last love and the news anchors called her Nancy. The names insulted him. He was offended by how the media spoke of his loves as though they knew them, used foreign names to label them and displayed pictures of their faces for all to see. They pretended, sitting in their studios and staring into cameras, that they held a connection to his girls. The truth, he knew, was that the media had done nothing but forget these creatures existed.

He walked up the stairs and threw his soiled shirt into the laundry basket. Instead of climbing back into bed, he took his pillow to the couch and lay down. Things needed to change, but he wasn't sure it was possible. Under the guilt and fear, beneath the ugly image of the latest one's bloated face zipped and stashed in black vinyl, was something else. He tried to ignore it, but knew he couldn't. However subtle at the moment, his thirst would grow. Unquenchable by the woman who lay upstairs, oblivious to his needs. It was a thirst for connection. For trust and dependency. He knew he would someday find it. Perhaps he already had.

And though the heavy burden of melancholy sat on his shoulders from the way things had ended with his last love, there was hope buried under those emotions. Hope and desire. He knew they were the dominant emotions that would prove victorious. For now, he would weather this latest storm and bide his time. Get through these missteps. Let things settle and calm. Then focus on what's important.

He tossed on the couch as he fell asleep. Night sweats found him as the image returned. The black vinyl bag uneven with her remains.

Chapter 36

Saturday morning, Livia was on the road before dawn. She passed the occasional eighteen-wheeler making a long haul from the north, but otherwise the highway was hers. She considered Casey Delevan, Nancy Dee, Paula D'Amato, Megan McDonald, and whether she could convince the police that a connection existed between them all. She wondered if Nicole played into that connection, and whether the delusional grandeur of a demented club had anything to do with all these missing girls.

Livia's mind returned to her fellowship interview, where she stored in her suppressed thoughts the idea that Nicole's body could turn up the same way Nancy Dee's and Paula D'Amato's had. She thought of Nicole's body being transported to her autopsy table, where it would silently beg Livia to find the answers it held and put to rest the many questions Livia and her parents still asked about the night Nicole disappeared. Instead, though, Casey Delevan had arrived in her morgue. And in place of answers, the case had only caused more speculation that sent Livia into bordering states searching for revelations about other missing girls.

As the sun crested the horizon behind her and stretched

the shadow of her car into a thin black ghost along the road in front of her, Livia realized she was chasing more than the ghost of her lost sister. Maybe it had taken Casey Delevan's decomposed body to force her into action. Maybe a year of denial and avoidance had finally run its course. Perhaps action was the only logical next step if forgetting about Nicole was the alternative. Whatever the reason, Livia knew she couldn't stop until she possessed the answers she craved. And if those answers didn't fully provide closure for herself, or quell the guilt about her flagging relationship with Nicole, perhaps finding a resolution for the Dee and D'Amato families would provide something else. A balm needed to heal wounds that would otherwise remain exposed and gaping.

She had pulled all the strings her feeble position as a fellow in forensic pathology allowed in order to convince the coroner of Decatur, Georgia, to meet her on a Saturday. The sun was at its peak by noon when she found the headquarters building of the Georgia Bureau of Investigation. The parking lot was mostly empty. Livia entered the front door and gave her name to the security guard behind the desk. He picked up the phone to announce Dr. Cutty's arrival, and a few minutes later a fiftysomething woman entered the lobby.

"Hi," she said. "Denise Rettenburg."

"Livia Cutty. Thanks for meeting me today."

"I've got a case, so I had to come in anyway," Dr. Rettenburg said. "Follow me. Thanks, Bruce," she said to the security guard before leading Livia into the building. They approached an elevator, where Dr. Rettenburg pressed the up button.

"So why is Raleigh so interested in Paula D'Amato?"

The doors opened and Livia followed Denise Rettenburg into the elevator.

"Maybe for no reason," Livia said. "But we've seen a few cases of young women with similar findings, so I wanted to have a look to see if we can make any connections."

"Sounds like police work."

"Right now, it's nothing more than suspicion. I need some facts before I take anything to the police."

Dr. Rettenburg smiled. "You *sound* like a Dr. Colt fellow. Facts first."

The doors opened and they shuffled out of the elevator and walked the empty hallway.

"So this is a personal inquisition, or does Dr. Colt know about it?"

"Dr. Colt is familiar with the case that got me onto my suspicions. A homicide case from late summer. But about the D'Amato case, I'm down here now on my own."

Dr. Rettenburg seemed to analyze this last statement. "Who are the other cases?" she asked. "The other girls you think D'Amato is connected to."

"Two others. One is a girl named Nancy Dee. You know anything about that?"

"No. A Raleigh case?"

Livia shook her head. "Virginia. But same MO as D'Amato—her body was found in a shallow grave in the woods. She died of an acute overdose of ketamine."

Dr. Rettenburg looked at Livia as they walked. "Ketamine?"

"Yeah. Tell me, was ketamine found in Paula D'Amato's toxicology report?"

"It was."

"Was that the cause of death? Ketamine overdose?"

"No." Dr. Rettenburg slowed and pointed to the doorway of her office. "She was beaten to death."

The autopsy photos were fanned out on Dr. Rettenburg's desk and Livia took her time studying them. They showed Paula D'Amato's body on the morgue table, her skin pale and blue and stretched in the same bloated way she'd seen so many other bodies in the last few months. Paula D'Amato had died recently, that was certain. Her body was not decomposed and death had come shortly before the autopsy exam.

"What sort of timing did you come up with?" Livia asked.

"About forty-eight hours at time of exam. In the woods for two nights, we suspect. The only thing that slowed down the carnivores was the body bag."

Livia leafed through crime scene photos next, which showed a black vinyl body bag lying in a wooded area heavily covered by leaves. Corners of the bag were ragged from the animals eager to get at the rotting flesh it held. The body sat on the precipice of a shallow grave, a mound of dirt next to it.

"What are the thoughts on the crime scene?"

"That's the million-dollar question," Dr. Rettenburg said. "No one quite knows what to make of it. Detectives figure the perp got interrupted in the middle of digging the grave. The site wasn't too far into the woods, so it's possible someone spooked this guy and he had to abandon the disposal. That's the working theory currently. Problem is, Homicide thinks the guy had lights set up."

"Lights?"

"Yeah, like he was getting rid of her at night. They found marks in the dirt that suggested some heavy-duty or high-powered spotlights, run from a battery or a gas-powered generator."

"Why is that a problem?"

"Because to break those down and move them takes effort. And time. If he got spooked by a passerby, it's hard to imagine he took the time to douse the lights and disassemble the stand but didn't bother to bury the body."

"Yeah," Livia said, still paging through the photos. "That doesn't make sense."

"Homicide is working to track down anyone who might've

been in the area over the last week or so. Haven't found any-one yet. But the fear is that if the only reason we found Paula D'Amato was because this guy got interrupted digging her grave, how many more girls are out there?"

Livia nodded. She pretended to continue looking over the photos, but her vision faded as Dr. Rettenburg verbalized her thoughts. The only thing Denise Rettenburg failed to men-tion was that one of those girls was Nicole.

"Are you okay, Dr. Cutty?"

Livia looked up from the photos, shaking the image out of her mind. "Sorry. Tell me about the autopsy."

Dr. Rettenburg slid a folder across her desk. She spoke from memory while Livia paged through the report. "We fig-ured she was dead for two days when she was found. Body showed signs of restraint, specifically chafing to the left ankle. Signs of sexual abuse, likely repeated and chronic."

"When did she go missing?"

"Two years ago."

"Christ," Livia said.

"Acute physical abuse," Dr. Rettenburg continued. "Bruis-ing to the face, head, arms, and torso. Damage to the strap muscles from manual strangulation. She fought, too. Broken toes from kicking. Bruising to her knuckles. Defensive wounds to her forearms."

"Were there signs of chronic abuse?"

"Sadly, yes. She had a poorly healed fibula fracture esti-mated to be from roughly a year ago, and a broken rib in the early phases of healing. Plus an array of abrasions and scars of various age. Sexual abuse was clearly chronic."

"So for two long years, the son of a bitch had his way with her until he decided he'd had enough?"

"I'll let the detectives determine that, Dr. Cutty."

Livia turned the page. "Can you tell me about the toxicol-ogy report?"

"We did find ketamine in her system, along with diazepam. It was recently administered not long before death, based on the level of metabolism. It looks like it was ingested in lemonade."

Livia shook her head. "The Virginia case was a straight ketamine overdose—both ingested orally and injected intramuscularly. No acute physical abuse. So, either by accident or with intent, he killed Nancy Dee by administering too much ketamine. Why not do the same here? Why give her the meds and then beat and strangle her?"

"Maybe the two cases are not related. We can only tell the story the body tells us, Dr. Cutty. Leave the speculation to the detectives." Dr. Rettenburg waited as Livia wrestled with the limitations of their profession. "What are the links to the other cases?" she finally asked.

"Ketamine is the strongest," Livia said.

"Yes, that was an odd finding. Usually used in veterinary medicine."

"Right, and I can link it to two other cases."

"The girl in Virginia and who else?"

"Megan McDonald."

"Megan McDonald of Emerson Bay?"

Livia nodded. "The night she escaped, she was found to have a large amount of ketamine in her system." Livia looked up from the report. "This guy OD'd Nancy Dee, perhaps tried to do the same to Paula D'Amato until he took measures into his own hands, and filled Megan McDonald with ketamine just before he meant to kill her. She escaped from that bunker and ran for her life until Arthur Steinman picked her up on Highway Fifty-Seven."

Denise Rettenburg slowly nodded her head. "That's some good detective work from a Gerald Colt fellow."

Livia paged again through the autopsy report. "The other connection comes from the fibers found in the girls' hair. The same fibers discovered in Nancy Dee's hair were discovered in Megan McDonald's the night she was brought to the hospital. From Megan's recounting of the night she escaped, we know a burlap bag was placed on her head. This bag was recovered from the bunker. Fiber analysis from the material in Megan's hair not only matched the bag they recovered, but also fibers found on Nancy Dee's body. It was the same burlap, at least."

"Well, now that's interesting." Dr. Rettenburg paged through the photos that sat in front of Livia, then slid one out into the open. "The D'Amato girl was found with a burlap sack over her head."

Livia looked more closely at the photo. She hadn't noticed it the first time. "A sack over her head *and* inside a body bag?"

"Correct."

"Did you run that sack?"

Dr. Rettenburg paged through a folder and slid the fiber analysis across her desk.

Livia pulled a copy of Nancy Dee's and Megan's fiber analyses from her purse and laid all three in front of her for comparison. "They all come back as hemp woven burlap. Same fiber width, same grade."

Livia looked up at Denise Rettenburg, who raised her eyebrows.

"I'd say you have a compelling case, Dr. Cutty."

Livia helped Denise Rettenburg reorganize the D'Amato file, then followed her out into the hallway and waited in front of the elevator doors.

"Gerald Colt was a year ahead of me in medical school," Dr. Rettenburg said.

"Oh yeah?" Livia said. "Dr. Colt is a great mentor."

"I hear he's doing wonderful things in Raleigh."

The elevator doors opened and they both entered. Dr. Rettenburg pressed the button for the lobby, and Livia waited for the doors to close.

"Is Gerald the one who made the ketamine connection?" Dr. Rettenburg asked.

"No," Livia said. "I found it."

"It's a great catch. I thought perhaps Gerald's wife played a role."

Livia started to say something, then stopped. Confused, she finally said, "This case wasn't on Dr. Colt's radar. Otherwise I'm sure he'd have picked this up."

"Of course," Dr. Rettenburg said. She pressed the button to hurry the process of the elevator doors closing. In the lobby, she walked Livia to the front door.

"Thanks for taking the time on a Saturday," Livia said.

"Good luck to you."

Dr. Rettenburg watched Gerald Colt's fellow drive away, then headed back to her office. She thought perhaps she'd misspoken in the elevator by suggesting Gerald's wife had helped make the ketamine connection. At her computer, Dr. Rettenburg typed her query into the search engine and waited for the results. She scrolled down and read. Yes, she thought she was correct.

Gerald Colt's wife was a veterinarian with a large clinic in Summer Side, just north of Raleigh.

Chapter 37

Butted up against Virginia, on the northern border of North Carolina, Tinder Valley consisted of eighty-two cabins set along a tributary to the Roanoke River. The cabins were made from galvanized log, and slept as few as two in the cozy models, and as many as eight in the larger ones with spacious floor plans. Located on the banks of the river, each cabin promised beautiful views of the water. Constructed in the eighties, Tinder Valley was, for a short time, a majestic lakeside resort where families escaped for long weekends. It was where kids steered paddleboats around the clear water while Mom and Dad watched from lounge chairs. Where couples walked the beach with dogs in tow, carving footprints in the sand. But Tinder Valley did not stay majestic for long. Over the years, poor management had allowed riverfront property to falter. Ownership changed hands many times, each new deed holder believing they could turn the place around.

The previous owner—an investment group from New York—could never turn a profit, and to come close required them to pay attention only to the most egregious maintenance concerns. During the last few years that the group clung to Tinder Valley, the cabins and the grounds slowly perished as paint peeled, windows cracked but were never re-paired, the dock skewed from sunken posts and missing boards, weeds and grass grew without restraint, and the beach bred a dense carpet of litter. The New York group eventually manipulated bankruptcy laws to free itself from the land. Finally, in a flurry of back-and-forth negotiations, the bank seized the land and the cabins and auctioned them off to the county. A three-year revamping plan was laid out by the county board to restore Tinder Valley to the majestic family-vacation spot it was always meant to be. The current clientele, however, until the revamp could get underway, were fishermen. And they cared little about aesthetics as long as the satellite dish worked and the toilets flushed.

Kent Chapple had long stopped believing a refurbished and rebuilt Tinder Valley could repair his family. He had stopped hoping to someday bring his wife and kids here to fish and kayak, laugh, and play board games, and drink wine with his wife on the cabin's front patio while the sun set across the water. That was an image he'd once held, but it was so far away now that he could no longer conjure it. Instead, he came to the *actual* Tinder Valley—ruined and weed-choked—to find something he could not find at home. He came to fill a void that was vacant and gaping the longer he stayed bound to his failing marriage.

But there was someone else now. Someone he'd allowed himself to think about. It was possible. The idea was not that crazy. He was, he convinced himself, worthy of her. She was new. She had different tastes and different interests and she was unique in her ways. He found himself thinking of her often. Maybe it was time to make that life change he was so desperate for. He felt certain doing so would allow him to focus on his happiness. Perhaps he'd stop making bad decisions. She'd come along at just the right time.

He parked his car outside cabin forty-eight. It was on the

corner of the riverbank, set back from the water and more se-
cluded than the others. It was dark. Only every third or
fourth lamppost was lit. He preferred it dark and quiet.
Standing from his car, he removed his duffel bag from the
backseat along with a container of food and supplies. He
headed for his cabin and felt, as he always did, the weight of
the world leave his shoulders as he approached the front
door. His blood vessels dilated and his skin flushed with
warmth. Could this work out? Could these feelings be a regular part of his life?

He walked up the front stairs and pushed through the
door.

Chapter 38

"It'll be okay," Megan said. "It's a long time coming, and I think this will help both of us."

Livia sat in the passenger seat of Megan's Jeep Wrangler as they drove through Emerson Bay. "How so?"

"People don't really know me. Some people know the girl from before the abduction. Because of the book, lots of people know the girl from the interviews and on the pages. But I'm not really either of those people. My dad, before all this happened, was the only person who totally understood me. We've lost that connection over the last year. I think this will help us."

"I hope so," Livia said.

A few minutes later, they pulled to the front of the Emerson Bay Police Department, where her father had served as sheriff for the past twelve years. Together, Livia and Megan walked up the stairs and into the building. A few people who would normally have protested two women walking unfettered through headquarters waved when they recognized Megan. When they arrived at Terry McDonald's office, he was busy with paperwork.

"Hi, Daddy," Megan said.

Terry looked up with surprise. "Hey. What're you doing here?"

Livia looked over Megan's shoulder and caught the sheriff's eye. She saw a sense of recognition in his expression. He stood slowly.

"Daddy," Megan said. "This is Livia Cutty. She's Nicole Cutty's sister and a medical examiner in Raleigh."

Livia followed Megan into the office. "I'm completing my fellowship."

Sheriff McDonald walked from behind his desk, his belt and holster jostling as he approached his daughter and Livia. "Under Gerald Colt?" he asked.

"Correct."

"I know Dr. Colt. We've worked together on a few cases." He shook Livia's hand. "I'm sorry about your sister," he said with a soft voice, holding her hand.

Unexpectedly moved by the remorse she heard in Sheriff McDonald's voice, Livia swallowed hard. "Thank you."

Terry turned to Megan. "What's going on?"

"Livia and I have been reviewing details about my case, from the night I disappeared and the night I escaped."

"Honey," Terry said in a controlled voice. "We agreed this was a topic best saved for your sessions with Dr. Mattingly."

"It has been, Daddy. But Livia, through her work in Raleigh, found some things we need to talk to you about."

"What things?"

"She's made some connections between my case and two other girls who have gone missing. And, we don't know, maybe others. She came to me with her findings and together we've gained some leverage and made some progress. But we need help, Daddy."

Terry McDonald stared at his daughter and then lifted his gaze to Livia. There was something in his eyes that took Livia a moment to define. But then it clicked. She made the connection to her own father, realizing every father who had lost a daughter to abduction likely carried a similar look of fright and guilt in his eyes. With Terry McDonald, though, there was something else. Something rooted, Livia was sure, in the fact that his daughter had been found, while Nicole and these other girls were lost forever. Had her own father appeared in the doorway, Livia got the sense that Sheriff McDonald would break down and cry.

"Other missing girls?" he finally asked.

Livia nodded. "Possibly, yes."

"You're working with detectives in Raleigh on this?"

"No, sir. Just myself and . . . Megan's been a big help, as well."

Terry McDonald looked at his daughter, then back to Livia. "Let's see what you've come up with."

They sat at the desk and Livia pulled from her bag each of the documents she had collected over the past few weeks. They spent an hour cross-referencing the information that tied Nancy Dee and Paula D'Amato together, and then spent time on the links to Megan's case—the ketamine and the burlap fibers. Finally, Livia presented what she knew about Casey Delevan, who had arrived on her autopsy table at the end of summer. She revealed the profiles of Nancy Dee and Paula D'Amato discovered in Casey's abandoned desk drawer, and told Sheriff McDonald everything she knew about the Capture Club. She revealed her guess that Casey played a role in the disappearance of the girls and was also present the night Megan and Nicole were taken from the beach party.

They covered the leg fracture and that it matched the height of Nicole's car bumper. Livia left out the tuft of Casey's shirt found under Nicole's car, and her theory about the barbecue set with the missing fork and the piercings to Casey's skull. To present everything she had found would be to implicate herself, and Megan, in evidence tampering. If it meant finding the answers she was so desperate for, in the end she would do it. For now, she'd use everything else she had to gauge Sheriff McDonald's willingness to help.

She presented her case for an hour while Terry McDonald listened with patience. When Livia finished her argument, he asked the same question his daughter had.

"But this fella is dead, right?" He pointed to Casey Delevan's picture. "He showed up in your morgue. So what are you looking for, Dr. Cutty?"

"Casey was killed more than a year ago. The last time he was seen was the weekend Megan and Nicole disappeared. Nancy Dee's body was found six months before Megan and Nicole were taken. But Paula D'Amato, who had been missing for more than two years, just turned up in Georgia. Dead for roughly two days, according to the ME down there. If we all agree these cases are connected, then there has to be someone still out there who killed Paula. Someone who was keeping her. Who abused her. I don't have all the answers, Sheriff. Just enough questions to make me suspect something is happening out there that needs to be sorted out. Enough questions so that I can't sleep at night. And enough suspicion to make me think there's someone who's still taking girls—other sisters and daughters."

Terry McDonald was silent as he studied the documents laid out before him. "How did you find out about this club? The one that does the mock abductions?"

"We talked to an old club member. He confirmed that Casey and my sister were members."

"When you say 'we,' who does that include?"

Livia looked at Megan.

"We talked to him together, Daddy."

Terry folded his hands and took a deep breath. "Megan, how long have you been doing this without my knowledge?"

"Daddy, it's fine. It's *good* for me."

He shook his head. "Look, I went over all this nonsense about the Capture Club during the investigation. It never led anywhere. All we ever found was a group of kids who pretended to kidnap each other. They talked about missing people, and got off by chewing on other people's misery. Unfortunately, there's no crime in that. I tried that summer, Dr. Cutty. I tried to find my daughter, and I tried like hell to find your sister. I looked at this club from every angle. And if you want me to open *my* books, I'll show you a hundred other leads we looked at that are much stronger than a bunch of burnouts in a secret club. I'll show you the sex offenders we are still watching. The three convicts paroled two months before Megan and Nicole were taken. One of whom is suspected in an assault outside of Raleigh. I'll show you the interviews with the informants we have inside the jails who tell us about anyone bragging about high-profile crimes."

"But now we've got more to go on," Livia said. "We've got the forensics. We've got science that shows these girls are connected."

"You're talking about getting three different states involved in the same investigation. Reopening old cases and getting everyone on the same page and moving in the same direction. Once we cross state lines, we're talking about involving the FBI. A very tall order. And you say you want *my* help? I won't be able to do a thing once the Feds are called in. Hell, once I get detectives from Georgia and Virginia involved, I'll be pushed to the side. I've been through that process before and I didn't like it."

"Daddy, that's why we're asking for your help. We know you can't do it all by yourself. I know if you ask for help from all those people—the detectives and the federal agents—they'll take things from you like they did before. But it wasn't your fault, Daddy. It wasn't your fault that I was gone for two weeks. It wasn't your fault that no one could find me. Nicole is not your fault. I know that, and Livia knows that. But you *can* help. You *can* make a difference. All Livia wants is some attention put on these cases. On Nancy and Paula. And on Nicole."

Megan ran her hand across the information on the desk. "All of this evidence will generate that attention. And I know it will bring attention to me, too. I'm okay with that. I *want* that. I want to be more than the girl who made it home, Daddy. I want to be the girl who found the man who took her. I want to be the girl who helped *other* girls, Daddy. *Really* helped them. Not in the way we're all pretending my book is helping them."

Terrence Scott McDonald ran his hands through his strawberry blond hair and slowly nodded his head. His eyes darted around the information and photographs on his desk. Finally, he looked at his daughter. "I'll make some calls. See what I can do and who I can convince."

Megan smiled and looked at Livia, grabbed her hand in victory.

"Thank you," Livia said.

Terry nodded. "Don't thank me yet. Let's see where this goes first. This is good work you've done."

Livia nodded a gracious *thank you* and packed her things. She stood and walked with Megan to the door while Terry McDonald remained at his desk.

"Dr. Cutty," he said. "If I could have brought your sister home that summer, I would have. I did everything I could to find her."

"I know you did."

Terry McDonald pursed his lips. "I'll be in touch."

Chapter 39

Megan sat Indian style in Dr. Mattingly's chair, eyes closed, arms resting on the overstuffed wings. In a deep mode of hypnosis, she could barely hear Dr. Mattingly's voice. She was careful not to venture too far on her own. His voice was her lifeline. Her safety net in case things went wrong and she needed to quickly exit this part of her brain where her suppressed memories were buried. But part of her, Megan knew, wanted to be free from the tether of his voice. Part of her wanted the liberation that came from venturing off on her own, without Dr. Mattingly's influence to guide her movements or control her destiny or limit her progress. Megan had grown frustrated during the last session when he so quickly pulled her back to consciousness just as she was ready to discover the thing that bothered her for so long. She could not tolerate being restrained when she was inches from unveiling the mystery buried in her memories. If only she were able to peel back the blanket of suppression that concealed it, that secret was waiting to be discovered. Megan just needed to get there.

For a moment now, in this session, Dr. Mattingly's voice disappeared. Megan felt like an astronaut on a spacewalk, leaving the familiar view that framed the earth to journey to the dark side of the space station. But, not able to advance farther due to the tether that held her, she unclipped herself to drift freely in space. The wrong move now would send her floating away with no way to return to safety. In her hypnotic state, Megan moved freely in the cellar of her captivity, released from the leash of Dr. Mattingly's comforting voice that she had always clung to during these sessions.

She stood from the bed. It squeaked as she rose, the springs expanding without the compression of her weight. She shuffled to the plywood-covered windows, her feet scraping against the concrete floor and her shackles clinking as the chain became redundant upon itself. Every noise, Megan noticed, was amplified now that she was free from Dr. Mattingly's voice—from the bedsprings, to her shuffling steps, to the shackle. She ran a hand over the plywood and listened to her skin skate against the grain of the wood. An airplane soared overhead and she listened to that familiar sound of jet engines high in the sky, having just made the long journey across the Atlantic and now on the descent into Raleigh-Durham.

When the plane was gone, she stayed still and continued to listen, unmoving and expectant. It came after a moment, that long, low whistle. Megan knew now, after hours of research, that it belonged to the freight train that ran through Halifax County. When the whistle was gone, eaten by the midnight darkness of the cellar, she turned from the plywood windows and walked blindly to the only piece of furniture she could reach—the small table near the stairs where he left her meals. She ran a hand over the surface, hearing her unclipped fingernails scratching the wood. She came to associate the food and drink left for her with a deep, groggy sleep that came afterward. The nourishment was where he'd placed the ketamine, Megan had decided. The drug that made her dance above her sleeping body. The preparation that brought hallucination and out-of-body experiences in that dark, lonely cellar. The medicine, which after two weeks of ingesting, she had worried she was coming to depend on.

She shuffled from the table, which was now bare, and made it back to the bed, lying on its thin mattress and hearing again the coiling of the springs under her weight. She lifted her legs onto the bed and heard the chain of her shackle clanking against the bedframe. She closed her eyes, which had little effect in the darkness. All the noises disappeared as she lay still. No planes. No whistles. No walking. She heard her breath leaving her lungs, but nothing more. No shackles, no chains. Dr. Mattingly's voice was nowhere in this place Megan had found. The place of her captivity. It was a new place without Dr. Mattingly. She knew, as she waited on her bed, that it had to be this way. Despite the desire to reach for the familiar voice that could so easily pull her to safety, that could rescue her in an instant, Megan needed this isolation from her therapist. She needed seclusion and loneliness, the way it had been for the two weeks of her captivity. She needed to be vulnerable. She needed to be back in the place where she had been, with no one to help her but herself. She needed to find her dying spirit and revive it. It was, she had determined, the only way to find what she was looking for.

Then, through the subtle sounds of her slow and calm breathing, she heard it. A car engine. Far off at first and then closer. Wheels crunching over gravel. Brakes crying in a small whine as the car came to a stop. The thump of the driver's-side door closing. The footsteps climbing outside stairs. The door opening and closing behind him.

She'd made it this far before only to be pulled back by Dr. Mattingly's voice, betrayed by her rapid heart rate and hyperventilating lungs. Megan had prepared herself for this moment, studying as she sat in the empty filing room of the courthouse the nuances of meditation and the methods used to calm her pulse and slow her heart rate and settle her lungs. She knew, even without hearing Dr. Mattingly's voice, that if her vitals went wild, the good doctor had ways of reaching a patient lost in hypnosis. So, in order to avoid being saved by Dr. Mattingly, Megan put to use all the tools of meditation she had learned during the long, boring hours spent at the courthouse.

Now, despite the fear that overwhelmed her as his footsteps thumped overhead and the cellar door opened and the stairs creaked, Megan worked to keep her heartbeat at a slow and controlled grandfather-clock rhythm, her breathing at a measured in-and-out, and her eyelids at a reasonable state of flutter as she listened to him descend the stairs.

His comings and goings had told her there were thirteen stairs into the cellar, and she listened to every noise, each sound that came and went as he made his way down them, closer and closer and closer.

Ten, eleven, twelve . . . thirteen.

Then he was there. But Megan had arrived as well. Finding after so long what she had been searching for. Uncovering that thing she needed. She let go of all her breathing techniques. Abandoned all the methods she had utilized to keep her heart from racing, and let her eyes run wild under her lids. It had the effect she wanted. She heard Dr. Mattingly's voice, not the calm, collected voice of her psychiatrist, but the hurried and troubled voice of a hypnotist who had lost control of his subject.

"Right now, Megan! I want you to come to my voice!"

But returning was not as simple as in the past. She was stuck in the cellar. Unmoved by the pull of Dr. Mattingly's voice. And her captor was there, in the darkness. Placing her meal on the table. Ready to make his advance upon her after she was properly sedated.

"Come to my voice, Megan!"

Megan shook her head, tried to move her arms as she sat up in the bed of the cellar.

She heard snapping and clapping. "Megan! Come. To. My. Voice!"

Her captor stood in the darkness. A black ghost against a black background.

Her eyes suddenly opened. Dr. Mattingly was kneeling in front of her in his tailored suit. Snapping his fingers and clapping his hands. His forehead was beaded with the same dots of perspiration that covered Megan's flushed face.

"What are you doing?" he asked. "You're supposed to respond to me when I engage you."

But Megan was paying no attention to her doctor. She had a bead on the thing she had so long searched for. That elusive item she knew was there in her memory but until now had been unable to reach. She stood from the plush chair and brushed past Dr. Mattingly.

"Are you all right?" he asked.

Megan ran a hand over her mouth, her eyes wide and wandering the room. She swallowed hard, her saliva rough against her dry throat.

"I've gotta go," she said, heading for the door.

"Megan. We need to discuss this. It's unhealthy to leave a session without vetting what was learned."

But without turning back, she was gone.

She tore out of the hospital's parking lot to a chorus of horns. The startle filled her with a burst of adrenaline, and the screeching tires brought Megan closer to consciousness. She had no memory of fleeing Dr. Mattingly's office. She could not recall if she'd taken the stairs to the lobby or ridden the elevator, and she had no mental picture of climbing into her car until the horns and weaving cars brought her focus back to the present. Her mind fought to retain what she had discovered in her rogue therapy session, but despite her efforts those images were slipping from her memory the more the world swerved around her.

The stimulus of the traffic and the highway suddenly became too much for her hypersensitive mind to tolerate. Without consideration she crossed two lanes of traffic, generating more screeching tires and blasting horns, to swerve onto the ramp that would take her to Points Bridge, across the Roanoke River and into West Bay. Her eyes were frantic and unblinking as she remembered the dark cellar from moments ago and the noises that were there. She fought against it, refused to go back there, while at the same time unwilling to let go of the images and sounds and smells she had discovered.

The battle lasted thirty minutes until Megan found herself in West Bay. As the images and sounds spinning in her head tugged her back to her therapy session, back to the cellar, her car slowly veered to the left and crossed the middle line. An oncoming vehicle squealed its brakes and slid onto the shoulder to avoid the collision. Megan jerked the wheel to her right and momentarily lost control of her car in a wild fishtail. The near miss finally brought her back, the trance passing entirely so that she became wholly aware of her surroundings. She pulled onto the gravel shoulder, setting loose a dust storm as she stepped too firmly on the brake pedal and skidded to a stop.

Taking deep, heavy breaths, Megan looked around and wondered how she'd gotten to West Bay. A sign told her she was outside a subdivision named Stellar Heights. It was nearly four p.m.; her session with Dr. Mattingly had started at two o'clock. Almost two lost hours. Megan pieced together what she remembered after she had untethered herself from Dr. Mattingly's voice and walked unfettered through the cellar of her nightmares. Assembling those memories was more difficult than she imagined, and after ten minutes she began to cry. She thought she'd found a way to locate the thing she was looking for, and she could briefly remember making a breakthrough while on her own in the cellar of her captivity. But now, parked on the shoulder outside a subdivision in West Bay, Megan felt no closer to the truth than she had the day before.

Chapter 40

Livia pulled to the curb of the dilapidated house again and knocked on the screen door. Daisy went berserk, barking and clawing at the front door. She heard scrambling and hollering until the Rottweiler was corralled, then Nate Theros opened the door.

Livia held up the book for him to see, as if presenting ransom money.

"Signed?" Nate asked.

Livia opened the cover of *Missing* to display Megan's signature.

"She even wrote you a note."

Nate pushed through the screen door and took the book. He read the cursive on the first page.

> Nate,
> It was great meeting you the other day.
> I hope you can help Livia with everything she needs.
> —Megan McDonald

"Cool," Nate said, reading and rereading the words.

"So, will you help me?"

Nate closed the book, ran his hand over the cover that depicted the dark woods and the bunker from where Megan had escaped. "Yeah. Let's do it."

Inside Nate's home, Daisy panted and whined as she did circles in her crate, her nails scraping against the plastic lining. The kitchen table stood in the middle of an epic explosion of waste and garbage. The countertops were invisible beneath dirty dishes, old pizza boxes, empty milk cartons, cereal boxes, and dog food. The table where Livia set her folder was sticky, and she got the sense Nate had just recently cleared the space.

There was no apology or embarrassment. Nate, she could tell, felt this was the way most people lived. And if it wasn't, he didn't care—it was the way *he* lived. Take it or leave it. The whole scene confirmed for Livia that Nathaniel Theros was a different breed. She hoped it would pay dividends.

He pulled a chair out from the table, spun it around, and sat on it backward, resting his arms over the spine. A smile came to his face.

"Let's see," he said.

Livia opened her folder, which contained everything she had gathered over the last few weeks about Nancy Dee and Paula D'Amato, and laid the contents in front of him. The detectives who work cases such as these utilize profilers—criminologists who review the details and come up with conclusions about the perpetrator. Livia had no privileges with the detectives on these cases, and no clout with any criminologists. She wasn't even sure she had Terry McDonald's full cooperation. She did, however, have Nate Theros's. Tattooed and creepy, he wasn't the perfect match for the job. But he had an odd fetish for following missing persons cases and studying the demented men who took women. He had a binder full of cases he'd followed through the years, and Livia was sure he possessed a vast knowledge—much greater than her own—about these women and the man she believed took them.

They spent two hours reviewing Nancy Dee's and Paula D'Amato's disappearances, cross-referencing everything Livia had collected about the two girls with everything Nate had stashed in his creepy black binder. Then Livia, to Nate's great pleasure, revealed all she had learned about the girls' crime scenes—the shallow grave in which Nancy was buried, and the would-be grave that had waited to swallow Paula's body but which remained empty, her remains waiting at the edge of the hole. Livia noticed Nate salivating, literally licking his lips and swallowing the excitement that manifested in a hyper-secretion of his salivary glands, as she laid out the crime-scene photos and autopsy shots. She allowed him time to dote over them and study them.

After a while, he ran both hands through his gnarly hair while he thought. Then he leaned forward, pressing his chest against the backward chair and resting his elbows on the table while he pinched the huge loops in his earlobes. Livia, seeing he was in some deep mode of concentration, decided to leave him with his thoughts. She stood and took a chance on the coffee that was brewed and waiting in the coffee-maker. She found what looked like a clean mug in one of the cabinets and poured a cup without Nate noticing she had moved. Nate Theros was gone. The photos, Livia hoped, had transported him into the mind of the man who took these girls. The man who might have taken her sister. The monster who was still out there, plotting, perhaps, to take other girls. Who had possibly buried more, their bodies waiting to be discovered by other joggers and their dogs.

"Here's what I got," Nate finally said.

Livia swallowed a rancid sip of coffee before abandoning the mug in Nate's overflowing sink. She sat at the table opposite him. "Let's hear it."

Nate was still rubbing his hands through his hair as he spoke, as if he had a frail hold on his thoughts. "Okay. With Nancy, you see." He moved a hand from his head to the crime-scene photo depicting Nancy Dee's body. He tapped the photo. "He OD'd her, right? On Special K. But I don't think he meant to. I think it was an accident."

Livia looked at the photo along with Nate. "Why do you think that?"

"Because he never hurt her. See? Nancy was never physically harmed. He took care of her. Loved her. Or wanted to love her. Maybe wanted her to love him back—that's a very common emotion with these guys. They're hungry for affection and can't get it from the real world, so they create their own world in order to find it. Problem is, no one exists in that world so they have to find people, like Nancy and Paula, and make them part of their world. Most of the time, that shit doesn't work. But from his perspective, it should all be fine. They should love being in this new world of his. They should be willing and eager to give themselves to him because he believes he's providing something for them that doesn't exist in the outside world that was so cruel to him. He thinks he's filling the same gap for these girls that he's trying to fill for himself. Problem is, the real world ain't like that for most of us. Our real world and his real world are different experiences. We have love and affection and relationships in our worlds. He does not. So when he takes these girls and transplants them into his make-believe world, they retaliate and fight. And he's shocked by their resistance. He can't understand why they don't love being with him. He can't understand why they don't love him the way he loves them."

"You said 'most of the time' it doesn't work," Livia said.

"Right. Because sometimes . . . it does. Sometimes, usually with people who are held for long periods, they *do* give in to their captors. They *do* develop a bond with them. And sometimes, they *do* end up loving them on some weird, very screwed-up level. My guess here is that's what happened with Nancy Dee. She was only gone for six months, but because he never physically harmed her, I'm guessing she was submitting to him. And to keep her doing the same, he was jacking her up on ketamine. He just messed up one day and gave her too much. OD'd her."

Livia stayed quiet while she restudied the photos of Nancy Dee. Finally, she asked, "What about Paula?"

"Totally different," Nate said, again with his hands running through his hair. "She was gone longer, right? Two years? But she never gave in to him. She was feisty. She wanted out. She never bought into this guy's world. He tried to convert her. Tried to convince her that he loved her and that she should love him, but without the dope and the sedation, she never gave in to him. She fought him, right? That's what the autopsy shows. Clawed at his face. Bruised her hands punching him? Broken toes from kicking him? Older injuries, too, found during the exam. Injuries suffered long ago, and healed by the time she died. A broken bone in her leg and a rib fracture? So he tried hard to break her. To convert her into one of the girls that gave in to him. But she wouldn't budge. She was a fighter. And what did he finally do? Strangled her and beat her to death. Nancy, he OD'd. Paula, he got violent. Two totally different victims. But here's the thing," Nate said, arranging the photos of each of the girls so they sat side by side. "Both had bags over their heads. So he killed them, each in different ways, but for both of them he put a burlap sack over their heads. Why?" Nate looked at Livia. "Why?"

Livia, lost in the narrative Nate was offering, finally looked up and noticed he was staring at her. "I don't know."

"Because he loved them. Because he couldn't stand to look at them after what he did. Had to put bags over their heads so he couldn't see their faces."

Nate went back to the photos and found the one of Paula D'Amato's body stashed in a black vinyl bag and resting at the edge of an empty grave.

"And here? Why didn't he dump her into that hole? Because he got interrupted? Bullshit! This guy is too smart to dump her at a time when someone might stumble onto him. It was because he couldn't do it. He loved this girl. He loved Paula D'Amato so much he kept her for two years before he gave up on her. And when he had to dispose of her remains, he got overwhelmed. He'd done it too many times before, and couldn't bring himself to do it again. This guy is filled with guilt, I'm telling you! He's barely hanging on."

Livia listened to Nate, who was on such a roll that she forgot about the tattoos and the piercings and the too-big earrings. He was a man with a fetish for victims of kidnapping and an obsession with their captors, a man who unknowingly possessed a criminologist's mind that was able to paint a picture of the type of person capable of stealing and stashing and raping and killing and disposing of women.

"He's filled with remorse. It's written all over these pictures," Nate continued. "He's on the edge. And with Megan? We see it again. Guilt. Sorrow. Regret. Why didn't he just kill her? She was doped up, right? Doctors found her high on Special K. He had her high as a kite, not able to defend herself. Why not strangle her like he did Paula? Because he hesitated." Nate pulled over his newly signed copy of *Missing*. "Read this and you'll see. He doped Megan, and moved her to the bunker. Maybe that's where he killed the other two. Maybe there're more girls out there that he brought to this bunker and then killed and buried. Maybe we find them later—weeks, months, whatever. But why didn't he kill Megan? Because he lingered. He took the steps—doped her, bound her, transported her to the woods, and then . . . he wavered. When it came time to kill her, he stopped and thought about it. And in that hesitation, she ran. Feisty girl ran like hell until that guy found her wandering on Highway Fifty-Seven."

Nate took a deep breath, as if the night had exhausted him. "So we got a guy who is lacking affection in the real world. A guy who wants love from the girls he takes because he can't find it elsewhere. A guy who is heartless enough to repeatedly rape the girls he takes, but remorseful when he kills them." He looked up at Livia, took another deep breath. "That help you at all?"

Now Livia ran a hand through her hair. "I'm not sure. But I know a hell of a lot more than I did a couple of hours ago. Your theories will help when I talk with detectives or federal agents."

Livia gathered the photos and reports and stashed them back into her folder.

"Thanks for looking at this stuff and taking so much time on it," she said.

"Yeah. No problem. Thanks for getting me a copy of Megan's book."

Livia nodded and headed for the door.

"Oh, one other thing," Nate said before she left. "Something no one mentioned in any of those reports, but I find odd. Whoever took those girls has access to body bags. Sort of weird that he took the time to stuff them both into vinyl after he killed them."

Chapter 41

Livia was at the desk in her bedroom, moving between the computer and her notes. She was starting a rotation through pediatric pathology the following week and was painfully behind on her readings. The fellows had been given thick binders and textbooks during their orientation week in July that outlined the subspecialties they would be exposed to during their twelve-month forensic fellowship. The first three months, from July through September, constituted their breaking-in period, where they concentrated only on general forensics. But starting in November they would begin integrating their skills in forensics with other subspecialties, which for Livia included pediatric path, neuro-path and derm-path. Preoccupied over the last several weeks with her extracurricular investigation, she hadn't yet touched her reading material. Tonight, however, she used the textbooks as a distraction to get her mind off her most recent, and slightly disturbing, meeting with Nate Theros. By midnight, she was deep into the intricacies of pediatric bone development when there came a knock at her door. She bolted upright in her chair, the bedroom lit only by the desk lamp and the rest of the house cast in shadows. She closed her textbook. Still in jeans and T-shirt, Livia waited until the knocking came again. She clicked on lights as she made her way to the front door, looked through the peephole, and saw Kent Chapple standing on her front patio.

She disengaged the dead bolt and pulled the door open.

"Remember that favor you owe me?" Kent asked through the screen door.

Livia did—from when Kent had let her leave early on the Friday of her ride-along week.

"Yes," she said with a wry smile.

"I need a couch for the night."

"It's that bad, huh?"

"Worse," Kent said. "No way in hell I'm making it until the kids are in college."

Livia took an exaggerated whiff of air through the screen door. "Investigator Chapple, is that whiskey I smell?"

Kent raised a hand, his index finger in the air. "Guilty."

Livia pushed open the screen door. "Come on in."

Kent slid past her and into her living room, where he collapsed onto her couch.

"Want to tell me about it?"

Kent shrugged. "I've tried to explain it to myself a thousand different ways. Make it sound like something other than what it is. Something that might be salvageable. I mean, when you're with someone since high school, it's hard to admit when it's over. It's hard to say that the first person you ever fell in love with is also the first you ever fell *out of* love with."

Livia walked into the kitchen. "Coffee, water, or soda?"

"I'll take a whiskey if you've got it."

Livia opened the refrigerator. "No whiskey, but I think I've got an old . . ." She crouched down to look on the bottom shelf. "Yeah. An old wine cooler."

She reached to retrieve it and when she stood up Kent was right behind her. "Oh God! You scared me."

"Sorry." Kent smiled as he stared at her.

Livia looked at the label. "Strawberry mango. Not exactly whiskey, but it's all the alcohol I have in the house."

Kent took it from her, eyes locked on hers. "Thanks."

Livia turned and closed the refrigerator, grabbing a mug from the cabinet. She filled it with hot water and dropped a tea bag into it.

Kent twisted off the top of the wine cooler and took a sip. "Tell me about this case you're so preoccupied with," he said.

Livia raised her eyebrows. "Am I preoccupied?"

Kent shrugged and sat down. "Had Jen Tilly on ride-alongs this week, and that's what she says. Says you're looking into some missing girls, or something, that you think might be tied together. That's why Colt murdered you in the cage just before ride-alongs."

Livia didn't remember telling Jen much about what she was working on, only that it had to do with her decomp from summer. But Livia knew well the ramblings and gossip that went on in the morgue van and could imagine Sanj and Kent egging Jen on to extrapolate on details.

"Don't know, really," Livia said as she sat down across from Kent at the kitchen table. "I guess you could say I've got as much crap going on in my life as you do in yours. Just different types of crap and different problems."

Kent stuck out his bottom lip and narrowed his eyes. He looked at his strawberry-mango cooler and then offered it to Livia.

She laughed. "Put it this way: If you'd offered me whiskey earlier today, I might've taken you up on it."

"Nah," Kent said, a slight slur to the word, like his tongue was swollen. "Docs can't tie one on like this on a random weeknight. All I gotta do is sit in a van with Sanj tomorrow. If I'm too hungover, he'll take the entire scene for me. We cover for each other like that. You? You gotta perform tomorrow. You gotta be *on*. Right? Can't be cloudy with what you do."

Livia smiled. "I'm going to get you that coffee after all. I think you need it."

"Don't bother," Kent said. "I'm gonna crash, if that's okay with you."

"Couch is all yours."

Livia watched him take another sip of wine cooler.

"Your job is very important, Kent. You shouldn't diminish what you do."

"It's not that. I love my job. It's just that I've got backup if I need it, that's all I'm saying." There was a pause in their conversation. "But that's what I do. I figure out crime scenes. I document what happened when someone dies." He paused again, as if reluctant to go on. "So that's why I'm asking about what you're working on. Maybe I can help."

"I'm not really working on anything. Not officially, and certainly with no supervision from anyone."

"Dr. Cutty's gone rogue?"

"Hardly. It's just something personal I have to look into."

Kent took another sip of strawberry mango. "It have to do with your sister?"

Now Livia squinted her eyes slightly, lifted her chin. Slowly, she nodded. "Yeah."

"Wanna talk about it?"

"I don't know."

Kent laughed. It sounded forced and Livia couldn't tell if it was real or fake. "Hey," he said. "I made you listen to my problems for a whole week in the van. I can at least return the gesture."

Livia lifted the tea bag from her mug and placed it on the table. She took a sip. "Fair enough," she said. "Girls have gone missing from this state and two others in the last three years. I think the same guy took them all, including my sister. If

I widen the search beyond border states, there have been others, too."

Kent stared at her with glassy eyes, mouth-breathing in the labored way of a drunk. Livia wasn't sure he'd remember a thing about their conversation tomorrow, but for thirty minutes she told him what she knew and what she suspected. Kent asked few questions while she talked, just sat and listened.

Finally, he said, "Those are some serious allegations. You talk to the cops?"

"I'm trying. But it's complicated with the girls being from different states. It means getting different police forces together, rival detectives pairing up and sharing information. It's a tall order for someone with no contacts. But I've talked with the sheriff of Emerson Bay. He was involved with my sister's case and sounded like he was willing to help."

"I know some of the homicide guys. We have drinks on the weekend. I could ask them for help."

"Thanks, Kent. I'll let you know what happens with Terry McDonald first."

Exhausted by one a.m., Livia stared at Kent. "Why don't you just tell your wife it's over?"

This brought Kent back from the place he'd been for the last thirty minutes as he listened to Livia recount her findings from the past few weeks.

When he didn't respond, Livia continued. "These last few weeks have taught me a lot. Mostly that keeping things inside and not expressing how we feel doesn't help anyone. Most of the time it ends up hurting the people we're trying to protect. I still haven't told my parents how guilty I feel about ignoring my sister in the months before her disappearance. Or about skipping her phone call that night. They haven't yet mentioned to me that they can hardly exist in the house that is a replica of the place it was before their daughter was taken. Megan McDonald won't tell her parents that the girl she was before she disappeared doesn't exist any longer."

Livia looked at Kent.

"If you don't think things are going to change between you and your wife, just tell her, Kent. Don't tell me. Don't tell Sanj. Tell your wife. We'll be there to listen, don't get me wrong. But tell your wife, Kent."

Livia stood and took the empty wine cooler from in front of him and dropped it in the garbage. "I've got an early morning."

"Yeah," Kent said. "Sorry to barge in like this."

"It's no problem. Thanks for listening to me."

"You too. Oh, one other thing," he said as he shuffled his body in the chair and reached into his front pocket. "I'm taking your advice." He pulled out his cigarette lighter, tossed it to Livia. "Keep that as a souvenir for saving my life. I picked up a stress ball."

Livia stared at the Bic lighter. "Good for you."

Later, after she got Kent settled on the couch with a pillow and blanket, Livia lay awake in bed. It was close to two a.m. She thought she heard the floorboards creak outside her bedroom, then heard Kent's snoring on the couch. Sleep felt far away. Maybe it was the fact that a man hadn't spent the night since she started her fellowship, or maybe it was the intimate pictures of Paula D'Amato and Nancy Dee that rolled through her head. Maybe it was Nate's chilling descriptions and insights from earlier. Whatever the reason, Livia lay in bed that night but never found sleep.

Chapter 42

Megan lay in bed, her window cracked with the chill of midnight whispering over the pane to cool her room. Under the covers her legs twitched as her mind flashed—dark, then bright—with images of the cellar. There were reasons not to venture too far into hypnosis. Her previous sessions, which ended smoothly in Dr. Mattingly's office under his guidance and tutelage, had never gone beyond the lush armchair that was her home while her mind explored the deeply buried memories of her captivity. But since the last session, when she unleashed herself from his voice and journeyed off on her own, her mind had been restless with images from the cellar. Dr. Mattingly had expertly prevented these suppressed memories from surfacing outside the controlled environment of his office and the isolated time frame of a single hypnosis sitting. But now, since Megan's rogue therapy session, every time her mind slipped into the unconscious state of sleep her thoughts and dreams were wild and saturated with the happenings of her captivity—disjointed thoughts and phantasmagorias loosely rooted in the facts she had established with Dr. Mattingly, but also rich with exotic pictures and fictitious characters.

In her current dream, Megan's ankle was still shackled to the wall, but the plywood was gone from the windows and the sunlight bright when she rose from her bed, springs echoing as she stood. Outside, she looked up to see the sky streaked with the jet stream of crisscrossing planes, white scratches against a blue sky. A loud whistle startled her as a freight train raced past the cellar. She felt its vibration as the long freight cars passed in a blur, one after the other, until they transformed into a commuter line—the windows spilling the blue glow of interior lighting.

The sun was gone now in her dream and it was dark but for the passing train and the aqua-lit windows. It sped past her cellar, and in the train's window Megan noticed an isolated figure profiled by the light. Each passenger car displayed the same image of the same person. Megan moved closer to the cellar window and squinted her eyes. The person in the train turned, as if sensing Megan's presence.

In bed, Megan's head and neck moved back and forth as she followed the saccadic motion of the train in her dream. She let out small whimpers as she slept, her mind straining to identify the person on the train. Then, the woman raised a hand in an easy wave and Megan saw clearly the face in the train's window, highlighted in the soft light. It was Livia Cutty.

"Don't go!" Megan cried.

But the train continued until there were no more cars. Until the night was black and quiet, with no planes and no stars and no moon. When Megan put her hand to the cellar window, the plywood was back.

"Don't leave me!"

She heard a voice and Megan shot her eyes open.

"Honey!" her father was saying as he woke her, shaking her shoulders. "Megan, wake up. It's just a dream."

Megan finally woke. She stared at her father, disoriented.

"It's okay, honey. I'm here. Daddy's here."

He held her close as she breathed heavily.

"This is why I didn't want you to start this again. This is what I wanted to save you from."

Megan wrapped her arms around her father, rested her head on his shoulder, and cried as the image of the blurry train passing the cellar window pulsed in her mind. Livia Cutty's easy wave as the final car passed. The feeling, again, of being alone in the dark cellar. And something else, too, that dug at the inner reaches of her brain, something difficult to identify as her mind fought fact from fiction. But eventually, as her mind settled and the images of her dream faded, one thing remained. A sound. It had not been present in her dream, but without doubt this noise was the missing element she'd worked so long to identify. It had been there in her last therapy session. She'd heard it just briefly before Dr. Mattingly forced consciousness upon her. And now, a week later, it finally manifested. It was no longer dancing and elusive in the foggy memories of her subconscious but, instead, clear and vibrant and ringing in her ears.

PART VI

"I know who took me."
—Megan McDonald

Chapter 43

November 2017
Fourteen Months Since Megan's Escape

After two weeks of no returned calls, Livia took her second personal day of her fellowship and headed to Emerson Bay. She parked in the lot of the Montgomery County Federal Building and entered the sheriff's office. At the front desk, she asked to see Terry McDonald. No, she had no appointment. Livia wasn't even sure he was in, but she was willing to wait, all day if necessary.

After a few minutes the secretary ushered her into the office where Terry McDonald sat behind his desk.

"Please," he said to Livia. "Sit down."

"Thanks for seeing me," Livia said.

"I was meaning to call you, just haven't had time."

"Is Megan okay, incidentally? I haven't been able to reach her for a couple of weeks."

"I'm glad you're here," Terry said. "Megan is another reason I was intending to talk to you. Since this little adventure you two have embarked upon—and I don't diminish it, that's not what I'm saying—but since Megan started looking into things on her own, her psychiatrist has told me some troubling things about her progress. She appears to have relapsed. Nightmares. Regression in memory during her therapy sessions. Withdrawal. Depression. All the symptoms she showed immediately after her ordeal."

"When did this start?" Livia asked. "I mean, I'm sorry that she's going through this, but the last time we talked she was doing well and was eager to help. I've had long conversations with your daughter, sir, about what she wants and what she still needs for closure."

"Dr. Cutty, I appreciate the forensic expertise you bring to Megan's case, and your sister's, but you are no psychiatrist. Am I correct?"

"Of course I'm not."

"Then please, I beg you, leave Megan out of this thing you are doing. I understand your need for answers, and your family's need. But you don't know my daughter. You don't know the hell she went through, and the long journey it's been for her to get back to some sense of normalcy. I will support you in any way my office or influence will allow. But please, leave my daughter out of it. She's come so far under Dr. Mattingly's tutelage, I won't allow that effort to be wasted. She was, until just recently, a different person than when she returned from her ordeal. She was, her mother and I were noticing, returning to the girl we remember. I want that girl back, Dr. Cutty. And seeing her with you, and the backward leaps she's taken in the last couple of weeks, convinces me that you're hurting her progress."

Livia stared at Terry McDonald, unsure how to respond. Livia knew things about his daughter that he did not. But Megan had been unavailable for days and had returned none of Livia's calls. Indeed, regression was possible but Livia wondered what suddenly brought it on.

"I'm sorry," Livia said, "if I've caused any problems. That was not my intent."

"Of course not. I'm simply making you aware of the situation. It's not healthy for Megan to pursue this. I will help you, like I said. In any way I can. As long as you keep Megan out of it. Can we agree on that?"

Livia slowly nodded. "Yes."

"All right," Sheriff McDonald said, shifting his focus and pulling open his bottom drawer to reveal a file folder. "I made some calls. Talked with detectives in Virginia and Georgia, as well as the guys here who ran Megan's and Nicole's cases. Brought them up to speed on your findings and suspicions. They're going to take a step back and look at it all. Don't expect immediate results, that's not how these guys work. But they were interested. Very interested." Terry nodded his head. "Despite my reservations about your judgment involving Megan, this is really good work, Dr. Cutty."

"I've got more," Livia said. Over the last few nights, she had documented and expanded on everything she learned from Nate Theros about the potential traits of the man responsible for Nancy Dee's and Paula D'Amato's deaths, as well as Megan's kidnapping and the botched transfer the night she escaped from the bunker. Nate's theories, organized by Livia's meticulous scientific mind, filled three pages. She pushed her work across the desk until it rested in front of the sheriff.

Terry McDonald took several minutes to read the report. "These are your conclusions?"

"No, sir," Livia said. "I had some help."

"From a criminologist?"

Livia shook her head. "Not exactly, but someone with an . . . odd hobby. He prefers to remain anonymous."

"Can I keep this?" Terry asked.

"Of course."

"I'll show it to our guys. Compare it against what they came up with." Terry placed the profile into his folder and returned it to the bottom drawer.

"So things are rolling now," he said. "I've made the calls, and we'll see what comes next. It will take these detectives time to clear their dockets in order to justify putting hours into a cold case. I'm going to do what I can on my own while we're waiting, and I'll keep you posted on any news."

"Is there a way for me to reach Megan? She hasn't been returning my calls."

"With respect, Dr. Cutty, I'd prefer you leave Megan alone for the time being."

Livia nodded. "Fair enough. Will you tell her I'm thinking about her?"

"I'll let her know."

Livia stood. "Thanks again for what you're doing. I know it's hard on you and your family."

"As well as yours, Dr. Cutty. I'll be in touch."

Chapter 44

August 2016
The Night of the Abduction

Nicole Cutty pulled her car into the parking lot of Emerald Cove, where the beach party was happening, an end-of-summer tradition for Emerson Bay kids. It was seven p.m. and the sun was at a steep slant across the water as Nicole and her friends primped in the parking lot, Jessica and Rachel fighting over the passenger-side visor mirror while Nicole smacked her lips in the rearview after applying a final coat of lipstick.

They stashed their makeup into small purses.

"No drama tonight," Jessica said.

"You sound like my sister," Nicole said. She had made a call to Livia after the incident on Matt's boat. Wanting to disappear, she'd asked Livia if she could come to Miami for a week. Of course, Livia was too busy with residency to consider it. Nicole had wanted to run to Livia and tell her about all the things that were swirling in her brain. She wanted, for just one week, to be a little sister and garner the attention she once had from Livia.

"*Just stay away from him,*" *Rachel said.* "*He's an ass anyway.*"

Nicole didn't answer. She'd been withdrawn, Jessica and Rachel noticed, since the incident between her and Matt the other day. Nicole refused to tell them what had transpired on Matt's boat, but it was assumed that he had broken things off for good now that he was with Megan. Jessica and Rachel knew their role tonight would be as peacekeepers. They'd work hard to keep Nicole away from both Megan and Matt.

The three walked through the parking lot and onto the beach, where a large bonfire was fighting off the first advances of dusk. Fifty other kids gathered in packs around the fire. A volleyball game was in full swing and a few boys threw a football down by the water. They waited for the sun to set and for darkness to cover the beach before they snuck beer and liquor from their hiding spots.

Jessica and Rachel merged with a group of girls by the fire. Nicole broke away and wandered down by the water. She pulled her phone from the back pocket of her jeans and checked again. Casey hadn't returned her text.

There was a loud holler from a group of boys by the fire and Nicole looked back. In the glow of the flames she saw that Matt had arrived, greeted by his friends. Holding his hand was Megan.

Nicole looked back at her phone and sent Casey another text.

Chapter 45

November 2017
Fourteen Months Since Megan's Escape

After handing Nate's profile off to Sheriff McDonald, Livia busied herself with work, escaping the anxiety of waiting for answers by delving into the bodies that came to her morgue. She no longer, as she admitted she had once done, looked at those bodies as a way to advance her career or as an opportunity to showcase her skills and outperform her colleagues. The last three months had taught her that each life deserved the proper respect of discovering the answers it left behind. For Dr. Livia Cutty, the only way she could find those answers was by examining the bodies that came to her. Respectfully and honorably, without ulterior motives of career advancement or personal gain but, instead, with a singular goal of providing information to the family about the cause of their loved one's demise. If she did that honestly, and to the best of her ability, the collateral rewards would come.

It took the last several weeks to plant the seed of this epiphany. And the last few days, after she handed over all her hard work and research to the authorities and entrusted them to find the answers she had come so close to discovering on her own, had reminded her that others were waiting just like she. Others were hoping for answers, and they had placed their trust in young Livia Cutty to provide closure. Livia would do her best to serve those people, and not herself. Perhaps it was a metamorphosis all medical examiners experience. Or maybe this insight was the elusive thing Dr. Colt hinted would come sometime during her training. Whatever it was, Livia was a different person today than she had been when she arrived at the Office of the Chief Medical Examiner back in July.

She prepared to bury herself in the riddles that rested on her autopsy table for as long as it took the authorities to examine her preliminary findings and turn them into something more substantial. This long haul was what she readied for. But as she paged through a textbook at ten p.m., a phone call changed her plans. She was surprised to hear Megan's voice.

"I need to see you," Megan said.

"Are you okay?"

"No."

"Sorry I haven't called. Your dad said I should give you some space."

"I don't care about any of that. I need to see you tonight."

"Tonight? What's wrong?"

"I know," Megan said. "I finally know."

Megan forced herself to lie still under the covers after she ended her call with Livia. Her mother was back on the prowl of late, since the nightmares started again, and had reacquired the annoying habit of peeking her head into Megan's bedroom to check on her. Stirring in bed would draw her mother's attention. Something tonight, more than any other, Megan needed to avoid. It would take two hours for Livia to make the drive from Raleigh, but Megan knew she couldn't stay still for long. It would be impossible to tolerate the throbbing in her carotid artery for much longer.

It had come to her. She had solved the last year of her life. The tumultuous fourteen months that had unfolded since the moment she saw Mr. Steinman's headlights on Highway 57 and sat in his car. More than a year of mystery had stretched along the road of her life since then, and now she finally had things straight. With her revelation, though, came an irrational fear that the secrets she had discovered buried in her mind would be broadcast to the world. That if she spent one more day attempting to tie up the details, her discovery would spill for the world to see and it would be too late. She thought of the girls Livia had discovered—Nancy and Paula—and the others who might still be out there. A nauseous ache turned her stomach. She couldn't risk waiting. It had to be tonight.

Forty-five minutes passed before the pulsing in her neck grew too great to bear. She considered briefly that her catharsis might be causing a panic attack. But Megan knew the throbbing vessels and beading perspiration were her sympathetic nervous system telling her to move. Her mind was preparing her body for fight or flight, and there was no one in her house to fight. So she ran.

Megan stuck three pillows under her covers for anyone who might check on her tonight, snaked into a pair of jeans, and dropped her phone into her pocket. She was careful when she slipped out the back door, took the stairs with silent steps, glided across the back lawn and into the night. Solving the mystery of her life had not answered all her questions. Why this had happened to her she couldn't quite figure. But her dream the other night, when she saw Livia in the window of the commuter train as it blurred past the cellar window, told her that no one else could help tonight. She needed Livia.

Megan made it to the intersection with more than forty minutes to spare before Livia would arrive. She stood in the shadows and tried to breathe. Tried to push from her mind the thought that with each minute that passed, the monster would learn of her discovery.

Chapter 46

She endured three hours of tedium while she waited. She stalked with people she had no interest in, and laughed at stupid high school humor she'd long grown bored of. She watched Matt deliberately ignore her, and listened to Megan giggle in her fake voice whenever Matt uttered a word. On a normal night, it would have been too much to handle. But tonight was anything but normal. Tonight was special. Epic, even.

She stood with Rachel and Jessica around the bonfire and pretended to drink beer. Pretended to be interested in them. Pretended to care which college everyone was off to in the fall. Her phone vibrated in her pocket and she quickly grabbed it.

Finally, Casey was ready.

Chapter 47

November 2017
Fourteen Months Since Megan's Escape

It was approaching midnight when Livia pulled to the intersection and saw Megan standing in the shadows of a building. The streetlight painted her face when she walked from the alcove, and even from such a distance Livia recognized the difference. When Megan climbed into the passenger seat, the dim glow of the car's dome light confirmed the startling transformation. More than two weeks had passed since they were last together, when Megan had squeezed Livia's hand in her father's office after he agreed to help them. Back then, Megan's eyes were filled with hope and elation. Now, Livia noticed vacant and wandering eyes, heavy with burden.

"What's wrong?" Livia asked.

Megan shook her head. "I know where he kept me. I figured it out."

Livia took a moment to decipher Megan's words. "The bunker?"

"Before that. I know where he kept me during those two weeks. The cellar. I need to go there, Livia. I need you to take me."

Parked on the side of a deserted road, dark and quiet in the middle of the night, Livia understood something cathartic was happening. She realized suddenly this girl's frailty, and she felt the heavy responsibility of Megan's well-being on her shoulders.

"Maybe we should talk to your dad, Megan. He told me you were having trouble with all this."

"No. Only you."

From her short stint through psych rotations during her internship year, Livia was familiar with different states of psychosis. She was certain Megan was in one now. "Maybe we should call Dr. Mattingly. Let him know about this."

Megan shook her head in the darkened car, then turned and looked at Livia. "Please, Livia. Take me there. Help me."

Livia stared at Megan, and in that moment another metamorphosis took place. Megan was no longer the girl who went to school with Nicole. She was no longer the other girl who had been taken that night. Megan was, in that moment, a friend who needed help. "Okay." Livia put the car into gear. "Where are we going?"

"West Bay." Megan shook her head in disbelief. "It's not far. Not far at all."

Chapter 48

Casey drove a rusted-out Buick Regal he kept covered and stowed in a storage unit in West Bay. He drove this car when he took the girls. The last time he put miles on it was when he journeyed to Virginia the previous year to steal Nancy Dee. Now tonight, nearly a year later, it came from storage once again. His insides exploded with fear and excitement.

Tonight was as exposed as he'd ever been, planning a take in Emerson Bay. But he was sure, with the ease of the others as reference, that he could pull it off. It was the perfect way to lure Nicole into his world. The perfect way to introduce her to the thrill. Their pasts were too similar for her to be without the same needs as he. So when Nicole came up with the idea to scare one of her classmates by enlisting Casey to take her and dump her in the shed behind Coleman's, he immediately understood the opportunity. He scratched his original plan to take the girl who worked at the high school three times a week—the girl named Stacey Morgan—who so perfectly fit the description of the latest request. He abandoned that original plan because even more perfect was the oppor-

tunity to bring Nicole to his dark and wondrous world. It was a world in which she would thrive, and he needed her there. He had unexpectedly fallen under her spell this summer. She was his perfect match, his exquisite accomplice.

He'd take Nicole's classmate where he'd taken the others. Deliver her to the cellar under heavy sedation, the same way he'd delivered the others. He'd show Nicole his methods tonight. He'd show her his work and watch the reaction in her face and in her eyes and in the black pond that also made up her soul, so similar to his. Watch her transformation. And then, sometime in the future, when another request came, he would not be alone in his dark world but accompanied by the only person who understood him.

He pulled now into the parking lot. He wore the clothes Nicole had purchased from the Goodwill store, receipt-less clothing and shoes that would leave untraceable fibers and prints. He heard music coming from the beach, and voices from the group of people gathered around the bonfire. He parked across from the Jeep Wrangler, his headlights bright against the spare tire on the back. He turned off the lights and waited. His heart was going at a good clip and he found he was more excited than normal. It took fifteen minutes before Nicole's text came. Casey pulled the burlap sack from the seat next to him, and grabbed the plastic zip ties. He scanned the parking lot to make sure he was alone. There was a pair of Porta-Potties off to the corner, which had been vacant for the past five minutes after three girls left them.

From the beach entrance, Casey watched the girl walk into the parking lot. She headed to the Jeep Wrangler and opened the driver's-side door. With the burlap sack and zip ties in hand, Casey started the engine, his headlights washing Megan McDonald and her Jeep in a blinding white glow. She shielded her eyes from the high beams and never saw him coming until the headlights disappeared as the burlap covered her head.

Chapter 49

November 2017
Fourteen Months Since Megan's Escape

It took half an hour to drive into West Bay. Megan gave directions from memory and Livia got the impression that while she busied herself this past week in the morgue, Megan, too, had been hard at work. The last few days had yielded a great discovery, and Megan was willing to share it with no one but Livia.

"Here," Megan said, leaning forward in her seat to gauge her location. "Pull over here."

Livia did so, pulling to the shoulder outside an undeveloped subdivision. Two red-brick posts stood next to each other, a long slab of pine hanging between them. Engraved in the wood and brightened by the lone remaining spotlight from three originals was the name of the subdivision: STELLAR HEIGHTS.

Livia pulled to the shoulder in the same spot Megan had skidded her car to a stop the other day when she fled Dr. Mattingly's office. She listened to Megan tell the history of this abandoned development.

"Erected during the housing bubble," Megan said, "Stellar

Heights was meant to be the western expansion of East Bay. Big homes, wraparound porches, long half-circle driveways. So in came the bulldozers and pavers and back fillers. Up went this giant berm."

Livia squinted through the windshield at the tall berm, covered by neglected trees and bearded with heavy weed growth that ran as far as her eyesight allowed. It encircled the Stellar Heights neighborhood.

"Up went the gates," Megan continued. "Tall, black, cast-iron gates that would keep out the unwanted West Bay residents until they moved along, pushed out by wealthy expansion. In came the winding road meant to meander through the beautiful neighborhood. Seventy-nine custom homes were meant to fill this subdivision. Seventy-nine magnificent structures, each five thousand square feet. The builder managed to erect six before the housing bubble burst. No one was buying giant homes anymore. The credit crunch pinched all the people buying homes with the bank's money. And when the banks stopped lending, the builder ran out of capital. So Stellar Heights, hidden from the world by the giant berm, was forgotten by all and sat abandoned for the last several years. Until a county ordinance a few months ago came through demanding the destruction of the six abandoned homes and the ghost town they sat in."

Livia watched as Megan opened the passenger-side door and walked past the Stellar Heights sign and to the tall, black gate. Highlighted by the car's headlights, Megan looked like a ghost floating toward the haunted town. She pushed the gates, which yawned open from the middle. The effect was dramatic and eerie, as if something sinister had just been released from within. Beyond the gates, through the mouth of the berm, blackness waited.

Megan sat back in the passenger seat and closed the door. "Let's go," she said. "I need to know for sure."

"Megan," Livia said. "Maybe we should call someone.

Your dad, or someone to meet us here. If you think this is the place you were kept."

"I don't *think*. I know."

Megan pointed forward, into the darkness of the abandoned subdivision. Livia thought of calling Kent Chapple to meet them out here. She knew he'd come in an instant if Livia asked. She thought of calling 911, but her mind stalled on what, exactly, she'd say was the emergency.

After a moment, she released the break and they slowly drifted past the gates and into Stellar Heights.

Chapter 50

August 2016
The Night of the Abduction

Nicole followed Casey as he drove from the beach parking lot. An odd thrill filled her chest from what she'd just witnessed. She knew Megan McDonald, at this moment, was terrified. And it served her right. Everything in her life had been handed to her. There had never been anything to challenge her or derail the perfect cadence of her life from grade-school star to high school princess and soon to college genius and medical-school scholar and eventually a physician who saved the world. No one should get everything they want in life.

So badly Nicole longed to be in Casey's car, listening to Megan cry and plead. But they both agreed it was too risky. Surely, Megan would identify Nicole, even with the burlap over her head. Should Nicole talk or laugh, as she was certain to do, the ruse would be over. It was a better option to follow Casey to the old brewhouse where the club's meetings had taken place. There, Nicole could watch from afar and muffle her laughs as Casey dumped her in the shed and slid the heavy latch down across the door. The same shed the club had used for Nicole's initiation weeks before.

When they finally let Megan go, it would take the princess an hour to find her way out of the Cove, and though Nicole would never have the satisfaction of telling Megan she had been the one who organized the prank, she would certainly enjoy the aftermath. Matt could comfort her all the way to Duke.

"Where the hell are you going?" Nicole said to herself when Casey turned left at Junction Avenue and headed to the other end of West Bay. The old Coleman's Brewery building was in the other direction.

She picked up her phone and called him. He didn't answer.

Chapter 51

November 2017
Fourteen Months Since Megan's Escape

Away from the streetlights of the surrounding road, the interior of Stellar Heights was an inky dark barely penetrated by the car's headlights. As Livia slowly drove the long, winding road that meandered into the heart of the abandoned subdivision, the vehicle's lights illuminated empty construction sites on either side of the smooth pavement. Gravel and boulders and large excavated holes meant to be the foundation for never-constructed homes came and went under the glow of Livia's high beams. With each passing minute she drove into darkness, Livia felt the outside world beyond the berm drift farther and farther away.

She was ready to abandon the journey, to drive Megan home and present this lost girl to her parents and ask for help. Even admit her mistake for bringing such a fragile girl into this search for answers. But as Livia lifted her foot to apply the brake, the far anterior reach of the headlights fell upon a home—a single home at the end of the tortuous road they had followed for the past few minutes. And then, under the scant moonlight, five other structures came to life. Each building sitting on two acres of undeveloped land, this string of six homes and twelve acres made up the whole of Stellar Heights.

Livia stopped the car and surveyed the house captured in the glow of her headlights. It could have been, Livia surmised, a magnificent home had construction continued. Red, vibrant brick made up the exterior of the two-story building. Above the beautifully trellised entryway was the framed glass that overlooked the foyer, reflecting back the lights of Livia's car. She could imagine the warm light of a chandelier glowing from within. Across the entryway where a beautifully stained pine door should stand was, instead, heavy construction plastic, gray and dusty and frayed at the edges.

Megan stepped out of the car and pulled a flashlight from her bag. Livia followed Megan to the front of the car and watched as she played the industrial-style flashlight over the big house, then turned and pointed the light at the neighboring home and ran its powerful beam over the brick. Megan turned in a circle, head tilted back, and looked up into the night sky. Livia knew enough not to interfere. Megan was on her own journey, and Livia was along only for support.

It was a few minutes before Megan spoke.

"There!" she said, pointing to the sky.

Livia looked up to see, high overhead, the lights of a jetliner blinking against the black canvas sky. Megan closed her eyes and listened, nodding her head. She looked back to the sky and watched the plane until it was gone from sight and out of earshot. Then she sat down on the hood of the car and closed her eyes. After twenty minutes, Livia grew anxious, standing in the dark, abandoned subdivision.

She was gathering the courage to ask some questions when Megan's eyes shot open, a faint smile finding her face. She began nodding. "Do you hear it?"

Livia listened to the dead night. "Hear what?"

"Wait. It will come again."

And it did. Faintly in the far distance, Livia heard a train's whistle.

Megan looked at Livia, locked her eyes with a triumphant stare. "This is where he kept me. In one of these abandoned homes."

"How do you know, Megan?"

"I've searched for months during my lunch hour. Searched for the right distance from the airport. The right flight pattern of the planes. The correct height of their approach. The volume of their engines. And I searched for that whistle. It belongs to a freight train that runs through Halifax County. I know, the best I can remember through the haze of my sedation, that it took about an hour that night to transport me from the cellar to the bunker. With these clues, I visited location after location, but none of them quite fit. Stellar Heights, though . . . it's the place that brings all those clues together."

Again Megan ran the flashlight around the homes, a point source of light in an otherwise black abyss.

"I'm sure, Livia. This is the place."

Chapter 52

August 2016
The Night of the Abduction

Casey watched the headlights in his rearview mirror, making sure Nicole was behind him. He'd ignored the chime of his phone. He was sure Nicole was calling to inquire why they weren't headed to Coleman's. The phone's ringtone— "Sweet Home Alabama"—was a melodious contrast to the crying and pleading from the girl in the backseat, bound and hooded, who went on in hysterics about her father. Casey turned the radio louder.

When he reached their destination, he jumped out and pushed open the cast-iron gates. Nicole yelled something through her open window but Casey did not acknowledge her. Instead, he climbed back into the Buick and turned into the darkness, following the winding road for several minutes. Finally, bathed in blackness and isolation, he stopped the car and shifted into park. Nicole stopped behind him. The girl's cries had begun to die down, the sedative finally taking effect. He quickly slammed his door and walked to Nicole's car.

"Where are we? This is creepy."

"Trust me," Casey said, sitting in the passenger seat of Nicole's car. "What I have planned is better than the shed at Coleman's."

Nicole looked around at the abandoned homes with no lights. "Think she'll be able to find her way out of here? I mean, where the hell are we, anyway?"

Casey ignored the question. He needed to give the ketamine a little longer. He turned the radio's volume louder.

"What did you think of my technique?"

"I think you're sadistic," Nicole said. "Is she freaking out?"

He didn't want to talk about the girl, so he slid a hand onto Nicole's thigh. "So it turned you on?"

"Sort of," she said. "When do we screw with her?"

Casey looked at his watch. "Twenty minutes."

He leaned over and bit Nicole's earlobe. They frolicked in the car, unaware of the sedan parked down the way, lights extinguished with the driver watching from the darkness. The man grew impatient as his body burned with anticipation. His delivery had arrived. A new girl. One he planned to love and care for more than any other. But his thrill of this night was overshadowed by the pulsing vessel in his neck.

The Buick Regal was not alone. A second car had trespassed into his secret world of Stellar Heights.

Chapter 53

November 2017
Fourteen Months Since Megan's Escape

Livia stared at Megan. The car's headlights were hitting them at thigh-level and gnats floated in their beam.

"Megan, tell me what you've learned."

"I know you think my kidnapping is related to Nancy Dee and Paula D'Amato," Megan said. "I know you've tried to find ways to link them and find all the similarities between us. And there are, Livia. So many things are the same. But only when you pointed out those similarities did I notice the differences. The startling ways our cases are unalike."

"I don't understand," Livia said. "What are you talking about, Megan?"

"The book," Megan gave a disgusted laugh. "It's such bullshit. My celebrity? Fake. Based on a lie. All the girls the book has helped? Nonsense. I used to help girls, back when I ran that retreat. I helped girls fit into high school. That was real. This? Everything I have now from that book, none of it helps anyone. It's all a lie."

"What's a lie, Megan? What lie are you talking about?"

"Nancy and Paula were both abused. Sexually assaulted, for months and years. It sickens me. Paula was beaten until she died."

"I know, Megan. It's awful."

"Yes. But why was I never touched?"

Livia squinted in the darkness.

"He never assaulted me, Livia. Never physically touched me. Dr. Mattingly initially believed I suppressed the abuse, hid it under the effects of the ketamine. But that's not it, Livia. The physicians who examined me confirmed there was no sexual abuse. No sexual intercourse. Dr. Mattingly speculated that I repressed the memory of other sexual abuse, and he has worked carefully with me during therapy sessions to tease these buried memories from me. The problem is, they don't exist. He never assaulted me, Livia. So much is similar between Nancy and Paula and me. But so much is different."

"I believe you, Megan. He never assaulted you. I believe that. But you never claimed he assaulted you. Not in your book or your interviews. That was never part of your story. You don't have to defend this point with me or anyone else. There was no lie, Megan. You didn't lie."

"Yes, I did. Not about the abuse. But it helps explain everything else. It makes everything else line up. It exposes my lie for what it is—a goddamn farce that's taken on a life of its own. For a while, even I believed it."

Livia walked closer. "Tell me. What lie, Megan?"

"About the bunker."

Livia waited as Megan continued to play the flashlight over the ghost houses around them. Clearly, her mind was confused and overloaded, processing too many things at once.

"No, Megan. You *were* at that bunker. There's proof of your being there."

"I *was* there. He brought me there. But I never escaped."

Livia watched Megan. Tried to read her eyes through the darkness and diagnose if this poor young girl had gone mad from the recent events and the possibility of her abduction being tied to Nancy Dee and Paula D'Amato, two girls who had turned up dead.

"Of course you escaped, Megan. You are here now. You're safe. There is no lie."

"No," Megan said, finally taking her eyes off the houses and staring at Livia. "You don't understand. I am here. I am alive. Nancy and Paula are not. But I'm alive not because I *escaped* from that bunker. It's because he let me go."

Chapter 54

August 2016
The Night of the Abduction

The headlights of Nicole's car shined into the backseat of the Buick Regal. The girl had settled down now. She no longer kicked at the door or pounded her shoulder into the window. Casey was certain she was lying on the backseat, sleeping in a coma-like slumber. He'd seen it before.

"Come on," he said. "It's time."

He climbed from Nicole's car and opened the back door of the Regal. The girl was indeed unconscious, lying like a drunk in the backseat, burlap over her head and zip ties securing her wrists behind her back, one leg splayed across the torn vinyl seat and the other limp on the floorboard.

"What's wrong with her?" Nicole asked. She and Casey were bleached by the headlights from Nicole's car, which also highlighted Megan's unconscious body.

"Just taking a little nap."

Nicole hesitated. "You give her something?"

"She'll be good as new in about an hour."

Casey reached in and pulled Megan—floppy-armed and

bobbleheaded—out of the car and over his shoulder. He clicked on a flashlight and headed toward one of the houses.

"What are we doing with her?" Nicole asked.

Casey didn't answer, just walked ahead. After a moment of hesitation, Nicole followed.

Away from the headlights it was pitch-black. Casey shined his flashlight onto the house numbers above the front door. 67. He'd delivered Nancy Dee, a year before, to the house next to this one. And a year before that, he'd brought the Georgia Tech girl named Paula D'Amato to the house two doors down. He'd never had the courage to revisit those homes to see what remained. He knew the Dee girl was gone. But the others . . . he never gathered the nerve to check.

He walked through the front door with the unconscious girl over his shoulder and Nicole following.

"What are these empty houses doing here?" Nicole asked.

Casey kept moving. Toward the cellar door, which he kicked open with his foot and then started down.

"Casey, stop! This is screwed up."

But he was gone a moment later. Swallowed by the dark stairwell.

Chapter 55

November 2017
Fourteen Months Since Megan's Escape

Megan took off, heading with her flashlight to one of the empty homes. Livia followed. Toward the dark house up the road from where Livia had parked, adjacent to the home bathed by the car's headlights.

"You ran from that bunker," Livia said. "The police know you were there. Your prints were found on the door handle. The burlap bag he placed over your head was found in that bunker. Your hair follicles were in the bag. That was a real thing, Megan. You did escape that night. You ran through the woods until Mr. Steinman found you on Highway Fifty-Seven."

Megan, a few paces in front of Livia, spoke over her shoulder. "Yes. The bunker was real. It was all real. The forest, the highway. Mr. Steinman, too. But not the escape. The media created that. Dante Campbell and all the others, they wanted the sensationalism. The whole country took that myth and ran with it. I did, too. Embellishing the details in my book until I believed the story myself. But it's not true."

She continued walking toward the house, the beam of her flashlight widening on the brick exterior. Megan jogged to the back of the house and shined the light onto the English windows of the basement. The light shined straight through the windows and into the empty basement. No plywood. She redirected the light to the next house, across two acres of construction and clay and rubble. She ran for it.

Livia worked to keep up, stumbling over the rubble as she finally came alongside Megan. "Tell me about the bunker, Megan. What's not true with your story?"

"I *didn't* escape. He left that bunker door open. He did it so I would run."

"Why? Megan, why would he do that?"

"Because there was no other way."

"Slow down and help me understand."

Megan made it to the rear of the next house and shined her flashlight onto the English windows at the base of the foundation. The light stopped at the yellow-brown plywood that covered the windows. Livia saw the boarded windows and remembered immediately the section in *Missing* that described such a thing. An eerie feeling came over her.

"This is it," Megan said, bewilderment in her voice. "I found it." She looked at Livia, locked eyes with her. "I know who took me, Livia. And this is where he kept me."

Chapter 56

August 2016
The Night of the Abduction

Casey's flashlight illuminated the bed in the corner, and he laid the girl onto the mattress. A chain slithered along the bare concrete, one end attached to the wall and the other to a thick leather cuff he fastened to her ankle. He pulled a knife from his pocket and snapped loose the zip ties that bound her wrists. She lay on her side, a deep, wheezing breath heavy with sedation expanding her chest every few seconds.

By the time he turned, Nicole had made it to the bottom of the stairs, staring at him in the darkness.

"Before you say anything," he said, "I have to show you something. Promise, then we'll talk. We just don't have lots of time."

She was shaking her head. "This is too sick. She's gonna freak out down here." Nicole looked at the boarded-up windows that were scantly visible in the residual glow of Casey's flashlight.

Casey grabbed her hand, kissed her deeply. He was intoxicated with the process, the take that was again so easy and

*fluid. It filled him with energy he could find nowhere else.
"Come with me."*

"Where?"

*"To my world. I promise you'll love it there. You're the
only one who would."*

He pulled Nicole up the stairs and through the house and
into the hot summer night, leaving Megan McDonald alone
and unconscious in the cellar that would haunt her dreams.
He pulled her as they ran, the flashlight bouncing through
the night. Holding hands, fingers interlaced, they hurried
past the house where he had deposited the Dee girl the previous year. He knew it would be empty. The next house came.
Above the entry was the number sixty-three. He pushed
through the door and stood in the entry foyer, listening. His
pulse was up, and had his hand not been locked so tightly to
Nicole's, he was sure it would be shaking. He knew not to
dote now, just have a look. Show Nicole. Prove to her that it
was real. Let her see the power he possessed, and allow what
they had just done to the girl from the beach party to fully
sink in.

He pushed open the cellar door and together they descended the stairs, led by the narrow beam of his flashlight.
When they reached the basement, Casey peeked around the
wall and brought his light up, pointing it at the corner. And
there she was. The Georgia Tech girl he'd deposited long ago
named Paula D'Amato.

It was a genuine startle, where nearly every muscle in his
upper body jerked, when Nicole screamed. She stared at the
girl in the corner, curled on the bed and staring at them with
glowing eyes blinded by the bright white light Casey shined
on her. In an instant, Nicole pulled her hand free and ran up
the stairs.

She made it to the top of the stairs and into the foyer before his hands came around her waist. She let out a fierce

scream as he grabbed her hard on the upper arm and lifted her off the ground, her legs still flailing. He finally corralled her, wrapping his arms around her so his chest pressed against her back.

"Shhh," he whispered into her ear. "It goes away. That feeling of filth and guilt. It leaves you, I promise. And eventually all that's left is the need to do it again. You'll see. You'll feel it, too. I know you will."

"What's down there?" Nicole asked through her tears. "What did you do?"

Casey put her down but kept his arms wrapped around her. "She's one of the girls I took," he said into her ear. "Not a take for the club. Not as an initiation. A real take." There was a moment of silence. "Paula D'Amato. We talked about her in the club. Do you remember?"

Nicole shook her head as she cried. "No, Casey. What have you done?"

"And soon, people will be talking about the girl we took tonight. People in this town and around the state. The whole country! They'll be talking about us, Nicole. You and me."

He finally unclasped his arms from around her chest. Nicole turned slowly, saw Casey's shadowed eyes alive with venom, some toxic stare that looked straight into her soul. In a quick, violent motion she pushed him away and ran. She pulled open the door and cut across the front yard that was strewn with clay and gravel. Without the aid of the flashlight the dark night disoriented her. She took several strides in the wrong direction until the silver tarnish of the moon reflected off her car and she righted herself.

Her legs hit the steering wheel as she scampered in and started the engine. Shifting into gear. The car jerked forward as she stepped too heavily on the accelerator and maneuvered around Casey's Buick in front of her, narrowly missing it. As she did, her headlights caught a glimpse of Casey as he appeared from around the front end of the Regal. Just a brief *blur of his green shirt. She felt a thud as the front bumper struck him, and then the sickening sway as the wheel displaced upward when she continued over his fallen body. The rocking stopped as the wheels settled on the gravel. Nicole couldn't see much in her rearview as she twisted a U-turn and sped away, back up the long, dark road she'd followed into this haunted place.*

The sedan rested in the darkness beyond the last home and crept slowly forward after the girl had hit the man. The driver rolled down his window as he pulled next to the body writhing on the ground. A quick assessment told him the man's femur was badly broken, bent as it was at a hockey-stick angle. A fortunate bonus. Had he needed to expend time subduing this one, the girl might be impossible to track down.

He stood from his car and stepped over the moaning man who begged for help, reached into the man's car, and removed the keys, just in case a lucid moment came over him and he controlled his pain well enough to start his car and drive for help.

"Please," Casey said.

Stoically, the man reached into Casey's front pocket and fished out his phone. He dropped it, along with the car keys, onto the passenger seat as he climbed back into the sedan. The taillights of the girl's car were still visible in the distance, far down the winding road that led out of Stellar Heights.

Nicole was breathing heavily as she tore out of the abandoned subdivision, her adrenaline so powerful she was barely able to control her hands as they gripped the steering wheel. Her mind was incoherent and unable to process what had just transpired. Running would get her only so far. She needed help, and checked off the people she knew she couldn't ask. Calling the police was not an option. There were so many reasons for this, but after considering only two—that she had assisted in kidnapping Megan and had also been involved in a hit-and-run—she stopped looking for more. She couldn't call her parents, for obvious reasons. Her friends, soft and hysterical, could handle none of tonight. Nicole knew she needed someone smart and level-headed. Someone who would look past her failures. She needed Livia.

The wheels screeched as she turned out of Stellar Heights and headed back to the beach party. She watched her rear-view mirror for a few moments, but she knew there was no way for Casey to follow her. Colliding thoughts of guilt and disgust came over her. She cried as the thud echoed in her mind from when she'd hit Casey, and her stomach rolled at the thought of Megan waking in the black basement. The image of Paula D'Amato burned her eyes and was there every time Nicole blinked. God, how long had she been missing?

There were no good solutions to these problems, and peeling back the events of tonight would be impossible. Still, she would try. It took twenty frantic minutes of speeding to find the frontage road that would lead back to the beach party. Twenty minutes to gather her thoughts. She'd go back to the parking lot, wait for Livia. She would do everything Livia told her.

As she approached a stop sign, she grabbed her phone. She dialed.

"Pick up, pick up, pick up. Please, Livia, pick up your phone."

As Nicole rolled through the stop sign, all her plans changed. She looked in her rearview mirror and knew nothing would be the same. The red-and-blue lights of a police car filled her mirrors.

Chapter 57

November 2017
Fourteen Months Since Megan's Escape

"I have to see for myself," Megan said, standing at the back of the house. The plywood covering the windows still bright under the glow of her flashlight. "Come with me, Livia. Come with me so I can be sure."

Megan was off again, headed toward the front of the house. Livia followed, stumbling in the dark over the uneven ground and chunks of concrete. At the front door, she hesitated before she followed Megan into the dark house. She caught a glimpse of the number sixty-one above the door. The interior was a hollow cove of high ceilings and vacant rooms barely visible in the rushed glow of Megan's flashlight.

When Livia caught up to her, Megan stood at the door to the basement. She noticed the beam of the flashlight quivering. Livia reached out and put her hand on Megan's arm to calm her tremor.

"Megan, stop and talk to me." Livia took Megan by the shoulders, the beam of the flashlight falling to their feet. "You said you know who took you. Tell me."

With the cellar door open, the staircase was a shadowless portal to a different world.

"During my last therapy session, I got further than ever before. He came down the steps and I heard it. I listened during that session, more closely than I ever did before. I heard it, Livia."

"You heard what, Megan?"

"And then, during my dream the other night when you were in the passing train, when you waved to me . . . I heard it again, just before I woke."

"Tell me, Megan. What was it?"

"That sound I know so well. That sound I've known from childhood."

Livia waited.

"Leather," Megan said. "I heard the leather holster of a belt."

Chapter 58

August 2016
The Night of the Abduction

Nicole heard Livia's recorded voice come through her phone as voice mail picked up. She ended the call as the flashing lights filled her rearview mirror. Part of her wanted to scream because she knew there was no turning back. Part of her wanted to step on the accelerator and flee. But another part wanted this, exactly what was happening. Wanted to be cornered with no choice but to tell the police what had gone on tonight.

She pulled to the side of the frontage road, her car pitching to a slight angle as the passenger-side tires settled onto the gravel shoulder. The officer came to her window as she rolled it down.

"You know you sailed through a stop sign back there, young lady?"

Nicole was crying. "I didn't see it. I need help."

"What's wrong?"

"I hit someone. With my car. I hit my boyfriend. And there's a girl who needs help. Two girls, maybe more. I don't know."

"*Slow down. Shut the engine off, please.*"

Nicole turned the ignition.

"*Step out of the vehicle, please. Tell me what's going on.*"

Nicole climbed from her car, crying hysterically now. The officer put his arm around her and led her to the patrol car.

"*Here, let's have those,*" he said, taking Nicole's keys. He opened the back of the car and helped her sit down. "*Wait here for a minute. We'll find out what's going on.*"

He reached for her other hand and gently took her phone.

"*Did you make any calls tonight?*"

"*My sister.*"

"*I see.*" The officer's voice was gentle and caring. "*Did you speak with her?*"

"*No.*"

"*Leave a message or a text?*"

Nicole shook her head.

"*Call anyone else?*"

"*No,*" Nicole said. "*No one.*"

"*Good girl. Sit tight, okay? I'll be right back.*"

The officer helped Nicole glide her legs into the backseat, and then closed the door of the squad car. Nicole watched as he walked a perimeter around her car, the red-and-blue lights highlighting the scene in front of her. He shined his flashlight into the backseat: something caught his attention. Nicole wanted to scream at him that they needed to hurry, but her voice had left her. All she could do was stare. She watched him pull a handkerchief from his back pocket, shake it open, and use it to pull open her car's door. Then she watched him lean in. He reappeared a few seconds later, something gripped in his hand. Only when he opened the patrol car's door and sat behind the wheel did Nicole recognize the object he'd taken. It was the long fork from the barbecue set.

"*I bought that at a Goodwill store,*" Nicole said through the chain link that separated them, although she wasn't sure why.

The officer doused the flashing lights and put the car into gear. He swung a rough U-turn and sped back down the frontage road.

"We have to go to West Bay," Nicole said, leaning toward the partition.

Their eyes met in the rearview mirror.

"Oh," Terry McDonald said. "I know where we're going. Don't worry, my Love."

Chapter 59

"Tell me again," Livia said. "A leather holster?"

"Yes. From my father's belt. He walked down these thirteen steps," Megan said, pointing to the cellar. "He did it nearly every day for two weeks. And he did it wearing his uniform and his belt and his holster and his gun. I know that sound, Livia. I've known it since I was a child. And once you and I started this together, once you filled me in on what you knew, slowly everything made sense to me. The twisted memories in my mind unwound themselves and all the madness of those two weeks vanished. He never touched me, Livia. Never assaulted me because I was never supposed to be taken. Casey Delevan abducted me. The way you discovered he took Nancy Dee and Paula D'Amato. He brought me here for my father, but he had no idea who I was. When my father found me, sedated and asleep, he knew his problem was immediate and immense. The man he hired to take girls had abducted his daughter. After his discovery, my father couldn't release me because I would lead authorities back to this house and to this abandoned subdivision. Too much had happened in these houses with the other girls for him to allow that. Too much was still happening, until recently, with Paula D'Amato. He couldn't have this place discovered. So he kept me sedated for two weeks, fed me sedatives in my food and in my lemonade. He allowed the town's search to die down. Bought just enough time for the pressure to lessen. And then, when he believed it was safe, he loaded my food with one more massive dose of ketamine, almost killing me the way he did Nancy Dee. I was nearly catatonic when he placed the burlap over my head and transported me to the bunker. I remember parts of the ride, almost an hour.

"The bunker, he knew, would make the perfect story. It would be the greatest distraction from where he'd actually kept me and the other girls. Once he deposited me, deep in the woods, he left me there with the door ajar. When I woke up and was coherent enough to walk, I found the bunker door cracked open. Through the haze of sedation, I ran for my life. I didn't escape, Livia. I did what he knew I would do. I found my way home."

Megan redirected her flashlight to the staircase.

"I have to see for myself."

"We shouldn't do this alone, Megan. We need to get help and sort this out. Make sure of the things you're saying."

"I've never been more sure of anything in my life," Megan said. "But I have to see this place again. I need to see that it exists somewhere other than my mind."

She shined the light at the thirteen stairs she knew would be there, and started down to the dark cellar.

There was nothing—not in her years of schooling, or her single year of internship, or her four years of residency, or the last three months of fellowship—that could have prepared Livia for what she saw when she reached the bottom of the stairs.

They had tried the light switch, but the house was not live

with electricity, so they had to negotiate the stairs under the guidance of the flashlight. When they reached the last step and sprayed the light across the basement, Livia screamed when she saw the two eyes reflecting back at her, like a cat in the bushes.

The eyes belonged to a skeleton of a girl who was draped in a ratty T-shirt many sizes too large. Her long hair was a knot of tangles, and her cheeks looked to have sunken like the elderly. The girl recoiled on her bed when the light found her, curling up into a ball with her knees to her chest and arms wrapped around her shins.

"Don't hurt me!" the girl shouted.

Megan, on her own quest to this point, turned suddenly into the young, inexperienced woman she was, looking to Livia with wide eyes and a frightened face. Livia took the flashlight from Megan and shined it away from the girl, realizing that as it was the only source of light, the girl had no idea who had entered the basement.

"It's okay," Livia said. "I'm a doctor. I'm here to help you."

"Is he here?" the girl asked in a panicked voice. "Is he with you?"

"No," Livia said, slowly approaching. "Just us. No one will hurt you."

The girl began rocking back and forth on the bed, still holding her legs to her chest. Livia couldn't tell what was happening; she thought perhaps this girl was having a seizure. But once she moved closer, she saw that the girl was smiling, laughing almost.

"Please help me," she said. "Please take me from here."

"I will, sweetheart. I will," Livia said. She put a hand on the girl's shoulder. The girl quickly took it and squeezed and reached for Livia's embrace. Livia hugged her and matted her coarse, dry hair as the girl sobbed on her shoulder. Livia allowed the embrace to last only a few seconds.

"We have to get you out of here," Livia said. "We have to hurry, all right?"

The girl nodded. "The chain is shackled to the wall. I've tried to loosen it, but there's no way."

Livia moved to the wall and crouched down to the chain that was anchored there. She grabbed the chain and pulled. It didn't move. She looked to Megan, who was stuck, unmoving, at the bottom of the stairs. "Megan! Come help me."

Megan snapped to attention. She shook her head. "You won't be able to," she said. "Not without a tool or a hammer."

Livia shined the light around the cellar. There was a table near the corner. She went to it and found a bottle of spray paint, noticing for the first time the dual X's painted onto the far wall, excess paint weeping down in long streaks to the floor. The sight sent an eerie flutter through Livia's gut. She resisted the morbid urge to examine this troubled place, and instead opened the drawers in search of anything that might help her pry loose the shackle. The drawers were empty.

"Okay," she said. She turned to the girl. "Sweetie, what's your name?"

"Elizabeth Jennings."

The name was familiar. Livia had searched during the last weeks for other missing girls in the area, and she vaguely remembered coming across this girl's story. She remembered, too, this girl's profile in Nate's black binder. She was another girl from a bordering state.

"Okay, Elizabeth. I have to go out to the car to—"

"No! Don't leave me."

"Elizabeth," Livia said in the darkened basement. "I have to get a tire iron so we can pry this chain loose. There is no other way. We'll be right back, I promise you."

The girl began to shake and cry.

"We are not leaving you. We'll be back. One or two minutes, I promise."

"No!" the girl cried.

"I'll stay," Megan said.

Livia paused. She knew what it would take for Megan to remain here on her own.

"Are you sure?"

"Go," Megan said. "But leave the flashlight."

Livia handed Megan the light and ran up the steps. Outside, she bolted for her car, which sat two houses away, parked at the end of the winding road that led nowhere and everywhere. She reached into her pocket as she ran, fished her phone out, and dialed.

"Nine-one-one. What is your emergency?" the female voice said.

"My name is Dr. Livia Cutty," she said, trying to control her voice as she ran. "I'm in an abandoned subdivision in West Emerson Bay. In one of the houses I found Elizabeth Jennings, a missing girl I believe from Tennessee. I need help right away."

"You are in a subdivision in Emerson Bay, is that correct?" the calm voice asked.

"Yes. In West Bay. Stellar Heights. Off Euclid and Mangroven. I found a missing girl. Elizabeth Jennings."

There was a short pause as the woman tapped a keyboard. "Elizabeth Jennings has been missing for two years. Is this who you're referring to?"

"Yes. I need an ambulance right away. And police."

"Officers are being dispatched now, ma'am. Would you like me to stay on the line with you?"

"No." Livia shoved the phone in her pocket and raced to her car.

The girl sat quiet and still on the bed. Megan stared at her in the shadow of the flashlight. She shuffled around the cellar in a way she was never able to do during her two weeks of captivity. There was nothing restraining her. She shined the light onto the painted wall.

"Three exes means he'd kill me," Elizabeth Jennings said.

Megan's eyes darted up and down the wall. Ever since her rogue therapy session things had been falling into place for her. With the lure of discovering the next bit of the mystery, she'd never stopped to piece it all together. Until now. Until she stood in the cellar with another girl her father had taken. A numbing sense came over her, and all the facts she had built up in her mind collided with the ache in her heart. She shined the light onto the thick bolt socketed to the base of the wall, and followed the chain to the girl's ankle. Could her father really be responsible for such a thing? Megan remembered Nancy Dee. She'd read the articles that chronicled her parents' desperate search. The shallow grave where her body was found. And just recently, she'd seen the leaked photos online that captured Paula D'Amato's body lying abandoned in the woods next to an empty hole that waited for her. Could the man who raised her have done those things?

"Will you hold my hand?" the girl asked.

Megan looked up from the girl's ankle, where her mind had wandered.

"Until the doctor comes back?"

Megan nodded. "Of course."

Chapter 60

Since the tragedy last year—when he made the horrible discovery after walking down those stairs to adore his new Love and found his daughter instead—everything had fallen apart. He could still feel the humidity of that warm summer night when he thought back. He had believed, for the short while as he sped back to Stellar Heights, that he could make things work. . . .

"Do you know," the girl asked from the backseat, "about what happened? I didn't mean to hit him. There's a girl, too. We need to help her."

Terry glanced down at the long fork on the passenger seat. It would solve his problem. He didn't know exactly what waited for him back at Stellar Heights, or how difficult it would be to finish the man whom he'd left lying in the street. Discharging his firearm was out of the question. It would require paperwork and explanation. Strangulation carried the risk of bruising or scratching his hands should the man still have the strength to resist. The fork was morbid, but the night was getting away from him and time was his greatest enemy. He could hardly control his longings to see the new arrival. He'd waited so patiently for her, and tonight's rendezvous was an untimely annoyance. But now, from potential disaster came opportunity. He had just settled another girl into the backseat. She was exquisite. The night was turning out pleasantly well.

"Do you know about the girl?"

Terry was finished talking to this one. There would be time to discuss the rules later, but he needed to stay focused for the moment. He slowed his patrol car as he came to the entrance of Stellar Heights, waited for an oncoming car to pass and disappear in his rearview mirror before he turned into the dark subdivision. He stopped the car and exited, closing and locking the tall, cast-iron gates behind him. When he shifted the car into drive and continued along the dark road, the girl went frantic.

"Why did you close those gates?"

Terry blocked her out, compartmentalized her pleas. The Buick Regal came into view as he sped along the winding road.

"Good," he said when he saw the man still lying in the street.

His first order of business from a long list in his head was to check his new arrival, make sure she was secure. He pulled the keys from the ignition and locked the doors. The girl in the back tried the handle but he knew she could go nowhere. He walked past the man in the road; he was still moaning but clearly unconscious from his deformed leg. Terry stepped over him.

He walked through the threshold of the home, number sixty-seven, and felt the familiar coital urge within him. He knew he wouldn't be able to act on those desires tonight. It was a shame, but this evening called for diligence and efficiency. He took the stairs quickly and turned the corner at the bottom, redirected his flashlight to the girl who waited. But something was wrong.

The hair and headband. The slope of her neck and angle of her jaw. The freckles and eyelashes. It was not possible. His urgings suddenly made him ill. She stirred on the bed, and he went for her before stopping himself. He couldn't. If she saw him, there would be no way to fix tonight. There was not enough time in a single night to hide his years of presence in the homes of Stellar Heights. And no matter how much he wanted to go to his daughter now and help her, he knew it was not possible.

From urgings to nausea, his emotions finally funneled to rage. He was a wild animal as he bounded up the steps and into the night, ripping open the front door of his cruiser and grabbing the long fork that was there. There was no thought as he approached the man lying in the road.

"Help," the man whispered.

"My daughter!" he said as he brought the fork down. He repeated his motion five times with his teeth gritted and eyes possessed.

"My daughter!" he repeated constantly until a noise brought him back. He looked around, panicked suddenly since there were never any sounds at Stellar Heights. The girl was screaming from the back of the squad car, staring at him through the window. He stood from his knees and kicked the front door closed to quiet her.

The man's shirt balled in his fist as he pulled his lifeless body behind one of the houses where the rubble was cleared and soft clay waited. Retrieving a shovel from the garage of one of the homes, he dug a hole. He sweated through his uniform until the grave was large enough, then kicked the man in and threw dirt over him until he was no more. . . .

Since that night, his life had been the rickety jerk of a roller coaster climbing to its peak. He knew, deep in his core, that he would eventually reach the top, hang for a moment, and then crumble downward. He didn't want to believe this, and did everything he could to convince himself otherwise. For a full year he'd managed to prevent the world from finding his secrets. After the release at the bunker and his daughter's triumphant return, he should have known to lie low. He had made a terrible situation workable, and the world bought what he sold them. The media attention was greater than he predicted, and for a time he had pulled back. But then, as if the universe were conspiring against him, Stellar Heights was slated for demolition, threatening to expose all the secrets he had stashed within those houses. He berated himself now as he considered all the mistakes he'd made.

In a panic, he had dug up the man's body and, without thought, disposed of it in the bay. The job was rushed and haphazard, without detail or clarity. It wasn't long before the fishermen made their discovery. The stress caught up to him later when he too severely punished his Love when she tried to escape through the window. This error forced him to bring her to the forest, and there his mind played tricks on him. His feelings for her were so great that his cloudy mind had caused him to leave her there, to be discovered next to her resting place. And now, the pathologist from Raleigh had shown up and was closer than she knew, offering him a profile that so closely described himself he could have authored it. This same woman had corrupted his daughter, filling her mind with things she should never have to think about.

Now, his hand was forced. Survival required him to make a move.

It was close to one a.m. when he pulled his squad car to the shoulder. The Stellar Heights sign glowed in his headlights. He tortured himself by replaying the last year, mulling each ill decision he'd made. He cursed himself for failing to control his desires. He'd spent hours playing out scenarios that would allow him to avoid what he was about to do. Hundreds of ways to prevent the proverbial roller coaster from reaching the top and sliding into free fall. The opportunities were many, but they all required clairvoyance. And they would require him, as much as he despised the thought, to end the only relationship that remained at Stellar Heights. He'd kept her the longest, and their bond had once been undeniable. But, sadly, the events of the last year had caused them to drift apart. With the homes scheduled for demolition by the county, his survival could not be achieved if their relationship continued. He could trust only one with such a burden. The special one. The one that meant the most to him. So tonight he came to Stellar Heights to make his final visit to the one the media would soon call Elizabeth. It was a wretched name that did not suit her in the least.

Then, before the wrecking crews descended upon them, the houses would need sterilizing. Despite their imminent destruction, he couldn't risk the discovery of evidence that might lead back to him. Too much had happened within those walls to hope that simply bringing them down would erase it all. The world knew about the ones they called Nancy and Paula. He'd make sure the world knew no more. And if he planned carefully enough, the one they might call Elizabeth would never be discovered. Four of the homes had, at one time or another, held girls. He would concentrate on them, expunge all evidence of their presence. Then, with breathing room, he'd tend to his daughter again and help her find her way back to the peace she was so close to reaching.

The plan, systematic and focused, would occupy many of the coming days. Time was both his enemy and savior. He needed to move quickly to erase his past. Taking too long would bring danger and exposure. But if he managed to pull off the first few steps—eliminating the last girl who resided at Stellar Heights and disposing properly of her remains, then making the homes immaculate before demolition—time would become his ally. He could concentrate on his daughter and help her heal. Days and weeks would tick past. Months and years, even. He would move further and further from his history. Stellar Heights would disappear and take with it all his secrets. His Loves would be missed, but with time the pain would resolve. He would be safe. His daughter would recover. The mysteries of the missing girls would fade. His heart would mend. Perhaps he could repair things at home and find a way to be happy again. He'd have to control the doctor. He'd have to placate her. He'd find a way.

His radio squawked and brought him back from his imaginings.

"We have a ten fifty-seven reported at Stellar Heights subdivision in West Bay. Request units and ambulance."

And just like that, it was gone.

Chapter 61

Livia pulled the heavy, black-metal tire iron from her trunk with the help of the dome light, and raced back to the house, leaving her trunk wide open. As she ran, she tried to concentrate on the house in the distance, its image dark and shaky in her tunnel vision. Up the front steps first and then through the opened front door, Livia finally bounced down the darkened stairwell. Megan was standing with Elizabeth Jennings, holding her hand.

Livia crouched down and placed the end of the tire iron into the eye of the bolt. She leaned back, pulling with all her strength. After ten seconds of grunting, she checked her progress and noticed under the glow of the flashlight that nothing had budged, or moved, or bent. Repositioning the tool, she stood and placed her foot on the tire iron, then transferred her weight onto the bar. When nothing happened, she tried to bounce to increase the force but this resulted in the point of the lever coming free and Livia stumbling to the ground, the metal tool rattling onto the bare concrete floor.

Megan tried for another minute or two, before Elizabeth began to cry.

Livia turned to her. "I've already called the police," she said. "Help is on the way. They'll be able to free you."

Livia watched Megan feebly work the pry bar against the bolt.

"In the meantime," she said in the best calm voice she could produce, "we wait. All of us. We're not going anywhere without you. Let me see how you're doing."

Livia passed the minutes by examining Elizabeth Jennings. She performed a cursory exam and determined the girl to be malnourished, underweight, and with signs of abrasions to her ankles and wrists as the method of bondage periodically moved to each extremity.

While Livia softly ran her hands over Elizabeth Jennings's body, checking for broken bones or signs of infection, the girl spoke.

"Did you find the other girl?"

Livia stopped her exam, stared at Elizabeth. Megan stopped fumbling with the pry bar and looked over.

"What other girl?" Livia asked.

"The other girl who's here. We talk to each other sometimes," Elizabeth said, pointing to the ceiling.

Livia looked up and followed the beam of the flashlight as Megan slowly raised it to the ceiling. The light came to rest on an air vent.

"We can hear each other," the girl said. "She's the one who saved me. He hasn't hurt me since she's come. When we're sure it's safe, we whisper through the vent. But I haven't heard her for a while. Not since he came last time."

Livia felt her breathing accelerate. "This other girl is upstairs?"

"Somewhere," Elizabeth said. "Wherever the vent leads. Her name is Nicole."

Chapter 62

Livia took the stairs two at a time, the flashlight's beam bouncing erratically.

"Nicole!" she yelled when she reached the top of the stairs. She listened for a reply but there was none.

"Nicole!"

She moved through the first floor, shining her light into each vacant room and finding no sign of life in any of them. Near the front entrance, she looked up the stairs. Livia headed up the steps and called her sister's name when she reached the top.

"Nicole!"

When no reply came, she oriented herself, picturing the vent above Elizabeth Jennings's bed and extrapolating where it might lead. She shined her light down the hallway and ran for the open bedroom door. Out of breath, she reached the doorway and brought the room to life with her light. Her heart broke when she saw the bed with wrinkled sheets, an armoire, and mirror. A shackle on the ground, the leather clasp open and free.

"Nicole! Are you here?"

Livia spent another minute futilely examining the other

vacant rooms on the top floor before she ran back down to the cellar.

"Is she here?" Megan asked.

"No. Elizabeth, I want you to think. When was the last time you talked to Nicole?"

"We don't talk. We whisper."

"When was the last time?"

"I'm not sure. A few days ago."

Livia wasn't sure what she wanted to hear. A year ago would make it easier. A few days meant she'd just missed her. A few days meant that if she'd worked harder or faster she might have run up those stairs and found her sister lying on that bed, just the same as Elizabeth Jennings.

A car screeched to a stop outside.

"Are the police here?" Elizabeth asked.

"Yes," Livia said, but her voice was filled with forced hope and relief. The noise outside was not what she expected. She longed to hear far-off sirens slowly growing louder, culminating in red-and-blue lights bouncing and flashing through the house. She wanted to hear ambulance horns waking the night. Instead, she heard a single car with no sirens and no lights. Absent were shouting or clamoring officers. There were no paramedics banging gurneys and equipment through the empty house and down the stairs. No radios squawking. Instead, Livia listened to a single set of footsteps as they walked overhead, pausing at the crest of the stairwell before finally descending, the glow of a flashlight preceding the strides.

Livia noticed, over the sound of the approaching footsteps, Elizabeth Jennings began to hyperventilate. She retreated to her defensive position with her knees tucked to her chest and her arms wrapped around her legs. Megan, too, was panicking. Livia pushed Megan behind her and stood in front of the bed as if she could protect them both from what was coming.

The light shined brightly in her eyes when he came around the corner, a fierce spotlight that brought the entire space to life and blinded them all as though looking into the sun. Livia dropped her own flashlight when the brilliant light found them. It clattered to the floor and pointed toward the corner.

The voice that came was strong and firm.

"Megan. What's happening, honey?"

"Oh my God," Megan said at the sound of her father's voice.

"Where's Nicole?" Livia said.

"Megan, I'd like you to go outside to my car."

"Where's my sister!" Livia yelled.

"I'm not sure what she's told you, Megan, but I'm here now. I'll take care of everything. Other officers are on the way. Go outside and wait for them in my car."

Megan began to move. Livia grabbed her arm.

"Right now, Megan! Go outside so I can gain control of this situation."

Megan walked past Livia, out of her grip.

"Good girl. Wait outside."

Trembling, Megan walked toward the bright spotlight, unable to see her father behind its powerful glow. When she drew next to him, instead of turning to climb the cellar stairs she reached for his gun. The holster strap was fastened and she fumbled while she tried to wrestle it free. Livia saw the light drop from her eyes. With her retinas bleached, she was still blinded. There were no rational thoughts to her movements. Adrenaline flooded her circulatory system and Livia ran at him. Their bodies collided in the center of the cellar, his much heavier and thicker than hers, reminding Livia of her sparring sessions with Randy. She saw Megan tumble onto the stairs, and Livia felt Terry McDonald's powerful grip throw her to the floor. She lunged at his feet and wrapped his ankles in her arms as she continued forward.

Falling to the ground as Livia tangled his feet, the powerful spotlight rattled and landed against the wall, dousing much of its brightness.

The bottom of his shoe found Livia's face and she felt herself propelled backward. They were both quick to their feet, Livia letting loose a side kick that landed to his ribs and took the wind from his lungs, doubling him over. She transferred her weight to her left foot, about to deliver another side kick.

Your kicks are lethal, but they get stale if you go to them too often.

Instead, she brought her right knee sharply upward and felt a clean connection with his nose. His knees crumpled and he fell in a pile to the floor.

Livia stood frozen with indecision. She wanted to grab Megan and run up the stairs, but she couldn't bring herself to abandon the lost girl on the bed. She heard a hiss, and the acidic odor of ammonia filled her nostrils even before her eyes registered the pain. She tried to shield herself in the dark cellar, bringing her hands in front of her as the pepper spray covered her face. The burning was immediate and intense and it drove her backward.

She felt him grab her by the hair, and Livia let out a gothic scream as he launched her through the air. She landed on the table by the wall and crashed into the corner of the cellar. Her eyes bled burning tears and her lungs wheezed as the irritant entered her system. Against protests, she raised her eyelids. The flashlight Livia had dropped lay still on the floor, pointing to the spot next to Livia and brightening her hip and the concrete and the thing she had felt when she careened across the table. It was a bottle of spray paint. Livia's mind flashed to the two strange symbols painted onto the wall. In a single motion, she reached into her pocket and pulled out the Bic lighter Kent Chapple had given her when he swore off smoking during his visit to her house the other night. She picked up the paint can with her right hand and lit the Bic with her left. Just as Terry McDonald reached her, she depressed the aerosol cap on the paint can and sprayed it through the flame. A giant fireball erupted, as if the canister itself were filled with flames. The horizontal blaze struck Terry McDonald in the face, igniting his hair. He recoiled immediately, turning away from the flame, but it was too late. First his hair, then his shirt took to flames. They were violent orange and lit the cellar brightly as the three girls watched his burning body stumble and turn. His screams were prehistoric and sickening.

He stumbled across the room, shrieking and moaning and slapping his face and head and chest. Megan ran to her father, pulling the blanket from the bed and throwing it onto his burning torso and head. He collapsed to the ground and she smothered the flames.

Semiconscious, he lay panting in the far corner. The smell of burnt flesh mixed with ammonia was worse than anything Livia had encountered in the morgue. Livia lifted the heavy flashlight that had landed in the corner. It provided all the light needed to see Megan staring at her incapacitated father, his face and chest burned black and greasy.

Livia worked hard to keep her burning eyes open as Megan unhooked her father's gun from the holster. For an instant Livia, lying in the corner, raised her hand and tried to speak *no*. But before she was able, Megan adjusted the gun, both hands playing over its surface until it clicked and clattered. Then she carried it to Livia.

"Here," Megan said. "Safety is off. Shoot him if he moves."

Megan went back to her father and pulled the radio from his shoulder. She twisted and adjusted the knobs, tricks of the trade, Livia guessed, learned from watching her father over the years. Megan pressed a button on the side of the mouthpiece and placed it to her lips. She knew the quickest way to draw police to a scene.

"Officer down at Stellar Heights."

Chapter 63

It took the first squad car six minutes to arrive. But soon after they surveyed the scene, the ghost town of Stellar Heights was alive with red-and-blue flashing lights, scores of headlights, ambulances, and fire trucks. After an hour, detectives arrived with stadium lights that brought the abandoned subdivision to life as if it were high noon. News helicopters hovered overhead as word spread.

Elizabeth Jennings was placed in an ambulance and brought to Emerson Bay Memorial. Terry McDonald was airlifted to Raleigh to be treated by the Duke burn unit. Megan was taken, under the supervision of Dr. Mattingly, to a private treatment facility undisclosed to the press. Livia, after being treated by paramedics who flushed her eyes with saline, stuck around Stellar Heights, refusing the suggestion of scans and observation.

They searched all six houses. Three appeared unused. The others showed signs of life, at one point in time. Each had similar characteristics of boarded-up basement windows with filthy living conditions in the cellars. The furnishings were consistent between all the spaces, and shared a common floor plan of a bed, a dresser, and a small table where it was determined meals had been placed. Each basement wall was graffitied with dual *X*'s.

Livia relayed to the police and the detectives Elizabeth Jennings's claim that she had been in contact through the ventilation system with a girl named Nicole. She was sure it was her sister, missing for nearly a year and a half. Livia showed the detectives the second-story bedroom where similar living conditions were found—bed, dresser, and shackle. Yellow tape went across the doorway and detectives waited for the crime scene unit to pick through the room.

The search for Nicole Cutty continued.

It was a week before Terry McDonald was able to answer detectives' questions. He was mummified in heavy white bandages, so that only his mouth and eyes were visible during questioning. It took three days at the hospital for detectives to put together the last three years. They found that Megan McDonald's father wanted to talk. Was eager, in fact, to rid his soul of sin. He confirmed all the facts Livia had brought to the detective's attention about Nancy Dee and Paula D'Amato. Elizabeth Jennings was pieced into the puzzle and tied with what Megan was beginning to divulge.

The only missing link, which they got to at the end of the third day, was the whereabouts of Nicole Cutty. Under tremendous pressure, he told them, with the coming destruction of Stellar Heights, he worked feverishly to find a new "home" for the girls who remained—Elizabeth and Nicole. But as pressure mounted and his ailing daughter began her nightmares, he was certain her memory would betray him. So instead of moving the remaining two "Loves," he disposed of them. Nicole first, Elizabeth Jennings meant to be next.

Two weeks of excavation, however, by the Montgomery County police force, who used donated Bobcats to dig up the forest where Terry McDonald had buried Nicole, produced no body. Pressed hard for details and location, he told detectives through tears that he was certain of the locale. He had, he confessed, in his haste buried Nicole without the protection of a body bag. Perhaps, it was suspected, animals had taken her remains.

When this news reached Livia, she listened with a stoic expression as detectives and social workers explained their theory. Livia tuned out after a moment. All she could concentrate on was that Nicole's body was no longer waiting to be discovered. There was no longer the chance that her sister's remains would come to her morgue and beg Livia to uncover the answers they held.

Livia slept that night under the red fan of her childhood bedroom, finding in her slumber both peace and angst that this opportunity was gone.

Chapter 64

Livia's jabs were crisp. They landed with a whistling pop each time she connected with Randy's headgear. He covered up well enough for her to know she wasn't causing any damage, merely keeping him at bay. She transferred her weight to her left leg and was ready to bring her right shin up to Randy's midsection when she noticed his arm rise in anticipation. Instead, she quickly spun to her right and connected solidly with a spinning elbow that caught Randy clean in the temple. He went down in a heap.

"Oh!" Livia said when his huge body crumbled to the mat. "Are you okay?"

But Randy was laughing while he lay on the mat, holding his head. "Thought you were going to the well with that side kick."

Livia crouched down. "Where'd I get you?"

"Right where you were aiming."

"Let me have a look."

Randy sat up. "No, thanks." He swatted her hands away. "You work on dead people. I don't want to be your patient."

"Okay." Livia lifted her gloved hands in surrender. "Tell me what hurts."

"My pride. Otherwise, I'm fine."

Livia offered a hand and pulled Randy to his feet. They both climbed out of the ring while the onlookers snickered.

"Yeah, yeah, yeah," Randy said to the crowd. "Get it all out."

This brought a few more laughs until the crowd returned to their workouts. He took a seat on the bench as Livia handed him a water bottle.

"How're you handling your fame, Doc? I keep seeing you on the news."

"I'm just filler. It's not me they want."

"I take you as a very modest person, but I hope you know you're a hero."

"Let's not get dramatic, Randy. I think that spinning elbow has made you delusional."

Randy pulled off his headgear. "I didn't expect you to own up to it. But I've heard you talkin' around here about how you look for answers to give the families of your patients. That girl you found in that house might not be a patient, but you saved her. And you answered the biggest question her family could ever ask."

"Maybe."

Livia took a seat next to him. Randy's hulking body seemed to dwarf Livia's more when they sat side by side than when they sparred in the ring.

"You know something?" she said. "You were with me in the house at Stellar Heights."

"I know that ain't true. I've seen the pictures of that place on the news, and you'd sooner catch this black man at a Klan rally than in that basement."

Livia smiled. She pointed to her heart. "You were in here. And up here," she said, tapping her temple. "I could have died if I didn't know the things you've taught me."

"Well, you just knocked a three-hundred-pound man on his ass, so there's nothing left to teach you."

Livia stood up. "You've taught me a lot more than how to fight." She kissed him on top of his head. "Thanks."

Livia headed for the locker room.

"Hey," Randy said. "Hope this weekend goes okay for you."

Livia smiled and nodded her head. "It will."

Nicole's funeral officially took place fifteen months after she disappeared. It was a quiet ceremony made up of family and friends. Jessica Tanner and Rachel Ryan spent the entire day with the Cuttys. The presence of Dr. Colt and his wife as they entered the church put a lump in Livia's throat. It was a short service that served a single purpose of closure, the atmosphere saturated with both torment and relief.

The church was nearly empty when Livia saw the old man walk through a side door and approach the closed casket. He ran his hand over the mahogany and bowed his head in prayer. It took Livia a moment to place him before it registered. She walked over and took a spot next to him, stared at Nicole's casket for a while before he noticed her.

"I'm very sorry about your sister," the man said.

"Thank you." Livia held out her hand. "Mr. Steinman, correct?"

He nodded and shook her hand. "I don't mean to intrude on such a private matter, but I've got a message from a friend of yours. She's very sorry to not be here. She wanted to come, but with the news cameras outside . . ."

"Oh," Livia said. "Of course. I understand."

"She wanted me to tell you," Mr. Steinman said, pulling a piece of paper from his pocket to make sure he got the message correct. *"Thank you for coming when I called you. And for being a good friend."*

Mr. Steinman handed Livia the note, the words written in curly cursive. Livia took the note, wiped her tears, and inhaled a long breath.

"She okay?"

"Getting there. She's helping me with my wife, who's ill. She's offered her help for as long as I've known her. I'm finally taking her up on it. She's a great caretaker, and come hell or high water, I'm going to get her to college and medical school."

"Tell her I'm proud of her, okay?" Livia said.

Mr. Steinman nodded.

"And I can't wait to see her again. When she's ready."

Livia returned to Raleigh on Sunday night. She wasn't sure she'd ever talk with Megan again, although the message from Mr. Steinman gave her hope. What would become of Megan after this ordeal, Livia couldn't begin to imagine. The media was frenzied. Elizabeth Jennings drew their peripheral attention, but the country was intimate with Megan McDonald. They wanted details about the night she faced down her father in Stellar Heights. They wanted exclusives. They wanted to see her on the morning and evening news discussing the fascinating details of her journey to Stellar Heights. But Megan, this time, stayed underground. She was nowhere to be found, and Livia had no intention of outing her friend.

Camera crews camped overnight in front of the McDonald home, scampering and running whenever the garage door opened and a car backed down the driveway. With microphones stuck on long poles and television cameras pointed through the windows, reporters shouted questions at the car's occupants. For the first few days it was Megan's mother and aunt, but like Megan, they eventually disappeared to undisclosed locations. A permanent crew remained at the McDonald home, just in case they returned. The rest scattered around and hedged their bets, some camping at Megan's aunt and uncle's, others at her grandparents'. There had not yet been a picture taken of Megan since her father was arrested. The networks were forced to loop old photos from her book tour, and the stale ones of Megan from before the abduction. But the media was growing restless. They all wanted a piece of America's renewed heroine. Dante Campbell promised that her audience would be the first to hear from Megan. She was, after all, a friend of the show.

In her absence, the hungry public ate up Megan's book. After the Stellar Heights discovery, *Missing* soared to the top of the charts. No longer simply the girl who made it home, Megan McDonald was the girl who brought her captor to justice. She was the girl who triumphed. She was, indeed, everything the audience wanted.

Chapter 65

May 14, 2018
Six Months Since Stellar Heights

The week before, Livia Cutty stood over the autopsy table. The body that waited had been her 232nd autopsy. With two months left in her training, she'd easily make the magic number of 250 postmortem examinations the program promised. Her autopsy times had come down to fifty minutes, and the mistakes and worries from the early months of her fellowship could hardly be recalled. She considered herself, after ten months of training, a medical examiner.

She walked through the front door of the OCME on Monday morning and rode the elevator to the third floor. As comfortable as she had become with her position as a senior fellow, trepidation brewed about the week ahead. She was scheduled for her last stint of ride-alongs with Kent Chapple, who had recently separated from his wife. Kent had shown up at Livia's the week before, drunk on whiskey like he'd been the last time. During an uncomfortable purging of emotions, he'd confessed his feelings for her. He liked her "more than a friend," he had said—stealing a line Livia hadn't heard since college—and asked her to dinner. Caught off guard, Livia politely rebuked his offer under the excuse that coworkers shouldn't become romantically involved. She suggested they talk when he was less emotional, and when his words weren't quite so slurred. Ten days had run past since that night, and the conversation had yet to take place. Their relationship, once easy and spirited, had grown awkward. A week together in the morgue van was sure to be what Jen Tilly would refer to as a hot mess.

But the angst about the coming week never settled in. There was no time. When the elevator doors opened, Kent stood in the hallway.

"We need to talk," he said.

Livia nodded. "Listen, Kent. The other night, I wasn't the most gracious—"

"Not about the other night," he cut her off. "We've got a call. White female discovered in a shallow grave in Emerson Bay Forest."

Kent walked into the elevator and handed Livia her OCME jacket. "You need anything else before we go?"

Livia shook her head. "How old?"

"Late teens, early twenties."

The elevator doors opened on the ground floor and they hurried to the morgue van out back, where Sanj Rashi waited behind the wheel. Livia had barely slid the side door closed before the van pulled from the back lot. Silence sat with them for the ninety-minute drive to Emerson Bay, only interrupted by Sanj's deep, New Jersey voice as he radioed their location to the officers cordoning the area. As they turned onto Highway 57, Livia spotted the squad cars parked at odd angles along the shoulder with lights flashing. Sanj pulled the van into the epicenter of the activity and, along with Kent, slipped latex gloves onto his hands.

The front doors opened as the MLIs climbed out. Livia stayed still in the backseat peripherally noticing the things around her—the squawk of police radios, the voices of the officers, the back door of the van opening as Kent pulled the gurney into the road, and the sound of Sanj prepping the scene investigation bag with everything they might need when they ventured into the woods.

"You okay?" Kent asked.

Livia blinked, noticing that he had slid open the side door. She nodded and climbed from the van.

"Morning, gentlemen," a uniformed officer said. He nodded at Livia. "Dr. Cutty."

Livia lifted her chin, tried to smile.

"My guys will take the gurney. It's a good walk, half a mile, over some dense stuff."

Sanj took the canvas bag from the gurney and draped it over his shoulder as he and Kent followed the officer into the woods. Livia stayed close behind, stepping over fallen logs and holding back branches for the officers who followed.

The moss-covered ground gave off a layer of fog as they got deeper into the woods, a faint odor of fall having been captured and preserved over the winter and now seeping from the floor of the forest. The sun was at a steep angle from the east and shone intermittently through the tall tree trunks, setting loose long shadows that crept through the forest. After a fifteen-minute trek, Livia saw officers in the distance standing around an area squared off by yellow crime-scene tape. As she approached, she noticed a white sheet lying over the body.

Sanj and Kent met with the officers and had a quick discussion to which Livia was deaf. Her concentration was on the snow-white blanket that had no place in this dark forest. Kent looked at her after a moment, raised his eyebrows.

Livia nodded. "I'm fine."

She walked into the cordoned square of sun-colored tape. Kent crouched down into the fog and grabbed the edge of the sheet. He glanced one last time at Livia, who took in a long, deep breath that she silently exhaled. Livia nodded again.

"Let's have a look."

In this gripping new thriller from #1 international best-selling author Charlie Donlea, a TV news host sets out to uncover the truth behind a brutal, decades-old murder . . .

Avery Mason, host of *American Events*, knows the subjects that grab a TV audience's attention. Her latest story—a murder mystery laced with kinky sex, tragedy, and betrayal—is guaranteed to be ratings gold. New DNA technology has allowed the New York medical examiner's office to make its first successful identification of a 9/11 victim in years. The twist: the victim, Victoria Ford, had been accused of the gruesome murder of her married lover. In a chilling last phone call to her sister, Victoria begged her to prove her innocence.

Emma Ford has waited twenty years to put her sister to rest, but closure won't be complete until she can clear Victoria's name. Alone she's had no luck, but she's convinced that Avery's connections and fame will help. Avery, hoping to negotiate a more lucrative network contract, goes into investigative overdrive. Victoria had been having an affair with a successful novelist, found hanging from the balcony of his Catskills mansion. The rope, the bedroom, and the entire crime scene was covered in Victoria's DNA.

But the twisted puzzle of Victoria's private life belies a much darker mystery. And what Avery doesn't realize is that there are other players in the game who are interested in Avery's own secret past—one she has kept hidden from both the network executives and her television audience. A secret she thought was dead and buried . . .

Please turn the page for an exciting sneak peek of
Charlie Donlea's newest thriller
TWENTY YEARS LATER
coming soon wherever print and e-books are sold!

Catskill Mountains

July 15, 2001
Two Months Before 9/11

Death was in the air.

He smelled it as soon as he ducked under the crime scene tape and stepped foot onto the lawn of the palatial estate. The Catskill Mountains rose above the roofline as the early morning sun stretched shadows of trees across the yard. The breeze rolled down from the foothills and carried the smell of decay, causing his upper lip to involuntarily twitch when it reached his nostrils. He wasn't sure if it was because this was his first case as a newly minted homicide detective or if it was because of some perverse fetish he had never known he possessed, but the odor filled him with a sense of purpose.

A uniformed police officer led him across the lawn and around to the back of the property where he found the source of the foul odor. The victim was hanging from a second story balcony, his feet suspended at eye level. The detective looked up to the terrace. A white rope stretched over the railing, tight and challenged by the man's weight. The twine disappeared through French doors that led, he presumed, into the bedroom. Walking closer to the victim he noticed the man's pants sagged on his left hip, exposing part of the buttocks. That the man wore no underwear was his first observation. The thin bruise marks that started at the waistline and surely covered the man's right buttock was the second. The contusions flared a faint lilac against the liver mortis blue hue of the dead man's skin and looked to the detective a lot like whip marks.

A spiraled bundle of rope wrapped around the man's ankles. Rigor mortis had bent his bloated feet at ninety-degree angles to his shins. The detective reached into his breast pocket and removed a pair of latex gloves that he slipped his hands into. He walked around to the back of the body. The man's right arm was swollen and stiffened at his side, wanting but unable to extend further due to the rope that bound the man's wrists together. The left arm was bent behind the man's back with a bundle of rope wrapped multiple times around each wrist. The length of twine connecting the wrists was stretched tight as rigor mortis attempted to bloat the man's arms away from his sides. Cut this rope, the detective imagined, and the guy would unfold to like a scarecrow.

He gestured for the crime scene photographer, who waited at the periphery of the lawn.

"Get close-ups of the wrists and ankles."

"Yes sir," the photographer said.

The crime scene unit had already been through the property, taking photos and video to log as the *before* evidence. This second time through would be during and after the detective had his first look. The photographer raised his camera and peered through the viewfinder.

"So what's the initial thought here?" the photographer asked as the camera's shutter clicked redundantly as he snapped a series of photos. "Someone tied this guy up and threw him over the balcony?"

The detective looked back up the second story. "Maybe. Or he tied himself up and jumped."

The photographer stopped shooting and slowly took his face away from the camera.

"Happens more than you'd think," the detective said. "That way, if they have second thoughts they can't save themselves." The detective pointed at the dead man's face. "Get some clicks of that gag in his mouth."

The photographer squinted as he walked to the front of the body and looked at the dead man's mouth. "Is that a ball gag? As in S&M bondage?"

"It would certainly go hand-in-hand with the whip marks on this guy's ass. I'm heading upstairs to see what's holding this guy in place."

Latex gloves covered the detective's hands and plastic wraps enclosed his shoes as he walked into the bedroom. The balcony doors opened inward and allowed the same breeze that had earlier filled his nostrils with the smell of death to gust through the bedroom. The pungent odor was less noticeable here, one story above where death hung in the morning air. He stood in the doorframe and moved his gaze around. This was clearly the master suite. A king-sized four-poster bed stood in the middle of the room with night tables on either side. A dresser sat against the far wall, its mirror reflecting his image back at him. Through the open balcony doors, the white rope curved up over the railing and ran at waist height across the room and into the closet.

He stepped into the room and followed the rope. The closet had no door, just an arched entryway. When he reached it, he saw a spacious walk-in filled with neatly organized clothes hanging from scores of identical hangers. Shoes filled the thick pine cubbyholes that covered the back wall. Against the far wall, amid the cubbies, was a black safe about five feet tall, likely weighing close to a ton. With an ornate knot, the end of the rope was tied to a handle on the side of the safe. The other end, the detective knew, was attached to the man's neck, and whether he jumped off the balcony or was pushed, the safe had done its job. It had not budged an inch—the four legs indented the carpeting with no adjacent depression marks to suggest the safe had moved from the weight of the man's body.

A large kitchen knife lay on the floor next to the safe. He pulled a flashlight from his pocket and shined it at the carpeting. Morning sunlight spilled through the balcony doors and trickled into the walk-in closet, painting his shadow across the floor and up the far wall. He was interested in the small fibers next to the knife. He crouched down and examined them in the bright glow of his flashlight. They appeared to be bits of frayed nylon from when the rope had been cut. Within the carpet fibers were three small drops of blood, and a fourth on the handle of the knife. He placed a triangle-shaped yellow evidence placard over the blood droppings and fibers, and another next to the knife.

He turned and walked out of the closet, noticing a nearly empty wine glass on the night table. He was careful not to disturb it as he placed another yellow evidence marker next to it, noting the lipstick that smeared the rim. High stepping over the taught rope, he walked past the mirrored dresser and into the bathroom. He slowly looked around and saw nothing out of place. Soon, the forensics team would be in here with luminal and black lights looking for hidden blood evidence. At the moment, the detective was interested in his first impression of the place. The toilet lid was open but the seat was down. The toilet water held a yellow color, and the faint smell of urine registering now as his nose caught up with his eyes. Someone had used the toilet but failed to flush. The lid was up but the toilet seat was down, and dry. A lone segment of toilet paper floated in the bowl. Another evidence placard found the toilet.

He walked from the bathroom and into the main area,

once again surveying the room. He slipped his suit coat off his shoulders and draped it over the chair next to the dresser, and then followed the rope out to the balcony. He looked down at the dead man hanging from the other end. In the distance, the Catskill Mountains were cloaked by early morning fog. This was the house of a very wealthy man, and the detective had been tasked with figuring out what had happened to him. In just a few minutes he had identified blood evidence, DNA from the lipstick on the wine glass, and a urine sample that likely belonged to the killer.

He had no idea at the time that all of it would be matched to Victoria Ford. And the detective could have no idea that in two short months, just as he had all his evidence organized and a conviction all but certain, commercial airliners—American Airlines Flight 11 and United Airlines Flight 175—would fly into the Twin Towers of the World Trade Center. In a single sun-filled, blue sky morning, three thousand men and women would die, and the detective's case would go up in smoke.

Manhattan, New York City

May 3, 2021
Twenty Years After 9/11

The New York City Medical Examiner's office was located in a nondescript, six-story white brick building in Kips Bay on East Twenty-sixth Street and First Avenue. If offices had occupied the top two floors they would provide views of the East River and the north end of Brooklyn. But the upper floors were not meant for the scientists and doctors who roamed the building. They were instead reserved for water and air purification systems. The circulated air within the world's largest crime lab was clean, pure, and dry. Very, very dry since humidity was bad for DNA, and DNA extraction was one of the crime lab's fortes.

In the cold, damp basement was the bone-processing laboratory. A technician opened the airtight seal of the cryo tank, releasing liquid nitrogen fog into the air. A triple layer of latex gloves protected the technician's hands. His face was safe behind a plastic shield. He reached into the tank with a pair of forceps and lifted the test tube from the fog. It was filled with a white powder that had minutes earlier been a small bone fragment specimen. The liquid nitrogen had been used to freeze the bone, and then the frozen specimen was shaken violently in the bulletproof test tube. The result was total pulverization of the original bone sample into fine powder. The technique allowed scientists to access the innermost portion of the bone, which made the chance of extracting usable DNA more likely. The concept was remarkably simple and had been developed based on two of the basic concepts of physics—the law of motion, and thermodynamics. If an apple were thrown at a wall, it would break into many pieces. But if the same apple were frozen solid by liquid nitrogen and *then* hurled at the wall, it would shatter into millions of pieces. When it came to extracting DNA from bone, the more pieces the bone could be broken into, the better. The finer the powder, better still.

The tech placed the test tube into a rack with a dozen others containing pulverized bone. With the nitrogen fog still spiraling from the latest tube, he dipped a titrating syringe into a beaker of fluid, drew ten ccs into the chamber, and added the extraction products to the pulverized bone. The next day, instead of bone powder, a pink liquid would fill the tubes. It was from this liquid that a genetic code would be procured—a sequence of twenty-three numbers unique to every human on the planet.

In the room next to the bone-processing lab, a continuous bank of computers lined all four walls. It was here where scientists took the DNA profiles generated from the original bone fragments and attempted to match them to profiles stored in the Combined DNA Index System databank known as CODIS. But this was not the national databank the FBI utilized to match DNA profiles gathered from crime scenes to previously convicted criminals. The databank searched here was a standalone archive of DNA profiles provided by the families of 9/11 victims who were never identified after the towers fell.

Greg Norton had worked at the Office of the Chief Medical Examiner for three years. Most of those years were spent in the computer lab. Each morning he was met with a stack of DNA profiles recently sequenced from bone fragments that had been collected from the rubble of the twin towers. He entered each sequence into the CODIS databank and searched for matches. In three years of employment he had never made a single match. But this morning, just as he sat down with his second cup of coffee and pecked away at the keyboard, a green indicator light blinked at the bottom of the screen.

Green?

A red light meant no matches had been found on sequences entered, and Greg had become so accustomed to misses that the red light was all he ever expected. He'd never seen a green indicator light during his tenure at the OCME. He clicked on the icon and two DNA profiles popped up onto the monitor—white numbers against a black background. They were identical.

"Hey boss?" he said in a careful tone, keeping his eye on the set of twenty-three numbers in front of him to make sure they didn't change.

"What's up?" Dr. Trudeau asked as he worked his fingers over a keyboard on the other side of the room.

As the head of Forensic Biology, Arthur Trudeau was in charge of identifying the remains of mass casualties from across the state of New York. For nearly twenty years it had been his mission to identify every specimen collected from those killed in the World Trade Center attack.

"We got a hit."

Trudeau's fingers stopped tapping the keyboard and he slowly glanced to Greg Norton's station. "Say that again."

The tech nodded and smiled as he continued to stare at the numbers on his screen. "We got a hit. We got a fickin' hit!"

Dr. Trudeau stood form his desk and walked across the lab. "Patient?"

"One one four five zero."

Trudeau pulled the keyboard from a standing computer station toward him and typed the numbers.

"Who is it?" Greg asked.

Other technicians had heard the news of a confirmed identification and gathered around. Trudeau stared at the monitor and the small hourglass that spun as the computer searched. Finally, a named appeared on the screen.

"Victory Ford," he said.

"Next of kin?" Greg asked.

Trudeau shook his head. "Parents, but they're deceased."

"Any other contacts?"

"Yes," Trudeau said, scrolling down the page. "A sister. Address in New York State."

"Want me to make the call?"

"No. Let's run it one more time to be sure. Start to finish. If it hits a second time, I'll give her a call."

"First one in how long, boss?"

Dr. Trudeau looked over at the young technician. "Years. Now run it again."

Connect with U s

Visit us online at
KensingtonBooks.com
to read more from your favorite authors, see books
by series, view reading group guides, and more.

 Join us on social media
for sneak peeks, chances to win books and prize packs,
and to share your thoughts with other readers.

facebook.com/kensingtonpublishing
twitter.com/kensingtonbooks

Tell us what you think!

To share your thoughts, submit a review,
or sign up for our eNewsletters, please visit:
KensingtonBooks.com/TellUs.